Student Affairs

Student Affairs

Book Three of The School of Dreams Series

Julia Sutton

Other books by Julia Sutton

The School of Dreams (Book 1 in the School of Dreams series)
Visions of the Heart (Book 2 in the School of Dreams series)

Dedication

For Katie – "good friends care for each other, close friends understand each other but true friends stay forever, beyond words, beyond distance and beyond time"

Acknowledgements

Big thanks to Creativia Publishing– always inspiring, open minded and encouraging!

Thank you to all the lovely people that have taken the time to read this series.

It was originally planned as a trilogy, but I have been unable to fit everything into three books so will be starting work on book 4 in 2018.

Thanks to my family and friends for your support, love and encouragement.

Thanks to all the kind, lovely people on social media – the writers and my social media friends who encourage me on the epic journeys I take into my imagination.

So, grab yourself a cup of tea (or wine if you prefer!) relax and welcome to the world of Chattlesbury....

Chapter One

The skies above Chattlesbury City were ablaze with a kaleidoscope of breath taking vibrant colours; splashes of scorching reds mingled with cool blues, that erupted against the back drop of a pitch-black night void. Stars pulsed like diamonds, revolving around a crescent moon, shining beams of silvery light through curling clouds onto the earth below. Fireworks whizzed and banged as they exploded, then dwindled to nothing; the remnants of ash and smoke that hung above the spectator's heads. The air was cloy with an array of pungent aromas; roasting onions, the sickly sweetness of freshly spun candyfloss, the acrid bitterness of petrol fumes vied with the smell of newly mown grass and the perfume of wild flowers. It was a night of fun, of rejoicing diversity and uniqueness. It was the annual summer carnival.

This particular August evening was perfect for the celebration. It had been a hot day which had stretched into a balmy humid night, an excellent environment for enjoyment and laughter. The streets rang with it; merriment and excitement. It was tangible in the atmosphere, an ambience that encapsulated the good vibes of a dynamic growing city which was celebrating another year of prosperity. There was hope surging within the crowds, hope for continued good fortune, health and happiness for its residents. The pavements were lined with people of all ages, who had come to listen to the mayor's inspirational speech and watch the carnival pass through the streets, now they surged and pushed to gain a glimpse of the final procession. Children clapped and laughed with delight as the characters on the flotillas waved exuberantly at them. The carnival snaked around in a giant horseshoe, passing shops, banks and restaurants. It was a hive of children's TV and book characters, exotic dancers and melodic musicians selected to participate in a carefree weekend jamboree.

Juliette Harris grabbed her daughter, lifting her up so she could see the feather covered ladies twirling. There was a cry of surprise, as one male dancer grabbed his colleague by the waist and threw her upwards. The crowd held their breath for a few moments until the smiling lady landed gracefully back into his arms, her legs splayed into a set of elegant splits.

"Wow!" cried seven-year-old Molly, her face suffused with excitement and happiness. Even cool and calm Harry looked impressed.

They had been standing here for an hour now and the procession was almost over. A group of musicians were the last to pass by, guitar strums and a drum beat accompanied an ebony skinned singer who owned the most exquisite voice. Juliette began clapping along, with hundreds of others, as she sang the last few words then bowed theatrically.

Suddenly the fireworks stopped, and bored looking police were encouraging the crowd to move on.

Juliette gazed at the car park and the hordes of people flooding towards it.

"Would you like an ice cream?" She decided, an excuse to stay out a bit longer and let the crowds disperse. They had had such a wonderful evening, Juliette was reluctant to go back to the concrete jungle of home.

"Yes, yes," came her children's eager replies.

Juliette took their hands, leading them back towards the shops. Thankfully the ice cream parlour was still open. A brightly chalked board advertised all sorts of delicious flavours.

"Can I have mint choc chip?" Pleaded a wide-eyed Molly.

"I should think so," Juliette teased, "and what would you like young man?"

She ruffled her son's hair. He looked up at her with a wide smile and dark eyes, so much like her own.

"Triple chocolate of course Mum," he replied.

They managed to grab a window seat. Juliette left them spinning on high stools with strict instructions not too fall off and hurt themselves. The girls behind the counter looked harried. They rushed around, multi-tasking and were extremely efficient. In no time Juliette was at the front of the queue and placing her order.

"Cone or pot?" The fresh faced young lady asked.

"Pots please," Juliette dug deep for the right change.

Her purse was feeling worryingly light after her summer holiday splurge; a week's trip with her sister and brother-in-law in a modest caravan holiday that had eaten into her wages, her family allowance and her meagre savings.

Thankfully she would be paid in four days' time and the end of the month couldn't come soon enough. Juliette thought back to the long sunny days spent at the beach and the fair. It had been a hot summer this year with none of the habitual flooding and it had been so lovely to swop the pollution and built up drab greyness of the city for rolling green hills, woods and clean, fresh air. Now they were back to reality; work and chores and the rush of everyday life. Juliette watched the assistant wedge chocolate flakes into the sweet cold mounds, "do you go to Chattlesbury uni?"

The question startled Juliette out of her reverie, "Yes I do: English."

"I've seen you in the refectory," the young girl replied, "I'm an art student. You hang around with a cute, dark haired guy, young?"

"Will," Juliette smiled, thinking fleetingly of him. How different it would be for him this year with a baby to care for.

"Do you know what you want to do after you've finished your degree?"

"Primary teaching hopefully," Juliette replied, "and you?"

"I'm moving to London with my friend. I want to be an illustrator; books, comics that sort of thing. My friend wants to work on a pop magazine. Our shared ambition is to become mega rich and famous," she laughed, and Juliette felt her financial worries slipping away to be replaced with a different kind of anxiety.

The second year of university loomed ahead of her. Juliette had already began poring over reading lists and deciding which modules she could take. The thought of seeing Ben Rivers again sent a shiver down her spine, even though the evening was warm. The last time she had seen him was at the end of May when she had participated in the class trip to Haworth. It had been a lovely day, interesting and inspiring to see the Bronte house and the pretty village where the famous writer sisters had grown up. Yet her memories were clouded with thoughts of their last conversation. Juliette had insisted they should remain just friends, so why was she constantly thinking of him? She sighed and picked up the ice creams, "come and say hi next time you're at uni." Juliette gave the friendly assistant a thankful smile and moved away from the queue.

"Thanks Mum," her children chorused as she set the rapidly melting desserts down on the table. Juliette watched with a wide smile as they dived straight in with their spoons.

"So, your Dad is taking you to Alton Towers then?"

"Yep," came Harry's emphatic reply.

"And pizza after," Molly reminded her.

"Is that okay Mum?" Harry's eyes were wide and filled with worry.

Juliette reached across to rub his arm, "of course it is love. Me and your dad, well we're sort of friends now and we just want what's best for you two."

"Cool!" Harry nodded happily.

"Daddy's got a girlfriend," Molly divulged.

"Oh, has he now?" Juliette wasn't surprised, Marty had always been attractive to the opposite sex, with his boyish good looks and bad boy image.

"Shush," Harry berated his younger sister, "Mum might get upset."

"Oh no, sweetheart," Juliette replied after a moment's hesitation, "don't worry, I'm happy for him...have you met her yet?"

"Nope," Harry scratched the bottom of the empty pot for any remaining dregs.

"Her name's Charlie and she's a hairdresser." Molly piped up, "Dad said she could do my hair when we get to meet her."

"Well that will be nice," Juliette said with a laugh as she held up her own wild, red curls, "maybe she could do something with mine."

Harry put down his spoon and looked at his mum with a serious frown, "Mum, me and Molls have been talking and we think it's time you got a boyfriend."

Juliette spluttered, "why on earth would you think that?"

"You never go out Mummy," Molly explained, "my friend Lola's Mummy was all on her own too and she was sad, but now she's getting a step dad and they all have lots of fun together."

"You think I'm sad?" Juliette's shoulders slumped in dismay.

Harry and Molly looked at each other then nodded.

"You pretend you're okay," Harry replied, "but I heard you crying on the phone to aunty Maz."

"And when you watch Disney films with *me* you get tears in your eyes." Molly wagged her finger.

"But...but, I'm going out this weekend, remember, with Aunty Maz and Uncle Dave and...and Clive."

Harry sniffed suspiciously, "is Clive your boyfriend then?"

"No." Juliette shook her head, "he's just a friend, but he's very lovely and I have lots of fun when I'm out with him."

There was silence. Juliette sighed, "I'm perfectly fine on my own with you two you know. We have lots of fun together don't we?"

There was reluctant nodding.

"Oooo-kay," Juliette decided to change the subject, "how's about we head home and watch a DVD together?"

It worked, Harry and Molly had immediately forgotten their Mum's love life and were bickering over whether to watch Disney, Transformers or Harry Potter.

As soon as she was back home and her children were settled in front of the television, Juliette tiptoed into her bedroom with the cordless phone. Marie answered after a lengthy twenty rings.

"You took your time," Juliette rasped.

"Oh, hello sis, I was in the bath and I am pregnant you know. I can't rush like I used to."

Juliette was contrite, "Sorry! I keep forgetting you're carrying my future niece or nephew. How are you feeling by the way?"

"Fine, apart from fat bloated ankles."

"You need to rest, especially in this heat," Juliette wiped at her perspiring forehead, "it's hot tonight!"

"How was the carnival?"

"Fantastic as always." Juliette swiped at a large fly, which was buzzing around her lampshade, "erm Marie, have the kids said anything to you about me having a boyfriend?"

There was a short silence then Marie chortled, "no, why?"

Juliette relayed the earlier conversation.

"It was almost surreal having romantic advice given to me from my own children, I thought maybe you might have put the idea in their head."

"Of course I haven't," Marie's tone was brisk, "they're not stupid you know Jules, you have been miserable just lately. Has a certain lecturer got something to do with it?"

"I am totally over him," Juliette shrieked, colouring at her own fib, "and I'm perfectly fine *on my own*."

Marie snorted, "who are you trying to convince? Don't you miss being intimate with someone?"

Juliette gulped, as her mind wandered to the night of passion she had enjoyed with Ben Rivers.

"Sex isn't everything," she sounded unconvincing, even to her own ears.

"Puts a smile on your face though," Marie let out a sensual chuckle, "and I think Harry and Molls are very astute. It's time you got off the shelf, life's passing you by. At this rate you're going to end up a lonely old spinster."

"But," Juliette was about to give her sister the prepared speech, all about independence, girl power, not needing a man to complete her life, but she realised a lot of it was bull. She *was* lonely, she *did* like male company, heck yes, she missed sex!

"Jules, they have given you their blessing to go find someone, love their little hearts, they just want you to be happy."

Tears sprang to Juliette's eyes, "I know," she sniffed, "maybe I'm not completely against the idea of finding true love."

"That's the spirit. You're beautiful Juliette, you know that? No, I don't think you do," Maz said in a firm tone, "Inside and out, upside and down, all the ways a person ever can be – you are kind and quirky and lovely and sweet all rolled into one. Why don't you forget about Ben Rivers? Yes, he's extremely attractive, but he has plenty of other students that already tell him that. He's heart-breaking and he's too dangerous for you."

"I" Juliette shook her head, "I, just find him irresistible and it's not just his looks, it's the way that he spoke to me, the things he said and the way he made me feel." Juliette gripped the phone, "I don't know what the hell is wrong with me, I'm usually so level-headed."

"Get your head out of the clouds. He's *all* shades of fifty that one," Marie decided, "did you like the trilogy by the way?"

"Yes! I did. I think E L James gets a bad stick, she's a good writer and extremely inventive."

Marie laughed, "I enjoyed it too! I think Dave's a bit worried that I'm going to tie him to the bedpost and cover him with squirty cream though."

They both laughed at the thought of it.

"Well it's not my usual genre but it was certainly entertaining." The conversation shifted away from books to socialising matters.

"Listen, about the weekend, I've booked us into a Thai restaurant. You know the one by the bus station that's been there for yonks. It has excellent reviews, I can't believe we've never tried it before." She then proceeded to rattle off some of the dishes from the menu.

"It sounds delicious," Juliette felt her spirits rise with excitement.

"Then Dave and I thought that we could all go back to ours. Watch some Saturday night television or a film maybe. I don't really fancy traipsing around pubs in this heat."

"Of course," Juliette replied smoothly, "I'll bring some wine for me, pop for you and beer for Clive and Dave, looking forward to it. Now you should go and rest. Call me if you need me."

"Okay sis."

Juliette cut the call and wandered into the kitchen, where she spent the next hour ploughing through a basket full of ironing. By ten o'clock she was exhausted. After shooing the kids to bed, she flopped down on her own, still fully clothed. The lamp cast a warm glow around the room, as Juliette snuggled into the duvet with a contented sigh. She reached for her current read; a light-hearted book on friendship and food by Lucy Diamond, but found it hard to concentrate. Her mind was whirring away and in frustration she reached for her phone. Her Facebook feed showed a vast array of new stories. Juliette scrolled through them, liking the pictures of adorable animals and children frolicking on beaches. Then she paused as she read over a few posts by Sophie. Feeling sad, the first one intimated, underneath which Sophie had written, single life is awful, I miss my husband. Then a few hours later, another status revealed that Sophie was feeling angry, how could he do this to me. There were over sixty replies, the majority of them sympathised with her, but a few who must be friends of her estranged husband Ryan, had pleaded with her to give him another chance. Then at the end, she noticed a succinct reply from Ann: 'forget the cheating git, you can do better, be strong and you'll get through this'. Juliette chuckled, the response was typical of Ann, straight forward and honest, it mirrored Ann's personality in real life, she certainly was a tough cookie but a lovely friend and person too.

It had been months since she had seen the university gang and she hoped that they were all okay, she missed their company, the fun and laughter they had shared. Thanks to social media, she knew that Hema had given birth to a baby girl. Will had posted a series of exquisite shots of them both, with the beautiful, tiny baby. Sophie had posted holiday pictures of herself with a happy looking Evelyn. They had been to Lanzarote; which Sophie had proclaimed to be the best holiday ever. In a few weeks' time they would be meeting up again. The registration for year two at Chattlesbury university had been allocated for mid-September. It would be great to see Ann, Evelyn, Sophie and Will - Juliette had missed them. They were all good friends and she enjoyed their company. University had become about so much more then studying. When Juliette enrolled, she had no idea that she would enjoy it so much. Over the past year, so much had happened, her head felt lightheaded when she thought of it. She had met some lovely people, learnt so much that her brain felt like bursting sometimes and then there was Ben. A brief fling with an English lecturer which had ended disastrously. Now they were just friends and it was a fresh start. A chance for new beginnings, a possibility to shine and prosper. Juliette's eyelids drooped and she found herself being pulled into a nightmare of epic proportions, with dragons and witches, snakes and gigantic rats. All of which she had to battle alone.

Chapter Two

"More tea?" Ann lifted the teapot off the tray with expectation and without waiting for a reply, poured the steaming brown liquid into three delicate china cups.

She offered around a plate of luxury cookies, brought especially to impress their visitor.

Her husband Jon took two off the plate, then proceeded to spoon three sugars into his brew.

"Not for me thanks," Rose the social worker lifted her hand but looked longingly at the biscuits, "I really shouldn't. I'm trying to diet after an all-inclusive two-week summer binge."

Ann glanced at the petite lady opposite and wondered why she was worried about her weight when there was so much horror and injustice going on in the world. Eating a cookie seemed insignificant in comparison.

"Have you holidayed this year?" Rose asked cheerfully.

"Paris," Ann confirmed, "for the fourth time. We love it there, don't we?"

She nudged Jon who was wiping crumbs from his lips.

"Paris is great," he responded with vigour, "so much beauty and history and just a hop over the sea."

"Ah, I'm ashamed to admit I've never been," the social worker leant forward and added in an excited tone, "but I've enrolled for a beginner's French class. You've inspired me Ann, all this talk of goals and achievement and I've always wanted to learn another language."

"That's fabulous!" Ann cried, "French is such a beautiful language; tres bon Madame."

Rose laughed heartily and stretched out a trouser clad thigh, "and how are your studies going?"

Ann sipped at her drink, "very well thank you. The second year will soon be starting and I have to admit, I'm looking forward to it."

Rose frowned, "it must be challenging for you?..." the question trailed off and the room grew silent, "sorry, that was insensitive of me," Rose looked away with embarrassment.

"You mean because of this?" Ann pointed to her wheelchair, on which she was seated, "not at all, the university have been very accommodating towards me and I can happily confirm there is full wheelchair access throughout. It's more about using this," she pointed at her head, "which is more of a challenge".

"You're a remarkable lady," Rose replied with warm sincerity, "brave and inspirational."

Not one for accepting compliments easily, Ann blushed, "I've had to be," she stated gruffly, "it's either wallow in self-pity or make the most of what life has dealt me."

"Thanks be to God," Rose lifted her eyes towards the ceiling and clutched at her glinting gold cross.

"I don't believe in..."

"So," Jon cut in briskly, throwing Ann a warning look, "we've passed all the tests then and the meetings have been going well?"

Rose shuffled her paperwork, "you have. We're very pleased with your progress. Oh," she jumped slightly in her seat and looked down at her feet. A white fluffy cat had wrapped itself around her legs and was purring contentedly.

"That's just snowy," Ann said as she clicked her fingers, "come here, you daft moggie."

Obediently the feline stretched, then padded across to jump up on Ann's lap.

Jon sprang to his feet, "it is okay for us to have a cat, isn't it?"

Rose looked up at the towering man with a frown, "of course it is Mr Stokes, please do relax, myself and my colleagues think you will be wonderful parents."

Slowly he lowered himself back on the chair, "that's great, erm, have you found anyone suitable?"

"I have," Rose bent to pull out a pair of lopsided spectacles and perched them on her upturned nose, "his name is Samuel and he's twelve years old."

Ann sucked in her breath, while the social worker unclipped a glossy photograph of a rather surly looking individual with blonde curls and piercing blue eyes.

"At the moment he's living with foster parents in Rocksley."

"I know it," Jon nodded as Ann passed him the picture, "I travel there a lot for work, it's not too far is it?"

"Not at all," Rose replied, "about a half hour car ride and there's a direct train that stops there."

"Where are his biological parents?" Ann asked.

"Both alcoholics, both in prison for theft and violent offences. They neglected him and neither of them wanted the responsibility of him."

Ann gulped, "the poor boy. Are there no other family members willing to care for him?"

Rose shook her head, "sadly not. The paternal grandparents are both deceased and the maternal grandmother is in a care home, suffering with dementia. There are no aunties and uncles."

Jon pushed a hand through his hair, "so how is he coping with all this... this upheaval?"

"As can be imagined not too well. He is a very quiet and withdrawn boy, who needs a permanent, stable home as soon as possible. You stated on your application that you preferred an older child?"

"We did," Ann confirmed.

"So, would you be willing and happy to meet him?"

Ann paused, mind whirring. This whole adoption business had progressed so much faster than she had anticipated. Then she noticed Jon gazing at her with wide, expectant eyes and she felt a tug of tender emotion for her husband.

"Yes," said Ann firmly, "we'd love to meet him."

Rose beamed at them both, "that's grand. I'll set the paperwork in motion and be in touch very soon. In the meantime, here is a dossier for you to read through, it tells you about Samuel's background, his likes and dislikes, hobbies, that sort of thing. I've also bought you some books on the adoption process and what further support there is out there for you."

"She's already got a shelf full," Jon pointed to the corner of the lounge, where a pile of books balanced precariously.

"Wonderful," Rose replied, "it's a good idea to be well informed." She rose to her feet and shrugged on her rain mac, "it looks like the summer is well and truly over."

Ann gazed towards the rain spattered window and thought about this young boy they could possibly be adopting. What on earth are we doing she wondered a little panicked, are we even ready for this?

"Would you like another drink?" Ann rasped. She was torn between wanting to wave goodbye to Rose and forgetting the whole idea, or alternatively begging her to stay and bombarding her with more questions.

"Good heavens no! I'm on my fourth already and it's only," she glanced at her wrist, "eleven o'clock."

"We're big tea lovers in this house too," Jon replied with a laugh, but Rose was staring at Ann.

"Are you sure you don't need some time to consider this?"

Ann swallowed and looked nervously at Jon, who was on his feet, eyes shining with excitement. After a moment's hesitation she smiled brightly at the kind social worker, "I'm just a little surprised at how quickly you've found someone. It seems that it took forever for the paperwork and checks to be completed and now, here we are…"

"It's sad to say that there are so many children stuck in the care system at this very moment, waiting for a loving home. Time isn't on their side I'm afraid. But if you would like more time Ann, please don't be afraid to say. We could postpone the meeting with Samuel until you are ready."

Ann was unable to meet Jon's eyes, she could sense the upset and disappointment emanating from him. Averting her gaze away from Rose, she stared down at her lap, at her trembling fingers, "I, I'm just not s-sure I can be the perfect parent this child so desperately needs." She stuttered the words, trying to verbalise her own internal angst on the whole adoption situation.

Rose clucked above her sympathetically, "nobody is perfect, that would be unrealistic to assume it of anyone, even the Queen, especially the Queen," the three of them laughed and the tense atmosphere abated a little, "Ann, I reiterate my complete support for you. My colleagues and I think you'll be great, both of you, and you have our support, one hundred percent. The adoption process is very vigorous, you've done well to come this far. You should be proud," she patted her hand soothingly, "now, I really do have to get to my next appointment. I'll be in touch, but in the meantime read through the literature, visit the websites. There's a wealth of support and advice out there for you Ann, and if all else fails, you can call a member of my team any time."

Ann smiled gratefully.

"Hopefully I have allayed some of your fears," Rose concluded, "now before I go, do you think I could use your toilet?"

Ann listened to the sound of the door squeaking open, as Jon went to let Rose out of the house.

"Well I think that went well," he bounded back towards her, a goofy smile on his face.

"But why are we listening to classical music?" Ann motioned towards the CD player, where a cacophony of violins soared around the room.

"Oh, I thought it would make a good impression," Jon flicked the remote and the noise filtered away, "I didn't think our usual Meatloaf ballads would create the right ambience."

Ann laughed, "you're right. I think Rose was impressed with concerto number five, or whatever it is."

Jon hunched down in front of her and planted a tender kiss on her mouth, "you were great today Ann. I love you Mrs Stokes."

Ann clasped his face in her hands and kissed him back, "love you too. Now, what shall we have for lunch? I'm starving."

"You're so romantic," Jon replied with a laugh, "how about we go out for a pub meal? A celebratory treat."

Ann cocked her head to one side, "you know what? I think I would much rather stay here, sit and read. It's not long until year two starts and I'd like to be prepared as much as possible."

"Whatever you want angel," Jon disappeared into the kitchen and set about searching in the fridge, while Ann wheeled herself over to the bookcase and pondered on which classic novel she could immerse herself in next.

Chapter Three

Evelyn picked up her handbag, checked her reflection in the mirror, then closed the front door softly behind her. The morning's milk stood uncollected on the doorstep and on closer inspection, she could see that a bird had been tapping away at the foil lid and siphoned the cream from the top.

"Good morning Evelyn!" A deep voice reverberated behind her, making Evelyn jump in fright. She spun around, her hand clutching her throat, then breathed a sigh of relief as she recognised Jacob striding up the path towards her.

"I didn't mean to scare you lass," he removed his cap and smiled widely.

"Jacob," she replied, "I wasn't expecting you," self-consciously she smoothed down her daisy patterned skirt.

"I can see that. I was just passing and wondered how you were. How lucky to catch you on your way out. Where are you off to on this lovely day anyway?" He stopped in front of her smiling. Jacob looked smart thought Evelyn, he was wearing a sky-blue shirt, navy trousers and it looked as if he had just had a haircut. Realising she was appraising him, her cheeks reddened.

"I'm going to see a friend. H-how are you Jacob?"

"Very well thank you," he replied with candour, his eyes bright and twinkling, "I hope you are okay?"

Evelyn nodded quickly, her lips lifting into a smile.

"I must say a tan suits you Evelyn," Jacob cleared his throat as his gaze roamed over her bronzed arms and legs, "how was your holiday?"

"Oh, it was lovely," Evelyn enthused, "I have to admit I was nervous, what with never flying before but it was so exciting to be up in the air. Can you believe it was my first time abroad?"

"You won't want to holiday in Britain again," Jacob chuckled, "the world is a big, exciting place Evelyn, so much to see and do." They chatted a while about holidays and all the exotic destinations Jacob had been too, before Evelyn reluctantly glanced at her watch.

"I do have to go; my bus is due any time now."

"Can I drive you?" Jacob asked, gazing down at her earnestly, "it would be no trouble."

Evelyn was touched by his chivalry and impeccable manners, "are you sure it's not out of your way Jacob? I'm going right across the other side of the city."

"I was heading that way myself and you would be pleasant company Evelyn," he held out his arm and steered her towards his small, red car.

Evelyn settled back on cool leather seats, clicking her belt into place as Jacob started the engine and pulled away, to join a steady stream of mid-morning traffic.

"How are you coping?" She knew the gently asked question was referring to the recent death of her mam.

"It's getting easier," she replied with a nod, "I still pour her a cup of tea sometimes though, and I haven't been able to bring myself to sort out her bedroom yet, but I think I'm doing okay."

Jacob removed one hand from the steering wheel and patted hers, "You're doing great."

A silence ensued, Evelyn became distracted by thoughts of her kind Mam. A snapshot of memories formed in her mind; Nora sitting in her high-backed chair, foot tapping as she sang along to the radio. Her Mam laughing with delight at old seventies comedies. Mam kissing and cuddling her goodnight when she was a young girl. Mam dancing around the living room on Christmas day. So many memories, so much joy and happiness, reminiscent of a much-loved lady. Evelyn grabbed at the locket around her neck, smoothing the gold, beneath which lay a photograph of her mam and dad, together again at last. They were stopped at a set of traffic lights when Evelyn realised that Jacob was speaking to her.

"... so, I was wondering if you would like to accompany me to the opening of the new art gallery. I thought we could go for dinner afterwards."

The invitation surprised her, "but how did you get tickets Jacob?" Evelyn was intrigued.

"The perks of working for the council. I think I'm the longest serving Chattlesbury employee there."

"I'm not sure..." Evelyn was suddenly undecided and nervous. She was very fond of Jacob, but it had been more than thirty years since she had accompanied a man on an evening out. The debilitating shyness which going to university had helped overcome, returned with a vengeance. Jacob glanced her way, intuitive and understanding.

"I would be honoured to take you," he explained softly, "but there's no pressure Evelyn. You have my number, please let me know if you would like to come."

"I will," Evelyn nodded, touched by his kindness. "I think we're nearly here." She gazed out of the window as they passed painted signs for the village centre.

"Sophie is your friend from university?" Jacob asked.

"Yes, and the lady I went to Lanzarote with, along with her two young adorable children," Evelyn pulled at a loose thread of cotton, hanging from her blouse, "she's going through a tough time at the moment."

Jacob looked at her with quizzical eyes.

"Recently separated from her husband, the poor dear. The ghastly man was unfaithful to her and more than once."

"Sophie, Sophie O'Neill, is that her name?"

"Yes, do you know her?" Evelyn was surprised.

"Only through the local newspapers. Ryan O'Neill is pretty famous as the main Chattlesbury Football Club striker. A wild man by all accounts."

"It seems that way," Evelyn shook her head with distaste.

Jacob put his foot on the brake and crunched the gears down to second, "Is this the right road Evelyn?"

"Yes, there it is," Evelyn pointed to a huge detached house encased by iron gates and bordered by a vast drive.

"That is some property," Jacob let out a low whistle then swivelled in his seat.

"Thank you so much, you're very kind," Evelyn picked up her handbag.

"It's been my pleasure Evelyn," Jacob replied, taking her hand, "it's been lovely seeing you again. Please consider my invitation, I'm sure we'll have a great evening."

Evelyn coughed, "I will, thank you. Good bye Jacob."

She waited while he tooted the horn, then chugged off up the quiet street.

She turned to peer between the metal bars noticing that the blinds were closed and covering all windows, even though the mid-day sun was shining brightly in a cloudless blue sky.

She fanned her hands in an effort to cool her perspiring face, then searched for a bell to ring, or an intercom to speak into. Ah, there it was, tucked away in a corner, half hidden by stems of climbing ivy and silvery cobwebs. She pressed the buzzer firmly and cleared her throat in anticipation. The minutes passed by, but there was no reply. Evelyn glanced at her wristwatch aware that she was slightly early, but still, Sophie was expecting her. They had only spoken two days ago to arrange the lunch date. Evelyn pressed the buzzer again with more force and heard the sounds of dogs barking in response.

"Are you after Mrs O'Neill?" A voice called from behind her.

Evelyn spun on her heels, surprised to see a woman peering at her inquisitively from an open car window.

"Yes, she was expecting me."

"Wait one moment," the lady in the red Fiesta pulled up the handbrake with a loud crunch then clambered from the car, puffing and panting.

She was small with ruddy cheeks and thick spectacles, that shielded a pair of tiny eyes.

"Mrs Pobble," she gasped, stretching out a chubby hand, "wife of Mr Pobble, the esteemed village vicar."

"Pleased to meet you," Evelyn smiled, gingerly taking her hand.

"Family member are you?" Mrs Pobble asked with an inquisitive sniff.

"No, no, I'm a friend, from Chattlesbury university."

"Ah, I see," Mrs Pobble shook her head, "it's a dreadful business," she motioned towards the house, "a huge scandal and in such a lovely village too."

Evelyn was puzzled, "I don't understand…"

"Why the O'Neill's of course. Tawdry affairs, gambling, drinking, illicit se…" she stopped, seemingly unable to voice the word referring to human copulation, "and that's just what we know about!" She fumbled for her glinting gold cross pendant.

"Oh, but that wasn't *Mrs* O'Neill," Evelyn felt compelled to defend her friend.

"They are heathens too!" Mrs Pobble rolled her eyes heavenwards.

"Sophie is lovely," Evelyn replied with conviction.

"I understand!" Mrs Pobble raised a hand gnarled by arthritis, "Sophie is your friend and your loyalty is admirable," she let out a wheezy cough, "if not somewhat misplaced."

Evelyn backed away slightly and glanced towards the house.

"Their behaviour has tarnished the entire village." Mrs Pobble continued with high pitched disapproval, "There are press constantly hanging around, asking our decent village members intrusive questions. They seem to think we're all at it," she fanned herself, "They even accosted my darling Mr Pobble while he was on his way to oversee a charity fete. It's jolly well not on."

Evelyn swallowed down a gulp of laughter, "I'm sure the press will soon lose interest and as a Christian Mrs Pobble, you surely must understand Sophie needs support and compassion at this difficult time."

"I am a *devoted* Christian," Mrs Pobble's tone became haughty and defensive, "I extend the hand of love and charity to all my parishioners. Of course I don't condemn her for past transgressions."

"That's good to hear," Evelyn replied firmly, "because Sophie really is the victim here and besides, she hasn't done anything wrong to be forgiven for."

Mrs Pobble pushed her spectacles further up her slippery nose, "I feel for the poor woman, really I do. To be married to such a devilish rogue must have made her quite ill. I've heard that he had, erm... dalliances with more than one woman and squandered money on all sorts of unnecessary frivolities. There are people begging on the streets of England and Ryan O'Neill throws his on the roulette wheel. Gambling really is a wicked vice indeed."

Evelyn nodded distractedly as Mrs Pobble continued her tirade, "Although Mrs O'Neill is not completely blameless you know. She seemed to positively relish their wickedly lavish lifestyle. Her and Mrs Lavelle have always been avaricious, they were *always* shopping. How many dresses does a woman need to own? These jodhpurs of mine have lasted me years," she pointed at her own sturdy attire, "and I certainly wouldn't ever consider going to a *spa!*" she hurled the last word in anger. "Maybe you could encourage Sophie to fill up a charity bag, although what use an African would get out of a designer ball gown is debateable. No, no, on second thoughts, tell her to send any unwanted items to the charity shop on the high street. I'm sure we would sell anything she owned, if only for the novelty value."

"Right, okay, I'll... mention it to her," Evelyn looked around for someone, anyone to intervene, but the street was eerily quiet.

"Now," Mrs Pobble sniffed loudly, "has Mrs O'Neill been christened? The good Lord shall set her on the right path again. You must encourage her to attend church. We can help her you know. Through the power of prayer and sermon, I'm sure that in time Sophie will heal. Maybe you could accompany her? Would this Sunday be convenient?"

"I think she has other pressing matters," Evelyn answered tactfully, her colour rising, "but I will certainly send her your well wishes. I'm sure that she will appreciate your kindness."

Mrs Pobble blinked, "of course, thank you. Now I really must go. I have numerous chores to attend to. I do like to keep busy. Idle hands spawn an idle heart you know. It was nice to meet you. Cheerio," with an elaborate wave, Mrs Pobble trudged back to her car and proceeded to disappear in a cloud of petrol fumes and vibrant exhaust clapping.

Evelyn shook her head in bemusement, then pulled her mobile phone from her bag, searching her contacts for Sophie's number. The phone rang for what seemed like an eternity and she was just about to cut the call and head back home, when a voice croaked, "hello."

"Sophie! It's Evelyn, I'm outside dear."

There was a sharp intake of breath, "I'll be down in a minute." Buzz, the line went dead.

A pair of magpies cawed overhead, Evelyn watched as they flapped onto the overgrown lawn, pecking at each other, as they foraged for worms. She could hear the faint sound of bolts being dragged open, the whimpering of excited dogs.

"Hello Evelyn," Sophie stood in the doorway, swathed in pink, lace pyjamas and furry slipper boots. The breath caught in Evelyn's throat, her normally immaculate friend looked so different. Her long, honey golden tresses hung lank and knotted around a face that was smeared with make-up. Dark shadows clung underneath her eyes and her cheeks were pale and dull. Sophie staggered towards the gate, her hands shook as she grappled with the iron locks.

"Sorry Evelyn," she mumbled, "I forgot you were coming."

"Oh, it's okay dear, you have a lot on your mind at the moment. I er, met your neighbour Mrs Pobble."

Sophie rolled her eyes, "poor you. The woman is nothing more than a judgemental, interfering hypocrite. A proper sticky-beak. Take no notice of her."

Evelyn grinned, "she wants you to attend church so they can cleanse you with holy water."

Sophie snorted, "as if! I've already been baptised once, thank you very much."

The gate creaked open and Sophie ushered her friend inside.

"Where are the children?" Evelyn asked, as she followed her friend back up the drive.

"They had a sleepover," Sophie sighed, "I had too much wine last night. My mouth feels like something has died inside it." She licked at her dry lips and led the way inside the lounge.

"Make yourself at home," Sophie said as she flopped down on the sofa.

Evelyn looked around at the discarded takeaway trays and stained cutlery. There was a strange odour lingering in the air; mustiness combined with spicy food, her nose wrinkled in distaste.

"Sorry about the mess," Sophie sprang up to remove a pile of glossy magazines from the opposite seat, "my housekeeper Heidi is in Germany visiting family."

"Ah!" Evelyn replied, "can I help you clean up?"

"No!" Sophie squinted across at her, "I'll blitz it later, when I'm not so hungover. Will you sit down Evelyn?"

Evelyn perched gingerly, "so, how are you coping dear?"

"Truthfully Evelyn? I'm a mess," she paused to exhale a shuddering breath, "I hate being alone. I hate being a single parent. I don't know how Juliette has coped for so long."

"You're not considering taking him back are you?" Evelyn fidgeted nervously.

Sophie threw an arm across her face, "of course not, I do have some self-respect left." She bolted upright, "I keep thinking about him with other women. It's driving me insane. How could he do it Evelyn?" She sniffed and rubbed at her tired eyes.

"You must keep busy," Evelyn urged, "try not to dwell on negative thoughts. University will be starting soon, that will help keep your mind occupied."

Sophie nodded. She looked thoroughly defeated and Evelyn was overcome by a swell of sympathy.

"Shall I make us tea?" Evelyn rose to her feet, determined to lighten the atmosphere.

"I suppose so, but ignore the herbal bags Evelyn., my body is in desperate need of a caffeine boost." Sophie sank back into the squashy cushions, "there's only a bit of sugar left, I haven't had chance to do a grocery shop."

Evelyn nodded, looking down at Sophie with concern. She looked so tiny and fragile, what she needed, decided Evelyn, was a little bit of tender, loving care and that started with a good brew.

The kitchen was in a worse state than the lounge. There were towers of dirty crockery piled haphazardly next to a dripping tap. The breakfast bar was covered with pictures of Sophie and Ryan cut into two and her marriage certificate had been torn into neat little squares. Evelyn sighed as she noticed a vandalised family portrait of the O'Neill's. Ryan's face was covered with ugly red spots and a pair of horns sprouted from his head. The word 'arse' had been scrawled over his grinning mouth. Evelyn opened a window to let in some fresh air then clicked on the kettle. On the vast fridge hung a collection of photographs; holiday snaps from their time in Lanzarote. Evelyn peered at the images of the bright blue skies, the golden sandy beaches which led to the rolling beauty of the wild ocean. There was a group photograph of them all together on Timinfaya mountain, with the rugged, volcanic landscape in the background. Looking at them transported her back to the balmy nights, sitting outside at relaxed restaurants, enjoying the Mediterranean food and fine wine. They had lain on the beach, with people from all over the world, while the children frolicked in the surf, watching a glorious sunset shimmer in the distance. It had been paradise. Now it was back to reality; life and all its tribulations.

"There's a packet of custard creams somewhere," Sophie broke into her reverie as she trudged into the kitchen and perched on a stool.

"I'm going to make you and the boys some homemade shortbread," Evelyn announced, "you'll never eat another shop produced biscuit again."

"That sounds nice," Sophie smiled, "maybe I should take up baking."

Evelyn busied herself making the drinks, "shall we sit in the garden dear? It's such a lovely day and the fresh air will do us both good."

"Yeah, okay," Sophie opened the back door and dragged the garden furniture out of the shade. They sat in silence for a while, enjoying the warmth and the quiet.

"This garden is beautiful," Evelyn commented, as she watched a squirrel hopping along the fence, bushy tail twitching.

"It's big, too big," Sophie looked around, "but yes, it is lovely. I've never really appreciated it before."

"That Buddleia is gorgeous," Evelyn shaded her eyes to peer across the lawn, "look at all the butterflies around it and I love the Master wort, it's my favourite summer flower."

"I'm ashamed to admit that I've never worked in the garden," Sophie sipped her drink, "I can't take any credit for it. We always paid other people to look after it."

Evelyn glanced across at Sophie, wondering what she could say or do to make her friend feel happier. She was certainly in a dark place; an unfaithful husband, a crumbling marriage, the responsibility of young children to care for and a vast house to keep running.

"I don't think I can cope Evelyn," Sophie's eyes filled with tears, "I feel utterly abandoned and I'm so constantly tired."

Evelyn set her tea cup down and reached out her hand, "you're not alone. You have me and I'll help in any way I can."

"Thanks," Sophie blew her nose into a tissue.

"Are you hungry Sophie?" Evelyn asked, "maybe we could go for a pub lunch or to a café."

"I suppose we could go to The Golden Goose," Sophie replied dully, "It's not too far."

"Excellent!" Evelyn beamed, "you go and titivate yourself, while I do a spot of sunbathing."

"Okay," Sophie's lips curved into a small smile.

When Evelyn was alone, she rummaged in her bag for her notebook and biro and began scribbling. The idea for a new novel had taken seed in her mind over the summer. It was completely different to what she had written previously. It was a bildungsroman and she had a book full of basic plot ideas and character lists, which she carried with her everywhere. Last week she had written the first draft of chapter one, on her brand new speedy computer. It had been a gift to herself, with some of Mam's inheritance money.

"I'll make you proud Mam," she whispered to the wind, as excitement coursed through her and she let her pen transport her away to magical worlds.

* * *

"What a beautiful view!" They stood at the crest of the hill, staring downwards at the prettily laid out village, bordered by the patchwork fields of the rambling English countryside. "How long have you lived here dear? It's charming."

"Since Ryan and I were married..." Sophie bit her lip.

"I love how it's all so natural and overgrown," Evelyn gushed, "just listen to the birdsong."

Sophie remained silent as they slowly began their descent, her mind was on other things.

As if sensing this, Evelyn chattered away, pointing out the numerous species of wild flowers which bordered the pebbly path.

"He hasn't even taken the boys out you know," the words suddenly burst from Sophie, angry and bitter, "they keep asking after him. I don't know what to tell them."

"Maybe you should discuss it with him, make arrangements."

"I could strangle him," Sophie kicked at the ground, creating a swirl of dust, "I feel constant anger towards him."

"It's understandable given the way he's behaved," Evelyn cleared her throat, "But Sophie alcohol isn't the answer."

Sophie sighed, "You're right, if anything it's making me feel worse. It just helps me forget for a while...I feel so desperately alone. I don't think I can do this single parent malarkey. I'm not strong enough. I'm beginning to think I'm just like my mother."

"You are not your mother," Evelyn replied gently, taking her arm, "and of course you can cope. It takes a while to adjust, that's all. Why don't you speak to Juliette, if anyone could empathise it would be her."

"I don't want to worry her," Sophie replied, "she has enough to deal with as it is."

"I'm sure she won't mind," Evelyn said, "think of your children, they need you now more than ever."

Sophie nodded, "I'll try," she mumbled.

"Good." Evelyn replied briskly, "now, which way is the pub? I'm famished."

* * *

When they entered The Golden Goose, a silence greeted them and all eyes turned to stare their way. A line of elderly men were propped against the bar, supping tankards of ale and rustling the days newspapers. A large group of women were gathered around three tables, gossiping and eating. Above them a wide screen T.V blared the latest pop hits.

"Come on," Evelyn took Sophie's hand, before she could turn and flee.

The bar-tender was bent over, restocking a fridge with cheap wine. Sophie winced as the thought of last night's excesses assailed her.

"What can I get you love?" He grinned cheekily at the pair of them, before turning to bellow at his wife, "turn that shite off Audrey, a man can't hear himself think over that racket."

"Just an orange juice for me please," Evelyn rattled the change in her purse.

"I'll have a lemonade, with extra ice," Sophie removed her glasses and peered around the dimly lit pub.

Audrey was balancing on a stool, swiping at a dusty window. She gave her husband a cool look as she pointed the remote control towards the screen. There were nods of approval from the men as Sky Sports appeared, but Sophie winced as she recognised the colours of Chattlesbury Football Club.

"Nasty business between you and your hubby eh?" the bartender leant on a pump and surveyed Sophie with a mixture of sympathy and distaste, "he was in here two nights ago, with that gardener of his. Blind drunk the pair of them. Flashing the cash he was, bought two bottles of my most expensive champagne and drank them both in an hour. I nearly threw them out for singing while the quiz was on. Couldn't shut them up."

"He's nothing to do with me anymore," Sophie snapped, quickly replacing her sunglasses.

"You're better off without him love," a woman holding a forkful of battered fish shouted at them, "once a cheat, always a cheat." Her friends harrumphed in agreement.

"I…" Sophie opened her mouth to reply but was quickly led away by Evelyn.

"Best not to respond," she mumbled, "it's none of their business. Let's sit over here."

They hid in a shadowy corner, at a wobbly, beer sodden table.

"I can't stand this," Sophie wrung her hands, "complete strangers knowing my business."

"They'll be gossiping about someone else tomorrow," Evelyn said sympathetically, "keep your head down, it will all blow over." She passed Sophie a menu and they perused it in silence.

"I think I'll have the steak," Evelyn decided, motioning to the hovering waitress.

"Me too," Sophie let Evelyn order for them and flicked through the diary section on her phone.

"Is registration next week then?"

"Wednesday," Evelyn confirmed, "I've spent the summer speed reading classics. I'm really looking forward to getting started and seeing everyone again and I think it will be good for you too Sophie. It will help keep your mind occupied and focused. Are you okay for childcare?"

"Heidi has offered to help more," Sophie replied, "I'd be lost without her."

There was a pause, "what about your mother dear?"

A look of irritation crossed Sophie's face, "too busy canoodling with my ex-gardener. We're not really speaking. Things are...awkward."

"She seems a nice person," Evelyn said gently.

"She acts like a teenager!" Sophie sighed wearily, "and she's completely selfish, no thought for other people's feelings. And messing with a married man, what's that all about? Are there not enough single men left in the world for her?"

Evelyn cleared her throat, "well they do say you can't help who you fall in love with, but anyway, Juliette messaged me. Her summer went well, but there's no sign of a reconciliation between her and Dr Rivers."

"That's a real shame, those two were so romantic together," Sophie sighed, "they reaffirmed my childhood belief in true love. What happened between them anyway? Jules was so shifty when I asked her about it."

"I'm not completely sure," Evelyn replied, "but I think a lot of it was down to other people's interference."

"Well I hope they work it out, oh here comes the food, that was quick," they chatted as they ate their meal. Sophie felt her spirits rising and was glad that she had Evelyn's company to distract her from thoughts of Ryan.

"You look better dear," Evelyn smiled her way, "shall we have a toast?"

"Why not."

"Here's to the future," Evelyn said as they clinked glasses, "whatever it may hold."

Chapter Four

"This is so gross," Will pinched the end of his nose and stared down at the soiled nappy in front of him.

"Here, quick!" Hema thrust a scented sack towards him, giggling as Will stuffed the offending item inside.

"Why do I always get the poo-ey ones?"

"She was sick on me yesterday," Hema said apologetically, "aw, just look how she is staring at you! Definitely a Daddy's girl."

Will grinned at Esme: his daughter, his little girl, his princess. He still couldn't believe that he had helped make her, he felt like he was dreaming and anytime now, Hema would pinch him back to reality. She was definitely his though, she had the Bentley dimples and her Nana's pointed ears. Everything else in her genetic make-up came from Hema of course; the golden eyes and dark, wavy hair. He felt like he was staring at a mini Mummy.

"Come here little lady," Will picked her up and cuddled her close to his chest.

Esme squirmed and let out a succession of sneezes.

"Is she okay Will?" Hema peered with worry at her daughter, "she might have a cold. Maybe we shouldn't leave her tonight."

"She's fine," Will nestled her in his arms and rocked her slightly. Her eyes closed as she slipped into a peaceful slumber.

"But she's only a month old. I don't like to leave her."

Will sighed, "stop worrying. We're only going out for a couple of hours, Mum and Dad are looking forward to babysitting. You know how besotted they are."

"Well okay," Hema sighed, "I suppose you're right. Ouch." Will looked up at Hema's cry of pain.

"I'm so sore," she sniffed, "and just look at the state of me. I'm leaking everywhere."

Dark patches stained the front of her top.

Will grinned, "they're certainly bigger, I'm not complaining."

Hema rolled her eyes and flopped down on the bed, "I'm not sure that cabbage leaves are such a good idea. I can't believe your poor Mum used these for six months," she wriggled underneath her top and removed two wilting leaves from her nursing bra, "I am *so* wearing black tonight."

Will clucked in sympathy, his adoring eyes back on Esme. Truth was that he didn't really want to leave her either, but he had promised Jimmy that they would attend his engagement party. The whole school crowd were going, it would be cool to see everyone again. Besides, Hema had bought gifts and fired off messages to all their friends; they were going whether he liked it or not.

"I have nothing to wear," Hema grumbled, "my skinny jeans are too tight. I'm a complete blob."

"Huh?" Will stared at her in disbelief, "you've just had our princess," he paused to kiss Esme's forehead, "you're perfect to me and that includes your leaky boobs."

"Come here," Hema opened her arms wide.

Gently Will placed Esme down in a broderie anglaise crib, then launched himself at Hema.

"Will. Stop, stop." Hema was curled up with laughter.

He lifted her blouse to tease her with his chilly fingers, "I have to get ready."

Will smothered her with kisses, "never mind that. Have we got time for?…"

"No!" Hema slapped his wandering hands away then groaned as his lips caressed the nape of her neck, "okay, maybe, but we'll have to be quick."

"Will…Will…phone call for you," Flora's melodic voice floated up the stairs.

Will let out a frustrated groan then buried his face in the duvet.

"Sorry lover boy, you had better answer it," Hema sprang up off the bed, "and I'm getting in the shower."

Will bounced down the stairs, whistling cheerfully. A few minutes later he wandered into the kitchen and found his Mum and Dad gazing at the steriliser.

"Is it finished do you think?" Max Bentley scratched his head.

"Looks like it," Flora carefully removed the lid, allowing a cloud of steam to puff upwards, "who was that love?"

"Oh, just Wayne from work. He wanted me to help out tonight, that's all," Will scraped back a chair, plonking himself down, "are you guys okay?"

"Just admiring modern technology," Max replied.

"Oh Will, I bought a present for Jimmy and Sadie, would you take it with you?"

"Course Mum, that's nice of you."

"Well you have been friends with him since primary school. The pair of you are so grown up now and I feel *so* old," she crossed to gaze out of the window, "you used to spend hours in that tree house. Can you remember Will? Your Dad made it when you were just five years old."

"I remember," Will stood behind her and placed a gentle hand on her shoulder, "now Esme can play up there."

Flora let out a melancholy sigh, "if she's anything like you, she'll be up there most days."

"Hopefully we'll have our own place by the time she's climbing," Will reminded his Mum.

"Course you will love," Flora patted his hand.

"So, are you ready for year two?" Max asked, as he filled the kettle.

"Sure," Will replied with a grimace. Inwardly the thought of going back to uni filled him with dread. His summer had been entirely devoted to Esme. He hadn't picked up a book since June. Essays and debates seemed a lifetime ago now. He found himself wondering again if he was doing the right thing by staying on. What he really needed was money, a steady income to buy everything they needed for Esme and to build a secure future for the three of them. Now all he could envision was uncertainty and a mountain of debt at the end of it.

"Want to swap?" Max queried, "I'll relax at uni and you can run St Mary's."

"No, definitely not," Will replied with a smile.

"It won't be long before school re-opens love, will it?" Flora asked, as she pulled apart a bunch of red grapes, handing one to Will.

"One week before the madness commences again," Max confirmed, "this term we have student teachers in. Oh, the joys of having optimism and eagerness back in my school again. And Will, your friend from uni – Sophie if I remember correctly? She never did apply for that teaching assistant position. I'm surprised, she would have been a strong candidate."

"She's had a lot of stuff going on," Will replied with a grimace, "personal issues. Probably not a good idea to be working at the moment."

"Oh well," Max shrugged, "I think the governors have already decided who's got the job anyway. A catholic parent no doubt. They do like to maintain the clique at St Mary's."

"How's your job going Mum?" Will asked.

Flora clasped her hands in front of her bosom, "oh Will, I'm loving it. Juliette's sister is such a nice boss. We have a big wedding order next week and Marie has said I can take charge! Get creative were her exact words." She slapped a glossy brochure down on the kitchen table and pointed out photographs of stunning wedding bouquets, "the bride is wearing a headband of real roses and the bridesmaids will be carrying posies. Then there are flower girls who will be scattering the aisle with flower petals. It's so romantic Will. I just want to make sure everything is perfect. What do you think of these flower stands for inside the church?"

Will bent his head and listened attentively as his Mum chattered away about colours and ribbon length, neither of them had noticed that Max had left the room until the door swung open and he wandered back in with Esme in his arms.

"She was crying," he explained, "is she hungry do you think?"

Will watched his Dad gazing adoringly down at his grand-daughter and grinned. Boy had he changed since Esme had been born. The 'M' for Max could literally be replaced with 'M' for mellow. It had been a long time since Will could remember actually liking his dad, but there it was, the therapeutic, healing power of a baby. And she was all his.

Flora hurried over to coo and cluck as Esme opened her eyes and emitted a cry.

"Can I leave her with you?" Will asked, glancing at the clock.

"Of course son." He bounded up the stairs, as Hema appeared in the doorway, clad in a fluffy bath towel.

"Will the time!" She pulled a comb through her tresses and they both rushed around, flinging on clothes in preparation for the evening's festivities.

* * *

"Text me when you want picking up," Max wound the car window up, then accelerated slowly off the sports and social club car park.

"How do I look?" Hema fretted, as she linked arms with Will.

"Stunning as always," Will dropped a kiss on her forehead, then led her towards the entrance.

"Yo Will," a figure moved out of the shadows and clasped Will's fist in a friendly greeting.

"Hello Harry," Hema smiled at the gangly youth, "how are you?"

"Alright I guess," he flicked a half- smoked cigarette on the floor, "man, I can't believe that you two are parents. Is it hard work?"

Will considered the question, "not as hard as I anticipated. In fact, Esme's pretty cool."

"I'll remind you of that when she's crying at three this morning," Hema chuckled, following the two boys inside, down a dingy corridor, where strip lights flickered and the smell of damp permeated the air.

The muffled beat of a dance song shook the scattered tables and chairs. They passed a group of elderly men, gripping dominoes close to their chests, while a harassed looking bar-maid bent over them, collecting glasses stained with froth and stale ale. The doors in front of them were festooned with balloons and banners. A recent photograph of Jimmy and Sadie in a passionate clinch had been enlarged and blu-tacked to the door. It was surrounded by paper hearts and smiley faces. They both looked so young, it made Will wonder why his best mate had taken a major step towards *the* biggest commitment. He remembered when he was a pupil at St. Mary's, trooping over to mass with the rest of the school. Squashing onto wooden pews, listening to the priest drone on about the sanctity of marriage, while inside his church, Michael the electrician was embroiled in an extra marital dalliance with Tracey the hairdresser and half of his female congregation fantasised over ageing pop stars and remorseless men in power. Anything to escape the doldrum of wedded bliss. Will was so relieved that Hema had shown no interest in *that* particular institution. He quite fancied the prospect of living in sin for the rest of his life.

Harry pulled the door to the function room open. It was full, with people queuing at the bar and lounging across leather sofas. A group of girls squealed and rushed towards them, overwhelming Hema with air kisses and demands to see pictures of Esme. Will glanced around, nodding at people he recognised. Then he noticed Jimmy, downing shots in a corner.

"Will!" Jimmy lifted his hand, beckoning him over, "how are you mate?"

"This is a great party," Will commented.

"Ere, get this down ya."

Will knocked back the glass of brown liquid, wincing as it burnt the back of his throat.

"Mum's organised it all," Jimmy coughed, "she's buying Sadie wedding magazines already. Anyone would think she wants shot of me."

They both laughed, but inwardly Will baulked at the notion of his best friend tying himself down at such a young age. Never-the-less Jimmy appeared happy, so Will was eager to show his support.

"Congratulations mate," Will grabbed his hand, shaking it firmly.

"And to you buddy. I still can't believe that you're a Daddy. Can we come and see her? Sadie's desperate for a cuddle."

"Course you can," Will nodded, "I'll message you next week, fix up a time."

Jimmy frowned, "I bet you're knackered, keeping you up is she?"

"Actually," Will explained, with a hint of pride, "she's golden and is only waking once during the night. She sleeps all the time."

"Must be picking up on your student vibes eh?" Jimmy teased. They grappled together good naturedly before they were interrupted by Jimmy's Dad. Mick was a cheerful Liverpudlian, covered in trendy designer stubble and gold bling.

"Will! Fancy training as a plumber? The company is looking for apprentices."

"Nah, but thanks for the offer – I'm sticking it out at uni."

"Why accrue all that debt, when you could be earning. A LOT," Mick rubbed his hands together.

"Yes Will," Jimmy nudged him, "what you planning on doing with an English degree anyhow?"

"No idea," Will replied non-chalantly, "but at least after another couple of years, I'll have a good qualification. Nobody will be able to take it away from me and I'd rather do it while I'm young, get it out the way. Jeez, now I sound like my dad."

"Come on," Jimmy laughed, pulling Will onto the sticky dancefloor, where Hema and Sadie were gyrating their torsos to a Snakehips song.

"Will!" Sadie threw her fake tanned arms around his neck and planted a sloppy kiss on his cheek, "isn't this cool? The old gang back together again."

"I suppose it is," Will replied, but his eyes were on Hema; the way her smile lit up her whole face. She looked happy and Will was glad they had made the effort to come. Although his thoughts were straying to Esme and wondering if she was okay. As if on cue, a text flashed onto his message screen.

'**Esme is fine**' it was Flora, as thoughtful as ever, setting his mind at rest.

Will jigged towards Hema, arms outstretched, "let's have fun," he shouted, as she twirled towards him.

* * *

Will's father had been waiting for them now for fifteen minutes. Punctual as ever, he had left the house with plenty of time to cruise across the city in his Audi A5 and was parked in a bay, revving the engine and texting Will, to alert him of his arrival. When there was no reply after two attempts, he clambered from the vehicle with a tut and walked towards a group of noisy revellers who were staggering outside the entrance doors.

"Anyone seen Will?" He enquired firmly. A few of the inebriated teenagers gulped as they recognised Will's Dad, the formidable head-teacher of St Mary's – a school which they had themselves attended.

"He's still inside Mr Bentley," the small group moved aside, to allow Max room to stride through. Balloons floated up and down the corridor, bouncing off the strip lights and peeling plastered walls. He pulled open the doors, scanning the room for his only son. Will was locked in a tight embrace with Hema. The pair of them revolved slowly, moving to a smoochy song. Her head was tilted onto his shoulders and his chin was resting on her crown. Young children skidded around them, chasing rainbow coloured party streamers, but they seemed oblivious to them; their eyes were tightly closed.

Then the D.J squawked into the microphone that it was time to go home and the darkness evaporated in a flick of a switch. The remaining guests blinked with surprise, at the illuminated world in front of them. Will spotted Max tapping his foot, looking as tense as ever.

"We'd better go," he mumbled in Hema's ear.

"Are we late?" Fretted Hema. As usual she wore no watch, but noticed the look of impatience on Max's firmly set jaw, "sorry, we were having such a lovely time."

Max waved the apology away, "we should head home."

After saying goodbye to Sadie, Jimmy and the rest of the school pack, Will fell in step beside his dad.

"How's she been?" He queried breathlessly.

Max smiled, "an absolute angel. We've hardly heard a peep out of her."

"Oh, that's great," Hema quickened her pace to keep up with them both.

They hurried past a youth who was bent over and retching in the corner of the stairwell. Max raised an eyebrow, "it was a good party then?"

"It was great," Will replied.

"And you're both sober," Max feigned a look of shock.

"We've had a few," Will admitted.

"Not too many though," Hema corrected, "Esme will probably have me up in a few hours."

"I'll do the night shift," Will pulled her close and Hema looked up at him with adoring eyes. Next to them, Max Bentley smiled.

* * *

After all their preparations for a sleepless night, Esme decided to have a lie in.

"Is she alright?" Hema asked, gazing with concern at her tiny daughter.

"She *looks* fine," Will answered, "blimey, it's past six o'clock," he poked her tiny foot with a gentle fore finger. Instantly she stirred, opened her mouth to emit a high-pitched cry. Then her arms and legs were punching the air in a demand for attention. Will left Hema to feed her and jogged down the stairs to make them both a strong coffee.

"Morning!" A deep voice resonated in the still kitchen.

"Morning Dad."

Will turned to look at Max who was seated at the kitchen table, furiously typing away, "you're up early – aren't you supposed to be on holiday?"

Max shook his head firmly, "term starts next week. I've got so much to do I don't know where to start. Got a bad head?"

"No," Will replied, "I'm just tired. Hema is too."

Max looked up from his laptop, "me and your mum could have Esme this afternoon for a couple of hours."

"What was that?" Flora slid into the kitchen, looking fresh and radiant in a summer dress covered with flowers.

"I was just suggesting we could have Esme, to give Will and Hema a rest."

Flora's face fell, "Oh I'm sorry Will. I'm working this afternoon, but it's my day off tomorrow. I'd love to have her then, if that helps."

"It's cool Mum – don't worry," Will tipped the steaming black coffee into a line of mugs, adding milk and sugar.

"I hope this job isn't going to make you stressed Flora," Max snapped, "you don't want to take too much on."

Will was just about to jump to her defence when Flora placed both hands on her hips and looked down at her husband.

"Of course I'm not stressed," she replied, "I'm thoroughly enjoying myself. It feels great to be earning again and it *is* only seventeen hours per week, so don't be such a grouch bag."

Max opened his mouth then closed it again. *Go Mum*, Will grinned at her with pride.

"Oh Will, Marie your friend's sister? She's such a wonderful boss. So patient and encouraging. I am now fully proficient on a state of the art, computerised till." Her eyes shone brightly as she spoke.

"Well done Mum," Will passed her a drink, "her sister Jules is a top bird."

Flora nodded, "I really should purchase her a gift, a thank you token for getting me the job."

"You did that all by yourself Flora," Max cleared his throat, "I'm sure that you were impressive during your interview."

Flora positively beamed at her husband, "How about bacon rolls for breakfast?" She asked, with a happy twinkle in her eye.

* * *

By mid-morning, Will and Hema were ready to face the day.

As it was so beautiful, they decided to take Esme out to the park.

"Let's have a picnic," Hema said with excitement. They raided the fridge, stuffing sausage rolls, slices of quiche and freshly made sandwiches courtesy of Flora, into a basket.

"I *think* we're ready," Hema said breathlessly, then slapped her forehead, "milk! Of course." She hurried over to the fridge, depositing two small bottles into a cool bag.

"Are there enough nappies in here?" Will prodded the bulging changing bag.

"Well I put five in earlier," Hema replied, biting her lower lip, "maybe I'll put a few more in, just to be on the safe side."

Off she scurried to grab two from the towering nappy stack.

"Are you *sure* we're ready?" Will scratched his head and stared down at the bags scattered across the kitchen floor, "I had no idea taking a baby out would involve so much organisation – so much *stuff.*"

"It's crazy," Hema agreed and they both chuckled.

"Who would have thought it – us domesticated – the cheeky chappie who only used to carry a house key and the dizzy girl who liked to travel light – with only a lipstick for company."

Hema lobbed a dirty bib at his head. Will responded by flicking droplets of water from the dripping tap. Then Esme let out an angry wail, putting a stop to their frivolities.

Will picked her out of the bouncy seat, placing her gently into her pushchair cum travel seat and they both gazed down at their pretty daughter, who looked extremely cute in a lilac sundress, with ribbon trimmed socks and a matching hat. She blinked up at them, eliciting a chorus of ah's from them both.

"Look at her face," Hema gripped Will's arm, "she's smiling!"

They both leant nearer, then suddenly a loud noise of flatulence made them jump.

"I'll change her…again," Will responded with good natured resignation.

* * *

"And we're off!" Will tipped the pram onto its back wheels and pushed Esme out into the glorious sunshine.

"Oh my, it's hot!" Hema was already perspiring, "which way is it? I'm still not used to this area."

"Take a left."

Slowly they walked down the street, underneath blossom trees bursting with colour.

"Well isn't that the cutest sight ever," Flora's friend Brenda was bustling across the road towards them, "how are you all?"

"We're fine thank you," Hema answered politely, darting a glance at Will.

"Little Esme is just adorable," Brenda peered down and clucked like an old mother hen, "my daughter Rose won't have children, says they're a bind. Puts her career before a family that one and here's me, desperate to be a Grandma. Your mum must be so proud."

"She is…thanks," Will went to move on, but she blocked his way.

"The church is very busy. You really should think about putting her name down for the christening as soon as possible dear."

Will's eyes narrowed behind his dark glasses, "what's Mum been saying?"

Brenda looked contrite and began pulling at a loose thread of cotton on her skirt, "nothing much Will – just that she was hoping to decorate the church when erm…I, I should be going. I've got a chasseur in the slow cooker that's probably burning as we speak." Brenda retreated into the shade and Will walked purposefully on.

"Will…" Hema's voice held a warning tone.

"I'll talk to her," he rasped, "let's just enjoy the day on our own for a change."

* * *

Hema found them a perfect spot on the newly mown grass, which was beside the lake and underneath two towering oak trees. They secured the patchwork blanket with large stones to stop it blowing away in the breeze, then lay back to gaze at a cerulean blue, cloudless sky.

"This is heavenly," Hema murmured, "I think I could get used to being a stay-at-home Mum."

"Do that then," Will shrugged, "there's no pressure. You don't *have* to go back to uni."

"But I really wanted to be a social worker," Hema sighed, "maybe I could stay home with Esme until she starts nursery."

"And maybe," Will grinned, pushed her back and rolled on top of her, "you could be my very own domestic goddess."

"Slave more like," Hema laughed and bucked underneath him, trying to throw him off.

"I should shackle you to the bed post and let you free just to make dinner," Will nipped at her throat.

"Will stop, stop!" Hema kicked her legs upwards and squealed as he tickled her.

Then Esme wailed and they both shot upright.

"She's due a feed," panted Hema, as she glanced at her watch.

"I'll do it," Will rolled onto his knees, heaving himself up.

"Here," Hema passed him the formula, then shielded her eyes as she looked around.

In the distance, she could see boats bobbing on a shimmering lake, clusters of geese floating towards her and a line of people queuing beside an ice cream van. Will followed her line of vision.

"Yes please," he said, before she could ask, "with raspberry sauce and two flakes."

Hema bent down to wipe at the clumps of grass which had stained her knees, "I won't be long."

He settled back to feed Esme, who was chomping on the teat fiercely. There were a group of young lads playing football nearby. He watched them kicking the ball to each other and thought back to youthful, carefree days. When he'd played in this very park with Jimmy. It had been flat fields then, now there were slides and climbing frames and zip wires; activities for all ages and here he was with his baby daughter, at just nineteen years of age – it was mad! But he wouldn't be without her, not now. Gently he sniffed her forehead, she smelt sweet, like melted chocolate and she was a warm bundle in his arms. Suddenly she pushed the bottle out of her mouth and gave him the brightest, sunniest smile he had ever seen.

"Hema!" He called, reaching frantically for his phone, "hold that pose princess." He took a dozen shots from different angles then searched the field for his girlfriend.

Hema was nowhere to be seen. Will scanned the throng of people next to the ice-cream van, then the lake, where had she gone? He wondered. Then he saw a flash of cream, long dark hair, being pulled behind a tree. Immediately Will was on his feet, his heart racing.

"Hema!" He shouted.

A frightened face came into view, "Will," she waved her arms and stumbled towards him, but two Asian men grabbed hold of her, halting her escape. They began shouting directly at her, jabbing at her, she looked petrified.

Will sprang into action, strapping a squealing Esme into her carry seat, then running with her across the grass, as fast as it was safe to do so. He was quick, reaching them a few moments later.

"Hema!" Will panted breathlessly, "are you okay?"

"Get lost," the taller of the two youths snarled at him.

Will glanced at Hema.

"Will…Esme," she motioned to her wailing daughter, "take her away please, I can sort this out."

Gently Will set Esme down, "leave her alone," he said firmly.

"That's what you need to do!" The other man shouted, He had dark penetrating eyes, a chin of stubble and a menacing countenance, "she needs to come home. She is shaming our family."

"She's with *my* family now," Will replied calmly, "we're looking after her."

"You two will never work," the man spat back, his face contorted with rage, "she'll soon get bored of you, she'll see sense eventually. Blood is thicker than water!"

"Oh yeah?" Will surveyed them both. They were taller than him and heavier built, but there was no way he was going to back down. There was no way he was going to let them bully and frighten her into submission. Instinctively he balled his fists into tight balls, as he prepared himself for a fight. The men surged towards him then halted as a voice boomed, "everything alright here?"

Will sighed with relief as a policeman strode over.

The ruddy faced officer glanced at them all, noting the tension emanating, "is there a problem?"

Will swallowed, "they were just leaving officer."

"You better watch your back!" One of them yelled in anger.

"Oi, oi," the policeman moved in-between them, "don't make threats now. You need to calm down." His dangling walkie-talkie blared in the sudden quietness, "move on now gents, go on."

The two men reluctantly turned away, kicking at stones and discarded chip wrappers.

Will watched warily as they stormed off down the winding path, heading for the park exit.

"Who were they?" He took a shaking Hema in his arms.

"My cousins," Hema replied with a sniff, "no doubt doing my uncles dirty work."

"Can I help you Miss?" The ruddy faced policeman was looking their way with concern.

"No…I,I, I'm fine, it was just a family argument."

"Hema," Will implored, "this is serious."

Hema abruptly pulled away from him, picked up Esme and began walking briskly back towards their belongings.

"Call this number if you need our help," the police officer handed Will a card with a local telephone number scrawled across it. Will nodded his thanks then broke into a jog until he reached her.

"Stop!"

Hema spun around, her cheeks were covered with tears, "it's never going to be okay is it Will? They're never going to leave us alone."

"Shush," Will soothed, grabbing hold of her, "I'm not going to let anyone hurt you. I'll sort it out…I promise." He kissed her forehead, her wet cheeks, her lips and they hugged each other tight, giving each other warmth and support and protection.

Chapter Five

"This is too sad!" Juliette sniffed loudly and wriggled her toes, trying to dispel the pins and needles that signalled she had been sitting in the same position for far too long. Three hours and fifteen minutes to be precise. Marie pulled a tissue from the box balancing on the arm of the sofa, blew her own nose, before thrusting a wad of scented paper Juliette's way.

"How many times have you pair watched Titanic?" Dave enquired, with relief that it was finally over.

"Five times together," Marie replied, flicking off the television, "and four times on my own."

Dave rolled his eyes, "Christ. Aren't you fed up of it?"

"No!" Marie and Juliette answered in unison, both of their faces blotchy from crying.

"Although we did fast forward the boring bits." Marie admitted, "What have you and Clive been up to anyway?" she placed one hand on her protruding stomach and struggled to her feet.

"Pool of course, that games room was the best investment we've made," Dave noted Juliette's empty glass, "fancy another?"

"Yes please," she replied, "has Clive gone home?"

"Of course I haven't," Clive replied, sticking his head around the door. He was smiling widely and his auburn hair was sprouting from his head in wild, untamed tufts. Juliette suppressed a chuckle, raised her glass his way and said, "here's to Saturday night."

They decided to move the furniture; shoving it back against the wall and making a square shaped space on the living room floor. Juliette inspected her sister's

C.D collection, "where are all the eighties?" She wailed, "all I can see is rock, rock and more rock."

Marie sniffed, "that's Dave's collection. Mine is in the dresser. Jules, you *know* how much I love Motown and dance. There's plenty to choose from, but I'm sorry to disappoint you – we don't listen to eighties music in this house."

"Well you should," Juliette grumbled, pulling the drawer open, "oh you have Diana Ross and The Jacksons too," she pulled out a couple of C.Ds and passed them to Dave to slot into the machine. 'Stop! In the Name of Love' rang around the room.

"Good choice," Marie said, tapping her feet in time to the rhythm, "now when are my niece and nephew back?"

Juliette pulled a sad face, "not until tomorrow afternoon, Marty's taking them clothes shopping first thing. They were so excited to be having a sleep over with him, but I can't help worrying. I feel like my arm is missing without them in the flat."

"Of course you're going to miss them Jules, but I suppose that is nice of him," Maz replied grudgingly, "about time he put his hand in his pocket."

Juliette decided to ignore that remark. She was well aware of her family's contempt for ex-criminal, ex-partner Marty, but since his release from prison last year, Juliette had to admit that he had been making a real effort with Harry and Molly. She found herself in a difficult position. Molly adored her dad and Harry was starting to thaw towards him also. Irrespective of what she thought of him personally, her children needed him in their life. He made them happy and that was enough for Juliette to make the effort to be more amiable towards him.

Just then Clive grabbed hold of her and twirled her around so fast her head was spinning.

"Whoops!" Juliette stumbled over the mat, "I think I need some fresh air." They left Marie and Dave bopping together and trooped out onto the dimly lit patio. The evening air was cool, clouds drifted across a sparkling full moon and hairy moths fluttered above them, attracted to the beam of the security light. Tendrils of smoke curled above the neighbour's fence; the remnants of an earlier garden fire, filling the air with a smoky, burnt acrid smell.

"I've enjoyed myself tonight," Juliette said, in-between hiccups, "thank you."

"You work too hard Jules," Clive said with a warm smile, "you should do this more often."

He brushed away a loose curl that had flopped over her forehead, Juliette gazed up at him, immobile and transfixed as he leant closer. Gently his lips touched hers, warm and soft, then his arms came around her and Juliette was kissing him back.

It was a pleasant experience, his mouth felt…nice and he was such a lovely bloke, such a nice friend. Friend – exactly what he was and nothing more! An image of Ben Rivers floated before her, making her gasp.

"Sorry," she mumbled, taking a step back, "I can't."

Clive's face fell with disappointment and a sad resignation, "you love him, don't you?"

Juliette nodded, "but I'm trying not to. How…?"

Clive shrugged, "Dave told me about him. The lecturer guy? Be careful Jules, he's not like you. He's not like us."

"I know," Juliette hung her head, "I am being completely unrealistic, completely foolish; over some guy who is way out of my league."

Clive gripped her arm, "don't you *ever* talk like that about yourself again. You are just as good, if not better than any of those academics," he frowned, "you understand what a struggle real life can be, you live it every day. You're inspiring and precious, you're everything!" He turned away from her, shoving his hands deep in his pocket.

Juliette swallowed, surprised by his outburst. Gently she touched his back, "Clive, I don't know what to say. I didn't realise you felt that strongly towards me."

"I shouldn't have said anything," he sounded annoyed, "just don't put yourself down – okay?"

"I promise," Juliette said with a fervent nod.

"Come on," Clive slung an arm across her bare, goose pimpled shoulders, "we'll have one more dance then I'll take you home. I'm completely knackered, it's been a long, busy week."

"I'm not the only one who works too hard," Juliette commented, noticing the weary lines around his eyes. She felt her heart strings being metaphorically tugged and was overwhelmed with guilt, for the way she had rejected him. "You're a lovely bloke Clive, but I…I'm just not ready for a relationship."

Clive laughed throatily, "Jules will you take a look at yourself, I'm sure I'll survive being turned down, although I have to admit it doesn't happen often and how can you be immune to my animal magnetism anyway?"

"Oh you!" Juliette knocked against him, "pass me my wine before I change my mind."

* * *

On Monday morning, before the sun had risen, before the traffic madness had commenced, Esme Bentley decided to rouse the entire household from its slumber. A bout of painful wind rocked her tiny frame, which resulted in a screaming pitch that lasted for a good thirty minutes. Will and Hema took it in turns to pace with their inconsolable child, trying to quieten her with a soother, a nappy change and a bottle of sweet tasting baby milk.

"Your poor parents!" Hema commented, as she struggled into her dressing gown.

The lights had snapped on in Max and Flora's bedroom, then the landing, leaving a bright trail down the stairs and into the kitchen, where the kettle was wearily clicked on. Then they were all in the same room, shuffling about and yawning, while a wide awake and extremely vocal Esme wailed and kicked her tiny limbs.

"In my day we gave them gripe water," Flora suggested gently, torn between wanting to help, but keen not to play the interfering mother-in-law.

Hema lay Esme down on the changing mat and rubbed tenderly at her daughter's distended stomach.

"They taught us this in baby yoga," Hema replied calmly.

Will stood beside her, shaking a brightly coloured rattle above Esme's head. It seemed to work, she spluttered with indignation, burped loudly then promptly fell fast asleep.

"Well done Hema!" Flora smiled with delight, "you're so good with her. Both of you."

Will grinned down at his daughter, who he decided now looked like an angel, "she's a sweetie, just like her Nanny."

"Of course she is," Max lifted the tray and the others followed him and the aroma of strong coffee into the sitting room.

"I've never watched television this early before," Hema said, as she relaxed on the floor next to Will, with Esme in her arms.

"It's always doom and gloom," Max complained, flicking through the world news channels.

He stopped on a programme entitled 'the nightmare neighbour next door.' They watched transfixed as Bob the bricklayer from Scunthorpe videoed his self-proclaimed 'lunatic neighbour' Frank, subversively digging *his* rose trees up in the dead of night.

"Oh my gosh," Flora's hand flew to her mouth as Frank struggled to pull the roots from the ground, flinging soil everywhere, "how can people act like that?"

Max shook his head, "Flora," he admonished gently, "that is tame behaviour compared to what goes on at St Mary's."

"Aren't you back today?" Will asked, passing a packet of biscuits around.

"Yes, I'm back," Max replied crisply, "along with the rest of the staff. Your friend has been invited too. The inset days are an important part of school life. As well as offering the opportunity for prep and training, they also give the staff chance to bond. I'm sure Sophie would like to get to know some of the other staff members."

"Or maybe not," Will replied with a roll of his eyes.

"I think they are very lucky to have such a driven and inspirational head teacher," Flora declared with a loving glance at her husband.

"Yes well, I'm hoping they see that," Max replied, "my predecessor was a complete and utter kn…" he paused as Flora peered over her glasses, "let's just say he was unscrupulous. A man who excelled at manipulation and mind games. Apparently, he lied to Ofsted, bent the truth to other significant institutions and spent most of his time performing in broom cupboards with more than the cleaner, if you understand my meaning." Max sighed at Flora's shocked face, "but worst of all he was pathologically jealous of other progressive schools within the borough and pathetically competitive towards other Headteachers who were doing a better job than he was," Max shuddered. "Oh, and I also heard that he was well known for concocting ludicrous conspiracy and bizarre theories to save his own skin and career. Really Flora you couldn't pay a person to believe what he got up to."

"Whatever happened to him?" Gasped Flora.

"He went off sick," Max replied with disgust, "squandering hard-working, taxpayer's money."

"Max!" Flora bolted upright, "it really isn't like you to be so angry!"

"Oh he deserves it," Max grumbled, dunking his biscuit. "Flora I've met a lot of headteachers, and believe me, this guy was up there as one of the worst, totally preoccupied with his own wellbeing; he was nobody's friend and under his watch the whole place became a den of iniquity. A real-life Sodom and Gomorrah. It's a wonder the school wasn't struck with fire and brimstone!"

Will chuckled, "sounds a fun place to work." Hema snorted with suppressed laughter.

Max rustled last night's newspaper, "it's not funny my lad, that man almost ruined the reputation of the whole school. Although I have to admit I do hold some sympathy for him; controlling large groups of females can be extremely challenging. We need more male staff at St. Mary's for sure, the women can be predatory – they hunt together in packs!"

"What?" Will threw back his head and laughed merrily, "like velociraptors?"

"Yes. Just like that, monsters with vicious talons," Max smirked and kicked off his slippers, "Flora – stay in your flower shop, you wouldn't last five minutes."

"I think you're being a bit sexist," Hema had stopped chortling and was glaring at Max, "surely you can't 'control' the female teachers. Aren't they every bit as professional as you are?"

Max closed his mouth, looking shocked.

"Way to go!" Will high fived his girlfriend, settled back to dunk his biscuit in the warm, frothy cappuccino.

"It must be terribly hard for Max," Flora felt compelled to jump to his defence, "and his deputy Marcia seems to make matters worse, isn't that right dear?"

Max nodded, sighed wearily, "Mrs Bent seems to be approaching that awkward age in a woman's life. She has been acting very strange of late."

"Maybe it's the world of education that's all wrong," Flora suggested brightly, "maybe they need to focus less on academic intelligence at teacher training universities and choose prospective teachers based on their emotional intelligence instead."

"Yes," Max nodded, "you could be right there love. So, any ideas on how I can start the new school year with a successful bang?"

"Motivate your staff more," Flora suggested gently, "you can do it love."

"I'm tired Flora," Max replied, "sometimes I think we should bring back the cane – and that's just for the staff!"

Will fell about, clutching his sides with mirth.

"It really isn't a laughing matter," Flora remonstrated, glancing with sympathy at her husband, "I'll make you egg sandwiches for lunch, on that crusty bread you love and I've got some fresh cress too?"

"Sounds divine," Max nodded gratefully, "I don't even enjoy the school dinners anymore – Jamie Oliver has a *lot* to answer for."

Then all eyes were back on the T.V, as Frank the nightmare neighbour was arrested and taken away in a blue flashing, siren wailing cop car.

* * *

The alarm woke Sophie at seven a.m. exactly. For the first time in weeks, she shot upwards and flung back the duvet with excitement. Today she was attending her very first INSET day at St. Mary's, the weather was warm, the sun was shining and the birds were hanging off her guttering and chirruping melodically. Sophie pulled off her silk pyjamas, flinging them in the washing basket on the way to her en-suite bathroom. The jet power shower rumbled to life, attacking her senses and ensuring she was fully awake. The night had been good; she had slept well, she hadn't woken crying for a change and if she *had* experienced nightmares, then this morning she had no recollection of them. She sang as she towelled herself dry and she sang as she brushed her teeth. The steam misted up the mirror, making it difficult for her to apply her mascara evenly. How long had it been since she had worn make-up? She wondered. Too long, her inner voice decided, but today she was back, today she felt energised and optimistic, ready to do beautiful.

On the way back into her bedroom she stumbled over a pile of ironing and stubbed her toe on a hardback book. Dust motes floated in the air, settling on her dresser and clinging to the heavy drapes covering her window. Sophie searched in her drawers for matching underwear, then pulled on a pair of grey bootleg trousers and hopped into soft suede ankle boots. Then she flung back the curtains and cranked open the window to allow the morning dew to freshen the musty air. Josh and Jake were playing their computer, she could hear them through the walls, shouting with excitement. Sophie squirted a cloud of expensive perfume around her neck and shoulders then pushed gently on their door.

"Boys are you ready for school?" They were perched on Jake's bed, a controller in each hand, faces staring intently at the vast screen, where a blue and red sportscar raced along a desert track. There was no reply, but Sophie could see that they were both dressed in their new uniform, with their hair gelled into spikes.

"Morning!" She hollered.

"Morning Mum," Jake replied with a cheeky grin, while Josh mumbled an indecipherable greeting.

"I'll make you breakfast, shall I?" There was no reply, just whooping at the T.V screen.

Shaking her head, Sophie snuck out and down the winding, opulent staircase, to be greeted by two playful dogs who jumped at her, almost knocking her sideways. She let them out into the garden, watching as they bounded through the overgrown grass. Marmaduke, the tabby tom cat peered at her from the garden fence, hissing at the dogs when they got too close. The sun was climbing in the sky, pushing the night clouds away. Sophie googled today's weather, pleased that it forecast mild temperatures. The summer flowers were still in bloom and the hanging baskets were ablaze with multi coloured Freesias and trailing Lobelia. She crossed to the cooker and turned on the hob. This morning's breakfast was going to be quick: scrambled eggs, the kids favourite.

"Good Morning!" Sophie turned as her housekeeper walked into the kitchen.

"Oh, morning Heidi," she greeted, stirring the beaten eggs with a wooden spoon, "I never heard you come in. Could you pass me the pepper please?"

Heidi removed her summer straw hat, placing it on the table, then passed over the pepper pot.

"It's a glorious day," Heidi remarked, as she turned on the cold tap to wash her hands.

"Gorgeous," Sophie agreed, "I'm off to do my voluntary work today, after taking the boys to school of course. I should be home after lunch though. Will you be okay on your own?"

"Of course," Heidi poured fresh juice into three glass tumblers, "I have lots to keep me busy," there was a pause, "have you heard from Mr O'Neill?"

Sophie grimaced, "he's messaged me. Wants to meet up to talk. I really don't want to see him, but I suppose we do need to discuss the children, finances, that sort of thing."

Heidi nodded, grabbing the toast which had just popped up.

As Sophie was spooning the eggs onto plates, the doorbell chimed throughout the house. The dogs rushed back indoors, yelping with excitement.

"Who could that be this early?" Sophie wondered, glancing at the clock.

"You want me to get it?" Heidi asked helpfully.

"No, it's okay," she set the saucepan down and hurried through the hall to the front door. A peer through the security peephole revealed her mother, looking immaculate, dark designer sunglasses snapped firmly over her eyes.

Sophie sighed, her good mood and positivity slowly draining away.

"Hello Mother," she said brightly, as she swung the heavy door open.

"Darling," Yvonne air kissed both her cheeks, before brushing past her, "I just thought I would drop in to see how you are, while I was passing."

"This early?" Sophie replied with surprise. Her mother was famous for her late nights and late rises.

"I'm concerned about you darling. You haven't replied to any of my messages. Derek and I have been worried."

Sophie tapped her foot, crossing her arms in a defensive gesture, "I've had a lot on my mind. And it doesn't help that you're letting Ryan stay with you. I feel like you're taking his side Mum."

"He's only stayed a few nights," Yvonne replied with a pout, "he's been at his footballer friends, Mickey? I think that's his name. As for taking sides, I think you're being silly Sophie. Ryan and Derek are extremely good friends, I can hardly turn him away now can I?"

"Why not?" Sophie shrugged, "he *has* cheated on me, your one and only child."

Yvonne steered her into the sitting room, "he's full of remorse," she explained, "I know he's done wrong, but it doesn't mean you have to divorce."

"That's exactly what I intend to do," Sophie said with conviction, "this is more than a drunken mistake, he was unfaithful twice, probably more. He's disgusting!"

Yvonne held up her hands, "okay, okay, I *get* it. You're angry and hurting, but Ryan is in bits. He's falling apart."

"Good," snapped Sophie.

"Please," Yvonne implored, "could you talk to him at least? Hear him out?"

Sophie sighed, "I suppose I'll have to eventually, for the boy's sake at least."

Yvonne clapped, "hooray! That's the spirit. Now where are my angels, I've missed them terribly."

"I was just going to call them," Sophie walked to the bottom of the stairs and hollered up that their breakfast was ready.

Julia Sutton

"Nan!" Josh and Jake charged down the stairs.

"Don't you look smart!" Yvonne appraised her grandchildren's gleaming white shirts and neatly ironed trousers. Their shoes were bright and shiny and their rucksacks were clean and new. She reached down to hug them both.

"I've bought you boys a present," Yvonne dug in her designer handbag, "it's only something little for your first day back at school." She passed them a stationery pack, full of pens, pencils, erasers and football stickers.

"Wow! Thanks Nan," they both cried with wide eyed delight.

"Breakfast!" Sophie pushed them gently towards the kitchen, "thanks Mum that was kind." She smiled at Yvonne, "I'm sorry I can't talk for too long, I'm at St Mary's this morning."

"It's fine," Yvonne waved away her excuse, "I must dash anyway, Derek and I are going to Manchester shopping, but Sophie how does a spa day sound?"

Sophie shook her head, "sorry, enrolment for uni is this week, I need to prepare and catch up on reading." Truth was pamper days no longer interested her, she would rather go to the library with Evelyn. Funny how one year at university had altered her so dramatically. Who would have believed that she would be separated from Ryan O'Neill, the famous Chattlesbury Football Club striker?

Yvonne tossed her glossy locks, "fine," she said crisply, "maybe I'll take your friend Amber."

"Good idea," Sophie replied, walking her to the front door, "I think Amber would love that."

"Well goodbye darling, don't forget about little old me," Yvonne air kissed her cheeks again, then flounced out, down the gravel drive to the thrumming red sports car, where Derek, Sophie's ex-gardener sat singing along to the radio. Yvonne turned once to wave theatrically, before they disappeared in a cloud of smoke and Sophie smiled, a sad, bittersweet smile and closed the door firmly.

Chapter Six

By the time Sophie arrived at St. Mary's the sun was shining and her good mood had returned. She parked up, checked her reflection in the mirror and then rushed to catch up with Andrea, the year one teacher, who was struggling across the car park, carrying a huge box.

"Morning!" Sophie called, "here, let me help you."

"Hello! Sophie it's lovely to see you," Andrea gratefully passed over a wedge of folders and paperwork.

"How has your summer been?" Sophie chattered away, glad that she had made the effort to come into school today. It would have been so easy to call up and make some excuse, but keeping busy was the best medicine, Sophie acknowledged, in her case anyway.

"Good," Andrea replied with a nod, "I've spent quality time with my children and I've been running."

"Running? Isn't that difficult? I mean I presume that you must be super fit to run."

"It's not too bad when you get used to it," Andrea replied with a chuckle, "The secret is too build it up gradually. I'm running the London marathon next spring – fancy joining me?"

"Me running?" Sophie burst out laughing, "are you joking?"

"No." Andrea shook her head, "I'm not. Why not Sophie? I could do with a running buddy and it's extremely good for you both physically and spiritually. Think about it?"

"I'll *think* about it," Sophie replied, "but I can't promise anything."

"I, erm…read about your husband in the paper," Andrea said awkwardly, "are you okay?"

Sophie bit her lip, embarrassed by the realisation that her entire personal life had probably been played out in the local media. For the past three months, she had refused to purchase any Chattlesbury newspapers, as she knew Ryan's infidelities would be front page news. She only had to walk down the local street, hear the shopkeepers whispering about her and women looking at her with pity. Plus, the press had been persistently hanging around, waiting for her to appear on the drive, asking ridiculous questions like 'how do you feel Mrs O'Neill?'

"Yes, I'm okay," Sophie replied quietly, "at least, I'm getting there slowly."

"Good," Andrea rubbed her arm consolingly, "and you've come back!"

"I have! And I'm looking forward to seeing just what really happens on a school Inset day. My friends and I always thought teachers sat around drinking coffee."

Andrea laughed, "we do that too, but honestly Sophie everyone is incredibly busy, we have so much preparation to plough through and displays urgh... they are so time consuming."

"I'll pop down to your class when I've finished in the nursery," Sophie promised.

"Thank you," Andrea pulled open the door and they stepped inside the warm school, "I suppose I should get cracking. See you in the staffroom for coffee," she winked and disappeared inside her class.

Sophie waved and carried on, heading towards the nursery. She could see Cara at the end of the corridor, leaning against the bare wall, talking to the receptionist about her holiday.

"We had such an amazing, worry free summer! The cruise was spectacular: around the Mediterranean in just under two weeks. Dan and I have already booked for next year, we're doing the Caribbean and I'm counting down already. Oh Sophie, you're here, I was worried you might never come back," Cara gripped her in a tight embrace, "where have you spent *your* summer? Wait, let me guess – the Seychelles?"

"Lanzarote," Sophie divulged with a wide smile, "and it was extremely hot – even for the Canaries."

"I've never been there," Cara tucked her arm through the hook of Sophie's, drawing her into the nursery, "Fuerteventura I loved, Gran Canaria was hilly but okay. Come and sit down and tell me *all* about it."

They chatted for a while about holiday destinations, before the teaching assistants arrived. Mrs King bustled into the nursery, closely followed by Gina, who collapsed next to Sophie puffing and panting.

"The traffic was horrendous. I didn't think I'd make it in time for Mr Bentley's welcome speech."

"Speaking of which, it's almost nine, shall we go up?" Cara picked up her notebook and pen and they trooped up the stairs to the staffroom.

Most of the staff were already up there, milling about with drinks in their hands, chatting and laughing. Cara and the teaching assistants headed straight for the kettle leaving Sophie clutching her water, not knowing what to do. She edged her way through a sea of bodies and slunk into a spare seat next to Rob the year six teacher.

"Howdy," he grinned cheekily at her.

"Hello," she replied politely.

"So," he said, leaning closer, "are you still hell bent on becoming a teacher? Or have you come to your senses yet?"

"I'd still like to give it a shot," Sophie replied, with a nervous laugh, "how long have you been teaching?"

"Too long!" Rob wiped a froth of coffee from his top lip, "you know, you're far too nice to be working in education, so some of the more jaded female staff members here reckon. In fact," he touched a tress of her hair, "you remind me of a princess. Have you considered applying for Disney instead?"

"Being inappropriate again are you Rob?" Cara rolled her eyes at Sophie, "make a formal complaint against him sweetie, we all have."

"You'll never get rid of me Cara, seeing me makes the monotony of nursery each day worthwhile surely?"

Cara laughed, "you are so bad," she squeezed next to him, placed a teasing hand on his knee. Then there was a clacking sound coming from the direction of the stairs, "look out, here comes trouble." There was a scurry as the rest of the staff rushed to find a seat. Marcia Bent flung the door wide and smiled icily as all eyes focused on her.

"Well, it is pleasing to see that *all* the staff have made the effort to come in early," she began, "…even the teaching assistants are here on time. Mr Bentley is just in the little boy's room, so I thought I would make a start." A muffled titter ensued, as Marcia took a deep breath and glanced down at her notes.

"That won't be necessary Mrs Bent!" Max Bentley skirted around her and opened his arms wide, "welcome staff! I hope you have all had a fantastic summer and are relaxed and ready for the new school year. It is lovely to see you all looking so refreshed and radiant and eager to inspire a new class of inquisitive young minds. Now then, before we go over the itinerary for the day, there are a few issues that need addressing. Myself and Marcia have this morning looked over the pupil enrolment numbers in the nursery and we are disappointed to put it mildly. We are *way* below expected figures."

"There are far too many schools in this borough getting outstanding," Marcia spat out, "they're pinching all the children in the damned city and we're getting overlooked!"

"Yes indeed," Max glared at Cara, "we need to be more welcoming to the parents, everybody needs to make more of an effort," the staff emitted a collective groan, "please smile more and when we have parents evening – maybe the teaching assistants could provide refreshments?"

Mutters of resentment resounded around the room.

"Maybe they're outstanding because they have super heads in charge," Rob smirked.

"Super-heads my arse." Marcia bit out.

"Marcia!" Max remonstrated, "Super heads are usually super because they have supportive staff, not back stabbers, er… where was I?"

"Of course, we rely on our strong moral ethos to draw *our* parents," Marcia prowled around the room, "we don't need to be in the local newspaper constantly winning some award or another," she raised her fingers in mock derisive speech marks.

"I think we've made our point Mrs Bent," Max said smoothly, "Before we have a morning blessing with Father McGregor, I just need to remind everyone that student teachers are due in this term. Myself and Cara both attended that peculiar I mean particular school of education and Marcia went urm, somewhere else…"

"Where was that?" Rob whispered in Sophie's ear, "the school of hard knocks?"

Sophie gasped and tried to hide her laughter.

"so, everyone needs to be on their very best behaviour," Max concluded with a warning look around the staffroom.

Marcia rolled her eyes heavenwards, "Why you ask? It means the education lot will be in here again, partnership tutors and lecturers, snooping about – trying to tell *me* what's what. There is *nothing* that I don't know about teaching – isn't that right Mr Bentley?"

"No one knows everything Mrs Bent, not even you," Max shuffled his feet, "especially you."

Marcia glared at Mr Bentley and then wagged her finger, "of course we should all take anything the university says with a pinch of salt, but just to be on the safe side be very, very careful indeed the way you behave around them. They are a dangerous bunch and *not* to be trifled with, no sir-ee. And please, do not disclose sensitive information that should remain within St Mary's with any of them. That could lead to all sorts of bother and repercussions and we need to maintain our high reputation with them, whatever the cost. Even if that means twisting information around a wee bit to suit our own agenda," she slapped her ruler sharply against her folder gazing at Sophie.

"Are you talking to me?" Sophie squeaked, feeling embarrassed, "No, no, no you've got it all wrong…I was never there…I study English in the Humanities school - remember?"

"Oh yes," Mrs Bent laughed, "I'd forgotten all about that…but anyway, of course, we must all remain focussed people, don't let yourself be distracted by any of these probing lecturers," she declared, clearing her throat, "although I have to admit, I myself have had one or two lapses in concentration…and they were extremely pleasurable indeed."

"Mrs Bent!" Max shouted, "please. Control yourself!"

Marcia trailed off, with a shocked and gasping staff staring her way.

Max held up his hand in an attempt to instil order, "what Marcia is trying to say is please, be professional. These are not people to be played with, I mean prayed with, I mean…just be careful! They have a LOT of influence and can be extremely persuasive," Max coughed, "within the Archdiocese for a start. We don't want them on our backs as well as the council, the governors, the PTA, Ofsted, the DfES …the list is endless!" Max wiped his brow, "I think I need a quiet sit down and Marcia you should accompany me. We both have plenty of work to attend to. Staff, you may take a quick tea break, but please do *not* eat all the chocolate hobnobs, they are Father McGregor's favourite and he likes to take a few back for the erm…nuns."

Marcia bobbed her head politely and they left the room, leaving the staff alarmed, whispering and racing for the custard creams.

"Oh God! Enthusiastic student teachers again – after *my* rightful job, now what can I do to discredit them?" Suzie the KS2 teacher blew out a long raspberry.

Cara patted her knee, "don't worry dear. I'm sure with your ambition and determined work ethic, you'll be *just fine*. We all have your back here you're one of us, and you have our full support. No matter what you get up to. No matter what you do." she thought for a moment, "well maybe not Marcia, her allegiance seems to be towards the fairer haired staff members, for some reason…"

"Stop waffling nonsense Cara," Winnie, a wild looking Modern Foreign Language specialist with a flowing afro chucked her mug in the sink, "in my day student teachers just got on with it. There was none of this namby pamby let's treat them like babies attitude. Resilience is what's lacking in today's student teachers. I do hope they put one of them with me, I'll toughen them up."

"Put them off teaching forever more like," Rob whispered out the side of his mouth.

"Winnie!" He said loudly, standing up, "I've missed your acerbic wit and general noise."

"Nothing wrong with shouting to make a point," Winnie replied with a smug, self-indulgent smile, "I *like* to shout – children, parents, other colleagues, that's my motto in life, don't you agree?" She glared at Sophie.

"Urm… maybe not?" Sophie replied, startled by the teacher's aggression.

"You know Winnie," Rob cracked his knuckles, "If, by any happy chance you're struck off teaching, you could always go into the protection racket. I reckon that *you* would make a fantastic bouncer."

Winnie glared his way, "*I* am a strong, independent woman with high morals. I have muscles in places you could only dream of seeing, *Rob*."

"Your tongue by any chance?" Rob cut in, "and let's face it we've all seen enough of that at this school."

Winnie shrugged, "that's the way to get ahead in life. Being nice gets you absolutely nowhere," she clattered out of the room with a wall stapler and reams of display backing paper in her arms.

"Don't be concerned or fooled by her Disney, her bravado soon disappears when a real man confronts her," Rob bent to tie his shoe laces, "she's a fawning sycophant and the complete antithesis to what a teacher should really be.

Whereas *I* am a sensitive, modern age practitioner, full of compassion and kindness. You won't catch me judging, stitching up a friend over a promotion or ruining a person's reputation for the sake of my own career. Unlike many here Sophie, I have some morals and conscience."

"Even if they are well hidden," Cara laughed and hugged Rob, "I only jest Sophie, Rob's a great bloke and if I wasn't married, well he'd have to watch out. Now, haven't you got some SATS to prepare for?" She grabbed the tea-towel and flicked it off his derriere. Rob chuckled throatily and made a dash for the stairs, where the other staff had begun piling down.

* * *

"That was lovely!" Was Sophie's verdict on Father McGregor's welcome speech and sermon on Christian compassion, which had been held in the main assembly hall. She trailed back into the nursery, following a yawning Cara.

"He is a darling," agreed Cara, "it's just his voice, it makes me all sleepy and relaxed. Now I'm ready for my bed. Mrs King – more coffee please."

They worked solidly for the next two hours, stapling paper on the display boards, labelling and sorting the new toys, generally tidying and reorganising. Then Sophie trooped outside with Mrs King to tackle the bike shed. Spiders scurried away in fright, as they emptied the entire container, binning mouldy cars and one wheeled trikes.

"That's better," Mrs King slapped her palms, creating a swirl of dust around them, "all ready for another year of fun. Shall we have another drink Sophie? I think we've earned it."

"Definitely!" A tired Sophie glanced at her watch, "it's almost lunch-time."

Mrs King ushered her back inside the nursery. Cara was up the step ladders stapling a new windchime to the ceiling.

"Would you like something to eat Sophie? We're ordering sausage sandwiches, my treat."

"That sounds delicious," Sophie nodded, "I'll have to leave straight after though."

"I understand," Cara backed down the wobbling steps, "thank you so much for your help today. For once I feel prepared for the new intake of children. Did you *hear* the comment management made about the low uptake figures? They make my blood boil, as if we haven't enough to do, without pandering to parents."

There was a murmur of agreement, "and to think I felt sorry for Mrs Bent this morning." Cara shook her head with disdain.

"You did?" Gina looked her way with surprise.

"I did," Cara's laughter was tinged with bitterness, "the three of them were gossiping about her in the school office again, running her down. It's a wonder her ears haven't sizzled right off! To put it bluntly they were making unkind comments about her being under the thumb that's all – and that we bear the brunt of her frustration." Cara paused, "I wonder what they say about me?"

"Oh Cara, don't you know; you're a spoilt Prima Donna who doesn't live in the real world." Gina wagged her finger.

Cara chuckled good naturedly, "those guys."

"Don't they like her?" Sophie clicked on the kettle.

"They don't like anybody," the nursery teacher divulged, "although Marcia does seem to enjoy being bitched about and at least it gives someone else a break. Of that we can be thankful."

There was a loud tut from the nursery teaching assistant, "serves her right I reckon. Have you heard about her being on the warpath?"

"Oh yes, that," Cara snorted, "Mrs Bent has a bee in her proverbial bonnet about one of the support staff. Apparently said lowly TA has far too much fun at work and doesn't take the world of education seriously enough," Cara sighed, "oh maybe they're right, I shouldn't really agree with the gossips, but she *could* be power-crazy after all."

"I kind of feel sorry for her," Sophie admitted.

"Don't Sophie, I've seen the way she's treated the staff over the years, she *is* a bully, don't waste your sympathy." Cara passed her a staple gun, smiling widely, "now, let's go and sort out the dining hall display board, then you can tell me all about your wonderful children and what it's *really* like to study for an English degree."

* * *

Ann couldn't sleep. She watched the ceiling fan revolve slowly above her, while sweat trickled down the side of her face.

"Why is it so humid?" She complained to Jon, who was wrapped tightly around the duvet, one leg sticking out at an odd angle.

"Huh?" He peered through the darkness at her, "do you want a glass of water?"

"I've got one," Ann replied with a sigh, "I just like complaining. Surely summer should be over by now?"

"I love the heat," Jon replied sleepily, snuggling himself further underneath the duvet.

"I know *you* do," Ann reached for a tissue, to mop at her damp brow. She could hear music drifting through the ajar window, "this is the fifth party in a month."

"What?" Jon struggled into an upright position.

"The neighbours," Ann blew out her irritation, "they complain about people parking outside their house, while they themselves keep the whole street awake regularly with shite music."

"What's really on your mind love?"

There was silence in the room. Ann thrummed her fingers on the mattress.

"I'm nervous about going back to uni tomorrow," she admitted.

"Why?" Jon looked confused, "I thought you were enjoying being a student?"

"I am...I mean it's because it's year two, the grades really matter. I'm worried I won't be able to keep up with all the reading and the A grade essays."

Jon shook his head, "You've always been too much of a perfectionist. Don't worry, *you* are going to smash it."

"I hope so," Ann inhaled shakily, "I'm also worried about the adoption." She heard Jon huff in response. "I know he'll like *you*, but what if he hates *me*."

"Come here," Jon opened his arms, allowing Ann room to snuggle against his firm pectorals.

"Stop stressing," he advised, kissing her forehead, "they warned us it might be difficult. Let's just go meet Samuel and see how things progress. He'll love you by the way. You're genuine and caring and a really nice person, you're going to make a lovely Mum."

"Not that you're biased?" Ann queried playfully, as she gently kissed his warm skin, "I'm not sleepy at all."

Their lips met in the moonlit room, Ann's body tingled with heat and pleasure, and her worries subsided, like the tide on a gently rocking sea.

"I can grab breakfast at uni," Ann decided the next morning, as she zipped up her cardigan and checked her bag for stationery.

"My wife the A grade student!" Jon smiled broadly, "are you ready?"

"Think so," Ann wheeled herself out of the front door and down the ramp. Mrs McInnis, her elderly neighbour was out on her drive polishing her Citreon Saxo.

"Ann are you off to school? I mean university?" She threw her rag on the tarmac, making a beeline for her.

"I am," Ann smiled politely.

"My grandson has started at Chattlesbury. A degree in forensics sounds awfully complicated to me, but he assures me that he'll have a spectacular job at the end of it. What are you studying again dear?" Mrs McInnis bowed her head, messing with the hearing aid attached to her ear.

"English," Ann replied in a loud voice.

"Splendid! I do love reading. Danielle Steele is my favourite, would you like to borrow some of her novels dear? I have a whole bookcase full."

Ann grimaced, "no, but thank you for the kind offer. We follow a reading list and I have a lot to keep me occupied."

Mrs McInnis patted her hand, "I think you are extremely brave. It must be difficult for you being in a wheelchair."

Ann swallowed, "it's fine. Actually, I very much enjoyed year one."

"Good. Good." Said Mrs McInnis, "these young students don't know how easy they have it do they? Well if you see Martin around on campus say hello from me and Mr McInnis. We hardly see him now-a-days. He's always off boozing and chasing women. Goodness knows how he's going to get any work done."

Ann was just about to reply that she had no idea what Martin McInnis looked like, when Jon appeared at the side of her.

"Morning!" He called cheerfully, pushing Ann quickly away from their neighbour "we have to dash, traffic can be horrendous can't it love?"

"Erm, yes," Ann gazed up at him gratefully. He helped Ann into the passenger seat then screeched away up the road, leaving Mrs McInnis searching desperately for her yellow duster and pondering on her Grandson's dubious choice in women.

Chapter Seven

Juliette kissed her children goodbye at the school gates, waved until they disappeared, before buckling herself back into Marie and Dave's car.

"Thank you so much for the lift guys," she panted, out of breath after the exertion of running across the main road.

"No problem," Dave replied, pulling smoothly away from the kerb.

"You're going to be early Jules," Marie commented.

Juliette smiled, "it's okay, I can grab a cuppa and people watch."

"Anyone in particular?" chuckled Marie.

"No," Juliette said firmly, "no one special."

She noticed the knowing look that passed between her sister and brother-in-law and decided to ignore it.

"Have you told Jules about the party?" Dave asked, as he accelerated through a set of green lights.

"Oh no!" Marie slapped her forehead, "My baby brain is making me so forgetful." She spun around in the seat, "Jules, I thought we could throw a surprise party for Mum and Dad's anniversary. They've been married forty years this year, haven't they?"

"You're right," Juliette replied, "isn't that ruby?"

"Yes, I thought we could make a fuss of them, organise a party – somewhere local?"

"That's a lovely idea. I could ask at the social club," Juliette suggested. She had been there last night, working the graveyard shift. It had been quiet though, so the bar manager Ted had insisted she leave early.

"Great," Marie nodded enthusiastically, "we could do the buffet ourselves and I could make them up a special bouquet. It's not until after Christmas, so that will give us plenty of time to get organised."

"Fab," Juliette cut in, "I'll organise the room and we can make a guest list. It will be nice to see all the family again, it's been too long."

Marie rubbed her protruding stomach, "and little one will be ready to pop by then."

Dave took his hand off the gear stick to place it gently over her belly, "can't wait," his voice was full of emotion.

"You two are so sweet," Juliette teased from the back.

"I know," Marie replied with a grin, "we're so cheesy and when you've met Mr Right, I'll be able to poke fun at you too."

"Not going to happen," Juliette stuck her nose high into the air, "men are off limits. I'm going to be too busy with my children and my books."

"Yeah right!" Marie rolled her eyes heavenward, "all work and no play makes Jules a dull girl."

Juliette pulled a face and stared out at the stationary traffic.

"Are you okay to jump out here sis?" Dave asked, "it's tricky parking by the uni."

"Of course," Juliette scrambled for her belongings and unclipped her belt, "well see you soon," she blew a kiss at them both then hopped out. Dave tooted his horn twice before being swallowed up in the line of commuter traffic.

Juliette cut through the church gardens, following a winding path bordered by multi coloured, pretty flowers. It was busy, people rushing past her clutching cups of coffee and briefcases. The city centre with all its banks, shops and wine bars was just a short stroll from here, it was the perfect location for students of all ages; in the centre of a vibrant, bustling metropolis. She gazed towards the university, appreciating the modern, tall glass building of the library, contrasting with the rest of the universities archaic architecture – the old, weathered bricks, heavy oak doors and the cooper plaques on the wall. There was a huge tower overlooking the universities main entrance, where a clock's iron fingers slowly ticked around and where birds cruised and hovered. Juliette swallowed, her breath quickening; She was here, she was back.

* * *

As anticipated this early in the morning, the canteen was quiet and sparkling clean after a summer of solitude. The tables sparkled with disinfectant, the cutlery gleamed, sunshine shone through the newly polished windows and the smell of freshly cooked breakfast permeated the air. Juliette poured hot water over a teabag, pausing at the counter to converse with the staff about the weather and holidays. She listened as Tina described her jolly jaunt to Blackpool; celebrating a hen do that sounded wild by all accounts. Then Max the chef appeared from behind his cooker and regaled them with tales of his expedition to Canada where he had visited the stunning Niagara Falls.

"Ere, have this on me," he passed Juliette a crispy bacon sandwich, "but don't tell anyone, they'll all blooming want one."

He ignored her protestations to pay, rushing off when his second in charge warned him that his best pork sausages were burning. Juliette chose a table near the doors, so she could be easily spotted and was just tucking into her free meal when the Mars bar security guard appeared at her side.

"Hello love, it's nice to see you again," he smiled warmly down at her, his moustache twitching.

"Hello," Juliette lifted her hand in welcome, "it's nice to be back. Where is everyone?"

"In bed probably," he said with a laugh, "the lecturers have been here hours though. Some important meeting with the Dean."

"Oh, have they?" Juliette's smile wobbled, "I'm waiting for my friends."

"Look, there's one now," he pointed his radio across the room.

Juliette glanced over, relieved to see that it was Wilomena Smythe, looking as bohemian as ever.

"Well I best get on with my rounds," the security guard hitched up his baggy trousers, "good luck Miss."

"Thanks," Juliette called to his retreating figure, "thank you."

She watched surreptitiously as Wilomena struggled to the till, her arms full of books and paper. Then as she was making her way to the exit she spotted Juliette.

"Good morning!" Wilomena headed towards her table, "it's Juliette, isn't it?"

"You remembered," Juliette replied with a smile, "hello."

"I *always* remember my best students," Wilomena winked, "besides, who could forget your striking red hair."

"I try too," Juliette laughed, pulling out a ringlet.

"It's stunning," Wilomena gazed at her, "you are extremely pretty."

Juliette blushed, "thank you. How has your summer been?"

"Busy. Non-stop. Although I did manage to squeeze in a break to Iceland. My sister lives there, teaches English."

"Wow! I would love to go there."

"The Blue Lagoon was beautiful, unfortunately I missed the Northern Lights – wrong time of year," Wilomena revealed, "and it's *so* damn cold. I prefer a warmer climate "Weymouth was hot this year," Juliette sipped her tea.

"I love that part of England," gushed Wilomena, "are you ready for year two?"

"I think so," Juliette nodded, "I'm prepared at least," she pointed towards her new folder, writing pad and posh pen that she had splashed out on.

"I suppose I should go and prepare for my upcoming lectures," Wilomena shifted her books to her other hip. Her face looked strained and uncomfortable.

"Can I help you?" Juliette asked, rising to her feet.

"Would you? That would be lovely of you Juliette. These books weigh a ton."

"Here, let me," Juliette took a pile out of her arms, "what floor is your office on?"

"The second, but let's take the lift anyway."

They walked out of the canteen and into the foyer, where a large group of staff were congregating. Wilomena stopped to talk to the Dean of the university; a small suited man with a soft, lilting voice. Juliette stood to one side, feeling awkward and wishing that her friends would arrive and rescue her. Then she saw him.

Ben had his back to her, but she would recognise his dark hair and tall, lean physique anywhere. He was talking to Helena Mulberry who looked ethereal and waif like in a floating white chiffon sundress. Juliette was glad that she had made the effort and donned a skirt for a change. It was a modest cotton number resting just above her knee, a bargain in the summer sales, but it showed off her shapely legs that tapered down to slim ankles and a pair of pretty wedge sandals that looked lovely on her nail polished, buffed feet.

Juliette was just considering sneaking away, when he turned around and stared directly at her. There it was again, that ridiculous fluttering feeling in her stomach. His slow gaze travelled over her, aware that Helena was observing them, she defiantly stared back. He looked so handsome, in a dazzling white shirt with the top unbuttoned and smart navy trousers. He lifted his arm to rub his stubble covered chin and she noticed the glint of expensive looking cufflinks. Juliette took a step backwards, ready to flee. He was too quick. A few large strides and he stood in front of her.

"Aren't you going to say hello?" he murmured, pressing his lips next to her ear. The musky, male scent of him overwhelmed her and she felt her treacherous body react to his closeness. Heat flooded her cheeks and other parts of her anatomy.

"Why are your pupils dilating?" He asked with a smirk.

"Maybe it's the light - it's a beautiful, sunny day," she squeaked, "hello Dr Rivers."

"Miss Harris," he returned, moving back slightly, "you look well. I trust you have enjoyed your holidays?"

Juliette cleared her throat, "yes it was lovely, thank you," she gazed up at his tanned face, "have you been abroad? You look so brown."

"Working in the garden," he replied, "I've re-landscaped it. You'll have to come see it."

Juliette thought back to the last time she had been there; a flashback of the meal she had cooked and being pushed back into the softest of duvets.

"I…maybe," she remembered the pleasurable feeling of his full lips on hers and shivered with longing.

Ben's jaw clenched at her words, "as friends of course."

She was saved from responding by the interruption of Wilomena.

"Oh, hello again Ben, shall we go Juliette, unless you need to speak with each other?" Wilomena looked between them, a puzzled frown on her face.

"I was just going," Ben replied, "see you in the lecture theatre Miss Harris." He turned away and Juliette looked longingly at his retreating figure.

"Are you okay Juliette?" Wilomena was appraising her with concerned eyes.

Juliette shook herself from the Ben induced trance, "yes, yes I'm fine. Shall we?"

They made their way up to Wilomena's office which was nothing like Ben's – it was neat and tidy and smelt of lilies.

"There are an awful number of students this year," Wilomena commented, looking out through the window at the people congregating in the courtyard and outside the library, "I'm going to be busy."

"This is a lovely view," Juliette stood next to her, "oh I can see my friends."

"Then you must go, thank you for your help. Hopefully I will see you in one of my classes?"

"Definitely," Juliette swung her bag onto her shoulder, "bye."

"Juliette," Wilomena stopped her as she was tugging on the door handle, "Dr Rivers seems very fond of you."

"He does?" Juliette was surprised and slightly embarrassed.

"Don't listen to the rumours that circulate here. Ben is a lovely man, but he's also very private. Maybe it's not my place to say but, I've never seen him so taken with anyone before."

Juliette felt her cheeks flame with colour.

"I heard about what happened at the end of year drinks," Wilomena explained, "take no notice of Dr Hodges, he's a good guy but sometimes he reads things wrong. They've been friends for years and I think he was just looking out for him."

Juliette felt a stirring of excitement growing within her, Ben liked her, he really did.

"I should go," Juliette said clutching her folder close to her chest, "but thank you Dr Smythe, thank you."

* * *

Ann was the next to arrive, closely followed by Will and Sophie, who sauntered in arm in arm. Evelyn was uncharacteristically late, apologising for over sleeping and bad traffic.

"Helllooooo," Sophie squealed, throwing her arms around everyone, "I've missed you!"

"Ditto," Ann's voice was muffled against her shoulder as she was gripped in a tight embrace.

"Will, your hair is so long!" Juliette stared with shock at his floppy mane, what have you been dousing it with? - Miracle Grow?"

They both laughed, "it's good to see you Juliette."

"How is the baby?" Evelyn asked, pecking his cheek, "and Hema of course."

"Both doing well...Esme's like a ray of gorgeous sunshine."

"How poetic," Evelyn returned his smile, "you must bring her in, we'd all love to see her."

"Oh yes," Sophie had a dreamy look on her face, "I adore babies. Juliette, you have legs! Come give me a hug."

"How are you?" Juliette asked. Sophie had lost weight, she could feel it in her frame as they embraced.

"Battling on," Sophie replied, trying to keep the bitterness out of her tone, "the summer's been shit, apart from the holiday to Lanzarote. Evelyn's been a fantastic support."

"How are Josh and Jake?" Juliette probed gently.

"Surprisingly resilient," Sophie nodded, "of course they miss their Dad and ask after him, but they seem resigned to the fact that we've split up. Half of their class have children from divorced backgrounds anyway, it's no big deal now-a-days."

"There's no chance of a reconciliation?"

"No way Jules! I *am* starting divorce proceedings, our marriage is dead, ka-put, gone. All I feel towards Ryan O'Neill is anger and disgust. He's despica-ble..." Sophie sniffed.

"Then you're doing the right thing," Juliette said quickly, "and I'm here if you need me, okay?"

Sophie nodded her gratitude.

"Well," Ann said loudly, her eyes twinkling "now we're all here, shall we go enrol for another year of learning and fun?"

"Yes," they all cried with excitement, surging forward with the rest of the crowd.

* * *

"Was it Freshers week last week?" Evelyn asked, as they took their seats in the vast lecture theatre.

"Yes," Ann replied, "Jon and I came to the library and there were loads of them, wandering about looking completely bewildered and lost."

"It must be hard for the younger students; moving away from home," Evelyn pondered.

"Are you joking?" Ann replied with a chuckle, "I bet they love the freedom, away from the prying eyes of Mum and Dad."

"I thought about moving away," Will cut in, "I liked the sound of York or Chester, but then I didn't want to leave Hema, get into even more debt and besides, Chattlesbury has a great reputation. A degree is a degree, wherever you go - right?"

"You're absolutely right Will," Evelyn replied, "and the English department here at Chattlesbury are brilliant."

"How's your writing going Evelyn?" Ann asked, as she offered round a bag of Maltesers.

"I've started a new project," Evelyn replied, with shy excitement, "and I've sent off my manuscript, as Dr Rivers suggested. It's costing me an awful amount in postage."

"Good luck," Ann replied warmly, "we're all rooting for you."

"How is the adoption going dear?" Evelyn enquired.

"Fast," Ann replied with a shake of her head, "we're due to meet a young boy this weekend actually. I should be excited but I'm so nervous."

"I'm sure you'll be fine," Evelyn replied, "oh look, isn't that Tarquin Haverstock?"

They watched as Dr Haverstock jogged down the steps, "hello everybody," he said in a loud, clear tone, he waited for the theatre to fall silent, before continuing, "welcome back to our year two and three English students. Myself and the other lecturers hope you have had a marvellous holiday and are ready for the torture of further study." There were groans around the room, Tarquin Haverstock held up his hand, "Our friendly admin team," he pointed to a row of ladies seated at tables, "are ready to enrol you for the new academic year, but before you do, feel free to come chat to myself or my colleagues about modules you're interested in, or any other general advice you may need. I officially declare this semester open," he bowed theatrically and laughter spread around the room.

"He's such a nice guy," Juliette whispered to Sophie, "don't you think?"

"Yes. He is," Sophie nodded with agreement, her eyes following Dr Haverstock as he was accosted by students.

"So it begins," Ann declared, leading the way through the excitable crowds to the front of the lecture theatre.

* * *

When Will arrived home, he was buzzing with adrenalin and eager to share his day with Hema, but she was out and had left Esme with Flora.

"Her friend rang," his mom explained, "to invite her on a shopping trip. I offered to babysit, you know how much I love to have her."

Will picked Esme out of her basket, kissing her gently on the forehead, "has she been okay?" He queried, overwhelmed with love for his child.

"Absolutely golden," came the happy reply.

Will pulled out a chair, sank into it with a sleeping Esme in his arms.

"Did your first day back go well?" Flora asked, tearing open a new bag of potatoes.

"It was good," Will confirmed, "the year two modules I've enrolled for sound really interesting."

"And how are all your friends?"

"Okay I think. Sophie is on about divorcing Ryan O'Neill."

Flora gasped, "the football player?"

"That's the one. He deserves it though, he's treated her like crap. I hope she takes him to the cleaners."

"What about the lady who was erm... courting the lecturer?"

Will laughed, "you are so funny Mum, who says courting now-a-days? I have no idea *what* is going on there. They couldn't keep their eyes off each other though. Although Juliette seems to be in complete denial, I overheard her telling Ann they were just friends."

"It must be awkward for them both," Flora reasoned, "he *is* her teacher after all."

"So?" Will was genuinely puzzled, "I don't see the problem, she's a mature student, not a school girl."

Flora began speedily peeling the potatoes, "not everything is as black and white as that love. Aren't there ethics involved?"

"Ethics?" Will waved the thought away, "to me it's simple - what they need to do is stop worrying about everyone else and go get a room."

"Will!" Flora chuckled good naturedly, then her smile slipped slightly, "son, I've been so worried about that incident in the park with Hema's cousins."

Will looked up, his Mum looked tense, he could see it in the stiffening of her spine.

"So, I tried to make amends..."

"What?" Will raked a hand through his hair, "what have you done Mum?"

The peeler slipped from Flora's hand and slowly she turned around.

"I took Esme to see her other Gran."

"You took...? Where did you take her Mum?"

"To the Kumar's shop of course," worry lines appeared on Flora's forehead, "I wanted her to see her, to see how beautiful she is..." she was gabbling now, trying to explain to an increasingly irate looking Will, "I thought I was doing the right thing. I thought I could sort things out for Hema."

"*What* happened?" Will jumped to his feet and began pacing.

"I've invited the Kumar's over for dinner. They're coming the weekend love."

The ticking of the kitchen clock seemed magnified in the ensuing silence.

"Will I'm sorry, I was genuinely trying to help." Flora was wringing her hands and close to tears.

Will stopped, looked down at his beloved daughter, so much like Hema, so, so pretty, "Mum," he sighed wearily, "*what have you done?*"

* * *

Hema had been surprisingly calm when Will tentatively explained what Flora had been up to.

"I'll tell her to go cancel it, first thing in the morning," he said resolutely.

"No." Hema had a determined look on her face, "let them come. Let them see how happy we are. Let them see how we love and cherish and care for her. Let them see the mistake they have made, let them see what they are missing."

"Are you sure?" Will reached out for her hand, "you don't have to do this. You don't *have* to prove anything."

They were lying on the bed facing each other, the rays of the setting sun shone through the window, casting a glow around the room. It created a halo around her, it highlighted her golden eyes. Will sucked in his breath, "I'm not going to let them hurt you again."

Quickly Hema shook her head, "they won't, not with you there beside me. What can they do Will? We have nothing to be ashamed of. They're the ones in the wrong and I'm going to let them know how wrong they are. I'm going to show them what real love looks like."

"Come here," Will took her in his arms, pulling her close, sharing his warmth with her, "you're so brave Hema." He kissed her gently, making her gasp.

"Love me," she murmured, lifting his shirt above his head.

Chapter Eight

"We should set off soon," Jon Stokes was pacing the living room, "the traffic might be busy and we don't want to be late." He adjusted his t-shirt for the fifth time this morning, then ran a hand through his hair, "shall I put on a shirt?"

Ann shook the magazine she was reading, "why? You look perfectly fine as you are."

"I want to make a good impression."

"He's a twelve-year old boy Jon," Ann replied with a sigh, "I don't think he's going to judge you on your dress sense."

"He might," Jon perched on the chair next to Ann, "some of my best dressed clients are teenage boys and they can be very critical of appearances."

Ann's attention was back on the magazine article. She was reading an interesting piece about inspirational women; a successful business woman who had started with nothing and made millions, a ninety year old grandmother of six who had been born in extreme poverty and was currently on her seventh sky dive, an author who had started writing at the age of seventy and had published ten bestsellers, a lady with life threatening cancer who had battled a terminal prognosis and was now in remission.

"What are you reading anyway? I thought you hated those magazines," Jon peered over her shoulder.

"I didn't *buy* it Jon," Ann snapped, "Sophie was recycling a whole heap of them. Apparently, she's had an epiphany over the summer and is on a mission to transform her entire life."

"I feel for her," Jon replied with a shake of his head, "but seriously, how could she have not known what a rat her husband was. Wasn't there any warning signs?"

"That's irrespective Jon, she's the victim here and maybe he was a good liar," Ann shut the magazine, "I'm just relieved we don't have to listen to anymore football anecdotes. So, shall we go?"

The jaunt on the notoriously busy motorway passed smoothly and they reached Rocksley half an hour early.

"I wasn't anticipating that," Jon said, "I thought it would be traffic hell."

"On a Saturday?" Ann raised both eyebrows, "please calm down."

"I am perfectly calm," Jon swung the car in front of a row of shops, "shall we buy sweets?"

"No!" Ann put her face in her hands, "how would that look in front of Rose and the foster parents? I know you mean well Jon, but *really?*"

"Maybe we should have purchased him a gift; a ball or something."

"You can't buy his affections," Ann stared at her husband with incredulous eyes, "we have to get to know him, take things slowly – okay?"

Jon nodded, unclipped his seatbelt, "I'm just going to get a newspaper." He disappeared inside the newsagents leaving Ann to fiddle with the hot air system. It had turned suddenly chilly, heralding the arrival of autumn. She peered through the misted windows at the boughs of a huge oak tree. The leaves were changing colour and fluttering to the ground. A small child was skipping through them, churning them up, kicking them high. Ann wistfully thought back to her youth; carefree afternoons spent with her sister, wrapped up warm and running through the park, with the family dog bounding at their heels.

"The cashier said there's a storm coming," Jon interrupted her reverie, "close your eyes."

"Why?" Ann was immediately suspicious.

"Hold out your hand," He instructed.

Ann muttered but grudgingly closed her lids and opened her palm.

"My favourite!" She glanced down at the packet of Murray Mints.

Jon grinned, rustled open The Guardian, "I knew *you* wouldn't turn down sweets."

Rose the social worker was already there when they arrived at their destination. She lifted a hand in greeting as Ann settled herself in her wheelchair.

"How pretty," Ann and Jon turned to gaze at number 65 Apple Orchard Drive. The house was a neat looking semi-detached, with a rainbow coloured front door and animal plaques adorning the bricks. Ann had never seen such a colourful property. She glanced around at the neighbours; standard double glazed bricks and mortar, with blinds and hanging baskets. This house stood out in a street of conformity. Ann decided she liked the owners already.

Rose was talking on her phone; her voice was terse and she looked uncharacteristically stressed.

"I'm so sorry," she said, as she cut the call rather abruptly, "it's my manager, seems to think I can be in two places at the same time. Our workload at present is crazy," Rose took a calming deep breath, "anyway, here we are! Are you both okay?"

"Very nervous," Ann admitted, reaching for Jon's hand.

The social workers face softened, "please *don't* worry. Come now, let's go meet some real life foster parents – they're lovely you know and I promise they won't bite."

Anton and Lulu were extremely welcoming and ushered Ann, Jon and Rose inside with wide smiles and warm embraces. They immediately had the kettle boiling and produced a delicious looking carrot cake and an oozing Sicilian lemon roll.

"All home-made of course," Anton said, as he patted Lulu's hand, "using eggs from our very own hens."

"You have hens?"

Anton nodded at Ann, "yes, we have four, in a pen in the garden."

"We love our animals," Lulu interjected, "would you like to meet them all?" She jumped to her feet with excitement.

Ann noticed Rose smiling, "you go," she said, "I'm acquainted with them all. I'll stay here and guard the cakes."

"Our oldest is Sebastian," Lulu led them down the hall and into a smaller room.

Ann anticipated meeting a geriatric dog or cat but was completely surprised to see a tortoise moving slowly inside a large tank.

"He's forty," Lulu said proudly, "passed to me from my mother, who can no longer care for him, bless her."

Jon scratched his head, "I thought tortoises lived in the garden."

"Oh no," Lulu remonstrated, "not in this weather. He's a very lucky fella – he has his very own fully heated and lighted vivarium."

"And this," Anton appeared in the doorway, "is Primrose." Ann stared in shock at the large, multi-coloured parrot perched on his arm.

"Say hello darling," Anton made a kissing sound.

"Balls!" Came the high-pitched response.

Lulu bent over with laughter, "oh that's Josh's fault," she explained, "he was our last foster child – had a very colourful way of using the English language."

"She is beautiful," Ann watched as the parrot ruffled her feathers and pecked lightly at Anton's ear, "what other animals do you have?"

"Let me think; a rabbit called Giles, a Russian hamster called Boris and a crested Gecko called Serendipity," Lulu listed them on her fingers.

"I'm impressed," Ann replied, "do you have erm, a cat or a dog?"

"Unfortunately not," Anton cut in, "I'm allergic to cat hair and the last dog we had, tried to eat Primrose here."

"As you can probably tell, we are big animal lovers in this house."

"Yes, I can tell," Ann nodded and saw Jon smirk her way. They went back into the first room, where Rose was slicing the Lemon cake.

Jon grabbed a plate for himself and Ann. The room was small but cosy, each wall was painted a different colour and the shelves were dotted with incense sticks and cinnamon candles. Ann noticed a small picture of a young boy, resting on the bookcase.

"Is that Samuel?" She asked, her interest piqued.

Lulu reached across to grab it, "yes, it is," she passed the photograph over to Ann, "it's his most recent school snap, he's handsome, don't you agree?"

Ann gazed down at him and felt a wave of sympathy for the poor, neglected boy.

"Where is he?" She asked quickly, "I'd like to meet him."

"He's gone to the supermarket with a friend, to spend his pocket money," Anton wiped bits of cake off his bushy beard, "he won't be long. So, while we're waiting...Jon and Ann, tell us about yourselves." The five of them chatted easily. Ann wasn't surprised to hear that Lulu was an artist and Anton a music teacher. They epitomised the liberal, arty type; Lulu had long violet and blue hair and reminded Ann of a seventies love child with her flowing hippy skirt and Doctor Martins.

"Is that your work?" Jon pointed to the canvas prints hanging from the walls.

Lulu nodded, "I make pots too."

"They sell awfully well at the local craft fairs," Rose commented, "she's really starting to make a name for herself."

"You're very talented," Ann gazed at the splashes of colour, "and Anton, where do you teach?"

"At the local comprehensive," Anton made a face, "it can be challenging, but it pays the bills I suppose. I play in a band as well, that's my real passion."

A sudden bang vibrated throughout the house. Lulu jumped to her feet, eyes sparkling.

"He's back."

Ann held her breath as she waited for Samuel to appear in the doorway.

"Come in sweetie," Rose called, "you have visitors."

Samuel edged slowly into the room, looking down at the floor. Ann bit her lip and glanced at Jon, who looked overwhelmed with emotion.

"Say hi Sam," Anton urged gently. There was no response.

Jon sprang up from his seat and held out his hand, "hello Sam, it's great to meet you."

A pair of huge, blue eyes looked up. Tentatively he took Jon's hand and Ann knew right at that moment, he had her husband: hook, line and sinker.

They spent an hour with him, but it flew by so fast that it seemed much shorter. Jon and Ann followed him out into the garden; which was gloriously over-grown and picturesque. At the bottom, past the greenhouse and the chickens, was a frame holding two swings. Samuel sat on one, dragging his feet and listened to Jon as he perched on the other, chattering about Chattlesbury Football Club.

"They're doing well so far," Jon said, "an unbeaten home record."

"Hasn't the football season just started?" Ann asked with a laugh, trying to lighten the atmosphere.

"I like Manchester United," Samuel mumbled.

"Good choice!" Jon nodded enthusiastically, "they have a cracking manager. Hey, maybe we could go see them play live, make a day of it. Ann, you could come too."

Ann cast Jon a warning glance, "do *you* play football Samuel?"

"I like to play in goal," Samuel was nodding vigorously, "and Billy, my friend, he's the striker, boom! Gets the goals in."

"I liked netball at school. My sister played it too, but between us, I was much better."

Samuel laughed, a lovely tinkling sound, Ann felt her spirits soar.

Then suddenly it stopped, "why are you in a wheelchair?" Samuel stared at her, his bottom lip trembling, he looked as if he was going to burst into tears and Ann felt a surprise rush of affection.

"I was in an accident; a car accident," Ann swallowed, she normally hated explaining this to people, but Samuel, he was different, he was just a little boy; a lost, lonely child, "the doctors tried really hard, but they couldn't... they couldn't fix my legs. So now I can't walk, but I'm okay Sam, I really am." Jon clasped her hand, mouthing the words, *I love you.* Sam nodded, seemed happy with the explanation and Ann smiled, acknowledging that she too was ensnared, by a golden-haired boy with the most piercing eyes, that seemed to be staring right into the depths of her very own soul.

* * *

As anticipated, Max Bentley was livid to hear of the impending meal Flora had arranged with the Kumar's.

"What *were* you thinking?" He shook his head in disapproval, tugged off his socks and hurled them into the washing basket.

Flora was sitting up in bed reading, her face covered in a cucumber face mask. She had deliberately stalled in telling Max of the impending dinner date, she already knew what his reaction would be.

"Well it's too late to cancel now, it's tomorrow love," she replied in a calm, soothing tone.

"But really... Flora, in our own home? After all the trouble and upset they've caused?"

"I'm trying to smooth things over Max. I was thinking of Hema and little Esme."

Max pulled back the duvet, clambering onto the high, springy bed, "you were interfering Flora," he berated, "not everything can be fixed! And what does poor Hema make of it all."

Flora swallowed, "she seemed fine about it. Oh, but Max I'm worried about her, Will too. Those cousins of hers sound like nasty people and apparently one of them is a student at Chattlesbury university. They could make trouble for him. No, this needs sorting, before it escalates."

"Stop exaggerating," Max sighed and picked up his latest thriller, "I suppose you mean well, but Flora it's a meal only; no after dinner party games and I want them gone, before nine o'clock."

Flora nodded happily, "okay dear. Maybe you could offer Mr Kumar a brandy – it might break the ice."

"My *best* brandy. The bottle I was saving for Christmas?" Max huffed and plumped up his pillow, "if I must...do they even drink alcohol?"

Flora chewed her lip, "I think so, maybe I'll pop to the supermarket in the morning and purchase a bottle of non-alcoholic wine, just in case."

Max snapped off the main light and snuggled down under the covers, "I hope you know what you're doing Flora...I really do."

Will was up early the next morning to warm Esme's bottle. He was surprised to see Flora in the kitchen, scrutinising a recipe book.

"Morning," he padded in, yawning and stretching.

"Morning love. Be a dear and pass me the onions."

"Bit early to start cooking, isn't it?"

"I'm making a base sauce for the curries," Flora explained, "it takes hours. Then I have the starters to prepare, the chicken to marinade and cook. It's going to be a busy day."

"Fair enough," Will popped the cold bottle of formula into a jug of hot water.

Flora glanced across at him, "Is Hema okay? About tonight I mean?"

"She's fine – calmer than me anyway. I'm not putting up with any of their bullshit though Mum, if they start..." Will warned.

"They won't," Flora said adamantly, "it's going to be a lovely evening, so relax son...leave it all to me."

By mid-afternoon pots of sauce were bubbling away on the cooker and the kitchen was full of the aroma of spicy food.

"Flora!" Max stared at the mountain of washing up, "have you used *every* single pot?"

"I'll help tidy up," Hema said helpfully, "Esme's fast asleep on Will's chest."

"Thank you," a grateful Flora passed her a tea-towel.

Max was helping himself to a nibble of the homemade onion bhajis, "are they supposed to be this colour?" he queried, "they look burnt to me."

"I forgot to set the timer," Flora stared down at the wire rack, "will they be okay?"

"I suppose they'll have to do. Woah, they're certainly spicy."

"Oh Max, you're supposed to dip them into the mint sauce," Flora tutted, "haven't you got work to do?"

Max nodded, "I'll be in my study, that's if...do you need a hand love?"

"Everything is under control," Flora replied smoothly, "I just need to pot it all up and then I can go make myself beautiful."

A few hours later and after a speedy dash to the supermarket, the meals were prepared and the table was set.

"Is the Queen coming?" Will asked, as he glanced over the posh cutlery and best crystal wine goblets, "you look lovely Mum."

Flora blushed, touching her freshly washed and styled hair, "Hema curled it for me, it's different to how I usually have it."

Max cleared his throat, "it looks very nice. Is that a new dress you're wearing?"

Flora laughed, "I've had it years Max, let me straighten your tie," she stood on tip-toe and fiddled with the knot.

"They're late," Hema commented, rocking Esme in her arms, "Mum and Dad are never late."

Will peered out of the window, "shall we go down the pub and leave the parents to get on with it?"

"You'll do no such thing my lad," Max snapped, "your mother has gone to a lot of trouble to plan this meal."

"Let's hope then the shit doesn't hit the fan," Will grimaced at his Dad, "fancy a beer Hema?" He disappeared into the kitchen, with Hema trailing after him.

"They're trying to help Will," Hema said, watching as he banged the refrigerator door shut.

"We don't need their interference," Will said tersely, "we're not teenagers any more. We can make our own decisions."

"Shush Will," Hema whispered, "let's be positive...try and enjoy tonight...for this little one?" Esme kicked her legs in approval and emitted the cutest yawn. Suddenly Ruby jumped up out of her bed and skidded past them, heading towards the hallway.

"Will," Hema's face contorted into a sheen of anxiety.

He reached out and pulled her into his arms, "united front, okay?"

Hema looked up at him with wide, troubled eyes, while in her arms, their baby gurgled and wriggled with innocent happiness.

"Please come in," Flora held the door wide open, smiling at their guests. Mrs Kumar breezed past, carrying with her the strong scent of jasmine. She was wearing a striking claret and gold sari, her make-up was immaculate and her thick, dark hair was piled into a high chignon. Mr Kumar followed her with his head bowed, hands behind his back. He looked smart in a dark brown suit, with a crisp white handkerchief poking out of his breast pocket.

"Hello Mum," Will heard the tremble in Hema's voice and immediately moved closer to her; a protective gesture, that did not go unnoticed.

"You've lost weight," Mrs Kumar's slanted eyes raked over her daughter's lithe figure, "are you eating enough?"

"Yes," Hema replied, "Flora has been looking after me and...and little Esme."

"Hello Hema," Mr Kumar's face softened as he gazed at her and then his granddaughter.

"Dad!" Hema stepped forward, kissing him lightly on the cheek.

There was an awkward silence, Will's jaw clenched in tension; they hadn't even acknowledged him or his parents. Remain calm, he reminded himself.

"Can I get you a drink Mr Kumar?" Max stepped forward, a forced smile fixed to his face.

"His name is Daljeet," Hema interjected, "and Mum's Shivani."

"What beautiful names," Flora clasped her hands together, "shall we go into the parlour?"

Will watched bemused as his Mum ushered them down the hall, *what the hell was a parlour?*

Max noticed his look and hung back to whisper to Will, "she's trying to make a good impression that's all. Will *you* need to make more of an effort."

"I get it Dad," Will shrugged him off.

"Now, we have wine, beer, cordial, coffee...what would you prefer?" Flora queried.

"Tea for me...please," Mrs Kumar burst into a succession of sneezes.

"That must be the chillies," Flora chuckled, "I didn't realise how potent they are when you cook them, I've been coughing all afternoon. Mrs Kumar, I mean Shivani, do you like your curry spicy?"

"I prefer it mild," she inclined her head, "and Mr Kumar is on medication for an ulcer, he has to be very careful what he eats."

"Oh," Flora looked disappointed.

"Did you not tell them Hema?" Shivani berated her daughter.

"I forgot," Hema looked contrite, "sorry Flora."

"Not to worry dear, I've made a variety of dishes," Flora threw her a smile of reassurance.

"I'll eat it," Will said with enthusiasm, "I love spicy food, it smells lovely Mum."

Max cleared his throat, "Mr Kumar, is wine okay?"

"Red if you have it," Mr Kumar replied with a nod.

Just as Max and Flora were about to disappear into the kitchen, Shivani thrust a box towards them.

"I made Gulab Jamun, a traditional Indian sweet, they are Hema's favourite."

"How delightful," Flora lifted the lid, "they look delicious. So, make yourselves comfortable and we'll be back..."

"How is business Mr Kumar?" Will asked, when the door was closed.

Will knew he had said the right thing; Mr Kumar's eyes lit up at the mention of his shop.

"It is good, the new factory has bought many new custom, thanks be to Shiva."

"We have had to take on another assistant," Shivani snapped, "now Hema is no longer working there."

Hema opened her mouth to speak but Will cut in, "she's busy with Esme now, our child is our priority."

Mrs Kumar's eyes narrowed into slits, but she remained quiet.

"Would you like to hold your granddaughter?" She smiled shyly at her father.

Mr Kumar held out his arms, "she looks like you Hema," he murmured, gazing down at Esme, "she is going to be a great beauty."

"She has Will's dimples," Hema laughed as Esme gurgled and kicked her legs.

"I heard it was a quick birth," the bangles on Shivani's wrist tinkled as she adjusted her sari.

"It was fast," Hema nodded, "they didn't even have chance to get me on the maternity suite, little lady popped out in Flora's car."

Mrs Kumar drew in a breath, "in full view of strangers?"

"It was dark," Will explained with a grin, "Hema was, well she was just fantastic. No stitches either,"

Shivani looked at him with cold eyes, "Daljeet waited outside when my children were born. It's not right for men to be there. It is a personal, female matter."

Will frowned, "Times have changed Mrs Kumar; Hema needed support and Esme is *my* child too."

"Yes Mum, men are so much more hands on now-a-days. Will is fantastic with her," she enthused, glancing at him with adoring eyes.

Shivani sniffed with disapproval, "are they looking after you?"

"Of course they are," Hema replied, sensing the tension emanating from Will, "they have made me feel very welcome."

Will held his breath, if there was any more negativity, then he might tell them to leave. Thankfully Flora bustled back in, carrying a tray of drinks.

"Here we go," she said, passing them around with a bright smile, "please come and sit at the table; the starters are ready."

They placed Esme in her cradle, where she promptly fell fast asleep. Max bought in trays of food, while Flora fiddled with the lamps.

"It's starting to get darker earlier," she commented, "the clocks will be going back and then soon it will be Christmas. I do love winter, when everyone's wrapped up warm against the cold. What's your favourite season Shivani?"

Will stared at his mum, she was definitely taking small talk to a new level, yet Mr and Mrs Kumar seem not to have noticed and were busy tucking into the poppadum's and mint sauce.

"We both like the heat, although in this country we are lucky to have any." Shivani looked around the room with interest, "I like the decor in here and that there, I presume you are religious?" She pointed to an oval table, on which rested a Bible, a pair of devotional candles and a statue of Mary. Above it hung a crucifix and a framed photograph of Max and Flora standing outside the Basilica of Saint Mary Major in Rome.

"Yes I am," Flora smiled, "my faith is very important to me."

Shivani nodded with approval.

"Of course, the popularity of the church within modern Britain has rapidly declined. This society is becoming more and more secular," Max looked around the table, "the Catholic church needs to embrace change, if it is to remain viable in today's society."

"In what way?" Mr Kumar looked up with interest.

"Well, for a start I believe that priests should be allowed to marry."

Flora nodded with agreement, "Father McGregor is such a lovely man, I can't bear the thought of him being lonely."

"Aren't they married to the church?" Will asked.

"Yes of course," Max agreed, "but a man has urges and needs. Romantic love and of course sexual pleasure are perfectly natural ways of attaining those."

Mrs Kumar gasped, dropping her onion salad.

"Sorry," Max rubbed at his temple, "I think Mrs Bent is rubbing off on me Flora," he looked towards his wife with disdain.

Flora reached across to pat his hand, "that's his deputy," she explained, "a very complex woman."

Will and Hema tittered surreptitiously, while Shivani wiped forcefully at her mouth.

"*I* believe in saving oneself until after marriage. This modern society is pre-occupied with gaining immediate pleasure and self-gratification. It seems that morals and restraint have been cast aside. What is so wrong with preserving traditions? Change is not always a good thing Mr Bentley!"

Max visibly bristled, "Mrs Kumar, as a headteacher, I embrace change. We can celebrate the past, but we do have to keep moving forward; questioning and improving, for the sake of our future generations."

Daljeet placed his cutlery down to signify he had finished, "as you mentioned our future generations, I would like to know what Will's intentions are towards my daughter and granddaughter."

Will swallowed his food, "my intentions?"

"He means are you going to marry Hema?" Mrs Kumar glared across the table, "and make a respectable woman of her."

"Now wait..." Max began.

"I don't think that's an appropriate question," Flora quickly cut in.

"She already is respectable," Will said through gritted teeth, "I don't need to put a ring on her finger to prove that."

"There is a stigma," Mrs Kumar continued haughtily, "I don't want my daughter classed as a single mother!"

"I'm not single - I'm with Will," Hema protested, "we're together and we love each other very much."

"Pah love, what do you really know of the term? As far as I can see you are, what do you Catholics like to call it? Living in sin!"

"That's enough," Will jumped to his feet, then Mr Kumar rose to his, closely followed by Max. All three men glared at one another. Tension crackled in the air, and as if on cue, Esme opened her eyes and wailed in pain.

"Please can everybody calm down," Flora was trying her best to dispel the friction. She glanced at Hema who was bent over Esme, trying to hide the tears in her eyes.

Mrs Kumar blushed, "sorry...Daljeet sit down." Her husband slowly sat back.

Will pushed back his chair, "are you okay?" He murmured, his hand on Hema's back.

Quickly she nodded, lifting Esme up and kissing the curls on the crest of her head. She turned towards her parents.

"Max and Flora have made you welcome in their home. They have spent the whole day cooking for you. You talk of manners and the correct way to behave, but you...you're both so rude and hostile – maybe you should just leave."

"Hema!" Shivani stared at her daughter in shock, "we only want what is best for you."

"Will is best for me," Hema's eyes glinted with determination, "you must both learn to accept that I love and want him."

"Fine," Shivani replied frostily, turning to Flora, "do you wish us to leave?"

Flora sighed, "that won't be necessary. Let me put on some music and we can enjoy the main meal. Will, can you help me?" She motioned towards the door, "Max please choose a CD; classical if possible."

Once they were alone in the kitchen, Will turned on his mother, "I knew this was a bad idea – they hate me."

"No they don't," Flora touched his arm, "they're just stuck in tradition and blinded by misconceptions, give them time love, it's obvious they are terrified of losing Hema."

"They've already lost her," Will cried, "I am so sick of them judging us; interfering and trying to make trouble. I bet they put Hema's cousins up to it the other day. I'm going to confront them."

"No!" Flora stepped in front of her headstrong son, "leave it be Will. Hema's upset enough as it is. Help me dish up the food...please."

Will let out a frustrated sigh, but followed her to the cooker.

"Now, I've made madras, bhuna and korma; do you think that's enough variation?"

"Yes," Will said tersely.

"Right then – Will, can you start spooning them into pots, while I sort out the rice," she glanced up at him, "and please, *calm down*."

"This is actually very nice," Max scooped the thick sauce onto his nan bread and smiled in appreciation.

Flora laughed, "you sound surprised love," she looked around the table and was pleased to note that everyone's plate was almost empty, "I think I've found my niche: cooking Asian food."

"It was very appetising," Shivani smiled stiffly and dabbed at the corners of her mouth. She watched Will as he rocked Esme in his arms, "could I hold her please?"

Will glanced up in surprise, "yes, of course."

He gently passed her over. Both Will and Hema sighed with relief as she smiled down at her granddaughter.

"She has a good, strong grip," Esme curled her tiny hand around Mrs Kumar's finger, "does she sleep well?"

"Not too bad," Will replied, "she's going longer between feeds now and seems to have settled into a routine."

"And does she keep you up?" Shivani's question was directed at Flora.

"Oh no, we don't usually hear her. Both Max and myself are deep sleepers."

"It must be a stressful occupation; being a headteacher," Mr Kumar said to Max, "a lot of responsibility I imagine. How long have you worked in education?"

"Too long," Max replied, "It's all I've ever done. I've gone from school to university then back to school again. Sometimes I wish I had done something else, different from teaching. When I was young I wanted to be an Olympic swimmer."

"You did?" Will gazed at Max in astonishment.

"I had my dreams too son," Max replied with a laugh.

"I wanted to be a train driver," Daljeet revealed, "and Will, what do you aspire to be?"

"Truthfully, I have no idea."

Flora tensed, preparing herself for another heated debate, but Mr Kumar just smiled.

"There is time. You are at university and that is a great start."

"Thanks," Will mumbled.

"So, shall we share the Indian sweets you have made Shivani?" Flora rose to her feet, a happy smile on her face.

Mrs Kumar patted her stomach, "I am full, but please, go ahead."

Flora passed the box round the table and they all commented on how tasty the *Gulab Jamun* were.

"Can I have another?" Max queried, helping himself.

Mrs Kumar looked pleased that her dessert had been so successful.

"Your house is very nice," she commented, looking round, "I do like the more traditional properties, they have more character, don't you think?"

"Absolutely," Flora replied, "the walls in these modern houses are paper thin. Would you like me to show you around Shivani?"

"That would be nice," Mrs Kumar rose to her feet and Hema trailed after them.

As soon as the men were alone, Mr Kumar wasted no time in bringing up the altercation between Will and Hema's cousins.

"It was not of my doing," he said to Will, "my brother is very traditional and headstrong, both myself and Shivani were extremely angry to hear of the incident."

Will nodded with relief, "that's good to hear, because I *will* protect Hema and Esme, I'm not going to back down, no matter who it is."

Mr Kumar nodded and appraised Will with respectful eyes, "you are a lion-hearted young man. Maybe my daughter chose well after all. I will talk to my family, it will not happen again."

Max smiled at his son, "would you like a brandy Daljeet, Will?" He crossed to the drinks cabinet and poured the brown liquid into three crystal decanters.

Max sat back down and raised his glass, "to Esme," he said. Will and Daljeet repeated her name.

"To her future: good health, happiness and success."

Chapter Nine

Juliette knew there was something wrong with Ben Rivers as soon as he walked into the classroom. The students were buzzing with start of year excitement and there was an upbeat atmosphere in the air. Some people were sitting on the tables chatting, while others were wandering around, mingling. So when he walked in with a down-turned mouth and worry lines etched on his forehead, Juliette felt a sense of alarm growing within her. He hadn't noticed her, sitting at the front table, twiddling her pen, while trying not to gaze adoringly at him. He looked deep in concentration, as he fired up his laptop and sorted through a pile of handouts. He didn't even look up when Melanie the effervescent note-taker bounded into the room; all wide smiles and cute, jet black plaits. She stopped to hug him briefly, before making her way over to Juliette's table, where she cast a sideways glance at her.

"Hi everyone," Melanie waved at the five of them, "I've missed you guys."

"You've dyed your hair," Ann commented, "it looks nice."

"Oh yes," Melanie settled in the vacant seat next to Ann, "Tasha persuaded me to go dark again, this is more like my natural colour, although I've dyed it so many times, I've forgot what that actually is," she chuckled, "so, are you all ready for year two?"

"No!" They all chorused together.

"I'm half way through Middlemarch," Evelyn pulled a thick book out of her handbag, "I'm reading it every spare minute I get."

"Christ!" Sophie stared wide-eyed, "is that on the reading list? It's a huge book - I'm never going to get chance to read that in twelve weeks."

"Watch the film," Melanie advised with a wink, "but you didn't hear that from me."

"Morning class," Ben cleared his throat and silence descended on the room, "welcome to year two and welcome to Realism and the Novel." The projector flickered to life, "the overwhelming dominant mode of representation in the eighteenth and nineteenth century novel is Realism. It addresses the contemporary and represents a recognisable social world, and is exemplified in the literature we shall be studying throughout this module," he cleared his throat again, Juliette looked up, was she imagining it, but did his voice sound shaky?

"Where was I? Yes, erm...the primary reading list is as follows: *Robinson Crusoe* by Daniel Defoe, The witty masterpiece, *Pride and Prejudice* by Jane Austen, the convoluted but brilliant *Middlemarch* by George Eliot, who, if you don't already know is a woman, then we have the extremely popular *Great Expectations* by Charles Dickens and finally the scandalous *Lady Chatterley's Lover*. An amazing reading list, don't you agree class?"

There were murmurs of agreement, along with a few groans of apprehension.

"This module sounds so good," Sophie whispered to Juliette.

"It does," Juliette frowned as she watched Ben rubbing his temple.

"Okay," he said, "just a word about the assessment. Fifty percent of the course marks will be taken from a 2,000-word essay and the remaining fifty per cent will be a closed book exam."

It seemed that the entire class groaned with dismay. Ben held up his hand.

"Try not to worry. It won't be as bad as you think and we will have lots of time for preparation. I'm going to be running an optional after class tutorial in preparation for the exam and I'm always available in my office or via email, if you need any one-to-one advice." He flicked a switch on his computer and the screen filled with his lecture plan, "so, let's discuss the rise of the novel."

An hour later, Ben drew his lecture to a close.

"Break time," he called, tugging off his jumper. Juliette stared at him and found herself transported back to her bedroom. Oh, she really wanted to...SNAP – the lead in her pencil broke where she gripped it too tightly.

"Tea anyone?" She jumped up and without waiting for a reply hurried out of the classroom, giving Ben a wide berth.

Evelyn peered over her glasses, "is Juliette okay?" She seems a little...flustered."

"She's lusting after Ben Rivers again." Melanie replied flippantly, "like an open book, that one."

Ann shook her head, "why don't those two just get back together? It's obvious he's not concentrating and neither is she."

Sophie tutted, "Jules can be stubborn when she thinks she's right about something. One things for certain though, she really cares about that guy…he's certainly made an impression on her."

"Yeah," Will drawled, "even I've noticed it. She goes completely moony whenever he's around."

Melanie sniggered mischievously, "why don't we get them back together?"

"Is that wise?" Evelyn asked, "it could cause trouble and push them further apart."

"Leave it to me Evelyn," Melanie's eyes twinkled, "I promise to be careful…I'll think of something."

* * *

After the seminar was over, they joined the queue for the lift to take them down to the ground floor.

"No need to wait for me," Ann said, "take the stairs, I'll meet you down there."

Evelyn stayed with Ann, while the others sauntered down the stairs. Will and Sophie were embroiled in a conversation about St Mary's.

"How you getting on there? Dad's always moaning about the place."

"I love being with the children but Will, some of the staff there are kind of strange and there's a weird atmosphere. I can't quite put my finger on it, but there's something not right about that school."

Will nodded, "I was a pupil there. There was one teacher who used to talk about hell and damnation and the devil sitting on your shoulder if you didn't behave. She sure was scary to a seven-year-old."

Sophie frowned, "I can imagine."

"Hasn't put you off teaching though has it?" Will probed.

Sophie swallowed, not wanting to offend her friend, "I'm keeping my options open."

Just above them, Juliette decided to broach the subject of Ben.

"Is he okay?" She whispered to Melanie, "he doesn't seem himself."

"Maybe he's missing someone," Melanie replied with a shrug.

Juliette sighed, "no, it's not that. It's something else…"

She was distracted by Will's exuberant chatter about Esme and they were pushed along in the swell of people rushing to grab the best seat in the refectory.

Ann and Evelyn had managed to grab a table with luxurious leather squashy sofas and waved them over as they walked through the entrance.

"I've just got to nip somewhere," Juliette said, as the others made their way to sit down.

She hesitated for a moment then mind made up, walked with determination back towards the lift.

His door was firmly closed so she placed her ear against the wood, listening for movement inside. It was all quiet, Juliette tapped four times, swallowing a nervous lump which had formed in her throat.

"Come in," it was unmistakeably Ben, but his voice sounded strange.

Slowly she opened the door and gazed at his back. When he turned round she noticed that his eyes were red rimmed and in his hands he clutched a photograph of his sister.

"It's my sister. She's sick."

"Oh!" Juliette's hand flew to her mouth, then impulsively she rushed over to comfort him, flinging her arms around him.

"I've lost Mum and Dad, I can't lose her too."

"It's okay," Juliette soothed, hugging him tight.

Bens arms encircled her waist and he buried his face into the softness of her stomach.

Then the door flew open and Brian Hodges stumbled in, carrying a pile of hard backed books.

"Oh sorry," he mumbled.

"I was just leaving," Juliette said, as she gently extricated herself from Ben.

"No! Please stay, I'll go," Brian looked down at the floor, shuffling his feet.

"Really, I have to get going anyway," she squeezed Ben's hand and smiled shyly down at him, picking up her discarded belongings.

"Juliette!" Ben called, waiting for her to turn around, "thank you."

As Juliette softly closed the door, she heard Brian Hodges say lightly, "just friends eh?"

* * *

"Where are we for Stylistics?" Ann was gazing at an upside down map of the university.

"According to my timetable, we're in room B104," Evelyn peered over the rim of her spectacles, "where is that?"

"Uh-oh," Melanie looked worried, "that's the basement."

"They have a basement?" Evelyn was surprised.

"It's mainly used for psychology," Melanie said with a nod, "it's where they experiment and keep all the crazy students," she chuckled heartily, "just kidding, come on."

Down they went in the lift, to a floor where the lights flickered and the corridors were eerily empty.

"I feel that we shouldn't be here," Ann whispered, "are you sure this is the right floor Evelyn?"

"She's right," Melanie confirmed, "the language department have been moved and I don't think they're happy about it. Ah, here we are; B104."

The classroom was empty, except for a lady in a stripy uniform, who was pulling a feather duster over the front desk.

"Hiya Gladys," Melanie waved at her, "have a nice break?"

The cleaner sniffed, "I suppose I did, until I got back here and found out they've changed me to the afternoon shift. Now when I get back home, my hubby's leaving for *his* job, we're like passing ships in the night; hardly get any time together anymore."

"Oh well look on the bright side," Melanie grinned, "surely you'll be retiring soon, then you'll have *too* much time together."

"Another blasted five years yet lass," Gladys swiped energetically at the projector slide, "now what the heck have you got on today?"

Melanie looked down at her attire, "What? You mean these beauties?" She straightened a leg that was covered in purple and black spots, "they're the new range of winter tights, don't you like them?"

Gladys chuckled, "I suppose they're okay for you young 'uns. Although my granddaughter wouldn't be seen dead in anything that wasn't designer."

Melanie grimaced, "you mean like the disgustingly over-priced, unoriginal sports labels?"

"Exactly!" Gladys shook out her duster, "although why she bothers is a mystery to me, she's about as active as a couch potato that one. Now, I best be on my way, is that dashing Dr Rivers teaching you this afternoon?"

Juliette's ears pricked at the mention of his name.

"Unfortunately not," Melanie replied with a laugh.

"Pity," Gladys sighed and looked at the others, who had settled at a table, "he's the university heartthrob. Reminds me of a movie star. *All* the women here fancy him like mad, but he's gay or bisexual. What he needs is a good, down-to-earth woman to look after him – not one of these puffed up, fancy lecturers who care more about their career than making a home…if he was my husband I would show him exactly what I could do with my feather duster, boy would I…"

"Let's not gossip," Melanie interrupted, whose face had turned red.

Will, Sophie, Evelyn and Ann exchanged horrified glances, while Juliette stared tight lipped down at her A4 pad. There was an awkward silence. Gladys mouthed a silent "what have I said?" to Melanie, who was trying to usher her out of the room.

"Bye," she said, closing the door on the cleaner, "she has a ridiculous crush on him that's all. One of these days she'll wake up and get over it."

"Poor Dr Rivers," Ann said, shaking her head.

"She means well," Melanie explained.

Juliette looked up, a small smile lifting her mouth, "well, I can categorically confirm that Dr Rivers is definitely *not* gay." Then she laughed and after a few moments hesitation the others joined in.

The room was half full when Wilomena Smythe peeped her head around the door.

"What a small class," she commented, "I'll just pop and get a coffee to allow for any late arrivals."

"I thought Helena Mulberry was taking Stylistics?" A confused Sophie asked.

"She's down as the module leader," Ann confirmed.

Melanie leant forward, "she's off sick," she whispered, "between us lot, there's a rumour going around that she has depression, caused primarily by the stress of this place."

"It's only the start of the year!" Sophie cried, "she's my personal tutor; now what will I do?"

"Check on the HIVE system," Melanie advised, "her students have been re-allocated to different lecturers."

Sophie scribbled herself a note to do just that, when she had a spare five minutes.

A few more students wandered in looking lost, "is this Stylistics?" One of the them asked.

"It sure is," Ann replied, "it should be starting anytime now."

"I'm here, I'm here," Dr Smythe bustled back into the room, clutching a polystyrene cup, "God I hate this floor; there's no natural light and no confectionary machine either, can't you lot complain and make my life easier?"

Laughter rippled around the class.

"I have no idea what I'm supposed to be doing by the way," Wilomena snapped on her spectacles and peered at the module handout, "so, according to Helena's plan, this is an introduction to Stylistics and what this module is about. In the following weeks you'll be learning about Coherence and Cohesion, Processes and Participants, Feminist Stylistics and Stylistics and Drama. The assessment is graded on an in-class writing exercise, half way through the module and then a case study which is due in the final week." She began passing the papers round, "there is a full list of the programme outcomes and assessment criteria for you to read up on, but for now, let me give you a brief introduction to what we mean by stylistics in language."

Sometime later, Wilomena called a break and the class dispersed in search of fresh air and refreshments.

"I need a cigarette," rasped Ann.

"No!" Evelyn was horrified, "you've done so well stopping Ann, here, have a toffee instead," she passed over a sticky, half full wrapper.

"I've stopped too," Sophie revealed, "thought I should make the effort to save some money, now I'm a single parent."

"How are Josh and Jake?" Juliette asked. They chatted about their children, while Will scrolled through Facebook and Evelyn and Ann discussed the reading list.

"Thank goodness there are no primary required reading, I don't think I could cope with *that* and the books off the Realism module list."

"We're going to be busy," Ann said with a sigh, "but I'm up for the challenge and I can't *wait* until we do our dissertation in year three."

"Any idea what you're going to do?" Will asked casually.

"Not yet," Ann replied, "but I *love* Angela Carter's work. Only trouble is, I think she's been done to death. Probably a good idea to look for something more original."

"Well, there's plenty to choose from. Here comes Dr Smythe," Evelyn picked up her pen in preparation.

Wilomena struggled to sit cross legged on her table, swinging her legs, as she carefully unpeeled a banana.

"Right then class," she began, "I suppose we should have some sort of seminar on what we've just learnt, but what the heck, how do you fancy a discussion on lexical choice? I presume we can still class that as a study of language and if not, I won't tell the Dean if you don't," she winked cheekily and there were murmurs of approval.

"There's an old saying that the pen is mightier than the sword, which basically means you should choose your words very carefully indeed," she hopped down to the floor and threw the fruit peel in the bin. "For example, there are certain words *I* dislike," she drew a red line down the centre of the board, "nice being one of them. Puppies are *nice*, chocolate cake is *nice*. People should never be nice! And woe be told anyone who utilises it in one of *my* essays." Wilomena paused to open her arms, "there are so many other interesting words to describe a person's character, don't you think class? Now passionate I like, scintillating I like, vivacious I like, bubbly I love. What about the word reckless – what does it connotate?" She looked around at the students expectantly.

"Danger," one woman shouted from the back.

"Okay," Wilomena nodded, "maybe..." she wrote it on the middle of the board, "is this necessarily a bad thing – or does it mean that you're alive?" Her eyes twinkled mischievously as she grinned at her shocked looking class, "so maybe we're not sure about *that* word, but tell me; what words fire you up? What words do you dislike?" She pointed her pen at Ann.

"Pity," Ann visibly shuddered.

Quickly Wilomena jotted it down under the dislike heading, "why do you dislike it so much?"

Ann cleared her throat, "it connotates weakness and superiority; condescension and domination over another person."

"Tres bien," Wilomena clapped her hands, "does anyone disagree?"

"Me," Evelyn tentatively raised her hand, "I think it can hold positive connotations such as empathy and compassion."

"It can Evelyn!" Wilomena scribbled the word again underneath the like heading, "I suppose it depends on who the pity is coming from. Juliette," she clicked her fingers, "where are you? Give me a word which you dislike."

"Oh erm, I…abandoned?"

"Quite! We don't *really* like that word at this university. Let's get rid of it. Let's chuck it in our vocab bin."

"Malice," Will shouted.

"God no!" Wilomena scribbled it down.

"Manipulation," a voice called from the left.

"Uh-oh – the tool of the fully conscious out and out bad." Dr Smythe jotted it down.

"Slander?" Sophie suggested, "and abuse," Sophie offered, feeling inspired by Wilomena's enthusiasm.

"Horrid words," the lecturer agreed.

"Vulnerable!"

Wilomena stopped scribing, "who said that?" She pointed at the student, "why not?"

"You're leaving yourself open to attack," the kind looking lad shook his head.

"Excellent," Wilomena nodded, "you lot are *very* perceptive. Stay sharp people, forget nice. There *are* people who want to harm you out there. In here of course, everyone is nice, oh balls I mean marvellous." Laughter rang around the room.

"Right that's enough doom and gloom. How about words you like," Wilomena cocked her head to one side and batted her eyelashes.

"Sassy!" Ann said, flinging her hair back.

"I *like* it," Ann chuckled.

A barrage of words flew around the room.

"Sweet."

"Sunshine."

"Fairy."

Wilomena held up her hand, "stop!" She declared, "where are we – primary school? Come *on!*"

"Aspiration!"

"Yes, yes," Wilomena spurred.

"Knowledge!"

"Bravo," the lecturer passed Juliette the pen for her to continue scribbling the words down.

"Humane?!"

"Yes, excellent – a manner in which we should *always* strive to treat others."

"Affectionate!"

"Oh my gosh – class, hug the person next to you – right now!"

There was a minute or two of total chaos.

"Lust?" The class erupted with laughter.

"I prefer love," Wilomena smiled, "is Fifty Shades love?"

"Pain," Juliette shouted, "it's pain...I erm... don't do pain."

Wilomena nodded, "no, I get that about you," she glanced at her watch, "okay class, you've worked really hard today and you've been extremely patient; considering I had no idea what I was doing, so I'm going to let you finish early – get off home or visit the library or the SU bar. That is unless anyone *wants* to carry on."

There was a noisy scramble as students jumped to their feet and began stuffing belongings back into bags.

"I guess that means this lesson is officially over."

Chapter Ten

The weeks rolled by and the remnants of summer were carried away on strong autumn winds. On impulse, Sophie decided to have a big sort out; a declutter, ready for Christmas. Ryan's belongings were thrown into boxes, sellotaped up and the word arse scrawled over them. He had been pestering her for weeks now, bombarding her with emails and messages through her mother.

"Is it wise to block him?" Yvonne asked, "there could be an emergency and you might need to contact him urgently."

Sophie gave a derisive snort, "he hasn't even made any attempts to spend time with the boys. Stuff him."

"He's not well," Yvonne countered, "the football club have dropped him for a younger striker and he seems to be sliding into depression."

"They have?" Sophie stopped scrubbing at the sink and pulled off her rubber gloves.

"Yes," Yvonne confirmed, "what are you doing anyway? Don't you employ a housekeeper to clean for you?"

"This is the new me," Sophie replied brightly, "I'm actually enjoying myself; I never realised that cleaning could be so therapeutic."

Yvonne regarded her daughter with tight lipped horror.

"I suppose I should arrange a meeting with him. I noticed that he's halved the maintenance payment this month – any idea why?"

"You need to speak to *him*," Yvonne replied haughtily, "it really isn't fair to involve me in your marital problems."

"Then I'll do just that!" Sophie strode decisively to her laptop and sent Ryan a succinct email, "now, if you don't mind Mum, I really need to crack on."

Sophie was having a short tea break when she received a reply. It said that he needed to see her as soon as possible. He'd even had the nerve to sign off with a line of kisses.

"if *he* thinks we're getting back together, *he's* in for a big shock," she murmured, through gritted teeth.

Their rendezvous was arranged for this weekend, at some wine bar in the city centre. Sophie pencilled it on the calendar, in-between a trip to the dentist and a start date to stop drinking wine. The other night she had almost polished off a full bottle of Prosecco. It had resulted in a hysterical bout of tears and a vent on Facebook that had accumulated almost 300 likes and comments. In the cold light of day she read over them, cringing with embarrassment. The majority of them were supportive, but one 'friend' had the temerity to post a mental health hotline on her wall.

"Well *they're* blocked for a start," she snarled at the screen.

What the heck! Why not deactivate the whole account. Her fingers hovered over the button, but then an image of Juliette, Will and Ann popped up on a 'friends who will miss you' thread, so she decided not to. Instead she was literally binning the alcohol. It was making her feel ill and maudlin and it had to go. Sophie deleted her vitriolic post on Ryan, hoping that her footballer friends had obliviously scrolled past it and wouldn't let on to her estranged husband and there was the real possibility that some stalkery types could even have screen shotted it. As she was studying her wall for any other implicating posts, Amber popped up on private messenger.

'**Hey babes ☺ are you okay?**'

'**Yes I'm fine thanks. How are you?**'

'**Fed up! Martin's off on one of his golf weekends – fancy a spa day?**'

'**Sorry I'm busy this weekend and funds are a bit tight.**'

'**I'll pay ☺ but if you're busy never mind.**'

'**Sorry. I'm meeting Ryan.**'

There was a pause then the cursor flashed again, '**are you getting back together?**'

'**No way! We just need to talk about finances and the boys.**'

'**Oh cool. Hope you're okay though, I was a bit worried after your last status.**'

Sophie shifted in her seat, '**I'm deleting it now. Ignore it, I was angry and upset.**'

Just then, another messenger box flashed onto the screen; it was Judith Bains, a school friend she hadn't heard from in over twenty years, enquiring if she was okay.

Then another popped up, oh my god, it was Charlie Brooks, wife of the Chattlesbury FC main defender, telling her that she too was having marital problems.

To top it all off, her hairdresser's face then appeared, asking if she wanted to go for a drink to '**talk things over.**'

A horrified Sophie quickly logged off, snapping the laptop shut. "What the hell have I done?" She mumbled, breathing deeply in an attempt to compose herself. Right, back to the cleaning.

* * *

On Saturday morning, Sophie decided to deliberately dress down. She pulled on her old, comfy leggings and piled her hair underneath a dusty sports cap.

"Just running a few errands," she said to Heidi, who was balancing on a stool, trying to catch a huge spider in a cup.

Josh and Jake were at a party and not due back until the evening; Sophie had planned an afternoon of uninterrupted study; she was determined to do well this year and show all those doubters that she *could* finish this degree. She threw a pile of books onto the passenger seat, then reversed backwards off the drive. On the way into the centre of the village, she was caught in a line of tooting cars. There were roadside signs advertising a car boot sale and Sophie noticed the vicar and his wife directing the traffic onto a mud saturated car park.

Mrs Pobble waved as Sophie crawled by and motioned for her to wind her window down.

"Thank you Mrs O'Neill, for the very generous donation of your clothes, we've been distributing them to a number of worthy causes; the homeless and women's refuge."

Sophie smiled, "I'm glad I could help."

"I'm sorry that you and Mr O'Neill have been unable to sort out your differences, I hope that you're coping okay."

"I really am fine," Sophie said in a firm tone, "I'm not the first and certainly won't be the last to go through a marriage break up."

Mrs Pobble sniffed, "yes well, as a Christian, I do believe in the sanctity of marriage; sticking together when times are tough and working things through. That seems to be the problem now-a-days; too many just give up."

"I try not to judge," Sophie replied crisply, "it really is nobody else's business but the two people involved," she pressed the button to slide the window back up.

Mrs Pobble shook her head and broke into a biblical rendition, "wives, submit yourselves to your own husbands as you do to the Lord, for the husband is the head of the wife as Christ is the head of the church, his body, of which he is the saviour."

Sophie papped her horn and waved at Mrs Pobble's figure in her mirror, "nutter," she mumbled.

Twenty minutes later she pulled onto the car park of Chattlesbury's trendiest new wine bar.

It was empty, except for a miserable looking bar man, who was stuffing pork scratchings underneath a row of shiny optics.

"Morning," Sophie said, as she perched onto a bar stool, "can I get a lemonade please?"

"Sure," the tousled haired youth popped a piece of gum, before flipping a glass, "ice and a slice?"

Sophie nodded and pulled her phone from her pocket. She was surfing the Amazon site for books when a shadow fell across the bar.

"Hi Soph," Ryan had his hands shoved deep in his pockets. His face was lined with a messy beard and there were dark circles underneath his eyes. He looked like he had lost weight; his clothes were hanging off him. In spite of everything, Sophie felt a stirring of sympathy for him.

"Hello," she replied stiffly.

"Shall we sit somewhere more private?" He motioned towards a corner table, Sophie hopped down and followed him across the dimly lit bar.

"You're looking well..." Ryan trailed off when he saw the anger flash in Sophie's eyes.

"Hardly," she replied, "I heard you've been dropped."

"I'm on the reserve bench," Ryan replied wearily, "they've signed a Portuguese lad, it looks like my days are numbered at Chattlesbury FC."

"What will you do?" Sophie asked, sipping her drink.

"Coaching maybe. I'm just trying to keep my head above water…things have been hard."

"Oh poor you," Sophie hissed, "maybe one of your groupies can help you out."

Ryan flinched, "you know how sorry I am, how many times do I have to say it and still get ignored."

"Maybe I want to make you suffer," Sophie slammed her glass down.

"I want to make it up to you," Ryan pleaded, "I love you. You and the kids are my world. Can't we get back together?"

"There's more chance of hell freezing over," Sophie rubbed her throbbing temple, "look Ryan, I'm here to discuss the kids, money, that sort of thing. I haven't come for the pleasure of seeing you, let's get things sorted, so we can move on with our own lives."

Ryan stuck out his bottom lip, "alright. Only thing is Soph, there's a problem…"

Sophie regarded him through suspicious, slanted eyes.

"I, er, there is, *no money.*"

"Don't be ridiculous," Sophie snapped, "you're rolling in money."

"No, I'm not," Ryan replied.

"You still get paid, even as a reserve, I'm not stupid Ryan."

"I had some," Ryan held up his hands, "now I don't – it's gone."

"What do you mean – it's gone?"

Ryan shifted in his seat and looked away, "It's not my fault, I'm an addict."

"Ryan…" Sophie's voice held a warning tone.

Suddenly he jumped up, "I've joined Gamblers Anonymous. I admit it. I have a problem but I'm trying to sort myself out."

Sophie glared up at him, "I know you've always liked a flutter on the horses Ryan, but a gambler, aren't you exaggerating?"

Ryan shook his head and slowly sank back down in his seat, "I've blown our savings," he whispered, "it's gone, all of it."

"What?" Sophie mouthed, the colour draining from her cheeks.

"That's not all," Ryan ploughed on, "I've run up a mountain of debts on credit cards and with loan sharks," he put his face in his hands, "I've screwed up, big time."

There was silence for a few moments, as Sophie digested the news, "but what will we do? The house, the mortgage, the bills. How will we cope?"

Ryan leant across the table and covered her trembling hands with his own, "we have to sell the house."

Sophie nodded, "I need to get a job," she pushed back her chair, "I'll have to leave uni. I'll have to...look, look for another house, a smaller property, a flat maybe."

"I can't pay you maintenance either, sorry Soph, at least not this month, I've got...nothing. The cars gone, my designer watch, the bling, the clothes. I had to catch the bus here."

Sophie almost laughed, "why didn't Derek bring you?"

Ryan shrugged, "working, or so he said. Your mum's been great though, proper looked after me she has."

"That's good," Sophie stared out of the window.

"Are you okay?" Ryan gazed up at her, "you're really calm. I thought you'd throw me through the nearest window...Soph?"

"I think I'm in shock," she admitted, "I'm not going to get mad, what good would that do? It's just bricks and mortar, right?" Her thoughts wandered to Juliette: stuck in ASBO central.

"I suppose so," Ryan rose to his feet, "so what now?"

Sophie let out a deep, shaky breath, "now we find the nearest estate agents."

* * *

On Saturday evening, Evelyn was watching a riveting documentary on wildlife in the Antarctic, while knitting a warm woollen cardigan for a children's African charity. Her weekend had been busy; she had been up at six to catch up on housework, then she had caught the bus into the city centre to do a spot of shopping. On her return, she had spent the afternoon baking scones and shortbread, she was giving a tin to Sophie, who was looking far too thin now-a-days. Her knitting needles stopped clacking, as a mesmerising shot of a killer whale jumped from the ocean, then crashed back down into a sea of bubbling surf. Above the noise of the raging polar sea, Evelyn heard a tinkling and realised that it was the phone ringing. She paused the TV and made her way into the hallway. She was surprised to hear Jacob on the other end of the line, enquiring how she was.

"Hello Jacob, I'm fine, thank you, how are you?"

"All good," there was a slight pause, "Evelyn, remember I told you about the opening of the Art Gallery? Well it's tomorrow night."

"Oh." Evelyn recalled him inviting her.

"Yes," Jacob cleared his throat, "I wondered...if...maybe you could accompany me?"

There was a short silence, "I mean, only if you're not too busy," Jacob surged on, "There is a bistro nearby that makes exquisite ravioli and sumptuous pistachio ice-cream. Will you come Evelyn?"

Her face softened, how kind of him to ask her, "yes Jacob, I think I would like that very much."

"That's grand!" Jacob sounded delighted, "I'll pick you up at five o'clock and Evelyn, I've heard it's going to be quite a fancy affair."

Evelyn's mind raced, now what could she wear? "Okay Jacob, well see you tomorrow then?"

"Goodbye Evelyn," he replied softly.

She placed the phone down and climbed the stairs to her bedroom.

Her clothes hung in a neat row, gently she prised the hangers apart and cast a critical eye over them. Trousers wouldn't do at all, she decided, neither would any of the various skirts she owned. No, this called for something special. At the back of the wardrobe, covered in a bag, was her most expensive item of clothing she owned. Carefully she unzipped the cover and pulled out the long, purple dress. The bodice was covered in tiny diamantes and the skirt was puffed out by a petticoat of black, lace netting. It was outrageously decadent and had only been worn once, but it was beautiful and just perfect for a special occasion. Evelyn hung it on the curtain pole and stood back to admire it. She could just envision herself now, floating about the new Art Gallery, holding onto Jacob's arm. As she was contemplating how she could style her hair, the telephone rang again. This time it was Sophie.

"Evelyn, I wondered if I could pop round tomorrow evening for a chat? I'll bring sherry and chocolate." Sophie sounded flat, not like her usual bubbly self.

"Sorry! I've made plans. But why don't you come around on the afternoon instead?"

"Okay, if you don't mind. Where are you going on a Sunday evening anyway?"

Evelyn smiled, "I have erm, a rendezvous, with a friend."

There was a chuckle from the other end of the line, "do you mean a *date* Evelyn?"

Heat flooded into Evelyn's cheeks, "I *mean* – a nice time with a friend, that's all."

"So, where are you off too?"

Evelyn told her about the opening of the new Art Gallery, "It's a posh affair. I've got the dress organised, but I have no idea how to do my hair and make-up."

"I'll do it for you," Sophie said decisively, "we can chat then okay?"

"Yes dear, that would be lovely," Evelyn smiled as she ended the call, then returned to her knitting and documentary, with a feeling of excitement fluttering in her stomach.

* * *

"Well sweetie, how shall we do your hair?" Sophie was holding a curling tong in one hand and a straightener in the other.

Evelyn laughed, "I'll leave it to you dear."

"Curly it is," Sophie decided, as she bent to plug the tongs in.

"Now then dear," Evelyn sat back in the chair and sipped her tea, "what's been happening in your life? Tell me all about it."

Sophie relayed the whole sorry story; of Ryan's crippling debts and their subsequent decision to put their house on the market. When she had finished talking she was close to tears.

"I think I might have to give up uni Evelyn, I desperately need a job and I really need to start looking for somewhere else to live."

"Don't make any rash decisions," Evelyn advised, "speak to Juliette and maybe a student rep, a benefit advisor would also be a good idea."

Sophie nodded, "I've had to let Heidi go too, I'm really going to miss her around the place."

"How are the boys?"

"Surprisingly resilient," Sophie replied, "Ryan came to see them Saturday afternoon. They seem okay that we're splitting. I haven't told them about the house yet though."

Evelyn patted her hand, "You're going to be fine Sophie. Things have a way of working out and maybe it will be for the better."

Sophie smiled at Evelyn's kind optimism, "I hope so. Now madam, your hair is finished, so let me start on your make up."

* * *

"Wow! This dress is beautiful," Sophie was helping Evelyn into her gown, "what shoes are you wearing?"

Evelyn pointed to a pair of strappy patent sandals.

"Perfect," Sophie nodded with approval, "you look stunning." They stared into the full-length mirror. Evelyn gasped, touching her hair.

"I've gone for the natural look," Sophie said, "you don't need too much make-up, you have a beautiful complexion already."

"Thank you," Evelyn stepped into her shoes and bent to fasten the buckles.

"Oh I almost forgot," Sophie dug in her bag, "this." She pulled out a silver butterfly slide, decorated with tiny crystals, "it was my Granny's, she passed it onto me on my tenth birthday; just before she got sick."

"It's exquisite," Evelyn bent her head slightly, so Sophie could clip the slide just behind her ear.

"Ta-da!" Sophie stood back to admire her friend, "you look gorgeous Evelyn."

"I do?" Evelyn's hand went to her throat.

"Absolutely," Sophie nodded.

Just then the doorbell rang, Sophie rushed off to answer it, leaving Evelyn alone to gaze again at her beautifully curled hair and carefully contoured make-up. She picked up a bottle of her most expensive perfume and squirted it at the pulse spots on her wrist and around her neck. Then she picked up her warm, woollen black shawl, wrapping it across her shoulders and arms. Her lace hand-kerchief and a bundle of twenty-pound notes was the last thing to be popped into her handbag, before she made her way down the stairs and towards a waiting Jacob. He glanced up as Evelyn descended and her breath caught; he looked extremely handsome in a black tuxedo and shoes that had been polished so vigorously, they shone.

"E- Evelyn?" He was gazing at her with his mouth open.

"It's me," she confirmed with a laugh.

"You look. You're breath-taking!"

Evelyn reached the bottom of the stairs, blushing uncontrollably.

"Isn't she just," a grinning Sophie regarded them both, "now Jacob please look after her, our Evelyn is very special."

"I've always known that," Jacob cleared his throat, "madam, shall we go?"

Evelyn took his arm, "Thank you so much Sophie, will you be okay?"

Sophie hugged her gently, "I'm going to be absolutely fine, now go and enjoy yourself and I'll see you tomorrow at uni."

* * *

Evelyn was staring at the most beautiful painting. It was a portrayal of a wild, rugged landscape with the rolling sea in the background and a stormy sky full of clouds, lashing rain and the white outlines of seagulls, cruising high above.

"Impressive isn't it?" Jacob said, as he stood next to her, "It's by a local artist, a Brandon White, extremely talented and a really nice guy."

"You know him?" Evelyn squinted at the signature in the right-hand corner.

Jacob nodded, "I know his family well. His father worked with mine at the brewery and his mom was a sister at the hospital, she would have given Florence Nightingale a run for her money; she was that good. Now she's retired, I take her to the daycentre each week."

Evelyn walked along to the next painting; a portrait of a young girl with her arms around a Red Setter dog. The mixture of the colours were stunning.

A waitress in a smart black uniform stopped beside them and offered them drinks. Evelyn took the flute of champagne and sipped it slowly. It tasted heavenly. There were quite a few people in the room and there was soft classical music playing from the overhead speakers, it was a nice atmosphere and Evelyn felt herself relaxing, she was so glad that she had made the effort to come this evening.

"The Mayor is making the official opening," Jacob glanced at his watch, "in about ten minutes time. Shall we find a seat?" He steered her out of the room and into a large hall with rows of chairs and a makeshift stage.

Evelyn sat next to a jolly looking woman, who had bright red cheeks and a beaming smile.

"Hello," the woman nodded at her and Jacob, "isn't this a wonderful art gallery?"

They chatted a few minutes about the paintings and pottery on display, then a tall, middle aged man hopped up onto the stage and introduced himself as Travis Star, one of Chattlesbury's key poets.

The audience listened as he reeled off a dozen or so of his poems; verses of love and heartbreak, grief and bravery. Evelyn looked through his biography on the handout and wondered if he'd ever lectured at the university, he was certainly articulate and confident enough to do so and was obviously very talented; most of the audience appeared spellbound by his soft, lilting, tones.

Beads of perspiration were forming on the nape of her neck, it was warm in here. Evelyn noticed that the lady next to her was nodding off; her head was on a slant and her eyes were drooping. But then the man had finished speaking and there began a polite clapping which turned into thunderous applause.

"That was wonderful," Evelyn said to Jacob, "we've just completed a module on poetry, it was very enjoyable, but this man is just as good as the poets we've been studying."

"He is talented," Jacob agreed, "oh here comes the Mayor."

A chubby man cloaked in the regimental red and gold council office colours, puffed and panted his way up onto the stage. He cleared his throat and began his speech; a dialogue that lasted for over half an hour. By the end, the men were shuffling uncomfortably in their seats and the women were fanning themselves with their free handouts. It was with some relief that the Mayor ceremoniously pulled open the red velvet curtains to reveal a large brass plaque on the wall.

"I hereby announce this Art Gallery officially open."

Jacob rose to his feet, "shall we mingle Evelyn?"

* * *

A little while later they left the building and headed across the busy road to the main strip of bars and restaurants.

"Here we are," Jacob held the door open, so Evelyn could scoot underneath.

The warmth of the restaurant hit her, colouring her cheeks.

"Table for two?" a waiter ticked them off his reservations list and led them to a beautifully decorated alcove, where vine leaves twirled on the walls and candles flickered on the table.

"Madam," Evelyn shrugged off her shawl and passed it over, before sitting down.

"Would you like the wine list Sir?" The hovering waiter asked.

"I think champagne would be better," Jacob replied.

"*Very good* Sir," the waiter bowed and left them alone.

"It's too expensive Jacob," Evelyn chastised, "a sherry would do me just fine."

Jacob waved away her protestations, "you can have sherry any evening. This is a special occasion and I want to treat you."

"Well thank you, you're very kind," Evelyn pulled open a swan shaped napkin, placing it on her lap, "so, you suggested the ravioli?"

Jacob nodded, "and maybe a sharing platter to start?"

The waiter reappeared, tugging at the cork, which proceeded to fly out with a loud pop. Evelyn sipped at the glass he had just filled and underneath the table she kicked off her shoes and wiggled her toes with contentment. Jacob ordered for them both and they settled into a relaxed conversation.

"How long have we known each other Evelyn?" Jacob asked.

"Oh it must be going on for twenty years," Evelyn replied, "since Mam started going to the daycentre?"

"A long time," Jacob toyed with the stem of his crystal glass, "I've always admired you Evelyn."

Evelyn chuckled, "that's the champagne talking."

"No. I mean it," Jacob's face turned serious, "I think you're a wonderful woman."

Evelyn's smile froze, *oh lord, where was this leading*? She wondered.

"Sorry," Jacob said, his face contrite, "I didn't mean to alarm you."

"You don't need to apologise," Evelyn replied hastily, "I've never been good at accepting compliments."

"You are a honourable, humble woman Evelyn, your Mam would be proud."

Tears sprang to her eyes, "thank you Jacob. You are a true gentleman and I bet that wherever Mam is, she's smiling down on the pair of us right now."

* * *

The starter was bought out and speedily consumed. Evelyn crossed her cutlery onto her plate and dabbed at her mouth, "my, that was delicious."

Jacob nodded in agreement, "your friend that was there earlier – Sophie?"

"Yes, that's right."

"Will she divorce her husband? There was rumours of it in the local newspaper."

"I think she will," Evelyn replied gravely, "between me and you Jacob, she is in financial ruin."

"Good Lord, I presumed that footballers were rich."

"He's been gambling," Evelyn whispered, "they have to sell the house just to pay off all the debts. The poor girl is worried sick."

"Where will she move to?" Jacob asked.

"I don't think she knows, she has no job, no savings."

"Could a relative help out?"

Evelyn shook her head, "the only family she has is her mother and they don't get on."

Jacob signalled to the waiter that they were finished and he could take their plates away.

"What about friends? Surely someone could put her up until she sorts herself out."

"I don't think…Oh Jacob, you are a genius!"

"I am?" Jacob looked across at her puzzled.

"She could move in with me!" Evelyn clasped her hands together, "my house is huge and I think it would be lovely to have some company. Why didn't I think of this before, it's the perfect solution."

"But Evelyn, she has children and animals – could you cope with the noise and chaos?"

Evelyn's eyes were sparkling, "of course I could! I've been on holiday with them Jacob and had a wonderful time. Her children are adorable, as for the animals, I love dogs and my garden is plenty big enough for them. Oh, we are going to have so much fun."

Jacob chuckled and looked at her fondly, "she hasn't agreed to move in yet."

"She will," Evelyn replied with confidence, "now I wonder which bedroom the boys could have…"

The remainder of the evening passed by quickly. As promised, the food was divine and Evelyn was thoroughly stuffed by the time she had finished eating. Jacob paid the bill, stoutly refusing to let Evelyn contribute, then they waited outside for the taxi to take them home.

"I hope you've enjoyed yourself Evelyn," Jacob said, rubbing his hands together to warm them.

Evelyn assured him that she had. Inwardly she was thinking how wonderful the whole evening had been and what great company Jacob was. They had talked non-stop about everything from politics to more personal matters. In fact, Evelyn was sorry to be going back to her huge, quiescent home. The taxi pulled up and Evelyn clambered in. As the cab bounced along the bumpy road, she found herself leaning against Jacob for support, he was warm and solid and it invoked in Evelyn a feeling of being protected. Jacob cleared his throat, "Evelyn, I wondered, would you like to do this again; go for another meal or on a daytrip somewhere?"

Evelyn's stomach felt warm and tingly at his words, "I would like that Jacob, very much."

Then he leant towards her and very gently brushed her cheek with his lips and in the darkness Evelyn smiled.

Chapter Eleven

"So this is what a real life university looks like." Flora was staring open-mouthed up at the imposing glass structure of the four storey library, "I never knew so many books existed."

"Oh yes," Hema said with a laugh, "there are books on every topic imaginable."

"Except for porn," Will said, scratching his chin, "they haven't got a section on that yet."

"Will!" Flora remonstrated, but her eyes were merry. She turned to her son and his partner, "thank you for letting me come with you today, I can't believe I've never been inside my own city's university."

"First time for everything," Will replied, manoeuvring the pram up the wheelchair access, "we should be thanking you anyway Mum, you've saved us a traumatic bus excursion." He gazed down at Esme, who was clad in a white snow suit, happily kicking her legs. "While you're here I'll show you around and introduce you to my uni friends."

Flora nodded happily and followed Will through the entrance, "it will be nice to put a face to a name. You can also point out the lecturers, I've heard some of them are very, erm, appealing."

"Ben Rivers is gorgeous," gushed Hema, "but totally besotted by Jules of course."

"And you're taken anyway," Will protested, feeling envious.

"You're still my favourite," Hema teased, winking his way. They flashed their ID cards at the security guard then proceeded down the long corridor, past the library entrance and out onto the courtyard.

Flora admired the neatly cut lawns and evergreen shrubs, the pretty, bubbling water fountain full of old coins.

"It's best in the summer," Hema explained, as they passed rows of deserted picnic tables.

"Yes, I can imagine, it's far too cold to sit outside now," Flora pulled the belt of her coat tighter and tucked a strand of escaped hair back underneath her woollen hat.

"There's Tarquin Haverstock," Will nodded towards a fair-haired man who was puffing on an e-cigarette, "he's the English course leader and also my personal tutor, a nice bloke."

"And *there* is Ben Rivers!" Hema almost squealed with excitement, as a taller man strode towards him, bent his head and began talking.

Flora looked across, her mouth hanging open slightly.

"Mum, you're drooling," Will shook his head with irritation, "he's not *that* nice looking."

Flora shook her head, "erm no Will," she turned towards Hema, "he is *gorgeous*."

Hema giggled with agreement.

"And your friend *dumped* him?" Flora was flabbergasted, "is she mad? He's better looking than Cliff Richard!"

"Oh stop it – the pair of you!" Will tutted, "there's a young child present," he motioned to Esme who was chomping on her fist, oblivious to her dad's annoyance.

Flora and Hema linked arms, trying to suppress their laughter.

The doors to the refectory slid open and Will scanned the room. He noticed Sophie first, brushing her hair, while chattering away to Ann and Juliette. Evelyn was nowhere to be seen. When they saw him, they began waving and beckoning him over. Sophie and Juliette were immediately on their feet, bent over the pram, cooing and clucking over his daughter.

"You said you wanted to meet her," Will pulled out a chair next to Ann.

"Oh she's adorable!" Sophie's face literally melted into the goofiest grin that Will had ever seen, "can I hold her?"

"Sure," he watched as she gently lifted her up, supporting her head, "oh my god – she's just like Hema."

Ann and Juliette peered at her, both agreeing with Sophie.

"This is Mum," Will pointed at Flora.

They all waved and said hi, but it was Esme who was centre stage, yet again. Will grinned at his daughter lapping up the attention, she was going to be a heartbreaker he acknowledged and he was definitely going to be playing the over protective Dad.

"Where's Evelyn?" He asked.

"Here I am," a voice called from behind him.

Evelyn rushed towards them, looking flushed and windswept; her cheeks were rosy and her eyes were sparkling.

"Grab some lunch," Sophie suggested, as she passed Esme over to Ann.

"I've just had some," Evelyn replied, a wide smile lighting up her face, "at the new Bistro, a very nice restaurant."

"Without us?" Sophie appraised her, "who have you been with?"

"Just a friend," Evelyn replied, after a slight hesitation.

"Anyone I know?" Sophie teased, knowing full well that it was Jacob.

Evelyn laughed, "Sophie I have to talk to you, I have a proposition for you."

"You do?"

"Yes," Evelyn continued, "we can talk later, after the lecture, if you have time of course."

"Oh yes, Journalism," Ann stroked Esme's cheek, "I'm looking forward to this module, it sounds really interesting."

Juliette glanced over her timetable, "Dr Hodges is the lecturer, which reminds me, I have an appointment with him in five minutes, I'd better go, will you wait for me?"

"We'll be here," Ann confirmed, while the others nodded their agreement.

Juliette swung her handbag onto her shoulder and wandered off towards the lifts.

"Doesn't Dr Hodges share an office with Dr Rivers?" Sophie asked, a smirk on her face.

The others looked at each other knowingly, "let's hope Jules remembers to come to her lecture after all," Ann commented drily.

* * *

Juliette knocked the door softly and was shocked to hear Ben's voice call 'come in.' Slowly she backed away and was just contemplating running back inside the open, waiting lift, when Brian Hodges appeared from the stairs entrance, puffing and panting and bent over.

"I think I need my inhaler," he rasped, "damn the Dean and his get fit, use the stairs initiative."

Juliette heard the door open behind her,

"Juliette?" She heard him say softly.

"Hi," awkwardly she spun towards him, "I have an appointment with Dr Hodges."

"Oh," Ben gazed over her shoulder, "well don't keep the lady waiting Brian."

Dr Hodges tutted, "excuse me while I collapse from an asthma attack. Go on in Miss Harris and take a seat, I just need to nip to the men's room."

Juliette slid sideways into the room, following Ben back in. She didn't know if she was relieved or disappointed that there was a young lady seated at his desk. Juliette made her way over to Dr Hodges untidy table and perched on a chair.

"Right," Ben cleared his throat, "where was I? Oh yes your dissertation, the outline is very good, I do recommend that you insert more references to literary theories, but other than that, it's coming along very well…"

Juliette tried not to listen to the conversation and resolutely stared out of the window. Fluffy clouds were so much more attractive than the hot Dr Rivers, *weren't they?* Bah! Who was she kidding, surreptitiously she sneaked a peek his way. Yes he was definitely as hot as ever, especially with that stubble, hmmm it made him look even more brooding and … dangerous! That was the word she was looking for – Wilomena Smythe and her lexical choice *would* be impressed! She suppressed a bubble of laughter and averted her eyes to Dr Hodges desk and what a complete mess that was! What was it with the male academics in this place? Maybe Gladys the cleaner could give *them* a lecture on tidiness. She drummed her fingers on her folder with impatience, *hurry up Dr Hodges,* she urged.

"Goodbye now," Ben was directing the student to the door.

Drat! Juliette thought, *now we are going to have to make mundane small talk.*

"Excuse me," she jumped at his words and close proximity, Ben was right beside her, tugging on the drawers of a cabinet.

Juliette inched away, the hairs on the nape of her neck prickling upright. Her gaze slid to his face and fixated on his firm mouth, that mouth that had suffused her with so much pleasure.

"Juliette…I,"

She was overwhelmed by the bold desire to plant her lips firmly on his, she'd had enough of speaking and listening. The trouble with this university, there just wasn't enough action…

"So Juliette," Brian Hodges noisily entered the room and the moment of madness evaporated.

"Let's have a chat about your progress."

* * *

The students were all very excited with the Introduction to Journalism lecture, especially Will, who had been really impressed when a guest speaker from the local newspaper had arrived to discuss the prospects of jobs within the media. A career in journalism sounded cool and he found himself wondering why he hadn't considered it before. He left the class feeling optimistic and full of excitement.

"Gotta dash," he waved to the others as he jogged to the lift, "work."

Melanie the notetaker paused to tighten her Doctor Marten boots, "so, have you heard about what the Student Union have organised?"

Ann, Juliette, Sophie and Evelyn looked at each other blankly.

"You lot are working far too hard," Melanie continued, "they've organised a fun night and I think we should all try and make the effort to go."

When there was no reply she huffed, "you *need* a break. Forget essays; focus on fun, inhibition and alcohol of course. Now, who's coming? I need a definite answer so I can get tickets."

"When exactly is this fun night?" Ann enquired.

"November 6th, a Saturday I think."

"Sorry no-can-do," Ann replied primly, "I'm going to a bonfire party and there's no chance of cancelling it."

"Oh," Melanie's face fell, "okay, well never mind, but Jules – tell me you can come and Sophie and Eve's too." She looked expectantly round at the circle of unsure faces.

"I suppose I *could* get a babysitter," Juliette replied slowly, "but I'm not going alone…if Soph and Evelyn can't go then…"

"They can!" Melanie announced, "ladies, trust me, this is going to be a night to remember."

"I suppose it looks like we're going then Evelyn," Sophie said ruefully.

"Well yes, but Melanie I can't stay too late," Evelyn warned.

"Don't worry Cinderella," Melanie replied with a wide grin, "I promise we won't be…late I mean, this is so exciting, we're going to have a ball."

* * *

Sophie woke with a sudden jolt from a horrible nightmare. It was the third night in a row she had experienced the same dream. In it she was homeless, living underneath a canal bridge with a carrier bag full of possessions and a meagre fifty pence in her purse. There was worse: a lot worse. Josh and Jake had been taken from her and were residing in a care home, waiting on a kind foster parent to take them in. Her mother had eloped with Derek and all her friends had shunned her. She was completely alone. No family, no home, no money, nothing. Sweat dripped off her nose as she struggled to sit upright and extricate herself from the tangle of the duvet. The clock informed her that it was only three thirty in the morning, *what the hell* Sophie thought, *please let me sleep!* She punched the pillow with anger, slid back down and clenched her eyes tightly shut. Then began the usual tossing routine; the left side of the bed was too cold and the right was too lumpy, lying on her back gave her indigestion and lying on her side hurt her arms. Finally she found a warm spot, where she coiled her body into a great shape that even a snake would be proud of. Slowly she felt herself growing sleepier and was just on the verge of unconsciousness, when an image of red final demand bills flying through the letter box assailed her. The electricity bill! Sophie shot upright, she should have paid it on Monday, it was now Saturday, but miraculously she still had power. Breathing heavy she snapped on her bedside lamp. Boom – there was light. *Thank Christ for that!*

Another hour passed slowly by, before Sophie finally dropped off. Then in no time the dogs were whining to be let out and the posse of birds on her guttering were singing away like some demented dawn chorus. She banged the window shut and watched with satisfaction as they cawed in fright and took off with an indignant flap.

"Ha ha, that showed *them*," Sophie turned around and jumped at the sight of her own reflection. Jesus, she looked like an apparition in her bright white nightie, with her hair sticking up and her milky white limbs on show. She missed the good old days of spray tanning; where her complexion resembled a satsuma and the boys laughed at her for being 'tangoed.'

"Fat chance of that," Sophie mumbled, looking around for her slipper socks. It was nippy this morning, she rooted through the clothes hanging off the door peg, baulking at the crazy notion of donning one of her seductive silk wraps. Her hands found the warmth and comfort of her oldest, longest, furriest dressing gown. Quickly she wrapped herself in it, revelling in the heat it cocooned around her. After checking on a still sleeping soundly Josh and Jake, she hurried down the stairs to open the back door. Freezing air invaded her kitchen, teeth chattering she waited for the dogs to relieve themselves, before whistling them back in and locking the frost and the ice out. As if on cue, the heating system burst to life and Sophie clicked the kettle on, she was parched and in desperate need of a cup of warm, sweet tea.

She sat at the table, thoughts racing through her mind; her broken marriage, her dire financial affairs, the well-being of her children. Sophie was really worried, her world was falling apart and she felt completely powerless to stop it, she felt like she was spiralling into a deep, dark abyss, with no means of escape. *How could I have wasted so many years at spas and beauticians?* She berated herself, *how could I have lived such a shallow life? I should have been frugal, I should have been working hard, I should have been saving money instead of frittering it away on nonsense.* Sophie put her head in her hands and wept; big, fat tears of loneliness and regret and anxiety slid down her cheeks and plopped into her drink. She felt a wetness against her ankle and looked down at her faithful dog, gazing up at her as he tried to nuzzle away her sadness. She wiped away the tears with a firm hand, reached for her phone and tapped out a message to Jules, hoping that she hadn't woken her. A few minutes later a reply pinged into her inbox.

'**Move in with Evelyn,**' it urged.

Sophie considered the advice. It had been so nice of Evelyn to offer her a home and if it was just her she might even jump at the opportunity of living with her dear friend, but she had Josh and Jake to consider and the pets of course. It wouldn't be fair to take over Evelyn's quiet abode, with her mad-cap noisy family. And it wouldn't be fair on the boys either – they needed their space to play and have fun. How would Evelyn cope with two growing boys running amok?

'**It wouldn't be fair on Evelyn,**' Sophie replied.

Then another reply whizzed into her messages, '**Evelyn would love the company! It would be a temporary measure until you get yourself sorted. Think about it Soph, it makes sense.**'

"Okay I'll think about it," Sophie mumbled to the empty kitchen.

"Mum," a sleepy voice invaded her thoughts, she gazed at the door, her heart constricting with love at the sight of Josh, tugging at his pyjama bottoms with one hand and rubbing his eyes with the other, "I can't sleep, Jake's snoring again."

Sophie rushed over to hug him, "neither can I honey, how about I make you a mug of hot chocolate, then we can watch a film together: your choice."

Josh gave her his trademark cheeky grin, followed by a big thumbs up sign and her anxiety slowly dissipated. She splashed cold milk into the saucepan, whistling a cheery Christmas tune as she cranked up the heat and watched the morning light dance in prisms across the frosty lawn.

* * *

After a rejuvenating shower, Sophie was feeling much more alert and positive. She dressed quickly, clipped up her hair and rapped on the boy's bedroom door. She could hear the sounds of electronic games and excited shouts coming from within.

"I need to speak to you guys," she called, flinging the door open.

Josh and Jake were lying side by side on their stomachs, their attention focused on the hand-held computers.

"Can you come downstairs please."

Josh sat up with a sigh, "we can't have a family meeting without Dad."

Sophie swallowed, "your Dad doesn't live here anymore, remember I explained about that."

Jake rolled onto his back and stared up at the ceiling, "are you and Dad going to divorce?"

"Yes love, we will eventually," Sophie wanted to be honest, "but right now we have other things to sort out...please come downstairs and we'll have a proper chat."

Josh and Jake huffed and puffed but jumped to their feet with resignation. They followed Sophie down the stairs, racing into the kitchen and hopping onto the high stools, where they began arm wrestling.

"I'm stronger!" Yelled Jake.

"You're a cheat," shouted back Josh, "your elbow was off the table. Mumm-mmmmm..."

"Stop boys," Sophie held up two hands, "we need to have a serious conversation."

The boys were silenced by the firmness of her tone.

"Okay," she perched opposite them, "firstly I want to tell you how proud I am of you both. I know that it can't be easy for you, with your dad moving out, but you're coping really well and I love you very much."

Josh and Jake exchanged awkward glances, "you're not gonna get all mushy again are you Mum?"

"No!" Sophie laughed, "I just want you to know that whatever happens in the future between me and your dad, we're both here for you one hundred per cent."

That last bit wasn't entirely true, Sophie acknowledged silently. Ryan hadn't been around much for Josh and Jake recently, it seemed that he was busy battling his own demons, but Sophie couldn't bear to upset her children, they were well behaved, well-adjusted kids and the thought of destabilising them terrified her. She was desperate to reassure them they were cherished by *both* parents, and if that meant romanticising their father, then so be it.

"Let's be open. Do you want to talk?" Sophie asked, "about anything?"

Josh was picking his nails, a sure sign of anxiety.

"I want to stay with you," he mumbled, "Dad's great and everything but he doesn't tuck us in when we stay over."

"He doesn't get marshmallows for the hot chocolate either," Jake interjected, his voice wobbling with outrage.

Sophie's insides turned to mush, as she was reminded how young and vulnerable they were.

"It's the little things that are so important," she acknowledged, clasping their hands, "of course you'll be living with me. I will always, always take care of you."

The twins glanced at each other grinning.

"Can we go back upstairs now?"

Sophie beamed at them, "In a minute. There's one other thing," she emitted a shaky breath, "we have to sell this house." She let her words sink in, luckily there was no dawning horror or hysterics. "It's far too big for the three of us and it's costing lots of money, that I just don't have."

In fact Josh and Jake didn't seem perturbed at all.

"We have to move out," Sophie rushed on, "as soon as possible."

"Will we have to move schools?" Jake asked, his face lit up with excitement.

"No!" Sophie's reply was emphatic, "that's if you want to stay there? I thought you guys were happy at school?"

"We like our friends," Josh responded solemnly, "but the teachers are cranky; they make us work too hard."

Sophie chuckled, "it's like that at every school."

"Even your school?" Doubt crept across Jake's face.

"Yes, even my big school, especially my school!"

Josh pushed back his chair and came and put his arms around his mom. She leant her head against his soft curls, he smelt good; full of the freshness of youth.

"It's alright Mum," he soothed, "everything will be okay."

Her eyes filled with tears, *talk about role reversal.* Then Jake was on his feet, cuddling her too.

"Don't worry Mum, it'll be Christmas soon, maybe Santa could bring us a new home this year."

"Actually," Sophie sniffed, "remember lovely, kind Evelyn, who we went on holiday with?"

The two boys nodded.

"She, erm... suggested we could live with her. Temporarily of course, until I can get a job and find us somewhere more permanent."

"You have to get a job?" Jake sounded horrified.

"Yes. I do." Sophie bit her lip to stop herself blurting out that their father was a feckless gambler who had landed them in a financial pickle. Of course she had to get a job, this was real life and everything cost money.

"We don't have to move in with Evelyn," Sophie said softly, "don't be afraid to say no, I'll understand."

"Grandma Fletcher!" Jake shouted, clicking his fingers "how come we can't move in with her?"

Sophie sighed wearily, "things are a bit tricky with Gran. She's busy with Derek and your dad stays over a lot. It just wouldn't work with us moving in there too."

"Is Del her new boyfriend?" Josh's nose wrinkled with distaste.

Sophie nodded, "and she has assured me that this is definitely the one."

"The one for what?" Jake looked confused.

"The one who's going to be make her happy," Sophie cajoled, "you know true love: hearts, flowers and cupid."

"Urgh!!" Both boys were in agreement, that it was gross to know too much about Grandma Fletcher's love life.

"So anyway, back to Evelyn," Sophie persisted, "what do you think?"

Jake shrugged and looked at his twin, "I think it would be cool."

Josh nodded enthusiastically.

"Yay!" Sophie felt like doing a happy dance around the kitchen, "she has a massive garden *and* she told me that you can have a bedroom each if you want to."

"Wicked!" Josh and Jake high fived.

Sophie rose to her feet, "I'll ring Evelyn now and tell her the good news. I must buy her flowers to thank her for being our saviour. Oh and boys, there are some people coming to look at the house a bit later, can you pur-lease tidy your room?"

"Yes Mum," they cried in unison, "can we go now?"

The boys zoomed off before Sophie could reply, racing each other back up the stairs.

Sophie sighed with happy relief, *this is the start of my new life*, she thought, *this is my second chance.* She picked up the phone and dialled Evelyn's number.

* * *

Sophie spent the rest of the morning hoovering and dusting, in preparation for the viewings which the estate agent had arranged. The first to arrive were Mr and Mrs Chan and their teenage daughter. Sophie showed them around, listening politely as they spoke about their family history. Mrs Chan, like many other Chinese women, was pretty and petite. She explained how the Chan family had moved to the UK ten years ago in search of prosperity and happiness. Sophie was impressed when she divulged that she was a scientist, working on the cutting-edge field of cancer research. Her daughter had been offered a place at Cambridge University and Mr Chan was some kind of financial genius.

They seemed impressed with the house and Sophie was shocked when they told her they would be paying cash in full.

"Well this is the garden," Sophie swung open the back door, leading them outside.

The daughter, who had been following in complete silence, gasped, "did Ryan O'Neill actually play footie here?"

Sophie flinched at the mention of her estranged husband.

"He did practice here sometimes, yes," she had a sudden vision of Ryan on the lawn in full Chattlesbury kit, performing ball tricks for Josh and Jake. *They idolised him, like so many others*, a bitterness gripped her, and she felt over-whelmed by anger and sadness.

Mrs Chan touched her shoulder, "are you okay?"

Sophie blinked away the image, "yes, yes... sorry, would you like to see the double garage?"

The next to arrive were a glamorous granny and her butch, toy-boy lover. Frederick had arms the size of Sophie's thighs and a bushy beard that seemed to be all the rage now-a-days in men.

"The bedrooms are large yar?" He enquired, in guttural, Dutch tones.

"Yes, would you like to see upstairs first?"

As they trooped up the winding staircase, Sylvie, who had to be in her late sixties at least, whispered that they had won a substantial amount on the Post-code Lottery.

"When we saw your house was on the market, we just had to come and have a nosy," she giggled girlishly.

Sophie surreptitiously rolled her eyes, she knew she would have at least one time waster, just here for the novelty value.

"We live on the council estate," Sylvie continued, "the neighbours are lit-erally green with envy. When I leave that dump I'm going to give the entire neighbourhood the biggest two fingered salute ever."

Frederick was caressing the wooden banister, "is good to slide down, yar?"

Sophie stared, "well my kids say so," she managed to reply, suppressing a bubble of laughter.

"He's into gymnastics," Sylvie winked, "extremely flexible."

Sophie cleared her throat, "then let me show you the master bedroom."

Her guests were in raptures over the imposing four poster bed and expensive decor.

"Real silk sheets," squealed Sylvie, "oh my god, is that a Chanel handbag?"

Sophie glanced at the designer bag that Ryan had bought her two birthdays ago; a monstrously expensive, red blingy number studded with real diamonds.

Sophie had been almost orgasmic with delight when she had torn off the wrapping. Now it was just another pointless bag to add to her large collection of other pointless bags, gathering dust and cluttering up the place.

"I don't use it much anymore," was all that she could muster, "can I show you the en-suite?"

"Those are real gold," Sophie pointed at the taps sitting atop a magnificent whirlpool bath, "and the power shower and bidet have been recently installed."

"This room," Sylvie looked around wide eyed, "is bigger than my garden."

"Really?" Sophie was horrified.

Frederick was inspecting the depth of the bath, "is good for making love? Yar?"

Sophie felt heat flood into her cheeks, "I...erm..."

"Frederick," Sylvie remonstrated, "you are embarrassing poor Mrs O'Neill."

Frederick hung his head, "very sorry."

"He's European," Sylvie muttered, "still acclimatising to British etiquette."

"You also European!" Frederick's voice rose an octave.

Sylvie looked aghast, "of course I'm not European silly. I explained all this; after the referendum result, Britain decided to become independent. We are no longer European!"

"What continent you from then huh?" Frederick's face and neck had turned red.

Sylvie looked startled by the question, "I don't think that's been decided yet. Get over it Freddy, we broke away."

"Pah," Frederick's top lip snarled upwards, "you English women all the same. You all think you perfect angels drinking tea all day, but you teases, deep down you all love the continental sausage hmmm?"

Sophie had heard enough, she twisted the cold tap forcefully, allowing a jet of freezing water to shoot out and shower them all.

"Fully working as well," she said briskly, wiping back a wet lock of hair, "follow me - I'll show you the ground floor."

By the time they had reached the kitchen, Freddy and Sylvie were friends again and were exchanging passionate kisses. Sophie gave them a speedy tour of each room and finally the gardens on their way out. After she closed the gate on them, Sophie leant on it for support, thankful that the boys hadn't met the funny couple. Two down, one to go, she thought as she trooped back inside and flicked the kettle on.

The last potential house-buyers to arrive were a loud Scottish man wearing a kilt and a quietly spoken handsome guy in a well-cut suit.

"This is James," the Scottish man boomed, "my husband of ten days."

"Congratulations!" Sophie shook their hand politely, "I love a winter wedding."

"We wanted to marry in James' local church; a marvellous piece of architecture, but he's Catholic, so of course, there was no chance of *that* happening."

"We married at a registry office and it was lovely," James explained, in contrasting gentle tones to that of his husband's rough brogue.

"Why don't you have a look around while I make you drinks," Sophie suggested. She was tired; her voice was hoarse from the use of too many uplifting adjectives and she had had enough of traipsing up and down the stairs.

"Good idea lass," Bruce and James wandered off, discussing wallpaper themes and structural surveys.

Sophie sat at the kitchen table with a pen and a piece of paper, moving list she wrote at the top, then she began scribbling down things that needed to be done. By the time the newlyweds returned, she had filled the entire page.

"Ach, it's a beautiful house," Bruce commented, "why are you leaving?"

"That's not your business," James said lightly.

"Marriage separation," Sophie replied, feeling numb, "he cheated on me and gambled away our money, I have no choice."

"The lowlife," Bruce said, sitting beside her, "you do know that you have a fortune wrapped up inside this house – designer this and that. Why don't you sell it all online or do a car boot sale?"

"Handbags," Sophie mumbled, "what a good idea!"

Sophie tore off a strip of fresh, blank paper: things to sell, she wrote at the top, in bold, red ink.

Chapter Twelve

"Remember, remember the fifth of November, the gunpowder treason and plot," Jon picked up the fireworks and carried them to the boot of his car.

"Don't forget the sparklers," Ann called from the front passenger seat, "and hurry, we're late!"

Jon went back to the house, pulling the door firmly shut. Above him a firework erupted with a loud bang, leaving a blazing gold trail in the black night sky.

"I think we're in for a explosive night," Jon said, as he strapped himself in, "all ready?"

"Put your foot down mister," Ann replied, glancing at her watch.

They pulled off the drive, turned right to begin the journey to Anton, Lulu and of course Samuel's house.

On her lap Ann balanced a box of toffee apples, freshly made this morning.

"These were mine and my sister's favourite when we were young," Ann told him, "they still are my guilty pleasure. In fact," she picked one up and pulled at the wrapper, "shall I?"

"Go for it," Jon replied as he fiddled with the car stereo.

Ann took a large bite, "hmm, this tastes so good," she proffered the apple to Jon, who took a sideways nibble as he manoeuvred the car around a tricky bend.

"Oh yes," he mumbled, "I think Samuel is going to love those." He flicked a switch and a spray of water shot onto the dusty windscreen, "so there's a party at the uni tonight?"

Ann nodded, "according to Melanie – yes, although I haven't seen any posters advertising it, they usually send a generic email to all the students when there's something social going on but not this time. It all seems a bit suspicious to me."

"Shame you're missing it," Jon remarked.

"I'm sure I'll hear about it on Facebook later," Ann replied drily, licking a blob of toffee off her finger.

"You know what food reminds me of my youth?" Jon said in a wistful tone, "pomegranates."

"Those round things that looked like a cross between an apple and an onion?"

"Yes!" Jon grinned, "Mum used to buy them on a Saturday from the local green-grocers. She would cut them in half and we would eat them using pins."

"Pins?" Ann laughed, "imagine the health and safety implications of kids doing that now-a-days."

Jon sighed, "I used to look forward to them. It was a real treat; pomegranates, lemonade and Saturday night T.V. Can you even buy them now in the shops?"

"Of course," Ann replied, silently vowing to pop a pack in the trolley next time she was at the supermarket, then she relaxed back in the seat and hummed along to the catchy number playing on the radio.

Jon just managed to squeeze his car into a tight parking space on a grass verge, some way back from Anton and Lulu's house. Ann contemplated the long line of cars stretching down the road.

"Are all these here for the bonfire party?"

"What?" Jon's head was in the boot, as he pulled out Ann's wheels.

"Never mind," she waited patiently for him to come around to her side door. Jon lifted her into his arms.

"You don't need to pick me up all the time," Ann tutted, "I am capable of getting myself into my chair."

Jon kissed the tip of her nose, "why so bristly? I pick you up because I love you. Doesn't every woman want to be swept off her feet."

"Not this one," Ann grumbled, "if I could actually feel my feet."

"Shush," Jon's mouth hovered over her own and her lips parted instinctively, "hmm, you taste of toffee."

"Funny that," Ann rolled her eyes, "are you ever going to put me down, Mr Romantic?"

Jon dropped her lightly onto the seat and they both turned to gaze at Anton and Lulu's bohemian house. Bright light was streaming through the windows and the front door was wide open. A small group of people stood chatting on the drive, bundled up with scarves and hats and gripping bottles of beer.

Ann shivered, "it's so cold," she exclaimed.

"Let's get you into the warm," Jon pushed her up the bumpy path.

"Jon, Ann, lovely to see you," Anton was standing at the side gate, "come on straight through," he led them into the garden, where more people mingled, "Rose couldn't make it," he divulged, "full of cold, but she sends her apologies."

"Oh that's a shame," Ann felt a pang of disappointment, she had been looking forward to seeing the kind social worker, "wow, you have a lot of fireworks."

Jon added his box to the collection.

"We have all sorts; Rockets, Catherine wheels, Roman Candles, Lulu went shopping with her mother and over-spent as usual, we do love Bonfire Night, Halloween is so American isn't it?"

"Where do you want this Anton?" Asked a tall man, with his arms full of logs.

"On the bonfire of course," Anton pointed to a large heap, "that is my piece de resistance," he said proudly, "the whole neighbourhood has contributed wood to it and Samuel helped me stack it."

"What about the chickens and the rest of the animals?" Ann asked, "won't they be frightened by all the noise and the fire?"

"We've locked them in the front bedroom," Anton replied smoothly, "no need to worry Ann, they'll be perfectly fine. Now, why don't you go and say hello to Lulu, she's in the kitchen and it's a lot warmer in there than it is out here."

Jon weaved Ann through the clusters of cold looking people and found Lulu chopping fruit and singing along to Heart FM.

"Guys! So glad you could make it," Lulu rushed over to hug them both. She smelt of lavender and was wearing a long, purple, crushed velvet dress and thick socks tied with ribbons. Her hair was piled high and decorated with butterfly clips. She looked wonderfully eccentric and extremely pretty. Ann felt boringly conventional in her faded jeans and thick fisherman's sweater.

"Would you like a glass of my fruit punch?" Lulu's kohled eyes twinkled as she spoke.

"Is it alcoholic?" Jon enquired.

"Of course," she laughed, "but I can't tell you what's in it – that's a secret family recipe."

"Not for me then," Jon held up one hand, "I'm driving, but I'd love a cup of tea."

"I'll have some," Ann cut in.

"Fabulous!" Lulu stirred the pot and poured a large ladle of red coloured liquid into a cup.

"There you go!" She wedged a piece of orange on the rim and passed it over to Ann, "could you be a love and make your own tea? While I prepare the hotdogs."

"Sure," Jon looked around the messy kitchen and finally found the chrome kettle underneath a tea-towel.

Ann sipped her drink, "whoa! That's got some kick."

"Should I dilute it?" Lulu chewed her bottom lip.

"Maybe a little," Ann coughed, "is Samuel around? I haven't seen him yet."

"He *was* playing with the boy next door," Lulu splashed a pint of water into her concoction, "I should warn you, he's had a bad couple of days."

Ann picked up a bread knife and began slicing the hot dog rolls, "nothing serious I hope."

Lulu frowned, "more desperately sad really. He wrote to his mum, but the letter has been returned unopened."

"The poor lad," Jon said softly.

"He's been very quiet," Lulu continued, "Anton and I have tried our best to cheer him up, but how do you explain to a twelve-year old that his mother simply doesn't care?"

The door swung open and a lady in a tight-fitting rain mac bustled in.

"Lulu, the boys have been wrestling again – on the garden of all places! Samuel is covered in mud, look," she stepped back to reveal a sheepish looking Samuel, his face covered in dark streaks and leaves twined through his golden curls.

"Oh Sam," Lulu sighed, "how many times have I told you not to play fight. One of these days you are going to be seriously hurt. I suppose I'll have to clean you up then huh?"

Ann put down the knife, "Could I help? That's if it's okay with Sam?"

"You're an angel," Lulu replied, "use the downstairs loo and Sam... please, no more wrestling."

* * *

"Thank you so much for picking me up," Juliette said, as she clambered into the back of the thrumming car.

Jacob smiled at her in the rear-view mirror, flashing pearly white teeth, "no problem."

In the front passenger seat, Evelyn was fiddling with her phone, "I've just text Sophie to tell her we're on our way," she turned towards Juliette, "hello dear, you're looking lovely as usual, who's looking after the children?"

Juliette sniffed, "my mum and dad. I've told them I won't be late, I'm not feeling too good, I was going to cancel."

Evelyn nodded, "I won't be late either, I'm really behind with my reading, but Melanie was adamant that we should come for some reason."

"What is this party in aid of?" Jacob queried.

"No idea," replied Juliette, "but she did mention something about some of the proceeds going to charity."

"Can I pick you up?" Jacob asked, "I've nothing planned for the night and I'd like to know that you've gotten home safe."

"That's very kind of you Jacob but we don't want to put you out."

He smiled at Evelyn, "it would be my pleasure."

"Oh Evelyn," Juliette leant forward, "Sophie told me the good news – she's moving in with you? That is such a generous offer. I know Sophie really appreciates you giving her a home. God, that makes her sound like an unwanted puppy."

"I know what you mean Juliette," Evelyn replied, "I'm just being a friend, which is what Sophie needs right now. To be honest I'm worried about her, she's not been sleeping with the worry of everything and the weight is dropping off her."

Juliette nodded, "I've noticed that she's not been eating much, it must be all the stress."

"You'll fatten her up in no time with that famous shortbread of yours." Jacob chuckled as he whizzed through a set of green lights.

"I intend to look after her," Evelyn confirmed, "what that girl needs right now is some tender loving care."

When they arrived at Sophie's she was waiting outside, leaning against the For Sale sign.

"Hi," she slid into the back seat. Juliette reached across to hug her and Evelyn turned to pat her knee.

"How has your day been dear?" Evelyn asked.

"Surreal," Sophie replied, "I've had three viewings on the house already and two more scheduled for Monday. There's so much to think about and organise, I feel like my head is going to burst."

Evelyn and Juliette exchanged worried glances.

"Not being pushy Sophie, but I sold my father's house when he died four years ago," Jacob said, "I'm pretty clued up on the financial and legal matters. If I can help or advise in anyway, please let me know."

Sophie smiled with gratitude, "I might just take you up on that," then her countenance grew dark, "Ryan is completely clueless. He seems happy leaving all the arrangements of the house sale to me. He hasn't contacted the children in days, he's become totally self-absorbed and my mother isn't helping matters, fussing over him. I think that she's forgotten that I'm the innocent party here."

Juliette regarded her sympathetically, "a night out with friends will do you good. Try and forget about it for a couple of hours," her phone beeped, "oh, I've just had a text from Melanie…it says to meet her outside the library."

Jacob pressed his foot down on the accelerator, "hold tight ladies, I'll have you there in no time."

* * *

"So, you like wrestling huh?" Ann wiped gently at a smudge of mud that was lodged underneath Samuel's nose. There was no reply, just the ticking of the clock in the hallway. "What other things do you like to do?" Ann persisted.

Samuel kicked at the crooked bathroom mat, "play my computer," he muttered.

Ann smiled, "I figured that. What about school? Do you like it?"

His face twisted into a scowl, "I HATE it!" He exclaimed.

"Oh." Ann drew back slightly, "I have to confess I didn't much like school either; all those boring subjects and the relentless homework, no thank-you! Apart from English, I suppose I liked English."

"You did?" Samuel asked dubiously.

"Yes Sam," Ann nodded, "I loved books, I still do." There was a pause, "what about you – do you like reading?"

"Dunno," Samuel shook his head, "I've only ever read comics."

Ann felt a tug of emotion, "I could lend you Harry Potter – I have the whole series, It's wonderful Sam."

Samuel glanced up from behind his curls, "okay."

Ann put down the damp flannel, "I'm helping Lulu organise the food, would you like to help too?"

He nodded and Ann was so pleased to see his lips curve into a small smile.

"Come on then, you can push me back."

They made their way into the kitchen, where Jon was picking pineapple wedges out of bowls and spearing them onto wooden skewers.

"So, what do you think of my fruit kebabs?" He held one up for inspection.

"They look very appetising," Ann placed one hand over her stomach, "all this food is making my stomach grumble."

"There's plenty more where that came from," Lulu rolled up her sleeves and thrust her hands into a bowl of warm, soapy water, "Sam, why don't you and Ann go outside and help Anton organise the fireworks."

"Okay," Samuel made for the door.

"He seems happier," Lulu whispered to Ann, "well done you."

Ann smiled and wheeled herself forward.

"Wait," Lulu called, "don't forget the sparklers."

"What do you think Ann? Fireworks or bonfire first?" Anton was standing on the uneven patio, scratching his head.

Ann glanced at the lopsided mountain of wood, "fireworks first definitely – do you have rockets?"

"I do," Anton's breath curled out of his mouth. He gathered a pile in his arms and trooped down to the bottom of the long garden, "Samuel bring the rest," he called over his shoulder.

Ann watched as they began embedding the fireworks into the earth.

"How's it going?" Jon appeared at her side, squinting into the darkness.

"Good," Ann replied, "Sam seems to have cheered up."

"You're doing really well with him," Lulu commented, as she placed a tray of food down, "he likes you, I can tell."

Ann's eyes sparkled in the darkness, "I like him too, very much," she grabbed hold of Jon's hand, "we both do."

"Maybe you could take him out somewhere on your own," Lulu continued.

"Would a football match be a good idea?" Jon queried.

"Yes," Lulu replied with a nod, "that would be perfect. He would love that, I don't think that he's ever been to a live football match before."

"Great!" Jon's voice rose with excitement, "could you ask Sophie for tickets love?"

"No," Ann snapped, "they're separated – remember?"

"Oh yes, sorry," Jon rubbed his stubble, "I'll nip up to the ticket office then."

"Don't you think you should ask him first?" Quipped Ann, "he's coming now, here's your chance."

Jon wandered off to greet him, two smoking hot-dogs in hand.

"How long have you been married?" Lulu asked, leaning on the table.

"Urm four years," Ann replied, counting backwards in her head.

"He's one of the good guys," Lulu said emphatically, "he has a kind aura."

"He's the best," Ann sniffed, "after the accident I was in a dark, dark place. Jon led me back into the light. He saved me."

"It's the same with me and Anton," Lulu said quietly, "I went off the rails when I was a teenager, tried to fit in with bad, bad people. Then I met Anton. He was so different to the other guys I'd dated, he's warm and loving and kind and not afraid to be unique."

"Originality is a rare attribute in today's society," Ann replied, "you should never be afraid of being different." A sudden beeping noise emanated from her pocket, "these damn Facebook notifications. I really don't want to know what my social media friends are having for dinner."

Lulu visibly shuddered, "we don't do social media in this house."

"Really?" Ann glanced her way, "I thought it was mandatory for every British resident to own a Facebook account."

Lulu laughed, "I can't see the positives myself."

Ann shrugged, "I suppose it's an easy method of keeping in touch with others, sharing interests and it *is* free advertising for anyone who has a product to sell, but some people seem to view it as a dating app – I've had numerous friend requests from American army generals with rifles and scary looking dogs. I've even had to change my profile picture to one of me and Jon – who is *not* happy because he loathes his photo on any social media and even then, it hasn't deterred some men."

"You're a pretty girl," Lulu replied.

Ann raised one eyebrow, "really? Then there's the posters who use it as a forum to preach, while in the real world, who knows what they're getting up to? And the political rants? Yada, yada, they really get on my tits."

Lulu nodded in agreement, "the dark virtual world has become the new religion."

There was a loud whizzing sound and a rocket erupted upwards, showering sparks all over the ground. Ann gazed at the cloudless sky, watching the firework arch overhead, before exploding into gold and scarlet splashes which scorched the inky blackness.

The crowds of people in the garden gasped. Jon turned to give Ann a big thumbs up sign, next to him Samuel was jumping up and down with excitement.

"Ann, have you ever had a tarot reading?"

"What?" Ann turned to stare at Lulu.

"Tarot cards, you must have heard of them. I could do you a reading. Free of charge of course."

Ann frowned, "I don't know…isn't it dangerous…isn't it…"

Lulu cocked her head on one side, "witchcraft?"

"Well I guess…I don't really know anything about it."

"It's not witchcraft Ann and it's nothing like using a Ouija board – now that can lead to some serious shit, so I've heard. Are you religious Ann?" Lulu passed her a piece of pineapple off her stick."

"I was when I was younger, who isn't? It's drummed into you from an early age but now, after what I've been through and seen, No way!" Ann popped the fruit cube into her mouth, "oh this is good, it reminds me of summer. But tarot cards, I've always associated them with darkness, death and…"

"The devil," Lulu sighed, "bad witches, demons and things that go bump in the night? Sin and hell? No Ann, their real purpose is divinatory."

"Oh."

Lulu laughed, "don't worry Ann, I'm not crazy and I'm not trying to lead you to the dark side. The tarot can be traced right back to Ancient Egypt. It was originally used as a card game and it's actually quite fun."

"Well why not? I'm open to anything that kicks against the establishment and it will be something else I can tick off my bucket list, but can we watch the fireworks first? It looks like the Catherine Wheel is just about to start spinning."

* * *

Juliette, Sophie and Evelyn were walking down the concrete ramp towards the library.

"It's so quiet," Juliette said, looking behind her, "where is everyone?"

The area was deserted, apart from a homeless man who was curled underneath a tea stained duvet. Evelyn dug in her purse and dropped a handful of loose change into his hat.

"Thank you angel," he mumbled.

They carried on walking. Lamps flickered and buzzed in the darkness and in the distance the muffled sound of beeping horns and a dog howling could be heard.

"I thought there was a party here tonight?" Sophie's heels clacked on the pavement, "I hope I haven't got dressed up for nothing."

"You look lovely," Juliette replied, casting a quick glance over Sophie's glittery jump suit.

"I can't hear any music either," Evelyn said, "maybe we're early."

"Surprise!" A high pitched squeal made all three of them jump.

"Goodness," Evelyn's hand flew to her chest, "Melanie, you gave me a fright."

"Sorry," Melanie stood with her hands on her hips, grinning widely, "it's so cool you're here. We need to head for the refectory, come on."

"The refectory?" Juliette's puzzled tone made them all stop, "I thought we were going to the Student Union bar – isn't there a disco?"

A guilty look flashed across Melanie's face, "er...no Jules, we're not going to a disco."

Juliette glanced at Sophie and Evelyn, suspicion growing in her mind.

"Why all the subterfuge?"

"Oh Jules, you are such a worrier," Melanie linked her arm through hers, "let's just call it a social gathering, a chance to mingle, an opportunity to meet new people."

A huge gust of wind lifted a poster off the wall in front of them, it flapped in the breeze for a few moments. Sophie squinted up at it, "speed dating night: 6th November, an evening of romance and fun," Juliette and Evelyn gasped.

Melanie released Juliette's arm, backing away with her hands in the air,

"I can explain," she mumbled.

There was a lengthy stretch of silence, "Well?" Juliette said, tapping her foot, "we're waiting Melanie."

"Look," Melanie began, "I thought if I told you the truth you wouldn't want to come."

"Too right I wouldn't," Juliette's cheeks had turned pink, "I'm not some desperado, I could be at home with my children."

"Dating is the last thing on my mind," Sophie said.

Melanie, looking extremely sheepish shrugged, "Evelyn?"

"I'm rather annoyed Melanie, I didn't come to university to meet men," she shook her head with disapproval and turned to Sophie and Juliette, "shall we go?"

They turned to leave.

"Wait!" Melanie's voice was high pitched in the chilly night air, "it's just a night of fun, I promise. Think of it more as a chance to chat to new people, it's only three minutes of your life ladies and it's for charity, the tiny little premature baby unit at the hospital. Please stay, at least for a while. If you hate it then you can leave, you can just get up and go."

Sophie sighed, "well if it is for charity."

"I suppose it's for a good cause," Evelyn nodded.

All eyes were on Juliette, "Oh okay, we're here now, but I'm warning you Melanie, if I get stuck with any sleazy guys, I'll hold *you* responsible."

"Yay!" Melanie jumped on the spot, "somehow Jules, I don't think *that's* going to happen."

Juliette glanced at her with suspicious eyes, then they were ushered inside by a gabbling and over-excited Melanie.

The refectory had been completely re-designed for the evening. The tables and chairs had been re-organised into rows and there were helium heart balloons dotted everywhere. Soft, romantic music filtered from overhead speakers and the windows were plastered with colourful posters, declaring that tonight was the night you could find true love.

"This is so cliched," Juliette commented, cringing at the 'find your soulmate' flashing neon sign.

"So," Melanie said brightly, "let's get drinks and then we can mingle."

As they waited to be served at the makeshift bar, the room slowly began to fill up.

Evelyn's stomach was stirring uncomfortably and she felt quite sick.

"Are you okay?" Sophie asked, frowning at her friend's pale countenance.

"Just a little nervous," Evelyn admitted.

"Oh Evelyn," Melanie said, looking contrite, "I really am sorry, I should have told you, but I didn't think you'd come."

"Sit down Evelyn," Juliette steered her towards a comfy looking, leather couch, "you don't have to participate, would you like to stay here and just relax instead?"

Evelyn nodded, sipping at the cold lemonade, which had been thrust at her.

"Don't worry Evelyn," Juliette soothed, "that's absolutely fine," she threw Melanie a stern look.

"Is there an eighties theme going on here tonight?" Sophie mused, as she watched a group of men with slicked back mullets cross the room.

Melanie laughed, "I don't think so."

Suddenly a burst of loud coughing emanated from the rear of the room.

The room fell silent as Leon Broome, the head of the Student Union strolled through, carrying a microphone and a clipboard.

"Evening everyone," he announced cheerfully, "thank you very much for coming to celebrate Chattlesbury Universities very first speed dating night."

There was a small round of applause.

"I can see you're all desperate to find true love, so let's begin, let's have fun and frolics, but please, no playing footsie," he chuckled into the microphone. Sophie and Juliette exchanged an eye roll, "ladies can you please take a seat." There was a scramble and a scraping of chairs, Leon cleared his throat, "now, the rules are simple. Men," he nodded towards the group of hovering, apprehensive looking males, "you have three minutes to wow the woman you are sitting with, but please keep it clean and chivalrous, remember we are a university that prides itself on our politically correct ethics, so no lewd seventies style behaviour." Laughter spread around the room, "ladies, in front of you there is a chart. All your suitors will be wearing a number, so if you like them feel free to give their box a little tick," he winked playfully and Juliette heard Sophie giggle next to her. Despite her misgivings she felt herself relaxing into her seat and her lips curved into a smile. Then she saw him and the smile froze on her face.

"Ah here come the lecturers," Leon nodded at the small group striding into the room, "Melanie our gifted notetaker managed to persuade a few of them to cast aside their books and boring academic research, to spend the evening with you lucky, lucky ladies."

Juliette's eyes narrowed into slits as she spun around looking for Melanie, who was strangely nowhere to be seen. Sophie was staring her way, hand over her mouth, trying to quell her giggles.

Slowly Juliette slunk down in her seat, vaguely aware that Leon Broome was still wittering on. She glanced up and was immediately ensnared by Ben's bold gaze. He looked as surprised to see *her* as she was to see *him*.

"I have here a bell," Juliette averted her gaze back to Leon, "when I tinkle it that means the men must move on, even if they don't want to, to the next waiting lady and please, we all must move in a right direction, remember that guys – move to your right!" He tinkled his bell, "and we're off!"

Juliette smiled brightly as a grey haired man in a tweed suit sat down in front of her.

"I'm Gerald," he held out his hand.

"Hello," Juliette replied politely.

"Well," Gerald began, "I must say that you are a fine looking lady." He wiped at a pair of steamed up spectacles, "bother, I knew I should have worn my contact lenses."

"It is warm in here," Juliette's eyes searched the room for him. There he was, chatting away to an extremely voluptuous blonde haired lady. He looked her way and she quickly refocused back on Gerald.

"And what do you study here Gerald?" Juliette leant her arms on the table.

"Biology, just for the fun of it of course, I'm retired you see." As Gerald explained about photosynthesis in plants, Juliette's attention drifted to Sophie, who was chatting amiably to a sporty looking guy with large biceps. By the look on her face, Sophie seemed quite impressed with tousle haired Dan.

"…so yes dear, as well as my studies here, I tend to a very large garden and a spectacular greenhouse which has a wealth of exotic plants, I do like the African lily's, their colour is just *magnificent…*"

Next to her, another lady off her English course was trying hard to suppress a yawn. *Oh Gerald is certainly going to send her to sleep* Juliette thought.

"Are you okay dear?" Gerald was looking at her quizzically. Juliette was mortified to realise she had laughed out loud.

"Sorry," Juliette replied, "your tale just reminded me of my parents awfully messy garden, it really is a tip."

"Well I could recommend an excellent gardener. If you want to leave your number with me…Ah," Juliette was relieved to hear the tinkle of the bell, "very nice to meet you dear." He got to his feet to move on.

"You too Gerald," Juliette cleared her throat, while sporty Dan took a seat. Out of the corner of her eye she noticed Sophie giving him a large tick and shook her head with amusement.

Then she noticed voluptuous blond giving Ben an even bigger tick and felt her cheeks redden with envy.

"Hi," Juliette batted her lashes and leant nearer to Dan, "so you're into sport?"

"Yeah," he drawled with a distinctive twang, "I was a lifeguard on Bondi for five years before I came here."

"*The* Bondi Beach in Australia?" Juliette's eyes widened, "my son watches that programme about lifeguards all the time."

"That's the one. I actually starred in a few seasons."

"Really?" Juliette was impressed, "could I have your autograph for my son please?"

Sporty Dan laughed, a very sensual chuckle that had Sophie craning her neck in his direction.

"Sure," he flipped a pen out of his shirt pocket and scrawled his signature on a tissue, "so you like it at this uni?" He stared at Juliette with eyes that were a very attractive blue.

"I love it," Juliette gushed, her eyes slid to Ben who was watching her over the head of his date.' "oh, erm...I mean the course is just fantastic."

"You study English right?"

"How did you know?" Juliette replied.

"Just a guess. You have that bookish, English look about you."

"I do?" Juliette squeaked.

"Yeah, that shy and sexiness, all rolled into one. *Very* attractive."

"Oh, thanks," Juliette moved back slightly, "and how long are you here in the UK for?"

"Just until I finish my degree," Mr Bondi played with his pen, "then I'm moving to the States, to experience the surf."

"I love the sea," Juliette said, "I went surfing down Cornwall once with an exboyfriend, it was a disaster. I lasted an hour tops. It's really hard work isn't it? I don't think people realise how strong you have to be to stand up on the sea."

Sporty Dan raised an eyebrow but remained silent.

"I mean," Juliette gabbled, "the sea... it's so powerful and cold and there's all sorts of things living in it, it's kinda scary don't you think?"

"I'm an adrenaline junkie," Dan said with a laugh, "nothing much scares me. I could take you to the seaside one of the weekends if you fancy it?" He cocked his head, his gaze travelling down to her breasts, "we could set up a camp fire, share some beers, share a sleeping bag underneath the stars, explore each other's bodies."

Juliette coughed, "thanks Dan but I have children and I'm not looking for a relationship."

Dan grinned, pearly white teeth flashing, "I'm not talking about a relationship."

Tinkle, tinkle went the bell. A flustered Juliette looked up as Dan rose to his feet, "think about it baby. Forget books for a while, focus on pleasuring your physical body."

He sauntered off leaving Juliette open-mouthed with shock.

"I hope you're not falling for his charm," Ben stood in front of her, looking angry.

"Of course not," Juliette looked up with guilty eyes.

Ben sat down opposite her, "are you trying to make me jealous Juliette?"

Juliette felt a surge of anger rise within her, "are you?"

"No I wasn't, but I can see that you are," he held up his hand as she started to protest, "jealousy is good...it means that you care. I'll admit I was jealous as hell seeing you with that guy. Do you know he's bedded three quarters of the women in the sports faculty."

"He has?" the shock reverberated in her voice.

Ben chuckled, "you are so naïve Juliette," he leant forward to stroke her cheek, "god you're lovely."

Juliette blinked, mesmerised by the closeness of him, "Ben," she whispered.

A muscle twitched in his cheek as she surveyed him. She longed to touch him back, her whole body ached with an over whelming feeling; lust, love a heady combination of both. She felt like jumping on top of him right here, right now.

"Everything okay?" Leon Broome asked.

Juliette jerked backwards, almost tipping from her chair.

"Dr Rivers, it's so good of you to attend this evening," Leon said, "but where is Helena? You're usually together."

"She's not well," Ben replied, his eyes firmly on Juliette. Leon circled his mouth into a silent 'o' and wandered off.

"So," Juliette snapped, "how many lecturers have *you* bedded then?" As soon as the words were out of her mouth she regretted them.

Ben's face darkened.

"You seem to think Miss Harris, that I'm the Don Juan of this university."

"Well aren't you?"

He leant towards her, "no." He said firmly. "I'll admit I've had relationships here, even a couple of one night stands and at the time they were very pleasurable."

Juliette crossed her arms and looked away.

"What did you expect?" He said softly, "I'm no monk, I'm a red blooded male."

"You don't have to explain," Juliette replied, "I understand, no one should be alone."

"But," Ben twined his fingers through her smaller ones, "I've never met anyone like you. I..."

Juliette gasped, "yes?"

"What I'm trying to say is, I..." he pushed a hand through his hair, "I've been waiting..."

Tinkle, tinkle went the bell, "all change please."

Juliette slumped back in her chair.

Reluctantly Ben got to his feet, "we'll talk later," he said tersely.

Juliette watched with frustration as he moved along. She looked at the pretty young student he sat opposite, she watched the way her eyes lit up at the sight of him, she saw the desire, the want, the craving. It was mirrored in her, it was her. Marie was right, Ben Rivers was utterly heart-breaking, he was breaking her heart. Again.

"I'm leaving Sophie," she slammed back her chair, picked up her handbag and ran, weaving round the tables.

"Jules," she heard Sophie shouting, "where are you going?"

Juliette carried resolutely on, not caring that people were turning to stare, not caring that Melanie was blocking the exit with a determined look on her face.

"Juliette Harris," she froze at the sound of Ben's voice.

Breathlessly she waited, scared to turn around. The whole refectory was silent except for Melanie, who was cursing at Leon Broome to turn the damned music off.

"Look at me," he implored.

Slowly she turned, her cheeks aflame with embarrassment. He was standing there smiling, his whole face suffused with happiness, "what I was trying to say was I've never met anyone so lovely and kind and gorgeous and perfect as you are." He swung his arms towards her.

"Ben," she mumbled, feeling mortified.

"I've been waiting for you all my life, just you," he pointed her way and the whole room broke into a chorus of ah's, "it's always been you."

"Me?" A tentative smile lit up her face as she stared at him.

"You!" He shouted, "I love you Juliette, I bloody love you."

Chapter Thirteen

Ann looked down at her beeping phone and stared with surprise at the message.

"Oh lordy," she said to Jon, "looks like there's been some kind of commotion at the university."

"What?" Jon had his eyes on a huge rocket that had just exploded.

Ann tugged on his jacket, "I said, according to Soph, Ben Rivers has just made a public declaration to Jules. Her exact words are 'it's better than Titanic,' whatever that means," Ann sighed, "you never know with Sophie, I'll text Jules in the morning."

"Cool," Jon nodded, "maybe her and Mr Lecturer will be getting it on tonight then?"

Ann shook her head, "is that all you men think about – sex?"

"Pretty much," Jon laughed, "oh maybe food and beer, footie too."

Ann noticed Lulu beckoning to her from the step of the kitchen, "Jon will you be okay for a while?"

"Yep," he replied, his eyes on devouring another hotdog.

Ann glanced at Samuel, who was mesmerised by the fizzing sparkler in his hand. She wheeled herself over the patio towards Lulu, who was opening the flat ramp of the utility door.

"Come Ann," her face was shining with excitement. They went through into the back room, where the heavy brocade curtains were pulled across and the room was dimly lit by a flickering banquet lamp.

"Very atmospheric," Ann commented, her gaze resting on the round, cloth covered table.

"Right then," Lulu pushed her forwards, "clear your mind Ann. It's hard for me to do a reading if you're having sceptic thoughts."

"Do you want me to chant too?" Ann asked, with a cheeky grin.

"That won't be necessary," Lulu replied with a huff, "so, before we start, let's hold hands."

She reached across the table and clasped Ann's hands, "close your eyes Ann."

Ann's eyelids flickered shut, she listened to Lulu's soothing voice, reciting a poem about reaching for the higher spiritual plane. Suddenly there was a loud noise, as the door banged shut.

"Crikey," Ann's eyes flew open, "have you got a wind machine under this table?"

There was a stamping of feet as a group of teenage girls ran down the hall.

"Oh sorry," Ann looked sheepishly down at the table, where Lulu was shuffling a deck of cards.

"Okay, this is called the Universal Waite Tarot," Lulu said crisply, "it's a classic deck and is quite simple and easy to understand, each card tells a story," she divided the pack and then placed three cards face down in front of them, "I'm going to do a simple, three card reading," she tapped the cards, "they represent the past, the present and the future. Are you with me so far Ann?"

"Yep," Ann replied, "let's do this."

"Turn over the centre card please Ann," Lulu urged, "this card represents what's going on in your life now – the present. Ah, the eight of cups. Well this is a card of letting go, of going in search of more fulfilment. See this figure," she pointed, "it means that you could be leaving something behind, moving on."

"Is that good?" Ann asked, with a dubious glance at Lulu, whose brow was furrowed with concentration.

"Yes Ann," Lulu continued, "it also symbolises challenges – trying something new – moving forward to freely embrace new opportunities. It's a strong card, it's a good card."

"Cool," Ann grinned.

"Would you like to look at the card of the future?"

"Absolutely."

"Oh perfect, the Queen of Cups," Lulu clapped with delight, "this is a powerful card, it symbolises confidence and energy. Basically it means that you are one self-assured badass," they both laughed, "it represents a future full of confidence, achieving your goals and making things happen. It is telling you Ann, that you are in charge, you are queen of your own life."

"Wow! I'm impressed," Ann said wide eyed, "and the last card?"

"The card of the past," Lulu turned it over, "the magician – another positive, empowered card. It means that you can draw on past experiences to move forward and to grow. Use your ability to create as a positive tool to focus on successes for the future..."

"Here you are," Jon stood in the doorway, surveying the scene before him with surprise.

"Hi Jon," Lulu said cheerfully, "would *you* like a tarot card reading?"

"Anton's just about to light the bonfire," he replied, looking at Ann with quizzical eyes.

"Fab, we can't miss that," Lulu crammed the cards back into their box and skipped out of the room.

"What are you doing?" He asked Ann, "you hate this kind of stuff."

"She persuaded me," Ann replied flippantly, "and I actually enjoyed it. Don't worry it was completely harmless. I still think it's a load of rubbish though."

Jon chuckled, "there's my Ann."

The bonfire was lit and the guests stood watching as the topaz flames flickered slowly inside. Ann glanced at the ragdoll, placed on the top wooden slat.

"Should we really be celebrating burning a man to death?" She asked Jon, with a whispered grimace.

Jon shrugged, "they were barbaric in those days. Same as Jesus innit?"

"Is it?" Ann puffed on her electronic cigarette, "I doubt that Jesus even existed and if he did he was probably just a profoundly wise humanitarian and not some Godly miracle worker."

"I agree Ann," Anton nodded with approval, "you won't find any religious artefacts in this house. As far as I'm concerned, religion is a tool of war."

"Oh Anton," Lulu interjected, "let's not start a debate tonight. Here," she passed him her phone, "go and take some pictures." Anton wandered off, fiddling with the zoom button.

"Did you ask Samuel?" Lulu's question was directed at Jon.

"Oh yes," Jon's face erupted into a wide grin, "he's coming to the next home footie match. He seems really excited. Would it be okay if we take him for a bite to eat after? We won't be too late."

"Of course you can," Lulu rubbed Jon's arm, "I think life is starting to look up for our little Sammy."

All three turned to watch Samuel. His eyes were glued to the bonfire, a look of rapturous excitement on his little face. Ann thought he looked like an angel, with his cherubic rosy cheeks and his golden curls, she was overwhelmed with a feeling of tenderness towards him.

"And life's looking up for us too," she said, linking fingers with her husband.

* * *

"Is that loud and clear enough for you?"

Juliette felt flames of embarrassment burn her cheeks as Ben strode towards her. All around the refectory there were gasps, nudges and murmurs of approval. Then a few claps began. She looked frantically for her friends; Sophie and Melanie were jumping up and down with excitement, giving her a big thumbs up of approval, while Evelyn was wiping away tears of emotion.

He clasped her hand and smiled down at her, "I think you need some fresh air."

They stood in the courtyard shivering, oblivious to the fine rain that had unleashed from a swirling sky.

"I need you," Ben whispered, "in the morning, afternoon, at night in my bed," his eyes glowered with desire, "come back to me."

"I...I," Juliette stammered, feeling overwhelmed.

"If you don't want me just say, we can still be friends," a muscle twitched in his jaw, "be honest Juliette. What do you want?"

There was a lengthy pause, Juliette let out a shaky breath, "you scare the hell out of me, but I want you. I always have."

Ben grinned and he looked so happy and boyishly carefree at that moment that Juliette knew she had made the right decision.

"Don't be scared," he kissed her forehead, pulling her close, "but if you agree to this, there's no turning back. You're mine now." His hands ran possessively over her hips.

"I've missed you," she blurted out, overwhelmed by a swell of passion.

"The summer has been interminably slow," his nose briefly touched hers as he dipped his head, "stay with me tonight."

Juliette wasn't sure if it was a question or an order, her breath quickened, "I have to ring home first. Give me ten minutes."

She broke away and walked quickly towards the ladies lavatories.

"Hurry!" She heard Ben call.

Thankfully the toilets were empty. She gazed in the mirror at her flushed, wild eyed reflection, then quickly turned the taps to splash cold water on her face. Then she rang the landline number, her mum picked up after a lengthy eight rings.

"Sorry Jules, me and your dad were playing twister," there was a short silence, "are you okay lovey."

"Yes," her voice sounded strangled, high pitched. "Mum, can I ask a big favour? Would you mind stopping with the kids tonight?"

"We'd love to," came Violet Harris' surprised reply, "are you having a sleep-over at your friends?"

"Yes," she bit out, silencing the voice inside that stated, *oh he is more than a friend, much much more.*

"Well okay, that's no problem at all. Give Sophie my love."

"I will, bye Mum," her hands shook slightly as she ended the call.

Ben was standing underneath a flickering lamp. His arms were crossed and his face registered a look of frustrated impatience. He looked so handsome that her breath caught in her throat. She stopped just to stare at him, her eyes raking over his tall, muscular frame.

"What are you doing Juliette?" He asked tersely.

"Nothing," she shook her head, embarrassed to be caught ogling.

He pulled her towards him, taking her face in the palm of his hands, "can you stay?"

Hastily she nodded, "do you…shall we go for a drink first?"

He regarded her for a moment, "so you want to make me wait?"

"Maybe," she smiled, "we have all night Dr Rivers."

He let out a groan of frustration, "come then."

He grabbed hold of her hand, then they were running – slipping and sliding up the icy path, heading for the bright lights of the city, their laughter echoing around the deserted courtyard.

The speed daters watched the two retreating figures, open mouthed with shock, noses pressed to the glass, as Bing Crosby crooned about singing in the rain and old fashioned love.

"Well," whistled Melanie, "that went far better than I planned."

"Are you sure Jules will be okay?" Sophie asked, feeling nervous for her friend.

"I think she'll be fine," Melanie replied, looking around at the group of lecturers talking in hushed tones, "one things for certain though, those two are sure gonna rustle a few stuffy feathers around *here*."

* * *

They stumbled through the door, kissing and tugging at each other's clothes.

"Ben," she laughed, as they hopped up the hall.

"What?" He tugged the shirt over his head, revealing a muscular torso which had her eyes alight with desire.

"Don't you want to go to bed?" She asked, her voice a hoarse whisper.

"Later," he promised, pulling her close and parting her mouth hungrily with his lips.

They backed into the kitchen; she was naked now, except for her underwear.

"You.are.so.beautiful," he unclipped her bra, his tongue circling a protruding nipple.

Juliette gasped, falling back against the wooden edge of a table. As his tongue ran over her breasts, she was vaguely aware of his fingers pulling down her pants. A feeling of shyness gripped her and her hands flew downwards to cover herself. Firmly he removed them, lifting her up onto the table. Oh it was cold. She arched her back, watching through heavy lids as he pulled off his belt. She reached for his zipper, but he grasped her wrist.

"No." He said huskily, "lie back Juliette."

She did as he instructed, squirming with desire, as his eyes travelled salaciously over her naked frame. Then he bent his head and Juliette succumbed to pure, intense pleasure.

* * *

Moonlight filtered through the gaps in the blinds. Juliette shifted in the warm bed, peering at the clock. It was three in the morning, but she felt wide awake and happy, so happy. Beside her Ben was fast asleep, his chest moving rhythmically, one arm was raised, covering his forehead and his lips were slightly parted. Gently she reached to push back a lock of tousled hair. He looked gorgeous; ethereal almost. She leant on her arm, gazing at him.

"I love you so much," she whispered.

Slowly he stirred, blinking at her in the darkness.

"I dreamt of you," he rasped, "you were an angel, you..."

"Shush," her fingers went to his mouth, "let me show you..."

Their lips met in the darkness and his arms encircled her, pulling her on top of him.

* * *

Something warm was touching her thigh, something soft was nuzzling her neck. It was Ben again. But she was so tired. Gently he pushed her onto her back, his warm fingers lifting the t-shirt she was wearing, raising it past her thighs, over her soft stomach and the curve of her hips.

"Oh God," he murmured, as her bare nipples hardened under his gaze.

Juliette raised her arms above her head, "Ben," she said sleepily, "we should use contraception."

"I'll be careful," his voice was a husky whisper, "I'm not going to make you pregnant. Not yet anyway."

The thought of making a baby with him had her suddenly wide awake. She gripped his arms as he nipped at her throat. Then his tongue was inside her mouth and a feeling of urgency grew inside of her. Her hands pulled him nearer, overcome with love and desire.

"Oh yes," she gasped, as he slid inside her.

Beyond the window, a golden sun rose in a scarlet stained sky, heralding the dawn of a bright new day.

* * *

Will had been pacing the bedroom now for twenty minutes and still Esme screamed.

"I'll go heat a bottle," Hema struggled upright in the bed, rubbing sleep from her eyes.

"No. I'll go," Will frowned at his girlfriend's pale pallor, "go back to sleep."

He planted a kiss on Esme's forehead, which was damp from the exertion of her angry outburst.

"Let's go see who's up shall we?"

The house was quiet, the muffled sound of a train whizzing along the nearby railway track permeated through the double glazing.

He wondered where Flora was, she was usually up and cheerfully pottering around. He found her in the kitchen, pinning a fascinator into her hair.

"Morning," Will balanced Esme upright, "say hi to Nana."

Esme let out a series of happy gurgles, which had Flora rushing over. "Hello my beauty."

"Where are you off to?" Will asked, glancing over her flowery dress and smart shoes.

"Church of course," Flora replied with a shake of her head.

"Is it Sunday?" Will scratched his head.

"Where have you been Will?" Flora chuckled softly, "Of course it's Sunday. Now, I've cooked sausages for you all, they just need heating and there's some mushrooms and grilled tomatoes in the pan. I'm leaving early to help tidy the church, Father McGregor has his hands full. There's been an influx of christening applications..." she trailed off, staring expectantly at Will.

"A baby boom huh?" Will shifted uncomfortably.

"Yes," Flora said crisply, "there's a waiting list and they're fully booked until spring – can you believe that? Who said religion is dead?"

Will laughed, "me."

"What?" Flora asked, a look of bemusement on her face.

Will sighed and moved away to click on the kettle, "she's not going to be christened Mum, it's not going to happen."

He heard her gasp as he opened the fridge door to remove a bottle.

"But...your dad and I, we presumed that she would be!"

"Why?" Will turned towards her, "you know I don't believe in any of it."

"Well what does Hema think?"

"She completely agrees with me."

"Oh." Flora looked down, trying to hide her disappointment.

"It's not going to make any difference to how she turns out when she's older you know," Will popped the chilled milk into a jug of bubbling water, "and if she's anything like you, she will be absolutely lovely, with or without Father McGregor's blessing."

Flora blushed, "I know that Will, I'm not trying to infer that non-christened children are lacking in any way, it's just my faith, it's so important to me, and Esme, well I wanted to be able to..."

"Take her to church?" Will finished off the sentence.

Flora nodded, chewing her lip, "I know that going to church on a Sunday isn't trendy anymore, but it really is lovely Will; the atmosphere, the people, the teachings."

"If Esme decides she wants to go with you when she's older, then of course she can," Will said firmly, "until then Mum, she's not being influenced in any way. Please don't buy her Bibles or crucifixes."

"Not even a guardian angel pendant to protect her?" Flora implored.

"I suppose that's okay," Will said grudgingly with a smile.

A mollified Flora turned to look in the mirror and began applying a light layer of lip-gloss.

"There's something else I wanted to tell you," he coughed, "she won't be attending a faith school either."

He watched her hands fly to her throat and a look of consternation cross her face.

"Will! Are you trying your best to upset me on such a beautiful Sunday morning?"

"I'm just being honest Mum," he replied, with a lop-sided smile.

"But your dad and I, we presumed that you would send her to St Mary's. You went there and look how well you've turned out."

"I was traumatised Mum. All that talk of sin and damnation taught by a bunch of immoral hypocrites."

Flora gasped, "then consider another faith school. Not all are like St Mary's. Please don't be bitter love."

"I'm not bitter in the slightest. What makes a faith school better then a community school, apart from some misguided sense of snobbery? Why would anyone *want* to send their children to a religious school if they themselves are non-believers, lapsed and not practising? What's wrong with this picture Mum, because I just don't understand it."

Flora swallowed, "because they do more than educate Will. They foster a child's moral and social development. They teach kindness, forgiveness, compassion and humanity, following the ten commandments and scripture."

"No. They don't." Will replied emphatically, "from my experience they take your spirit and they crush it and you don't need to follow scripture to be a good person."

"Will!" Flora was visibly shocked, "I-I had no idea you harboured so much antipathy towards the Catholic church."

"That's not it," Will shook his head, "I'm talking about specific experiences...I'm talking about choices and Hema and I choose *not* to send our daughter to a faith school. I don't believe in the Bible Mum – it's a collection of fairy-tales created by mankind to oppress and subjugate and as a means of controlling the populous." He stuck his chin out defiantly, "there is *no way* I'm going to let anyone brainwash or indoctrinate my daughter. She's going to have her own mind, her own opinions and if she does follow a religion when she's older, then that will be her choice and it will be fine with both me and Hema."

Flora's cheeks were ablaze with colour, "okay son, I understand, you're right," she pulled at her fascinator, "maybe *I* should stop going to church too."

"No Mum no," Will replied firmly, catching her by the hand, "if anyone should go to church, it should be *you*. You symbolise all the goodness of religion," his tone softened, "you skip through life, searching for the good in everybody and we all love you for it."

Flora shook her head, "I've always been too soft, too kind."

"That's not a weakness, that's a strength. They should have christened you Pollyanna," he stepped towards her, pecking her on the cheek, "go to church Mum, please, go on," gently he pushed her towards the door and Flora wandered outside into the bright sunshine, feeling slightly dazed and ruminating on her son's very own unique brand of philosophy.

Chapter Fourteen

Evelyn was sitting at the kitchen table, sipping hot coffee and absently reading the morning's newspaper, when the flap on the front door rattled open. From her place at the kitchen table, she watched as a bundle of envelopes fell to the floor. Music from the morning show on Radio 2 crackled from the radio; The Boomtown Rats reminding her that they don't like Monday's. She stood to rinse her mug under a stream of hot water, before ambling down the hallway to pick up the crumpled envelopes. Her breath quickened as she recognised a London postage mark; its red lines blurred by the damp. Her novel! Quickly she tore open the envelope. The crest of Bloomsbury Books, one of the leading UK's publishers adorned the top of the thick, expensive paper. Her eyes devoured the words and as they did, her mouth fell into a downward curve.

"We like your lively, energetic style," she read aloud, "but unfortunately, in today's strained economic climate, we do not feel that we could represent you. Please do not be disheartened, as other publishers / agents may feel differently. Good luck for the future, we hope that you are successful." Evelyn slumped in the chair and opened another London marked envelope.

It was another rejection; a shorter, more succinct one, which offered no feed-back. The other mail was flyers and charity bags. Carefully Evelyn pinned the letters to her cork noticeboard, sighing with resignation. She cast her mind back, trying to calculate how many publishers she had contacted. A dozen maybe? There was still hope then.

She glanced at her wristwatch and flew into a flurry, her appointment was at nine thirty, she was late! Thankfully the bus was early and she managed to arrive at the university with plenty of time to grab a bottle of water and a teacake. The refectory was quiet and restored to its former glory after the weekends speed dating event.

On her way out of the canteen she bumped into Doctor Rivers. He was carrying a large box, full to the brim of papers.

"Year three essays," he informed Evelyn with a grimace, "a feminist critique of Dracula."

They made their way up to his office. Evelyn stood in the doorway shivering as he shifted a pile of books off a revolving chair.

"Please, sit down Evelyn."

"I've had my first rejection," she told him, crossing her ankles.

"Keep going," Ben said briskly, "the publishing world's a tough business to crack, but you definitely have the talent."

"I do?" Evelyn chewed her bottom lip.

"Yes," Ben replied, with an emphatic nod, "now, I know I have a pen on this desk somewhere."

Evelyn glanced over the clutter, "here," she pulled a silver biro from underneath a pile of papers, "are you okay Dr Rivers?"

He seemed distracted, "Yes Evelyn, just incredibly busy. Have you lectures today?"

"Romanticism. We're meeting in the canteen… Ann, Sophie, Will, Juliette…" she trailed off, smiling as his lips curved upwards.

"That's a great module – Byron, Shelley and Visionary Individualism?"

Evelyn looked at him blankly.

He laughed, "enjoy Evelyn and whatever you do; don't give up on your writing."

"Thank you," she rose to her feet, her spirits lifting, "bye Dr Rivers."

* * *

Juliette was walking through the courtyard, gripping her folder tightly against her chest. The sun was shining high in a cold winter sky and frost covered the floor in a silver sheen. Her phone beeped in her gloved hand and she glanced down to read the message.

'Morning. I love you.'

She gasped and a warm feeling settled in her stomach. Was this love? She guessed so. Marie was right, she'd never truly been in love before. How could she have thought she loved Marty when she felt like this for Ben, after such a short time? She tugged one glove off and typed out a reply, '**I love you right back. Morning. xx**'

A minute later a reply whizzed into her inbox, '**I can't stop thinking about you.**'

Juliette's toes tingled with excitement, "don't do this to me now Dr Rivers," she mumbled, as a group of chattering students passed her by. She glanced up at the windows on the top floor. Maybe she could sneak upstairs before class started, maybe they could...

"Juliette!"

Will was slipping and sliding down the path towards her.

"Hi!" Juliette smiled warmly, her breath fanning out in curls.

"How's your weekend been?" Will blew into his palms, "are you okay?"

Juliette snapped out of her loved up daydream, "it's been pretty perfect actually. How's yours been?"

"Oh, you know, nappy changing, midnight pacing, baby sick."

Juliette laughed, "I know exactly what you're going through and I was on my own for most of it."

Will surmised her with raised eyebrows, "you are one badass."

"Co-eee!" Evelyn was beckoning to them from the doorway, "I've bought tea-cakes, would you like one?"

"Sounds delish," Will replied. They followed her into the refectory where Will pulled out chairs out for them all.

Another text from Ben pinged into Juliette's inbox, '**can you come to the hospital with me this afternoon? My sister has had her op.**'

Juliette gasped, she had forgotten all about his poorly sister, she'd been so wrapped up in her feelings for him, these past few days she hadn't been able to think straight and the kids had noticed it too.

'**Of course,**' she messaged, '**shall I meet you after my lecture?**'

'**Yes. I'll come get you. Enjoy Romanticism.**'

"Juliette?" Evelyn was looking at her quizzically.

"Oh, sorry Evelyn, what was that?"

"Will was telling me about a Christmas party, here at the university."

"The Tinsel Disco," he pointed at a colourful poster stuck to the wall, "Hema fancies a night out. It sounds alright."

Juliette nodded eagerly, "definitely, count me in."

"You know," Evelyn sat back in her chair, "I never thought that coming to uni would give me such a great social life. I've met so many wonderful people here. You've all become very dear to me."

"What a lovely thing to say so early in the morning," Sophie stood behind Evelyn, her hands resting on her chair, "hi everyone. So," Sophie flopped onto a seat, "I have some very, very exciting news. Evelyn, I've only gone and sold my house!"

"Whaaaaatttttt!" Evelyn looked flabbergasted, "so soon Sophie?"

"Yep," Sophie took a bite out of Will's teacake, "Mr and Mrs Chan are paying cash for it – can you believe that? They are unbelievably wealthy."

"Wow," Juliette said in a quiet voice, "I've had trouble finding my rent this month."

"That doesn't make them better people Jules," Sophie said with a frown, "money can't buy you happiness and neither can possessing a big, fancy house. Look at me," she shrugged, "I've learnt that the hard way and I'm happier now I'm alone and broke then I ever was spending Ryan's thousands."

"We'll ask you that again in six months' time Soph," Will said, with a cheeky eye roll at Juliette.

Evelyn leant across the table to pat Sophie's bare arm, "well I think it's wonderful. Does that mean you and the boys will be with me for Christmas?"

"Looks that way," Sophie confirmed, "they want to move in as soon as poss. Is it okay though Evelyn? Are you completely sure you want me and my madcap family underneath your feet?"

"I am sure," Evelyn threw her a firm look, "it will be a pleasure to have you all with me and Sophie, you can stay as long as you need to."

"Ah," Sophie wrapped her arms around her friend.

"I can't cope with all this sweetness," Will joked, "time for me to take a loo break I think."

On his way out, he bumped into Jon and Ann, who were accompanied by a frazzled looking Melanie.

"Will!" Jon thrust out his hand, "how is Hema and the baby?"

"Oh Jon," Ann tutted, "I've told you loads of times; her name is Esme."

Will laughed, "she is doing great, they both are."

Melanie gripped his arm, "have you seen Doctor Rivers this morning?"

"Er, no," Will replied, a little nonplussed, "we haven't got him for lectures today."

"Oh," Melanie looked around, "what about Juliette?"

"She's right over there," Will pointed to her back, where red curls cascaded.

"Is she okay?" Melanie was chewing her lip.

"For God's sake," Ann let out an irritated sigh, "can no one get to the point around here? Melanie decided to do a spot of matchmaking to get Jules back with Dr Rivers and now she's worried that it has all backfired on her."

Will spluttered with laughter, "Really? Well she seems quite happy actually."

Melanie emitted a sigh of relief, "that's good. Maybe I'll just pop upstairs and check out my timetable for the week."

"Oh no you don't," Ann cut in sharply, "you're supposed to be with me for romanticism. What are you worried about Melanie? I'm sure Juliette will be stoked that you've been meddling in her affairs."

Will and Jon bent over with laughter.

"It's not funny," hissed Melanie, "I was trying to help. Those two were meant to be together...I just gave them a friendly push."

"Well let's hope they don't give you a push.... off a cliff." Ann shook her head, but her eyes twinkled with humour, "come on Melanie, you've got to face the music sooner or later."

They made their way into the canteen, with a nervous Melanie hovering at the back.

* * *

"Romanticism promises to be extremely romantic," was Evelyn's verdict on the lecture they had just attended, "I adore Byron; so wild and heroic." Ann and the others nodded in agreement.

Juliette was backing away in the opposite direction, rummaging through her bag for her phone.

"Jules?" Sophie was gazing at her expectantly, "aren't you joining us for lunch?"

"Sorry no. I've got an appointment, but I'll see you guys later in the week, ok?" She disappeared behind a set of heavy doors before anyone could wish her goodbye. Then she was rushing down the stairs. Somewhere between the fourth and the ground floor she bumped into Ben. With nervous apprehension she waited for him to bound up the stairs towards her.

"Hi," he raked a hand through his thick dark hair and smiled widely.

"Hi," her heart was racing, as if she had climbed up the stairs herself instead of going down them.

"Are you okay?" He asked breathlessly.

Juliette nodded. In her mind she was thinking about the weekend; sharing his warm bed, wrapping herself around him.

He gazed into her eyes for a lingering moment, "we should go. Visiting hours have already begun."

"Yes." Juliette stepped back slightly, "can we stop at a shop on the way? I'd like to buy your sister a magazine and maybe some sweets."

"She'd like that," Ben smiled down at her, "come." He held out his hand, waiting for Juliette to slip hers inside his warm palm. Then he was pulling her next to him and they were hurrying down to the ground floor. At the bottom Juliette stopped, pulling her hand away.

"People will see," she whispered, colouring underneath the fluorescent lighting.

Ben shrugged, "I don't care. Juliette, they know anyway, everybody does; staff, students. Don't worry"

Still she stood there, biting her bottom lip.

"Are you ashamed of me?" His countenance grew serious.

"Of course not," Juliette was flabbergasted that he could even think that, "I don't want you to get into trouble. I don't want people to…"

"Gossip about me?" Ben finished her sentence, "let them. They'll soon grow tired of us. It'll be some other poor person next week."

"Okay. You're right." Juliette straightened her shoulders, "let's give them something to talk about."

Ben laughed, pulling her into a tight embrace with one arm and opening the door with the other.

Students milled about, a few paused to appraise them, but the majority sailed on by.

"See," Ben mumbled into her ear, "little miss worry knickers."

Juliette felt herself relax and then gulped as she noticed the Dean talking to a group of suited men just beside the exit doors. Ben noticed them too.

"Come on Juliette," he said through gritted teeth, "we've got nothing to be ashamed of." He tugged her hand, propelling her forward.

"Well hello Dr Rivers," the Dean fixated on Ben, making a beeline for him, "I was just finishing off my tour of the university to some very important business men." He glanced at Juliette, "and who are you my dear?"

Juliette's knees bobbed down, "I'm a student," she replied, inwardly cursing her spontaneous curtsey, "English, second year."

"Ah," he nodded with approval, then his eyes grew suspicious, "you're one of Dr Rivers students then?"

"Dr Smythe's actually and Dr Hodges and Dr Haverstock's," Juliette gabbled, her forehead growing clammy.

"Yes, she's one of my students," Ben confirmed, pulling her closer, "but we don't let business get in the way of pleasure." Ben strode past him, a mortified Juliette hopping along.

"A chat would be good Dr Rivers," the Dean called after them, "very soon!"

"Oh my God. Ben!" Juliette glanced over her shoulder, where the Dean was still staring, shaking his head and peering over his spectacles.

* * *

"Her name is Alice and she's three years younger than me," Ben finally pulled into a parking bay on the hospital car park, next to a dirty Landrover and a shiny motorbike. They had been cruising around for ten minutes now, looking for a space.

"I like that name. Alice," it rolled from Juliette's tongue, "is she a lecturer like you?"

"No." Ben smiled and her stomach flipped over.

"Alice and I are polar opposites – she's a gardener; has her own business, loves getting her hands dirty, owns a motorbike like that one actually. She's very feisty, a real rebel, whereas I am mostly laidback, quiet, subdued…" he trailed off as Juliette burst into laughter.

"I wouldn't say you're any of those things Ben," she checked her reflection in the mirror.

"No?"

"No! Passionate would be a good term to describe you. Maybe you're more like your sister than you realise." She looked across at him quizzically, "didn't you landscape your garden over the summer?"

"Yes, with Alice's help! Shall we go?"

Juliette slid from the car, following him over to a ticket machine. They stood behind an elderly couple, waiting patiently for them to pop their pennies in.

"Thank you for coming with me," Ben lifted her hair, kissing the nape of her neck.

A shiver ran down her spine, "oh," she moved away slightly, "it's my pleasure…I mean you're welcome."

The elderly lady turned towards them, "my what a beautiful couple. How long have you been married?"

"We're not," Juliette answered, glancing at Ben, who looked extremely amused, "married I mean."

"Ah Frank they're courting."

The man next to her turned around, touching the peak of his cap, "the best move I ever made was marrying my April."

"Fifty-two years together," April divulged, her cheeks dimpling into a smile, "through good and bad; weathering the storms of life together."

"My parents are the same," Juliette said, "they're devoted to each other."

"I wish the same good fortune on you both," April replied, "be happy." The friendly pair shuffled off, arm in arm.

"Right," Ben said with a wide grin, "looks like I need to marry you then."

* * *

They passed the busy Accident and Emergency department and followed the signs for the Oncology Ward. Down a spiralling ramp they went, into the boughs of the hospital. It was quiet, deserted and smelt strongly of antiseptic. They came to a set of doors, through it a lift took them up a floor to a reception, where two nurses sat, filling in paperwork. Juliette hung back as Ben explained who he had come to see.

"The operation went well," the nurse nodded, "she's currently on the recovery bay. Take a seat and we'll show you to her room when she's brought down."

"That sounds positive," Juliette said, as they sat on a plastic bench.

"Hmm," Ben looked down at his hands, his forehead was creased into lines of worry.

"A school friend of mine had breast cancer," Juliette said gently, "she went through a really rough time, but that was years ago, she's fine now. Has your sister opted for breast reconstruction?"

"Yes," Ben replied, "the doctors have told us she'll need chemotherapy as well."

Juliette nodded, "how are the children taking it?"

"Not too bad surprisingly, it's my brother-in-law who's struggling."

"Children are resilient," Juliette said with a nod, "are they visiting too?"

"James is. The children are coming later tonight." Tears glistened in his eyes.

Juliette felt a swell of compassion for him and placed her hands over his, "everything will be fine Ben. You have to be strong for Alice."

He gazed down at her, "I'm so glad you decided to come to university. I lo..."

"Mr Rivers," the young blonde nurse was beckoning him over.

Juliette watched as he went to speak to her, noticing the flirtatious way she leant across the desk and twirled her hair. Juliette looked away, watching a tired looking doctor stride up the corridor. It must be such a rewarding job, she thought, saving lives every day.

"She's on ward O3," Ben said, "let's go."

* * *

Alice looked so small and vulnerable in the hospital bed that Juliette thought for a moment that Ben must have got it completely wrong portraying his sister as such a tough cookie.

"She's sleeping," Juliette whispered, "maybe I should wait outside."

"No," Ben said firmly, "she insisted that I bring you. She categorically said that if I didn't, she'd set the kids on me."

Juliette laughed, "okay." She sat down on a high-backed chair, while Ben paced the room, his hands shoved deep in his pockets.

Juliette gazed at Alice, shocked by the resemblance she held to her older brother. They shared the same dark hair and long lashes, resting on pronounced cheek bones. They really were both gorgeous specimens, she felt a pang of sadness as she thought briefly of their deceased parents; she wondered who they looked like and whose temperament they had inherited.

"James," the figure in the bed was stirring, moving her head slightly towards the window, where afternoon sunshine filtered through the half-closed blinds.

Ben was immediately striding across, to bend over and take her hand, "he'll be here soon."

Alice swallowed with difficulty, "thirsty," she croaked.

"I'll go get a nurse," Juliette said, springing to her feet and hurrying out the room to accost the ward sister.

After the nurse had helped Alice take a few sips of water, checked her blood pressure and administered a cup of pain killers, she left them alone, with strict instructions not to over exert her patient.

"Feeling rough huh?" Ben joked, perching on the bed.

"Just a bit," Alice blinked and a tear slid down her cheek.

"Hey," Ben said gently, "the op went well, you're going to be fine sis."

"I thought I was going to die," Alice sniffed, "I was so scared Ben, all I could think about was the kids and James. How they'd cope without me." Ben planted a kiss on her forehead and held her hands tight.

Juliette shifted in her seat, feeling embarrassed that she was intruding on a private sibling moment.

"Sorry." Alice wiped her eyes with the back of her hand, "you're Juliette?"

"Yes." Juliette smiled, "please don't apologise, I've bought you magazines...for when you feel better."

"Thank you," Alice grinned, "so you're the one who's captured my brother's heart?"

"Oh...I..." Juliette looked down at her plum polished nails.

"Of course she has," Ben replied smoothly.

Alice frowned, "Ben, can you go get me some mints, my mouth is so dry."

"Mints?" He ran a hand through his already tousled hair.

"Yes. Mints," Alice let out an exasperated sigh, "there's a shop one floor down. Juliette can stay with me."

Ben glanced her way and Juliette smiled. When he'd gone Alice beckoned her closer.

"He's been talking about you all summer, I'm so glad you're back together."

"He has? You are?" Juliette's stomach flipped with happiness.

Alice nodded, flopping back against the pillows.

"You should rest," Juliette noticed her pallor had taken on a greyish hue.

Alice winced then closed her eyes, "be careful Juliette, my brother's love isn't for the faint hearted, it's all consuming, he'll capture your heart, he'll possess your soul as well..."

With that she promptly fell fast asleep, her chest moving rhythmically in time with the bleeping machine next to her.

Chapter Fifteen

The following Monday Sophie was busy at St. Mary's nursery preparing re-sources for the children to make Christmas cards.

"Isn't it a bit early for Christmas?" She asked Cara, who was stapling a painted figure of a fireman on the cloakroom door.

"Absolutely not," Cara replied with a chuckle, "preparation is the key to the running of a successful nursery."

"Here, here," Mr Bentley strode into the room, glancing around at the mess all over the floor, "and that applies to all primary key stages of course."

"What can I do for you Mr Bentley?" the nursery teacher looked up, her nose and cheeks were covered in glitter, making Sophie smile as she carried on with her work.

"I'm just reminding you of the lunchtime meeting," Mr Bentley replied.

"Yes, I saw it on the computer and have it pencilled on my calendar. Prevent training?"

"Terrorism and unhealthy use of the internet," Mr Bentley elaborated, "and you are welcome also Mrs O'Neill, all participating staff will be issued with a certificate which you may find beneficial for future use."

"Thank you," Sophie smiled, "I'll be there."

Mr Bent nodded his approval.

"Cara," he continued, "I need to talk to you about another issue."

They moved away slightly.

"*What* are we going to do about Mrs Bent?"

Sophie noticed Cara roll her eyes, "what has she done now?"

"Shouting at colleagues in corridors again for a start. Belittling others, making rude nasty noises at the happier staff members. Manipulating the weaker minded to do her dirty work. The woman is out of control Cara, I think she has been spending far too much time with the key stage two children, she's forgotten how to behave like a grown adult. If she's not careful I'll have another grievance on my hands to contend with."

"Have you spoken to her?" Cara was stifling a yawn, "sorry. I was up into the early hours with sixty reports to write."

"She's hardly the most approachable person now is she? Come, come Cara why so heartless? I know it may be hard for you to accept that your oldest, dearest friend was involved in the malicious thrill of that unbelievably cruel incident in the assembly hall, but a line has been crossed both professionally and morally. She needs to be held accountable, so for starters I'm sending her home for the rest of the day. I think she may be in some sort of mental distress."

"Maybe she has the start of some kind of virus; swine flu?... it could be all the stress of being a deputy."

"Yes quite," Mr Bentley shook his head, "we need to keep an eye on this and of course offer her support if she's struggling professionally. I dread to think *what* she gets up to when she's not at work." He turned on his heel and strode back out, muttering something about meetings with troublesome parents.

"Don't become a member of Senior Leadership Team Sophie, far too much responsibility and the extra pittance they pay us – pffttt!" Cara emitted a heavy sigh, "now, before the children appear, tell me all about your house move."

* * *

At lunchtime the entire staff trooped down to the computer suite.

"Whoopee, more training," Rob said with bad temper, "what the hell is Father McGregor doing here?"

Sophie could see the priest through the pane of glass, talking animatedly to Mr Bentley.

"And what is Marcia still doing here? I thought Max was going to send her home," Cara bit into a Golden Delicious apple.

"She refused to go," Rob replied, "there's no getting rid of the blasted woman."

"Come in, come in," Mr Bentley swung open the door, "grab yourself a seat at a computer; there's plenty to go around."

Sophie sat down at a console between Cara and Rob and flicked on her screen.

"Just before we begin our Prevent Training on how to spot terrorism and internet safety, Father McGregor has very kindly offered to bless us with a prayer."

The priest moved into the centre of the room, casting a warm smile all around, "let us pray."

Sophie automatically closed her eyes and then had a peek to see who else had. She was shocked to notice that some of the staff were on their mobile phones, but thankfully Father McGregor seemed oblivious to their blatant rudeness.

"Father," he began in a lovely lilting tone, "I lay down my self-imposed responsibility of judging the heart, motives, intentions and actions of the people in my life. You have instructed me in this and I will obey you. I remove the back-breaking burden of being the judge, and I repent of the pride in my life that is evident every time I have a critical, judgemental thought. You have commanded me to walk in forgiveness and love, to rise above offenses and to walk humbly with you. I choose that road today. I submit my thoughts to you – each and every one – for approval, choosing loving thoughts and not condemning thoughts, compassionate thoughts not critical thoughts. And kindly removing the log in my eye. Thank you. In Jesus' name and with the help of the Holy Spirit, Amen."

There was an echo of amen's around the room. Mr Bentley squeezed past Sophie's chair to pat the priest on the shoulder as he left.

"I would just like to add my own opinion on Father McGregor's prayer," Mr Bentley addressed the room, "of course judging someone does not define who they are; it defines who you are. Come, come staff, as a Christian school we all must surely appreciate that no one in this establishment is perfect. We are all guilty of some peccadillo or another, so let us try to cast aside any feelings of self-righteousness towards others right now."

He paused to take a gulp of water, "I'd also like to point out that there are far too many staff members here that like doing things in secret," he stared pointedly at Mrs Bent, who was sneezing into a tissue.

"Mr Bentley, aren't we supposed to be talking about internet safety?" Mrs Bent snapped.

"Yes, yes. Now then, we've discussed the danger of Facebook – which is bothersome enough within the teaching profession."

Groans resounded but Mr Bentley carried on, "I'm not going to lecture you on that today, but please let us consider for a moment these cloak and dagger secretive educational forums."

Sophie noticed how Mrs Bent had significantly paled and suppressed a titter.

"If you have a story to tell...I would advise you very strongly...not to do it on those websites," Max shook his head with disapproval, "and you should be very wary of anyone on the internet who claims to be posting for support, to highlight a concern or some noble cause. More often than not they ain't. Many are driven by their own agendas, their own personal axe to grind," Max bent his knees and the crack resounded around the deathly silent room, "of course if you want to genuinely support or inform a person, you don't need to be a keyboard warrior – you go around to their house for a cuppa and a chat, you email them, you even pick up the phone."

One of the staff members tentatively raised her hand.

"Yes, yes," Mrs Bent boomed, "speak up, don't be shy."

"Mrs Bent..." Max warned.

"They can make you paranoid," she began with a gulp, "I was concerned about posts on a forum which I believed were somehow linked to me."

"Thank you for being so honest. So, what happened?" Max asked with interest.

"For quite some time I was convinced that the poster was a person I had worked with. A proper Jane Austen type baddie."

"Tell us more!" Marcia urged, eyes shining with the prospect of gossip.

"Well...I heard that a Teacher Training establishment had barred her and in retaliation she took her incandescent, aggrieved rage out on me, posting vile, aggressive poison in a late night attack for everyone to see. The irony of it was that she was the lucky one, she was the one who got off lightly."

"Oh dear that doesn't sound good at all," Mrs Bent shook her head with disapproval, "what drove this person I wonder?"

"Possibly a primal need for self preservation? Ambition? Certainly no consideration for the true injured party."

"So *was* she someone you knew?" Mr Bentley queried.

The staff member shook her head with firm resignation, "Truthfully? No. I didn't know her at all. I was told by an expert who looked over the posts that those were really nothing to do with me and that it was a troll, a random stranger. It's all about your own personal interpretation apparently."

"A lesson for us all," Mrs Bent clapped her hands, "stay *away* from those forums."

"Read a book," Max advised, "now staff, let us all proceed with the online Prevent training before we break for a well-deserved lunch."

* * *

"So, Ryan O'Neill's not playing today?" Ann asked, as they pulled up outside Anton and Lulu's bohemian abode.

"I've heard he's been dropped...permanently," Jon replied, switching off the thrumming engine.

"Good," Ann sniffed, "I might have had to shout profanities at him for the way he's treated Soph."

Jon was gazing into the right-wing mirror, watching Samuel running towards the car. "Here he is." They both turned in their seats, bright smiles on their faces as Sam flung open the door and clambered into the back.

"Hello mate, buckle yourself in," Jon helped him pull the seatbelt across, making sure it was clicked firmly into place.

"You have a scarf," Ann grinned, "so does Jon."

"I got a t-shirt too, I bought it with my pocket money from the club shop," he unzipped his jacket to reveal a red top with the Chattlesbury logo printed across the middle.

"Wow," said Ann, "that looks awesome!"

"Who do you think will win then Sam?" Jon indicated and moved into a space on the busy road.

"Us! We're gonna stuff 'em 2-0."

"Yes," Ann punched the air, "come on Chattlesbury FC."

"They're expecting thousands from Reading," Jon disclosed, "it should be a good match. Both teams are doing well."

"We haven't got Ryan O'Neill anymore though," Samuel said glumly.

"No," Jon conceded, "but we have got Abubaki. I would bet that he's going to score more than O'Neill ever did."

Ann tore open a bag of lemon bon-bons, offering them around, "how's your week been then Sam?"

"Okay," he mumbled, his mouth full of sweet, "I won a spelling competition."

"Well done!" Ann cried, "that's wonderful."

"I hate school," Sam grumbled.

"I never liked it much either," Ann replied, "what's your favourite subject?"

"English I suppose."

"Good choice. That reminds me, I brought you this," Ann produced a bag of books which she passed over to Sam, "it's the entire Harry Potter in hardback series."

"Awesome!" Samuel was immediately pulling out the books for inspection.

"Let me know what you think," Ann said, her face crinkling with happiness as she watched Samuel flicking through them.

"Can I text you?" Samuel asked eagerly.

Ann glanced at Jon, "well we'll have to check with Anton and Lulu first, but I can't see why not."

"Wicked!"

"Uh-Oh," Jon said with a shake of his head, "looks like we're hitting traffic."

They moved at a snail's pace, following the long line of vehicles heading towards the city centre, all three debating which of the Harry Potter movies was the best.

* * *

Jon had managed to bag them fantastic seats at the side of the pitch in the bottom tier of the accessible area. It was an exciting first half; one of Reading's key strikers received a red card for a dangerous tackle and was subsequently sent off the pitch to a round of boos and hisses. Then Chattlesbury FC netted the first goal off a seriously impressive right volley that bent the ball at a flying angle over the defenders' heads and smashed it past the open- mouthed goalkeeper into the back of the net. The crowd erupted; the whole stadium exploding into cheering and yelling. Next to Ann, Jon and Samuel jumped up and down, whooping and high fiving each other with glee. The furore eventually abated; spectators sat back in their seats, but the sound of jubilant singing still rang around the stadium.

After the referee had blown the whistle to signify half time and the players had disappeared down the tunnel, a friendly disability liaison steward enquired if they would like any refreshments. Jon ordered three hot dogs, with extra ketchup for Samuel and bottles of pop for them all. In no time the steward was back, revealing that he had managed to "jump the queue." Ann organised napkins for them all, smiling as Samuel took a hearty bite and let out a mumble of approval.

"These are the best hot-dogs I've ever tasted," Jon commented, in between mouthfuls.

Samuel was looking down at his t-shirt which had become streaked by a huge blob of sauce, "sorry," he said, looking contrite and nervous.

"Hey, it's fine," Ann soothed, "don't worry, it will wash out."

"And it's red anyway," Jon continued, "you can hardly notice it."

Samuel relaxed back in his seat, "what do the players do during half time? Do they practise inside?"

"I don't think so," Jon replied, "they probably have a sit down and a drink, maybe eat a banana to give them some energy? Who knows?"

"Maybe the manager gives them a telling off if they're losing, or in this case, a pat on the back," Ann swallowed the remaining edge of the hot dog and took a hefty swig of pop that fizzed at the back of her throat.

"This is so awesome," the twinkle had returned to Sam's eye, "wait till my mates hear where I've been the weekend."

"We can do it again Sam," Jon enthused, "and maybe next time you could bring a friend."

"I could?"

"Yes!" Jon and Ann chorused together.

"Thanks," Samuel was staring at a female steward who was helping an elderly gentleman back to his seat. His mouth had tilted downwards.

"What is it Sam?" Ann asked, concerned by the change in atmosphere.

"She," he pointed at the same lady, "looks like my mum."

"Oh." Ann gazed over at the petite, blonde haired steward, "she's very pretty."

"She has warts," Sam announced, "you can't see them from far away, but when you get close they're on her nose and her chin. Just like a witch."

Jon and Ann knew that he was referring to his biological mother.

"What's her name Sam?" Ann asked gently.

"Heather." Samuel crossed his arms, "a horrible name for a horrible person. I hate her."

He looked so vulnerable and alone that Ann wanted to hug him tight. Instead they were distracted by the fanfare that announced the return of the players.

"Here they come," Jon said brightly, as eleven super fit men ran back onto the pitch. The crowd went wild.

* * *

After the mention of his mother, Sam was quieter for the second half, even when Abubaki scored another goal. He jumped along with the rest of the crowd, but the smile didn't quite reach his eyes and Ann was left trying not to judge a woman who could abandon her own flesh and blood in such a heartless manner.

"Fancy some tea?" Jon asked, looking at his watch, "we've still got two hours before you have to be back, and I've heard they do a cracking fish pie at the local pub."

Sam nodded, following Jon as he pushed Ann out of the large gates which had been opened at the back of the stand.

"Do your legs hurt?" Sam asked, gazing at Ann with curious wonder.

"No Sam," Ann replied firmly, "they're actually completely numb."

"You're brave," he mumbled.

"No. *You're* brave," Ann insisted gently, catching hold of his arm and giving it a squeeze, "Jon and I have really enjoyed today Sam. In fact, we love spending time with you."

"Really?" Sam's cheeks had turned pink.

"Really," Jon reiterated, "and we'd love to spend *more* time with you… if that's okay Sam."

"That would be okay," Sam said with a huge grin, "that would be awesome, you two are cool."

The three of them made their way to Jon's shiny car, their laughter and chatter ringing across the car park.

* * *

"*This* is to die for," Ann pointed her fork at the chunks of cod and salmon, topped with creamy cheese mash, "I need to make one of these, don't you think Jon?"

"Absolutely!" Jon wiped his mouth with a cherry coloured napkin, "I'll consult Delia when we get home."

"Who's Delia?" Sam figured it must be a Grandma or another elderly relative.

"A famous cook off the tele," Ann replied, "I have a few of her recipe books Sam, I'm sure there's a fish pie in one of them."

"Bound to be," Jon said, "more drinks anyone?" He rose to his six-foot frame, picking up the empty glasses.

Ann gazed up at him, her eyes lingering on his large biceps. Her husband was a fine specimen of a man; gorgeous, kind and funny and if it hadn't been for that awful accident, then she never would have met him, maybe life wasn't so bad after all. She watched him saunter up the bar, all testosterone infused confidence. Sam meanwhile had slunk down in his seat and was fiddling with the chipped edge of the table.

"You okay?"

There was a pause, while Sam pondered whether to disclose that his current crush was sitting directly opposite them.

"It's just a school friend," he said eventually.

Ann peered round, "the girl?"

"Uh huh," Sam nodded, "her name's Beth, she's a year above me, she's in the gymnastic team and she's really cool."

"Do you want to go say hi," Ann smiled.

"No! That would be totally embarrassing."

"Well, it looks like she's coming over here Sam," Ann watched the dark-haired girl push back her chair and walk gracefully towards them.

"Hello," she was looking at Samuel, her hands clutching a mobile phone.

"Hi," Sam looked up and Ann was taken aback by the dazzling smile he projected at Beth.

"You won the spelling gala then?"

"Yeah."

"That's cool. What you up to?" Beth popped a piece of fruity gum into her mouth.

"Just been to the match…and you?"

"Out with the folks," she motioned to the middle-aged couple behind them, "we're going to the pictures a bit later."

"Cool," Sam nodded and then as if just remembering that he was with Ann, "this is my friend Ann."

Ann glowed under the unexpected praise of being called a friend, "hello Beth, would you like to sit down?"

"Hello. No but thanks, I suppose I should get back," she cast Sam a shy glance, "so I'll see you at school?"

"Yep," Sam waved as she wandered off.

"She seems a lovely girl," Ann said.

"I guess she is," Sam replied nonchalantly, his eyes following her moves.

"Maybe you could ask Beth next time we go out then," Ann suggested.

"Not the football though," Jon chipped in, as he set the drinks down, "bowling? Cinema? You can choose."

Samuel sat back in his chair, a wide grin on his face as he daydreamed about letting Bethany Hope Miller beat him at ten pin bowling.

An hour later they dropped him at home, turning down the offer of a beverage with Anton and Lulu.

"We've had such a lovely afternoon," Ann told Anton and Lulu, after Sam had ran off into the house, waving manically, "he's such a good kid."

"You're fantastic influences on him," Lulu replied, with a warm smile, "he's forever talking about you both."

Jon and Ann looked at each other, both faces tinged with happiness, "can we take him somewhere next weekend?"

"Of course!" Lulu replied clasping her hands, "Sam's happy when he's with you and that makes us happy."

Jon started the engine.

"There's one more thing," Ann said, "he wants my number to message me – is that okay?"

"That's absolutely fine," Lulu replied, "I'll let you contact each other directly then to make arrangements."

Jon papped the horn as he pulled away and Ann watched Anton and Lulu with their arms around each other, disappearing in her side mirror.

"It's going well," Ann said with a smile.

"It's going great," Jon said, clasping her hand, "I've got a feeling that we're going to have a plus one in our family in the not too distant future."

"Let's just wait and see," Ann replied with nervous excitement, "we've got meetings with social services and more training before we can think about Sam…Sam moving in with us."

"Being it on darling," Jon replied adamantly, "bring it on."

Chapter Sixteen

As usual on a Monday morning, the queue at the village Post Office was long and busy. It snaked around the aisles of the tiny newsagents, passing the tilting magazine rack and the temporarily defunct ice-cream freezer. Sophie stood on the edge of the doorway, shivering as a cold December wind buffeted her back.

"Come on in love," a kind lady in front of her wearing a bright yellow anorak moved forwards so Sophie could squeeze in.

"Thanks," Sophie shook her hair, damp from the sudden torrent of fine rain, "it's so cold isn't it?" She blew on the tips of her red fingers.

"Yes sweetheart, but this weather doesn't bother me," the lady winked, "I've been around eighty-three years and I've seen some bad winters. Four foot of snow we had it once girl. This is tropical in comparison."

"You look fantastic for your age," Sophie exclaimed with complete sincerity as she gazed at the ladies youthful looking visage.

The other woman chuckled, "thanks love that'd be the yoga. I've been going twice a week for thirty years now."

They moved forward in the line. Sophie was considering coming back later. She had forgotten it was pension day and there was only one assistant working the till, but then the lady in the yellow mac was still chattering away and Sophie felt compelled to stay.

"You going to that?" She asked, pointing a thumb at a flyer advertising the Christmas Fair, "Mrs Pobble arranges it every year."

"What do they sell there?" Sophie asked with interest.

"All sorts. People pay for a table to sell their wares; clothes, household appliances. Then there's the Christmas stalls which are nice; Christmas crafts, food, decorations, gifts – you know the like."

Sophie nodded, her mind was whirring like cogs in a clock factory, there was so much unused stuff dotted around her house and now here was a perfect opportunity to get rid of it and make some cash at the same time.

Once she was home she contacted Mrs Pobble to reserve a space and table and then searched around for the things to sell list she'd made the other day, adding four more words at the top of the page, '…at the Christmas Fair.'

* * *

After hearing about her plans for the weekend, Juliette and Evelyn popped round Friday night to help her make the price tags, stickers and sort all the jumble into organised boxes.

"You have a lot to sell," Evelyn said, as they surveyed the covered lounge floor.

"I know," Sophie replied, "I've even got baby stuff from years ago that I've kept."

"It's designer too," Juliette said picking up an exquisite cot throw, "this stuff is going to sell in no time."

"I hope so," Sophie replied, "I need to make as much money as possible."

Juliette looked around her with a wistful sigh, "this house sure is beautiful. Won't you be sad to leave?"

"God no," Sophie replied, "It's a money leeching monstrosity and I'll let you in on a secret; I've never really liked living here anyway. It's more of a showcase than a home. Bricks and mortar that's all it is Jules, bricks and mortar."

Evelyn laughed, "Sophie! You've changed so much since we first met."

"In a good way I hope?" Sophie questioned, her face serious.

"Yes. Absolutely, I mean you were erm…lovely before, it's just now you've…" she trailed off blushing.

"Come to my senses?" Sophie finished, "course I have. I feel like I've been dormant and sleepy for so many years, but now I'm back, and living in the real world again."

"Like a real life Sleeping Beauty," Evelyn said, as she affixed a tag to an unopened pack of baby romper suits.

Sophie laughed, "but minus the Prince. I don't need a man to save me anymore, I'm quite capable of saving myself."

Juliette clapped and looked at her with admiring eyes, "not even Tarquin Haverstock?"

"No. Not even the course leader," Sophie replied glibly.

Just then the doorbell chimed. Sophie hurried down the hall and opened the door to Mrs Chan and her daughter.

"Hello," Sophie exclaimed with surprise.

"Mrs O'Neill, sorry to bother you, I just wondered if I could possibly measure the bay windows. I'm having a seamstress make the drapes and she's been pestering me for the sizes."

"Of course," Sophie swung the door open, "come on in. The house is in chaos I'm afraid."

"I understand," Mrs Chan replied with a smile, "may I start upstairs?"

"Go ahead," Sophie confirmed, "do you need a tape measure?"

Mrs Chan delved in her handbag and pulled out a metal contraption that shot out a bendy measure when she pressed the button.

"I'll pour you a glass of wine," Sophie said with a laugh, "my friends and I were just about to open a bottle."

* * *

Will was pushing Esme down the street. It was late afternoon and she had been screaming for the past half hour now. To give them all a break and to try and placate little one, he had volunteered to take her a walk in the dwindling sunlight. He strolled through the park, pausing to watch a group of youngsters having a kick about on the grass.

"When you're big you can go on those," he pointed to the weather-beaten slide and the swings which were moving lazily in the breeze. Esme gurgled in response, then chomped on her fist. He carried on past a row of towering oak trees and bushes covered in winter berries, following a winding path that took him out of the park and onto a quiet residential street. At the end, Will could see a convenience store, where he would be able to purchase baby milk, nappies, spur of the moment flowers for Hema and a bottle of wine for them to share later.

Flora and Max were going out for the evening, which meant they had the house to themselves. He planned on watching a film or listening to music, spending some quality time with Hema, on their own for a change. And hopefully this walk in the fresh air would zonk his princess out for a while.

The shop was quiet. As he was gazing down at his daughter with pride and love, the assistant left her counter and stood next to him, gushing over Esme. Then the cleaner put down the mop and peered in the pram, closely followed by the broody shop manager. Will managed to escape twenty minutes later with his purchases swinging from the handle. He walked quickly home and as he slotted his key into the lock and opened the door, he heard the shower running from above. He guessed it was his dad and he was right; Hema and Flora were in the kitchen, sitting close together at the table, giggling over their phones.

"You okay?" He asked Flora, who was looking extremely flushed.

"Your mum has joined Facebook," Hema said, with a wide triumphant smile, "I've helped her set up an account and I've just been giving her a very basic run down on how to use it."

"Facebook?" Will was amused and surprised, "how many friends have you got then Mum?"

Flora looked at the screen, "erm, fifty-four including Hema. They're mostly friends from church but Jimmy's sent me a request too." As she looked up, Will noticed her eyes shining with excitement.

"She's also had a few stranger requests," Hema said, as she bent to pick up Esme.

"Oh Will," Flora gasped, "I've had two American Army Generals send me a request and I...a young man with his t-shirt off sent me one too!"

Hema chuckled, bouncing a wide-awake Esme on her hip, "He had a set of really impressive pecs."

"My mother's a MILF," Will said, grinning widely.

"What?" Flora replied, her eyes wide, "what on earth is a MILF?"

"Really Flora!" Max said reprovingly, as he strode into the room.

Will was immediately on the defensive, "chill Dad. Mom's joined Facebook that's all."

"Have you Flora?" Max spun to stare at his wife.

"I talked her into it," Hema began, "I thought..."

"I wanted to join dear," Flora interjected firmly, "Brenda's been on it for ages and did you know that the Pope has a Twitter account!"

"Oh Flora, you don't really think that the Pope sits there in the papal chambers tweeting do you? It's probably one of his many aides." Max shook his head, while Hema and Will exchanged an eye roll.

"Well anyway," Flora refused to be deflated, "*I* think social media is exciting. Who writes letters anymore? It's all done online via the internet now-a-days and the flower shop has its own designated Facebook business page. Hema's been showing me how to share links to help advertise it."

"Well okay," Max sighed, "just be careful Flora, there are a lot of strange people on the internet. And please, make sure all your privacy settings are set to private, I don't want anyone from St. Mary's seeing what you're up to."

"Don't you think you're being a bit paranoid Dad?" Will said with irritation, "Mum knows what she's doing."

"Of course I do love," Flora glanced at Max, "you don't need to worry."

"Very well," Max nodded.

Flora collected the dirty mugs from the table and took them over to the sink.

"Flora," Max continued, "…you look lovely by the way."

"Oh," Flora smoothed her grey woollen dress down, "thank you. I treated myself, it was in the sales."

The doorbell rang and Flora hurried out to let in her brother and his 'friend.'

"Howdy," Evan boomed, making everybody in the kitchen jump, "ready to be thrashed at the quiz are you Max?"

"We'll see about that," Max said smoothly, "I'm a teacher remember; my general knowledge is inexhaustible."

Evan laughed loudly before making his way over to Will to slap him heartily on the back, "how's the new Mum and Dad coping?"

"Alright Uncle Evan," Will smirked.

"They're doing fantastic," Flora cut in, taking Evan's lady friend Grace over to see a yawning Esme.

"She sure is a beauty," Grace said warmly, "just look at those amazing eyes."

Evan nodded in agreement, "have you got a real job yet then?" His gaze focussed on Will.

"I'm still at uni," Will said between clenched teeth.

"You know he is," Flora berated her brother, "Will's staying with us until he finishes his studies."

"Then he's going to get a magnificent job and make me and his mother delirious with pride," Max said.

"I *am* here," Will cut in, "I can talk for myself."

"Only jesting boy," Uncle Evan swiped at his steamed-up spectacles, "but if you ever decide you want a career in the armed forces, then you know who to come to for advice."

Flora was aghast, "Will doesn't want to go in the army!"

"No, he wants to use his brains. Evan, leave the poor lad alone," Grace was shaking her head with disapproval, "Flora, shall we go?"

"Yes," Flora pulled on her jacket, then turned to Will and Hema, "have a nice evening lovey's."

"Bye little one," Grace stroked Esme's rosy cheek before pushing Evan towards the door.

"Thank Christ for that," Will mumbled, running a hand through his tousled hair.

Hema glanced at him sympathetically, "you're brilliant Will, you do know that don't you?"

"Am I?" Will's smile had slipped from his face, "maybe I should train to be a plumber. At least we'd have plenty of money."

"And you would hate it," Hema placed a warm hand around his waist, "you're a fantastic Dad, the most perfect boyfriend and a really lovely bloke who is going to smash this degree and do whatever he bloody wants to do – okay?"

"Okay," Will kissed the top of her head, pulling her close, wrapping his arms around his gorgeous, loving, supportive girlfriend and their beautiful baby: his world, his everything.

* * *

Evelyn was up early on Saturday morning. By seven o'clock she was showered, dressed and sitting at the table eating hot porridge covered with a generous dollop of syrup. Sophie was due to pick her up soon, then they were going to collect Jules, before setting up Sophie's stall at the Christmas fair. Thankfully the weather had stayed dry but cold. Underneath her boots she wore two pairs of socks and around her neck she had arranged her new, glittery black snood. It had been a flamboyant purchase during a late-night shopping excursion with Jacob. Another example of Evelyn's recent impulsiveness. To the delight of great aunt Gertrude, who had been down visiting, Evelyn had been seeing much more of Jacob. She enjoyed his company immensely and the feeling seemed to be reciprocated; meals, day trips, he had even cooked for her, and this Sunday they were going to the theatre.

Evelyn pondered on her Mam's last words on this earth "find love" she had urged her only daughter. Evelyn had dismissed the idea at the time, but now,

now as she was growing fonder of Jacob with each passing day, the romantic notion no longer seemed so far-fetched. Jacob was kind-hearted, he was chivalrous, he was decent, honest and dare she admit it handsome? Yes, she was growing very fond of him indeed. A quiver of excitement ran through her as she thought of the gentle way he had kissed her lips the last time they had met, the way he had smiled at her as he told her how beautiful she was. She felt transported back to her youth; feeling like a giddy teenager whenever he was with her. Evelyn wondered if Juliette felt the same about Doctor Rivers? Maybe she could ask her. Maybe she could confide in her or Sophie about her growing feelings for Jacob Morley. The sound of papping jolted her from her romantic reverie. Evelyn slid into her warm, cashmere coat, popped on her matching hat and gloves set, then locked up the house.

"Morning sweetheart," Sophie said brightly, as Evelyn opened the car door, "isn't it a glorious day?"

"Morning Sophie," Evelyn replied, peering out of the window at a bright, cloudless sky, "it's beautiful, are you all ready for the Christmas fair?"

"I sure am," Sophie stuck the gear into first and revved the engine, "let's get Jules and go make some money."

It took them four trips to the car before they had emptied it and organised everything onto the fold up tables and the clothes hanging frame. Juliette gazed in wonder at a black Versace dress, with a corset style bodice and a sexy, revealing side split.

"Have it," Sophie decided, taking it off the hanger, "it will fit you Jules."

Juliette started to protest but Sophie held up her hand, "call it a thank you present," then she turned to Evelyn, "what takes your fancy Evelyn – the vase?" She had noticed the reverential manner that her friend had placed it in the box last night.

"No Sophie, it's too much!"

"Of course it isn't," Sophie removed it from the table, wrapped it in tissue and handed it over, "you have both been so good helping me, please have them as a token of my love and gratitude." A group of women holding onto already bored looking children wandered inside the large hall, "here we go ladies, brace yourselves for the rush!"

And what a rush it was. In less than an hour almost all of the garments had gone.

"Sophie – you are going to make a fortune at this rate," Juliette whispered, tucking a wedge of twenty-pound notes inside her combat style trousers pocket.

"That's the plan," Sophie said with a wide smile, "can I help you madam?"

The baby equipment was the next stuff to proverbially 'fly off the shelves.' A Winnie The Pooh bouncer, a revolving baby gym, a fold away high-chair, clothes, sterilisers, even the bibs were being grappled over.

"I forgot Esme," wailed Sophie, during a break from the hordes, "Will and Hema could have had first pickings."

"Maz said that Flora has been ordering them things brand new from the baby shop on the High Street." Juliette divulged, "I wouldn't worry Sophie. Besides, you need to sell your stuff, not give everything away!"

"I suppose so," Sophie said, chewing her bottom lip, "maybe I'll just put this aside for them anyway." She folded up a swing that played lullabies as it rocked, "this came all the way from America, I've never seen it in any of our stores."

"You are extremely generous," Evelyn rubbed her arm, "and a great friend."

Sophie wandered off, muttering about being desperate for the lavatory.

"Is she okay?" Juliette asked Evelyn, "I mean what with her marriage separation and now this huge house move, as well as family life to contend with and university too."

"She's under considerable stress," Evelyn agreed, "but I think this is the making of Sophie. I honestly think she's going to be fine." There was a pause, "how are you getting on Juliette? Dr Rivers seems very taken with you."

Juliette poured them a drink of tea from a flask, "is he? I hadn't noticed."

"Oh you tease," Evelyn scoffed, "of course you know how much he likes you, even I've noticed that, but are the feelings reciprocated?"

Juliette swallowed the milky tea, her mind casting back to last night; his sweet murmurs as they had made love. Should she admit to how much she adored him? How quickly she was falling?

"I care for him very much," she disclosed, with a flushed face and neck.

Evelyn didn't press the matter further, instead she changed the conversation to talk of the modules they were studying at university and the essays and coursework which were all due before the Christmas break.

Chapter Seventeen

"I think I need to give this volunteering business a knock on the head," Sophie was pulling on her trousers and looking down at her faithful dog, "time for me to get a job paying real money – what do you think huh?"

Her black Labrador barked in response and wagged his tail.

Sophie stooped to pat his head, "I suppose I've got time to take you and your sister a stroll around the block." She slipped into her running shoes, tying them tightly, "come on then boy." Down the stairs she jogged, clipping leads onto her two faithful friends before swinging the door open onto a beautifully glorious sunny day.

Forty minutes later she was pulling onto the car park of St Mary's, her mind made up that this was to be her last visit here. Hopefully Mr Bentley would agree to writing her a reference which she could forward to any future prospect employer. She found him in the corridor inspecting wall displays, he looked really tired, in fact Sophie might even go as far to describe him as haggard.

"It's the Christmas term," he disclosed, after she asked if he was okay, "a tremendous amount of stress on the staff."

Sophie told him her plans and he assured her he would be happy to give her a reference.

"But what of your plans to go into teaching?" He asked, "I hope we haven't put you off."

"No, no," Sophie said with a laugh, "just a change of circumstances, but truthfully, I don't think teachings for me."

"What will you do?" He enquired with an understanding nod.

"Start looking for jobs as soon as possible," she swiped back a tendril of her hair which had escaped from its ponytail, "maybe see a careers advisor at the uni."

"Could you take my son as well?" Max Bentley laughed, and it was such a lovely sound coming from someone who looked so stressed, "he just doesn't seem to know *what* he wants to do."

"I still don't know," Sophie admitted, frowning at the look of worry on Max's face, "Will's doing great at uni. He's so good at the journalism module, maybe he's found his niche after all."

"Journalism," Max rubbed his chin thoughtfully, "thank you Mrs O'Neill, thank you." He wandered back towards his office, leaving Sophie to go say her goodbyes to the rest of the staff.

* * *

The Learning Centre or library, as Will referred to it, was full of English students working on their journalism projects. A harassed looking librarian carrying a pile of books to be returned to the shelves, tutted loudly at the sight of Will's feet propped up on the table.

"Sorry," he mumbled, flicking his chair back onto four legs.

Opposite him, Ann looked up from her scribbling to frown his way.

"Had a sleepless night?" She asked sympathetically.

"One of many," he replied with a yawn.

"How old is Esme now?"

"Four months. She's cutting her first tooth, not a happy girl. And Hema is exhausted. She reckons it's harder being home full time with a baby, than being a student."

"I would agree with her there," Ann said, "babies are relentless; even the golden ones."

Will pulled out his phone to show Ann a series of selfies he had taken early this morning; a happy Esme pulling his nose, trying to chomp on his chin.

"She is beautiful," Juliette cried, dumping a book on the table, "I managed to find one, I think it's the last copy in the entire library."

They all stared at 'Writing Feature Articles: A practical guide to methods and markets' as if it were a chunk of real gold bullion.

"Right," Ann slipped into bossy, organised mode, "Will, you look through it and see what quotes we can use and remember they need to be relevant to our project, don't just pick out random facts."

Will picked up a pen and pad and began flicking through the textbook.

"I suppose someone should tell Sophie we've found it, where is she by the way?" Ann peered around.

Juliette shrugged, "last time I saw her she was on the third floor being chatted up by the drinks machine."

"She could be a while then," Ann grimaced, "we really need to get this finished by the end of the week."

"What's the rush?" Will complained, "the deadlines two weeks away yet."

"It's almost Christmas Will, won't you have presents to get, parties to attend?"

Will nodded, "the Tinsel Disco – awesome!"

"Exactly!" Ann said, "which is this weekend – we don't want to have to worry about coursework when we're all hung over. Where is Evelyn by the way? Am I the only one who's bothered about getting a good grade for this module?"

"There she is," Will motioned towards the entrance, where Evelyn was talking to a man with sandy coloured hair. From the looks of it, they seemed quite close.

"Morning!" A flustered looking Evelyn rushed over.

"Hi Evelyn," Juliette waved across the table at her, "is that Jacob?"

"Yes that's my friend Jacob," Evelyn gabbled, "he bought me this morning, there was an awful accident on one of the A roads so we came the back way."

Ann raised her eyebrows in surprise, but remained silent.

"Are you bringing him to the Tinsel Disco?" Juliette asked.

"I hadn't thought about it," Evelyn gasped, "I could I suppose, but haven't the tickets sold out now?"

"Nope," Will was leaning back again, "Hema's coming, so is Jon, and Melanie's bringing Tasha. The more the merrier I say."

Evelyn nodded, "okay I will," her face was lit up with happiness.

"Right then," Ann looked over her reading glasses, "now everyone's social life has been organised, can we please finish this blasted project?"

* * *

"I love independent study," Sophie declared, licking the sugar from the top of a jam oozing donut. They had walked into town for lunch and were sitting in a cafe that specialised in extravagant desserts.

"We should get back soon," Ann said, as she glanced at her watch, "if we work hard this afternoon, we should have the article finished in draft form."

She rolled out a glossy sized A3 paper, flattening it down on the table, "how do you think it looks so far?"

The criteria of the journalism project was to design and create a magazine article of the student's own choice. Ann had reservations on the group work aspect of the criteria, truthfully she like to work alone, but to be fair, between them they had produced a snazzy little article. It was Sophie who had inadvertently come up with the feature topic. She had been lamenting on her children's hay fever allergy to Juliette, whose own two children suffered from an allergy to penicillin. Ann had been struck with inspiration and the idea of a health feature with the angle on allergies had been borne. They had all contributed; Sophie had written a piece about hay fever, Juliette had interviewed a friend who suffered with a banana allergy, Evelyn had written a section on the effects of allergies on the body and the different types of medication used to combat it, Will had overseen the critical summary of the piece and Ann had been officially designated as the group leader; she had compiled the module log, edited each person's work and slotted all the sections into an impressive two page spread that would be perfect for any of the women's weekly magazine.

"Wow!" Sophie nodded her appreciation, "fantastic work."

"Well done everyone," Evelyn said, smiling widely, "I think we may get an A grade for this one."

"Good I desperately need one," Sophie replied.

"You did get a B for your poetry module," Juliette pointed out, "your grades have improved massively."

Sophie's eyes gleamed with happiness, "I did think of jacking it all in at one point but I'm so glad I stuck it out. Only one more year after this one guys."

The conversation drifted into talk of dissertation choices and exam worries, then when they had all finished their lunch, they had a slow walk back through the city centre for their afternoon lesson: Realism and the Novel, with the delectable Dr Rivers.

* * *

Juliette was trying hard to concentrate on the handout in front of her, but it was extremely difficult when her lecturer boyfriend was pacing a few feet away from her, pen in hand, looking hot and intelligent and smart and extremely distracting. She doodled on her pad; a spiral which turned into a heart, *what the hell* she thought, *how old am I?* Feeling embarrassed, she closed the pad and leant back in her chair listening to Ben. Thankfully he hadn't noticed her regression back into teenage hood. He was talking about the novels of Jane Austen.

"The single most significant economic problem for women in Pride and Prejudice is a lack of fortune." He then went on to elaborate how the novel highlights the importance of making a good match in marriage and how a woman can raise her status through it.

Feeling bold Juliette raised her hand. Ben glanced at her, a small smile lifting his lips, "yes?"

"I feel that Jane Austen is making a clear critique on marrying without love!"

"Give me an example?" Ben retaliated.

Juliette thought for a moment, mind racing, "the character Charlotte Lucas marrying Mr Collins and the negative manner they are depicted."

"An excellent example, well done," Ben walked away to the other side of the room, "anyone else have an opinion on this?"

Hands shot up across the room and the debate continued.

At break time Juliette left the others on the pretext of 'finding a drinks machine', she knew Ben was following her down the corridor, weaving around the many students. Then he was next to her and his hand was brushing hers.

"Want to play a real game Juliette?" He asked huskily.

"Playing for keeps?" Juliette asked breathlessly.

"Absolutely."

Then they were parted by the oncoming hordes and Juliette carried on walking, determined not to look back. If she would have done so, she might have been shocked by the look of love on Ben's face as he stared at her retreating figure.

Chapter Eighteen

"Eight hundred and seventy-five pence exactly," Sophie dropped the last silver coin into the almost full bottle, "not bad for a Christmas jumble sale huh?"

Evelyn was sitting opposite her at the breakfast bar, paperclipping twenty-pound notes into neat piles. "An excellent days work."

"Evelyn I should give you and Jules some of this, after all your help."

"Nonsense!" Evelyn cried, "you've already given me a beautiful, expensive vase and Juliette a designer dress too. Keep it for you and your children. You need it now more than ever Sophie."

"Thank you," Sophie said quietly, tears shimmering in her eyes as she looked around her vast kitchen, "looks like I won't be here for much longer."

"I can't believe how fast this house sale has gone through," Evelyn commented, "so next weekends your definite leaving date?"

"Yes," a tear trickled down Sophie's cheek.

Evelyn rose to hug her, "oh dear don't upset yourself. I thought you were okay with leaving here?"

"I am," Sophie sniffed, "it's the memories. Some of them are bad, but a lot of them were very good. I remember standing here just after we'd brought the twins home from hospital, crying with all this overwhelming new mother emotion. They took their first steps in here too. Ryan and I used to waltz around when we were both a bit tipsy, all the parties we used to have," Sophie shook her head, "it seems a life time ago."

"You're moving on," Evelyn said softly, "but you can still take the good memories with you. Leave the bad one's here in the past where they belong."

Sophie nodded, "I should go get ready. Can I do your hair Evelyn?"

"I thought you'd never ask," Evelyn let out her relief in laughter.

* * *

"Are you sure I look okay?" Hema was standing in front of their full-length mirror, twisting and turning, biting her lip at her reflection.

"Honestly?" Will said scratching his head, "you'll do I suppose."

Hema turned to glare at him.

Quickly he held up his hands, "that was a joke. You look stunning."

A mollified Hema picked up her handbag, "well I guess I'm ready then."

"How do I look?" Will preened in the mirror, blowing kisses at his own reflection.

"You joker," laughed Hema, "you look as handsome as ever. My boyfriend the heartthrob."

Will nodded his agreement, "true," then ducked as a pillow narrowly missed his head.

They clattered down the stairs, their laughter ringing throughout the house. In the living room, Max was settled on the sofa watching MTV television, as a hungry Esme chomped on a bottle of milk. Her eyes followed her youthful parents as they danced around the room.

"Anybody would think you're excited," Max commented drily.

"Why have you got the music channel on?" Will asked in surprise.

"Little Esme likes it, look..." he pointed to her wiggling toes.

"Ah," Hema was immediately on all fours, bent over her daughter, kissing her forehead.

"Are you ready?" Flora stood in the doorway, jangling her car keys, a happy smile on her face.

Will tenderly kissed his daughter before following his mother to the front door.

"Will Dad be okay on his own with her?" He asked dubiously.

"Of course love," Flora scoffed, "your father was very hands on when you were a baby you know. Babies haven't changed that much in twenty years – surely?"

"Fair point," Will laughed, pulling Hema close, "let's go party."

* * *

"There she is," Ann pointed to a figure standing underneath flickering lamplight.

"Is that Juliette?" Jon gaped through the window screen, "she looks different."

"I think it's her," now Ann was unsure. Then the figure turned to stare straight at them and there was no confusing Juliette's porcelain complexion and her striking red hair. Why she looked so different became obvious, her hair had been perfectly styled and was sitting atop her head in a mass of glorious ringlets.

"She looks gorgeous," Ann commented, "watch out Doctor Rivers."

"Indeedy," Jon replied, slipping the gear into first, as she opened the door.

Close up Juliette looked even more beautiful; her lips were coloured a striking red and her sparkly eyes had been cosmetically widened with the help of mascara and liner. She wore a long coat wrapped at the waist and trimmed with a fur collar and cuffs.

"You look like a model," Ann mumbled as they waited for her to clamber into the rear of the car.

"My sister's been working her magic again," Juliette replied, "she should be a beautician instead of a florist."

"She must have a good eye for colour."

"Yes, she's always been the creative one. I was always more academic."

"Speaking of academics," Ann grinned, "is Doctor Rivers accompanying you this evening."

"I'm meeting him there," Juliette replied, "about five minutes ago actually."

"Oh it's fashionable to be late," Ann said looking at Jon, "I was always keeping you waiting wasn't I?"

"Still do," Jon grumbled looking at the clock on the dashboard.

"Well look slippy mister," Ann urged, "let's get Cinderella to the ball."

* * *

Jon managed to squeeze his car into the last remaining disabled bay just outside the front entrance of the university. As they were making their way up the ramp to the sliding doors, there came a squeal from behind that sounded like Sophie. Juliette turned into a warm, tight hug.

"Hi guys," Sophie waved manically, Evelyn and Jacob lagged behind her, arm in arm.

While Jacob was introduced to Ann and Jon by a proud Evelyn, Sophie took Juliette's arm and they clattered on ahead, laughing and chattering. The university looked so pretty in the darkness with the draped tinsel and the twinkling

Christmas lights. They stopped in a line for security to check their bags and relieve them of their tickets.

"Keep your stubs," A jovial looking man in a bright orange jacket boomed, "just in case you need some fresh air or alternatively if you wanna poison yourself with cigarettes." He pointed to a shelter where a dozen or so smokers huddled close together.

"Have you still stopped?" Juliette asked.

"Yep, for months now, aren't I good?" Sophie's smile beamed liked a star in the moonlight.

Into the lift they trooped, heading for the basement and the Student Union bar.

"Are we going to leave our coats there?" Ann pointed to a makeshift cloakroom.

"Jules, I've never seen you wear such a long coat," Sophie said, "what have you got on underneath?"

Juliette blushed slightly as all eyes turned upon her, "I wasn't sure I should wear it…but my sister insisted." Slowly she unbuttoned the coat and shrugged it off.

"Oh my god!" Sophie's mouth was open, "is that the dress I gave you."

"That's the one," Juliette twirled around and as she did the long slit revealed a section of glossy thigh. A few passing men slowed down, ogling at her impressive cleavage, enhanced by the tight-fitting bodice.

Sophie whistled, "it looks a helluva lot better on *you* than it ever did on *me!*"

An unsure Juliette was biting her lip, "I've never worn anything so expensive and revealing and designer before."

"You look beautiful," Evelyn cleared her throat, "I'm sure everyone would agree on that."

There was a chorus of approval.

"You lot coming inside?" Melanie stuck her head around the door, "I need a dance partner."

They hurried into the room which was already packed full of students.

"I managed to grab us a couple of tables," Melanie shouted, "can someone help me with the drinks?"

Jon wandered off after her, leaving the ladies to organise the seats. Then Tasha, Melanie's girlfriend, was pulling them all onto the dance floor.

Juliette was bopping away, her eyes scanning the room, she couldn't see him anywhere. She glanced at her watch, wondering where he was, then she noticed Sophie grinning at her crazily and felt a slight tap on her shoulder. Of course he was behind her, looking so handsome it made her stomach flip over.

"Ben!" She threw herself against him, wrapping her arms around his neck, "How is your sister?"

"She's fine, steadily recovering. She told me to get outta there, in fact she was adamant I should be with you."

They stared into each other's eyes.

It was Juliette who reluctantly broke the spell, "shall we go get a drink?"

"In a minute," he replied huskily, "that dress you're wearing Juliette – what are you trying to do to me?"

"This old thing?" Juliette batted her lashes in a teasing manner.

"You look gorgeous," he replied, his hand running up her thigh, "what are you wearing underneath?"

"Later," she whispered into his ear, her hand sliding over his firm buttocks, "I might show you."

* * *

"Have a great night," Flora called from the car, "are you sure I can't pick you up?"

"We'll be late Mum," Will replied, "don't worry about us, we'll find our way home somehow."

Flora shook her head, smiling at her carefree son as he sauntered away, tugging his enamoured girlfriend with him.

"Will they be okay with Esme in their room for the night?" Hema fretted.

"Of course they will," Will replied with a shrug, "we're only down the hallway anyway."

"I better not drink too much then," Hema said.

"Enjoy yourself," Will stopped, pulling her to face him, "I'll take it easy. I'll get up. I'll look after her."

"Will," Hema touched his face, "I..."

They were interrupted by the sound of harsh laughter.

Will turned to peer through the darkness, his heart sank as he recognised Hema's cousin standing alone in the smoking shelter. The same cousin who had threatened them months ago, purely for being together, for being in love.

"You two skanks still together then?" He snarled, plodding heavy footed towards them, "I thought you might have got bored by now," he growled at Will, then looked towards Hema, "and I thought you might have come to your senses, you stupid girl."

"Go away," Will replied wearily, "just go away and leave us alone." He was happy, it was Christmas and he was so sick of her family's bullshit and strife. He didn't want to fight; not tonight, not with anyone.

"Oh yeah? Make me then," he prodded a finger at Will's chest. Automatically Will pushed him back.

"Stop it!" Hema got in between them.

"You stop it Hema, come back to your family. We love you. He doesn't know the meaning of the word," he spat on the ground in front of Will.

That was the last straw: Hema saw red.

"How dare you!" She shouted, "you don't know what real love is. You don't know how kind and loving Will is; how good he is to me and Esme. I love him with all my heart, but I hate you Akesh, I hate your spite and malice, your envy and your cruelty and your blinkered religion that teaches you nothing but prejudice and hate. I hate you." She raised her fist, "I disown you, I disown *you.*" Tears were pouring down her cheeks. Her cousin stared, open mouthed at her, but Will edged closer to her, taking her hand in his.

"Leave us alone. We don't ever want to see you again." This time Will spoke, clearly and forcefully.

Akesh blinked twice, "you haven't heard the last of this," he murmured quietly, before turning and walking away.

"Are you okay?" Will asked, gently taking her face in his hands.

Hema brushed away her tears, "that told him huh?"

Will kissed her forehead, "do you wanna go home?"

"No!" Hema was adamant, "I'm okay Will, really I am."

This time it was her tugging him towards the entrance where a brass plaque assured them 'welcome to Chattlesbury University; where learning enables us to be free.'

* * *

An hour later the party was well under way. Hema and Will were on the dance floor bopping to Taylor Swift and Ed Sheeran's funky 'End Game.' Sophie was chattering away to Evelyn and Jacob. Ann and Jon were telling Melanie and

Tasha all about their adoption journey and Ben was trying to talk Juliette into going over to say hi to the English lecturers who had their very own table; right by the bar.

"They won't like me," Juliette mumbled, feeling embarrassed, "I'm not clever like them."

"What are you *on* about?" Ben pushed a hand through his hair, "you're one of my hardest working, most talented students."

Juliette laughed at his wink, "I mean...they're all so intellectual, I bet they talk about French subtitled films and discuss Russian politics. What would I have in common with them Ben? You've said yourself that I'm so girly."

"That's what's nice about you," Ben shook his head, "you're like a breath of fresh air. There's no one like you in my life Juliette: no one. And nobody in the English department talks about Russian politics, Tolstoy maybe; you remind me of Anna Karenina actually. Now come on."

"Okay, If I must," Juliette rolled her eyes like a belligerent teenager "and stop dropping references to literary works I have never heard of."

Dr Rivers laughed, "I'll read it to you in my bed Juliette."

"Really?" An unconvinced Juliette gave him a sardonic smirk.

There were about eight of them sitting around two pushed together tables. Wilomena Smythe, looking lovely in a crushed velvet burgundy dress, was chatting to the course leader Tarquin Haverstock.

"Hello," Wilomena looked up, smiling at Juliette, "sit down," she patted the empty chair to the left of her, "we were just discussing holiday destinations in the UK. Tarquin here has never been to Weymouth – can you believe that Juliette?"

"I spent my summer holiday there this year," Juliette exclaimed. Tarquin was all ears and behind his back Ben was grinning and mouthing the word "see."

Juliette had such a lovely time chatting to Ben's friends, she didn't realise that she had been sitting with them for over an hour, the time had flown so fast. She'd learnt that Wilomena and Malcolm Pickett, the Creative Writing lecturer, were an item. This news surprised her as she'd heard about his reputation from Tasha; apparently he was a little too popular with the younger female students. Juliette had wrinkled her nose in distaste as he leered over her, complimenting her on her dress. Then Ben had intervened and he had thankfully backed away.

Ben had introduced her to an older lecturer called Samuel Brown. He was a softly spoken man with impeccable manners who specialised in Film Studies.

"I'm taking a film studies module next semester," Juliette gushed, "Hollywood and the American West?"

"An excellent choice," Dr Brown had replied, "I think you will enjoy it Juliette. It's a very popular module."

"What films do you analyse?" Juliette asked with interest, sipping her wine.

"My Darling Clementine, Stagecoach, The Searchers, High Plains Drifter?"

"Clint Eastwood," Juliette nodded, "is my dad's favourite actor. He has an impressive collection of his western films."

"Then I recommend you watch some over the Christmas break, it will give you a head start."

"I will," Juliette replied, her voice full of enthusiasm. She noticed Ben had moved seats and was talking to Helena Mulberry who was resting her hand on his arm and leaning a little too close for Juliette's liking. She looked away and was just contemplating re-joining her friends, when Ben beckoned her over.

"You've met Helena?" He queried.

"Yes, I was in her class last year," Juliette smiled at her.

"Ben," Helena said, "be a darling and get your friend and me a drink."

Juliette bristled, her eyes darting to Ben, whose mouth had set in a firm line.

"Juliette's my girlfriend," he replied.

Helena draped an arm over his shoulder, "since when?"

"A while now," Juliette was inwardly seething at the other ladies frosty manner.

"Good luck with that," Helena turned away from them both to lean across the bar.

Ben pulled her away, "sorry," he mouthed, "wine always makes her confrontational."

"I hadn't noticed," Juliette's sarcasm quietened Ben and the other lecturers.

"She's not been well," Ben explained.

"She's a drunk," Wilomena said quietly.

"Oh. I'm sorry to hear that," Juliette felt sympathy rise within her, "how does she cope working as a lecturer?"

"She doesn't," Brian Hodges shook his head, "she's had a lot of time off sick, been through capability, tense meetings with the Dean, observations, that kind of shit."

"Talking of our leader," Wilomena cocked her head towards the doorway, where the Dean stood inspecting the room.

"He seems okay?" Juliette ventured.

"He's had his share of problems," Wilomena divulged, "his wife accrued an enormous amount of debt on credit cards and then ran off with his neighbour apparently. Poor man's been obsessed with work ever since."

"Eye up," Brian Hodges took a swig from his beer bottle, "looks like we've been spotted."

"Ah, the English department," the Dean glanced over them all, "and a staff member I don't recognise?"

"I'm a student," Juliette replied, trying to tug her hand away from Bens, who refused to let her go.

"Oh yes of course," the Dean smiled stiffly at Ben, "enjoy your evening."

He walked away with a slight limp, Juliette sighed with relief.

"You are so stubborn," she chastised Ben, "are you determined to compromise your career?"

"Some things are more important," he replied, stroking her cheek.

"She's on her way back," Brian muttered.

Juliette turned around to see Helena Mulberry staggering towards Ben. She tried to grab hold of him but missed and fell into the table, knocking glasses all over the floor. Wilomena and Brian helped her to her feet.

"I'm going back to my friends," Juliette whispered in Ben's ear.

"Dance with me," Ben replied. The music had slowed right down and there appeared to be a lot of smooching going on.

Juliette followed him onto the dancefloor. Beams of light shone over the oak veneer and balloons floated around, creating a dreamy, romantic scenario. She noticed Evelyn in Jacob's arms and an inebriated Hema gazing dreamily up at Will. Then Ben's arms were pulling her close and she rested her cheek against his chest, listening to the dull thud of his heartbeat.

* * *

191

"Esme is fast asleep," Hema mumbled against Will's chest, "your mum text me five minutes ago."

"Good," Will replied, blowing into her hair, "I've been thinking Hema."

"Uh-oh," came Hema's cheeky reply, "did it hurt?"

"Ha ha, you're so funny," Will chucked her underneath the chin, "seriously, I thought we could go see your parents tomorrow, take Esme."

"Really?" Hema pulled away slightly, "I mean yes, I'd love to see them."

"I know you would and it's important for Esme to know her other grand-parents too, so let's do it, let's make more of an effort with them."

"We need to tell them about Akesh too Will. It's starting to worry me, all this hatred towards us."

"Your mum and dad are cool though aren't they? Maybe they could talk to him, help sort it out."

"Maybe," Hema rested against him, "I'm so happy Will. You and Esme, you're my life, you're my world."

"Mine too." Will kissed her forehead and they revolved slowly, listening to the lyrics of the song that was playing. Balloons floated lazily around them, the DJ was speaking softly into the microphone about the magic of Christmas and peace and love. Then Will saw Akesh and his eyes widened in fright. He was advancing on them, pushing his way through the crowds. His face was con-torted in anger, but it was his eyes that scared him the most. They seemed to glower with rage and hatred and they were totally focused on his girlfriend.

Will stepped in front of Hema, pulling her behind him, just before he saw a flashing of silver in Akesh's right hand. Then he felt a cold pressure on his stomach and his legs were buckling and Hema was screaming over and over. He fell on his back, his hand reaching down. It was covered in blood and the shock made him shudder. Strangely he didn't feel pain just a cold numbness as his eyes flickered shut and glitter from an exploding balloon settled on his cheekbones.

Chapter Nineteen

The bar was in complete pandemonium. Students were running for the exit, pushing and falling in the stampede to escape.

"What the hell is going on?" Ann asked, staring around her in bewilderment.

Then she could hear Hema screaming and could see Juliette bent over a figure lying on the floor.

"Someone's been hurt Jon," she said with urgency, "I think it's Will."

Jon jumped to his feet and ran to the scene. It was Will, he was lying on his back, his eyes closed, and Juliette had her hands on his stomach. Jon could see a knife sticking out of his abdomen and blood seeping through his white shirt.

"Check his pulse," he instructed Ben, as he quickly tugged off his jumper. Juliette moved back allowing Jon room to apply pressure around the knife wound.

"Someone call an ambulance," he yelled.

"They're on the way," a doorman replied, his arms out to hold a few grisly spectators at bay.

Ben lifted Will's head slightly so he could slip his jacket underneath his neck. Juliette looked down at her hands, swallowing back nausea, they were covered with blood, it was trickling from her fingers and Hema was still screaming.

"Stop!" Juliette shook her by the shoulders, "you need to stay calm."

"Talk to him Hema," Jon suggested, "keep him awake."

Hema stared down at Will with horror.

"Hema!" Jon urged, "he needs you."

Onto her knees she sank, "Will," she said gently, her face a picture of wretched dismay, "he can't hear me," she wailed.

"He can," Jon insisted, "keep him calm."

"Will," she began again, "you're going to be okay. The ambulance is on its way," she grasped his hand which felt cold, so cold, "I love you Will Bentley, I love you, I'm right here. Stay with me, look at me Will, look at me."

His eyes flickered open, his lips moved slightly, but no sound came out. Tears cascaded down Hema's cheeks as she moved closer to him, "Esme's waiting for you at home Will, please hang on, hang on darling."

It seemed a lot longer but ten minutes later paramedics arrived on the scene. Juliette held Hema in her arms as they worked on Will, lifting him onto a stretcher.

Evelyn, Sophie and Ann hung back on the edge of the dance floor, hugging each other as they cried.

"Is he going to be okay?" Hema shouted, "please...make him okay."

A tall, dark haired paramedic rose to his feet, "we need to get him to the hospital as soon as possible. Are you a relative?"

"I...I'm his partner, can I come in the ambulance?"

"Of course," the paramedics motioned for her to follow them.

"But...but his parents," Hema looked around wide eyed, "I need to tell Flora!"

"We'll go," Juliette assured her, "just be with Will."

Hema ran after them, leaving a stricken Juliette searching frantically on her phone for her address contacts, "where is it?" She cried.

Ben took the phone off her and calmly flicked through her contacts, "got it." He grabbed her hand, making for the exit, while the others waited behind for the police.

Outside the university, the ambulance had gone but there was still a large number of students hanging around looking shocked. The press had got whiff of the story too and were snapping cameras and thrusting voice recorders into people's faces.

"Can you tell us what happened Sir?" They called to Ben.

"No." Ben strode past them flicking a switch which unlocked his car from an impressive distance.

"I can't believe this has happened?" Juliette said, slipping into the passenger seat, "and to Will, he's so lovely and popular! Why would anyone want to hurt him?"

"I heard Jon saying it was some relative of Hema's. He's been having hassle off them for some time. Family politics gone bad by the sounds of it."

Juliette was searching in her handbag for a tissue, "this is awful. Do you think he'll be okay?" She was wiping at her eyes which were full of tears, "poor little Esme."

"He's in good hands," Ben replied, as he typed Will's address into the sat-nav, "try not to worry." Ben pulled sharply away and sped through the city out into the suburbs.

"There it is; number seventy-two," Juliette pointed to a large detached house surrounded by a high privet hedge and an iron gate. Ben swerved across the road, depositing his vehicle half on the kerb.

"What shall I say?" Juliette waited for Ben to walk round to her.

He grasped her hand, "just explain what happened. Do you want me to talk to them?"

"No. It's okay, I think it will be better coming from me."

Ben gave her hand a gentle squeeze and pulled open the gate.

They both stopped at the sound of laughter. It was coming from inside the house. A man and a woman's, loud and playful; happy. Juliette swallowed, walked up the path and quickly rang the bell, then rang it again and rang it for a third time. She heard the sound of a chain being pulled across, the door creaking open and a man's face appearing in the dim light. It must be Mr Bentley she thought as she surveyed him. His mouth was curved into a smile, his hair was sticking up and he was wearing stripy pyjamas.

"Yes," he said, looking from her to Ben with a puzzled expression.

Juliette stood rooted to the spot, her brain was refusing to send a message to her mouth, no words came out.

Max Bentley frowned, "Are you religious callers or sales people?"

Still Juliette remained silent.

"Why are you knocking doors at this time of night?" He demanded, sounding angry now.

Ben stepped forward, "Mr Bentley…"

"How do you know my name? Who are you?"

"Who is it darling?" Juliette was relieved to hear Flora's voice. She appeared behind Max, carrying a wide awake, smiling Esme. Juliette felt her stomach lurch and thought of Will lying on the floor covered in blood.

"Is that?" Flora squinted in the darkness, "Marie's sister?"

"Yes," Juliette's voice sounded high pitched.

There was a moment of silence as the two women stared at each other.

"What is it? What's wrong?" Flora's face had drained of colour.

"Who are these people Flora?" Max snapped.

"They're friends of Will's from university," Flora stated flatly.

"Oh." Max replied looking tense, "Will's not here, he's at a party…"

"What's happened?" Flora interjected.

"It's Will," Juliette blurted, "oh God I'm so sorry he's hurt, he's been stabbed, he's …" She stopped at the sight of the tears sliding down Flora's face.

"No!" Flora gasped, "not my son, not my Will."

"He's been taken to hospital," the words felt like they were bombs dropping from Juliette's mouth, "Hema's with him."

"Hema." Max's face darkened like a thundercloud.

"Here." Flora bundled Esme into her husband's arms, slipped on her shoes and then pushed past Juliette and ran down the path and onto the street, ignoring Juliette's calls for her to wait and Max bellowing her name.

"Mr Bentley stay here with the baby and we'll go and find Flora and take her to the hospital," Ben had his hands on the shoulders of a very shocked Max Bentley.

Max nodded, "will you call me as soon as you get there?"

"Of course," Juliette replied softly, "are you going to be okay on your own?"

"Yes," he said distractedly, "Esme is due a bottle, I need to heat one up for her and then I'll change her, I…"

"We have to go now," Juliette said, "we need to find Flora."

They backed away.

"Wait." Max's voice was full of emotion and close to cracking, "Will's okay isn't he? He's not going to …?"

Juliette glanced at Ben, swallowing back a lump of emotion.

"Your son is a fighter Mr Bentley," she replied, grabbing hold of his hand, "I'll call you."

Then Ben was pulling her away and they were both running to the car.

"She can't have gone far," Ben said, as he zoomed down the quiet, residential street, churning up dust and dead leaves, "left or right?"

"Right," Juliette decided, "that takes you to the main road into the city."

Juliette eyes were scouring both sides of the street. They slowed down as they spotted a figure in the distance, it was a late night dog walker.

Juliette wound down her window, "excuse me," she called, "have you seen a lady on her own wearing a dressing gown?"

The man huffed, pulling his dog to heel, "I saw her alright. She was crying like a banshee, scared me stiff she did."

"What direction did she go?"

"Over there," the man pointed towards the subway, "is she deranged? Shall I call the police?"

"No!" Juliette shouted, "she's had some distressing news, she's no danger to anyone."

"Alright lady keep your hair on," the man grumbled.

Juliette slid up the window, "hurry please Ben. That subway is dangerous, there's druggies and all sorts hang around there."

Ben cursed as the lights turned to red and a line of cars sped in front of them.

"Oh God Ben I can see her, she's already there," Juliette swung open the door, "I'll go get her, meet us at the other side of the island." Before Ben could protest Juliette was running after Flora, yelling her name, just as she disappeared into the tunnel of the subway.

Juliette slowed as a few minutes later she followed Flora down the ramp. Her stomach was throbbing with an acute attack of stitch and she was puffing and panting with the exertion of running.

"Flora!" She yelled, as she spotted her near the end of the tunnel.

The figure in front of her stopped and a bewildered Flora turned around to stare as Juliette finally caught up with her.

"Oh thank God," Juliette bent over, resting her hands on her knees as she caught her breath, "We're going to take you to the hospital Flora, Ben's car is just over there."

"Will needs me," Flora sounded bewildered, "I have to be there for him."

Juliette put her arms around her shoulder, "you will. We'll get you there I promise. Come on now."

They walked quickly through the centre of the subway and up a set of concrete stairs, passing a spaced out man slumped against a urine stained wall.

"Keep going," Juliette said, looking straight ahead. Inwardly she was cringing at the thought of sweet, naïve, gentle Flora being alone underneath here.

"Just look at me," Flora declared, pulling at her floral dressing gown, "I'm covered in baby sick. Esme drank too much again, she's a guzzler; just like her daddy was."

The man on the floor had woken from his stupor and was shouting at them, "got any spare change ladies?"

Juliette pulled Flora to the top of the steps. They were out on the other side of the ring road now, she was so relieved to see Ben she could have kissed him.

"Are you alright?" His voice was tinged with concern.

Juliette nodded and helped Flora into the back of the car, "I think she's in shock," she whispered.

"We'll be there soon," he promised.

The drive to the hospital was only five minutes from where they were, but never-the-less they managed to get stuck behind a bus and then delayed by a broken down bin lorry whose rotten cargo had spilt all over the road.

"Come on," Ben thumped the steering wheel in frustration.

A siren blaring police car arrived on the scene and a police man waved them around the debris.

Finally Ben could put his foot down on the accelerator and for the first time that night the road ahead was clear; a straight line which took them directly to Ambleside Accident and Emergency.

Ben swerved outside the entrance like something from a seventies cops and robbers series.

Flora was out of the car running to the sliding doors with Juliette in close pursuit.

"Will," she shouted, "I'm here." They both fell into a packed room. No one seemed concerned with Flora's night attire or Juliette's wide-eyed anxiety. They stepped around a drunken youth who was grappling with a porter and a toddler who was playing on the floor with a plastic train.

A buxom nurse bustled over towards them and began chastising the inebriated man.

"Behave yourself," she warned, "there are sick people here. If you don't want our help I suggest you leave."

"I'm injured," the man protested, arms flailing, "look at me."

Juliette glanced at him, his face was a sorry state indeed, blood was seeping from two large gashes above his eye.

"You'll have to wait your turn," the nurse said frostily, "and anymore gip and you're out. We don't accept any verbal or physical aggression towards our staff." The injured man slumped down on a seat, crossing his arms over his chest like a truculent child.

"Excuse me," Juliette stepped forward and explained briefly what had happened to Will.

The nurse consulted her ream of notes, "he's in surgery," she said, her tone a little softer, "are you family?"

"I'm his mum," Flora replied, wiping her wet cheeks.

"There's a waiting room over there," the nurse pointed to a door opposite.

Flora and Juliette made their way over. They could hear the sound of soft crying emanating from the room.

"It's Hema," Flora said, "she must be beside herself."

When Hema saw them she jumped to her feet with a strangled sob and hugged Flora tight.

"Is he okay?" Flora held her face in her hands, "tell me he's okay Hema."

"I don't know," Hema shook her head, "they took him straight into surgery, I haven't heard a thing since."

Flora nodded and perched on a nearby chair, "what happened?" Her voice was trembling with emotion.

Hema swallowed, "it was my cousin Akesh, he attacked Will. It's my family again Flora, this is my fault, it's all my fault."

"No, no," Flora soothed, taking her in her arms again.

"He wouldn't be here if it wasn't for me. I should have done what my family wanted. I've been selfish and now Will he's...he's going to..."

"Don't you dare," Flora's voice shook, "Will is going to be okay. I'm going to pray Hema, God will help him sweetheart, have faith."

Hema didn't look convinced but she let Flora cover her hands and sat quietly as Flora recited the Lord's prayer and the rain pattered gently on the misted up window pane.

* * *

Will's body felt incredibly heavy and cold: he was so cold. His limbs ached, even his eyelids hurt and for some reason he couldn't open them, he couldn't move his limbs; not even his fingers and toes. But he could hear faint voices, they seemed to be coming from above and to the left side of him. He was so tired, he just wanted to sleep and there was a warm light directly in front of him. It grew steadily brighter, warming his bones, relieving his pain, inviting him in and he wanted to go so desperately. He wanted to be free of the pain and the darkness. He reached out in his mind, 'let me go' he said to everyone, 'I can't fight anymore' but suddenly there was a loud clap and in the light he could see figures. Were they angels? He wondered, were they real? Or was he dreaming? No it was his mum. Flora was dressed in black, she was carrying a white rose, she wasn't wearing her cross – why wasn't she wearing her gold cross?

"Will, Will," she whispered, "come back," she held out her hand, "come back darling. I would lie down and die for you Will, I would die for you, I would die." Then she was revolving, spinning around so fast that she disappeared and Hema stood there holding Esme. They were both crying, so many tears cascading all over the floor like a lake, then they slipped under the water and disappeared and Max stood there, both fists raised. He was shouting, his face and neck were bright red, the veins in his arms were protruding with the exertion, "fight Will Bentley fight. Don't you dare leave us Will. I love you Will. Don't you go. Don't you go."

"Fight!" The lips left Will's mouth. Boom! The light imploded. Will sucked in a huge lungful of air. His fingers moved, his toes tingled. His eyelids snapped open and a lady with golden hair and caramel coloured eyes was bending right over him, staring at him, smiling, "he's back."

Chapter Twenty

"Mrs Bentley," somebody was shaking Flora from a beautiful dream of light and love and Will. Her eyelids flickered open.

"He's going to be okay," Doctor Munroe was smiling at her, "your son is going to be okay." Flora gripped the arm rest, her legs wobbled slightly and her head spun. Thankfully she was sitting down; or she may have tumbled over.

"Thank you God," she mumbled, "thank you Doctor."

Juliette rubbed the sleep from her eyes and looked across at Flora and the doctor as they talked.

"Ben," she whispered, shaking the slumped form next to her, "Will's okay."

"Fantastic," Ben replied, sitting up, "Christ, what time is it?"

"Three in the morning. Where's Hema?"

Ben shrugged, "Let's go find her. Tell her the good news."

Juliette could hear the doctor explaining to Flora that Will had had a blood transfusion and his stomach stitched. He was weak and in pain, but other than that he was going to be okay.

"Can I see him?" Flora asked, giddy with relief.

"Just for a short while," the doctor replied with a kind smile, "he does need complete rest."

Flora nodded and looked around, "oh Hema's gone to ring Max. I need to find her..." she trailed off.

"We'll go," Juliette assured her, enveloping her in a warm, soft hug, "be with your son Flora."

They found Hema outside puffing on a cigarette. "I haven't had one of these since I was fourteen. I guess I needed it huh?" Her eyes were red and puffy, Juliette noticed her hands were shaking. She hastily told Hema the good news.

"He's going to be okay?" Hema's voice trembled with incredulity.

"Yes," Juliette smiled, "and if you're quick they'll let you see him."

Hema threw the half smoked cigarette on the floor and ran back into the hospital.

Juliette sagged against Ben, "I'm exhausted."

"Let's get you home," Ben steered her towards his car.

Wearily she slumped onto the passenger seat, "I need to send a few texts. People will be worried." She fired off messages to Sophie, Ann and Evelyn then relaxed back as they whizzed along the deserted streets. Five minutes later Juliette was fast asleep.

* * *

The following day Will was up and walking slowly about. A kind nurse who was checking his temperature and blood pressure told him that he would probably be allowed home tomorrow. Will was relieved, he'd hardly slept since he woke in the early hours, it was so noisy in here and the heat was unbearable. Then Doctor Munroe and a group of student doctors appeared on their rounds and Will thanked her for saving him.

"No need for thanks," she said crisply, "you were lucky Will – you're young and fit and the knife wound wasn't too deep, luckily it missed your organs."

Will picked at his tray of food and watched the clock tick slowly round until it was the afternoon and visiting time.

Hema came rushing through the door clutching car magazines and his favourite: Dime bars.

"Hello," she squeaked, hugging him gently.

Will kissed her lips and watched as Flora entered followed by a stricken looking Max.

"Are you okay son?" He was by the side of Will, clasping his hand.

"Sore," Will winced as he tried to pull himself up.

"Let me," Flora gently leant him forward, plumping the pillows behind him.

"How's Esme?" Will asked, coughing slightly.

"She's fine," Hema replied, "she's with Brenda your mum's friend."

Will nodded and sank back.

"I made you a video of her this morning when she was having her bath. Look." Hema perched on the edge of the bed and showed Will her phone. He watched an adorable Esme kicking her legs in a tub of frothy water, she was gurgling and smiling. Then a nurse came in and berated Hema for sitting on the bed and she switched the footage off.

There was an awkward silence and then they all spoke at once.

"Love shall we leave Hema with Will for a bit," Flora suggested brightly.

"Okay," Max mumbled, allowing himself to be ushered out of the room.

"So you can leave tomorrow?" Hema said, "that's great news."

"I'll be glad to go home," Will admitted, "I miss Esme."

"She misses you too Will," Hema gushed.

There was another silence, beep, beep went the machine next to Will's bed.

"My mum and dad send their love," Hema bit her lip and tears glistened in her eyes, "Dad's disowned his brother and his family."

Will sighed, "they've caught him then?"

"They didn't need to," Hema answered, "he walked into the nearest police station and admitted to everything. He's going to go down Will... for attempted murder."

"Why doesn't that make me feel better," Will said glumly.

Hema grasped his hand, "we are okay aren't we Will?"

Will lifted his head to gaze at her, "why wouldn't we be?"

Hema looked down at the floor, "I'm ashamed Will. I'm ashamed of my family. You must hate them."

"No," wearily Will shook his head, "and I don't blame you Hema. This isn't your fault."

"I don't deserve you," Hema cried, "I'm so sorry Will. I'm so sorry you were hurt because of me."

She leant towards him and he lifted his arms around her, "I love you Will Bentley. You're my hero."

* * *

"Is this the last one?" A burly removal man with a shock of black curls picked up the sellotaped box, "family photo's eh?" He read Sophie's scribble, "can't forget them now can we?"

Sophie stared around at the empty house, which looked huger than ever now it was devoid of furniture.

"That's the last one," she replied, her voice a tremulous echo.

The removal man backed away, he was used to tears off his clients but this one seemed more melancholy than usual, he wondered about the reason for her leaving but then reminded himself not to get involved. It was important in his line of work to stay professional. Get the job home, earn himself a generous tip and then get off home to the wifey.

"I'll leave you alone for a bit," he said, clearing his throat, "don't be too long mind lady, we need to get this all unpacked at t'other end."

"I won't," Sophie sniffed, "I just need a minute."

Sophie stood in the centre of the dining room. In her mind she could hear and see the memories; the twins opening their presents on Christmas day underneath a towering tree. The dogs chasing them around in their pyjamas. Ryan posing in his new football kit; kissing her underneath mistletoe. So much laughter and happiness, so many wonderful memories.

Then came the bad one's – the arguments, the deceit and lies, the sham that had become her marriage. Sophie squared her shoulders; this was a fresh start for her and she wasn't going to be maudlin, she was going to be positive. So she picked up her handbag, looking round once more before walking out with a new determination to be happy and to make the remainder of her life a success.

Once outside she was dismayed but not surprised to see Ryan. He had been emailing her a lot over the last week; asking her to change her mind and to forgive him. This time he'd brought her mum with him for back-up and support no doubt. Sophie felt a flicker of annoyance that Yvonne was still siding with her unfaithful husband.

"Why are you here?" She asked with a sigh.

"That's it then?" Ryan was staggering across the footpath and as Sophie neared him she could smell whisky. His clothes were crumpled too, he looked a sorry state and so different from the famous last season's Chattlesbury striker. *No longer the flavour of the month* Sophie thought.

"It's all over then, twenty years of marriage just thrown away like that?"

"We were married eleven years Ryan," she replied, *typical that he couldn't even get that right.* "And you threw it away Ryan, none of this is my fault."

Now Yvonne was out of the car, "why don't you try to forgive him darling, otherwise it will eat away at you."

"I have forgiven him," Sophie replied brightly, "now the house is sold, I finally feel I'm able to move on."

"Pah," Yvonne flicked her wrist, "what magazine did you get that line from? You won't manage on your own Sophie, you and me are very similar. We both need men in our lives to take care of us. You'll never cope alone!"

Sophie stared at her mother, "that's where you're wrong," her voice was icy cold, "I've never been like you; I'm like my Dad."

Yvonne Fletcher paled, "your dad?" She let out a sharp laugh, "was a feckless gambler. He deserted you remember?"

Sophie winced, "maybe...but I know that he loved me with all his heart. It's you I'm not so sure of." She pointed a finger at her mum.

"What's happened to you Soph?" Ryan spluttered, "you used to be so happy and carefree until you went to university. That bloody place has warped your mind."

"Don't be stupid Ryan, I hadn't been happy for a long time, before I started at university."

"Oh yeah?" Ryan sneered, "those buddies of yours are the stupid ones. The broad with the red hair who's so desperate she shags a lecturer, then there's the mouthy one in the wheelchair – no wonder you've gone funny, it's mixing with them...those feminists."

Yvonne clapped along with agreement.

"And that lad?" Ryan continued, warming to his theme, "what kind of nonce hangs around with a bunch of old, dried up women."

"Don't you dare mention Will. You leave him alone," Sophie hissed.

"Why, hit a nerve have I?" Ryan turned to look triumphantly at Yvonne, "see, she's the one who's been unfaithful."

Sophie surged forward, "he nearly died protecting his partner, you silly, silly man. Don't you dare run him down again, he's worth ten of you."

Ryan chose to ignore that remark and held out his arms, "please come back to me Soph, give me another chance. This time I'll get it right I promise. We can renew our vows, we can go away, just me and you. Anything you want me to do, I'll do. We can work through this."

"No," Sophie replied with determination, "I don't want to. I'm sorry Ryan but I don't love you anymore. Our marriage is over." She walked past him, looking for the removal man.

Then she was grabbed by the arm and pulled around, "you'll regret this Sophie. You'll realise what a good catch I am and maybe then it will be too late for you."

"Too late *for you* and I doubt it," Sophie snapped, "go away Ryan, sober up and sort yourself out."

"You okay love?" The removal man tapped her lightly on the shoulder, "is he giving you grief?"

Ryan glared up at the other man, and then backed away as the man advanced towards him.

"I'm okay thank you," Sophie replied, "he's nobody."

With those parting succinct words she clambered into the high van and stared straight ahead while they drove away from Thistledown house, once home of the famous Ryan O'Neill, now in full ownership of the lovely Mr and Mrs Chan.

"Never did care for those big fancy footballers mansions," the removal man said with a laugh, "where to Madam?"

"The future." Not once did Sophie look back.

* * *

As usual Ann had left her Christmas shopping to the last minute and was now flapping like someone demented. This had accumulated in a weekend trip to the huge indoor shopping mall where she could blitz everyone on her list and at the same time purchase a new tree to replace their old shabby artificial one of ten years.

"I don't know why we can't have a real one," Jon grumbled, as he reversed into a prime disabled space.

"We had one once can't you remember?" Ann shook her head in exasperation, "the cat pounced on the angel and almost tipped the whole thing over. It made you sneeze and me miserable because of the pine needles it kept shedding. Anyway, an artificial one is better for the environment."

"Fair enough," Jon said, looking mollified with Ann's explanation, "so where to first?"

Ann glanced down at her list, which was longer than last years, "I think the football shop."

It was busy in the main precinct. Jon weaved Ann around the many shoppers, pausing to listen to a group of hat and scarf toting carol singers warbling 'Silent Night'. Nearby, a Santa's grotto had been erected, complete with tinsel, flashing lights and a paper maiche reindeer. There was also an array of takeaway food stores selling hot pork baps, jacket potatoes and hot dogs. It was all very festive and cheerful. They paused in front of a giant map of the precinct, looking for the football merchandise store.

"Ah," Jon hummed, "there it is," he pointed straight ahead where a group of gangly youths hung about.

The shop was packed; a long line of people waited to be served and excited children ran about whooping and laughing.

"How about this?" Jon picked up a Chattlesbury FC mascot teddy.

"No Jon!" Ann said, "Samuel's twelve, not two."

"Yes, but his girlfriend might like it."

"Damn, I knew I'd missed someone off my list," Ann looked at the teddy, "it's kinda cute, put it in the basket."

Jon lobbed it in and the search resumed for a suitable present for Sam.

"I think this," Ann ran her hand over a furry fleece, "it's the new seasons."

"Perfect," Jon agreed. In the basket it went.

"We have got to get him one of these!" Jon threw a case ball high into the air, it landed on his head and then into his hands.

"Go on then," Ann replied with an eye roll.

A pen and notebook and a calendar was added to the pile and half an hour later they were finished and at the till with their purchases.

The rest of the morning was spent buying presents for family and friends, which included the university gang. Ann decided on perfume for Juliette, Evelyn and Tasha, and an inspirational book on fulfilling your potential for Sophie.

"What about Will?" Jon asked.

"You decide," Ann replied.

After a jaunt around the bottom floor of the mall, Jon chose a voucher for a music and film store and a selection of around the world beers.

"Poor guy deserves to be spoilt," he said, "I hope he's taking it easy."

They retraced their steps back to where they had come in. The car park was much busier now.

"Crikey," Ann exclaimed, "there must be thousands here."

Her breath curled out in front of her, it was chilly, a hard frost clung to the ground and grey clouds rolled ominously above them.

"I've heard off Jules that Will's okay, no lasting serious damage, apart from a scar, which should fade over time."

"He's a brave lad," Jon said blowing his hands, "there's not many who would stand up to others the way Will does."

"I agree," Ann replied, "so why don't we make a detour on the way home. Let's go see him, wish him a merry Christmas."

* * *

Ann was surprised to see Will up and about, mixing bottles of formula for Esme.

"Hello," he said brightly, "this is a nice surprise, fancy a cuppa?"

He made them cups of steaming, bitter coffee and led them through into the lounge that was festooned with hanging Christmas decorations.

"How are you?" Ann asked, wheeling herself around a magazine rack.

"Not too bad considering," he replied, with a lopsided grin, "can't keep me down for long."

"We've been worried and it hasn't been the same without you at uni."

"Did I miss much?" Will asked sipping his drink.

"No," Ann replied with a smile, "just tying up loose ends really; giving in essays, preparing for semester two."

"Did you manage to finish the journalism project?"

"Yes," Ann replied with enthusiasm, "it looks pretty amazing."

"Hopefully we'll get an A," Will replied with a cheeky wink.

Ann looked around, "it's so quiet Will, where's the baby?"

"Hema took her a walk with Mum, they should be home anytime now."

As if on cue the doorbell rang and Will went to let them in. Flora wandered into the living room unwrapping a long scarf from around her neck.

"Hello," she exclaimed, "it's lovely to see you." She perched on the sofa and began chatting to Ann.

Will closed the front door and lifted Esme from her pram. Hema stood on tiptoe to peck his cheek, "were you okay?" He asked.

"Of course," Hema replied, "we only walked to the park and back. It's so cold out there…"

"I mean did you see anyone, was there any trouble?" Will's face looked strained as he uttered the words.

"No Will," gently Hema touched his arm, "we didn't see anybody. Please don't worry, he's in custody, he can't hurt us anymore."

"It's the rest of your family I'm worried about," Will muttered.

Hema gasped, "you can't think my mum and dad would deliberately hurt me or agree with what he did?"

Will shrugged, "how do I know?"

"They are disgusted and horrified," Hema said firmly, "please Will they want to come and see you."

Will shook his head, "I'm not ready. Hema I think it would be wiser for them to stay away. I feel so bloody angry, I don't think I can make small talk with your family."

"This isn't their fault," Hema implored, "I know my parents have been a bit antsy in the past, but I really think they're starting to like you Will."

"A bit," Will snapped, "your parents have been a complete nightmare. Have you forgotten how they ostracised and abandoned you Hema? What kind of people do that?"

"It's their culture," Hema shrieked.

"Stop!" It was Flora, poking her head around the door, "Will you have guests."

"Who is it?" Hema demanded.

"Ann from uni and her husband."

"Oh that's okay then," Hema said with a sarcastic twang, "sorry but I don't feel like entertaining today," off she flounced up the stairs.

Will rubbed his temple, his head hurt as well as his abdomen. He was suddenly overcome with tiredness and wanted nothing more than to lie down in a dark room.

"Are you okay love?" Flora touched his arm, "she feels guilty Will."

"I know."

"We're going to go," Ann and Jon appeared in the hall looking awkward, "I've left a present underneath your tree, please take care of yourself."

"Thanks," Will bent to kiss her cheek, "and cheers for coming over."

"Merry Christmas," Ann blew a kiss at Esme who was still fast asleep in his arms.

Flora hugged them both and then stood with Will watching as they left in their car.

"Mum, can you watch Esme for an hour, I need to sort this out."

Flora nodded, "go on darling."

Will bounded up the stairs and into their bedroom. It was dark, silver moonlight shone through the window, shining on the figure curled up on the bed. Her shoulders were shaking gently as she wept.

"Hema," he said, rolling next to her, "don't shut me out."

She turned to snuggle against his chest, "I'm sorry Will. I'm so sorry."

The tears streamed down her face as she reached out her hand to touch his stubble lined face.

"I thought I'd lost you. Will I couldn't carry on if you had d…" she trailed off.

"I'm alive," Will whispered against her hot forehead, "and I'm not going anywhere."

Chapter Twenty-One

The music swooned around the room, Juliette lifted her arms and swayed her hips in time with the tempo. She knew she was tipsy, she knew Ben was watching but she really didn't care.

"Dance with me," she said softly, holding out her hand.

"I'm enjoying the floor show," he said, sinking further into his leather sofa.

"You are?" Juliette teased.

"I am," he said with a laugh, "the dancers hot: very hot."

Juliette lifted the hem of her top, pulling it slowly over her head, "now will you dance with me?" Her sultry whisper had Ben on his feet and pulling her into his arms. His lips found hers and they were kissing passionately.

"Stay with me tonight," Ben said huskily against her mouth.

"I can't," she murmured, "it's Christmas Eve, I have to go home to Molly and Harry."

Ben nodded reluctantly, "I hate being away from you." Then, "when am I going to meet your children?"

"Soon." Juliette put a finger to his lips.

Ben let out a growl of frustration then lifted her into his arms.

"Put me down," she protested with a giggle.

"I thought your curfew was midnight Cinderella?"

"It is," Juliette glanced at her watch, "we have two hours left Dr Rivers – do you want to talk?"

"Later," he promised, kissing the tip of her nose.

Quickly he carried her up the stairs and deposited her on his vast bed.

"Ben!" Juliette gasped as he unbuttoned her jeans and pulled them down her thighs.

"I love you," he unclipped her bra and sucked her nipples into hard peaks.

"I love you too," Juliette wriggled underneath him, reaching for his belt.

He stopped her with his warm hand, "not yet." He moved his fingers down and Juliette grasped the pillow and cried out with pleasure as he touched her.

"So soon," he tutted after she'd opened her eyes, "really Juliette, you need to learn some self-control."

Perspiration glistened on Juliette's forehead and above her upper lip. She licked it away, "let's see how much self-control you possess Doctor Rivers."

Quickly she rolled onto her knees, then straddled him either side, "lie still," she instructed. Ben gazed up at her, a small smile lifting his mouth. The breath caught in her throat; he was so handsome and sexy and he was all hers.

"I love you so much," she whispered, easing herself onto him.

Ben gritted his teeth and grasped her hips.

"Oh yes," she moved above him; fast then slow, teasing him with her naked body.

"Fuck," Ben groaned, thrusting inside her faster. He called her name and tensed, just as Juliette's world exploded and the stars fell around her.

She lay pressed tight against his chest. His one arm was wrapped around her shoulders and the other arm rested possessively over her bare thigh. Juliette stared up at the ceiling, watching the shadows dance across the ceiling.

"What are you thinking about?" Ben asked, softly caressing her leg.

"How happy I am," she replied, smiling against his dark chest hair, "how totally loved up I feel when I'm with you."

Ben kissed the top of her head, "what will you do tomorrow?"

Juliette sighed, "the usual crazy Christmas morning with two young children, followed by cooking dinner, washing up, inserting batteries into toys, playing, watching family films," she paused, "oh and thinking about you."

"I'll miss you," he replied quietly.

"Are you still having your sister here?"

"Yep. I'm cooking everything from scratch too. Turkey with all the trimmings and a homemade trifle."

"I'm impressed," Juliette laughed, hugging him tight.

"Can I see you boxing day?" he asked.

"I'll try," Juliette replied kissing his chest.

"Try harder Juliette," he rasped, "speaking of which…" they both looked down and shook with lusty laughter. Then Ben leant over the bed to pull his drawer open, "here's your present."

Juliette gazed down at the rectangle box covered in glittery paper and a cute little bow.

"Can I open it now?" She felt a surge of happy excitement rise within her.

"Of course," he pulled himself upright in the bed and looked at her expectantly.

Juliette tore off the wrapping and stared down at a burgundy box. Her heart quickened as she slowly opened the lid. Inside lay the most exquisite gold heart locket she had ever seen.

"It's beautiful!" She gasped.

"It's engraved," Ben said, pulling the necklace out and passing it to her.

She turned it over, grinning at the inscription which read 'love always, Ben'

"Oh Ben," she kissed him fiercely, "I've got you a present too, but it's so small in comparison. I didn't have much money left after everything else I've had to buy."

"I don't care," Ben shrugged, "you didn't need to buy me anything. I've got the best present lying next to me."

Juliette touched his face, "you're so lovely." Then she sprang up, "let me go get it." She pulled his t-shirt over her head and went in search of her handbag.

"Here," she passed him a gift bag covered with Christmas trees. Ben grinned and then pulled off the sellotape.

"A mysterious box," he said peeking inside.

Juliette watched his face as he opened it and looked down at the posh, engraved pen, "do you like it?" She fretted.

"I love it," he replied, lifting it and studying the inscription, which read 'with love Juliette.' "I won't take it to uni, I'll keep it here for best."

"I thought you could use it for the book you want to write."

"And that shall be my new years resolution," they snuggled down in the bed. Next to them the radio played gentle Christmas tunes, lulling them both into a gentle, restful nap.

* * *

On Christmas morning, Sophie was up early with a pair of exuberant twins. She encouraged them to tiptoe down the stairs so they wouldn't wake Evelyn, then made them mugs of hot chocolate with whipped cream and marshmallows.

"Can we go see what Father Christmas has left?" A wide-eyed Josh asked.

Jake shot him a withering look, "it's Mum you fool. There's no such thing as Father Christmas."

"Oh Jake, don't spoilt it for him," Sophie said, annoyed that his belief in Santa had been shattered. Last year he had solidly believed; insisting on leaving a mince pie and a carrot for Rudolph. But that was last year and so much had changed since then.

Take this house for instance, who would have known that Sophie and her brood would be living in a Victorian style detached with a dear lady she had only known for eighteen months. Yet Sophie felt she had known Evelyn for ever; she was a kind and gentle soul, Sophie had adopted her as the surrogate mother she had always craved.

Sophie had baked for the very first time last night, following Evelyn's recipe which had been passed down through the generations. A tub of mince pies rested proudly on the kitchen table, ready to be devoured.

Jake's hand snaked towards them, "can I have one?" He pleaded.

Sophie conceded, "go on then." The boys bit into them, showering crumbs all over the floor, sending the dogs into a scrap sniffing frenzy.

"Can we open our presents now pur-lease?" Josh pleaded.

Sophie stood up, "why don't we take Evelyn a drink up first. Wait for her to get up and then we can open them all together."

The boys nodded, happy with this course of action.

Sophie made her a tea and instructed Jake to plate up a mince pie with a few extra biscuits. They went up the creaky stairs and knocked gently on Evelyn's bedroom door.

"Come in," Evelyn warbled. She was sitting up in bed, bathed in lamplight, rubbing her eyes.

"Good morning," the three of them sang out and before Sophie could stop them the twins had jumped up on the bed.

"Boys," Sophie chastised.

Evelyn held up her hand, "it's okay Sophie, they're excited and who can blame them, it is Christmas after all."

Sophie perched on the bed and reached to peck Evelyn on the cheek, "merry Christmas."

"Merry Christmas to you all," Evelyn replied with a smile, "I'll put on my dressing gown and then we can open our presents but first, let me sample one of your delicious looking mince pies."

The Christmas tree stood in the bay window twinkling and gleaming with presents of all sizes and shapes underneath it. There were a lot less than normal, but the boys didn't seem to notice and gasped with delight never-the-less. While they began unwrapping, Sophie poured herself and Evelyn a small glass of sherry from a crystal decanter.

"Cheers," they clinked glasses and watched the twins' rapturous faces as they opened Lego, DVD's and giant colouring sets. There was also a pair of snazzy, top of the range roller boots from her mum, Derek and Ryan and a large tub of flying saucer sherbet sweets. Yvonne had dropped them off last night while they were watching an explosive scene in Eastenders. The atmosphere between mother and daughter had been strained but they had at least managed to be civil. Unsurprisingly Ryan was spending Christmas with Mum and Derek, which would turn into a booze binge no doubt.

"Is Dad coming over today?" Josh asked as he pulled on one roller boot.

"I'm not sure honey, maybe," Sophie made a mental note to text him and ask him what his plans were later.

"I think I should make a start on the turkey," Evelyn rose to her feet.

"Wait Evelyn," Sophie called, "this is for you, off me and the boys."

Sophie passed her a large square present.

"Oh my," Evelyn pulled back an edge of paper, "what on earth can this be?"

Slowly she unwrapped it, gasping at the contents. It was a canvas painting of a seaside town, with the sea and a busy harbour in the background.

"How wonderful," Evelyn gushed, "thank you very much," she peered at the signature in the right-hand corner, "is that *the* Brandon White the local artist?"

"Yes," Sophie replied with excitement, "I remembered you talking about the art gallery opening and how much you liked his work."

Evelyn nodded, "it's beautiful, thank you Sophie."

Now it was Evelyn's time to pass round her presents. The boys were excited over the new Jurassic Park DVD she had bought them. While they sat on the floor amidst paper, boxes and bows, eyes glued to the screen, Sophie and Evelyn sneaked off into the kitchen and began preparations for a sumptuous traditional dinner. Christmas music filled the room and they both jigged around, laughing and chattering.

"The crackers!" Evelyn cried, "I forgot the crackers."

Sophie pulled open the pantry door and pulled out a box of eight, "ta-da! They're luxury ones too."

While Evelyn basted the turkey, Sophie went to dress the table. She'd kept the candelabra that Ryan had hated. It looked so pretty in the middle of the table with the gold confetti and the red napkins. The whole room looked lovely and cosy, so different from the cold extravagance of Thistledown House. Sophie lit two winter spice candles and hung mistletoe above the doorway. Then the doorbell was ringing and Jacob arrived, looking windswept and ruddy cheeked.

More gifts were passed around; a gorgeous pearl chain for Evelyn and luxury chocolates for Sophie. He had also bought kites for the boys; one red, one blue, with dinosaur faces on. They eventually sat down to indulge a most veritable feast; turkey, gammon and an array of buttered vegetables and appetising condiments. They pulled the crackers and sipped flutes of real champagne, sang carols and laughed over cheesy jokes. Then Evelyn brought in a gold platter on which sat a decadent Christmas pudding and a pot of freshly made brandy cream. They all watched, mouths watering as she lit the stem and clapped as it sparked.

"I am so stuffed," Sophie sank back in the chair, patting her stomach, "did I really need to eat five pigs in blankets?"

"Mum's a pig," Josh and Jake whooped with laughter.

"We have after dinner mints to come yet dear."

Sophie shook her head, "maybe later Evelyn, I don't think I could eat another morsel."

"I suppose we should clear up," Jacob glanced over the plates, dishes and cutlery strewn across the table, "ladies I'll wash up."

They all pitched into clear up, even the boys. Finally, when everything was pristine clean and back in its rightful place they pulled on coats and hats and trudged up to the common, right to the top of the hill where Jacob helped Josh and Jake unravel the kites and ran with them to lift them high in the air.

It was a windy day, Sophie watched the diamond shaped kites ducking and diving above her and thought how happy and content she felt surrounded by her children and real friends. Sophie looked down at the city spread out in front of her, in the distance she could see the massive structure of the university, proud and imposing against a cloudy skyline, lines of traffic slowly crawling around it and through the streets of Chattlesbury. The dogs skittered around her ankles, dropping muddy sticks for her to lob far and high. By the time they had walked back down the hill and reached home they were both filthy. Yet Sophie wasn't bothered in the slightest, she cleaned the dogs off, hung her coat up and then joined the others flopped in front of the television, with a hot cup of tea and the Christmas TV guide to pore over.

* * *

For the first time since they had been a couple, Jon and Ann found themselves having to explain to close family members that they wouldn't be available to participate in the Christmas day festivities. This year they were doing something completely different; an alternative Christmas as Jon repeatedly referred to it. Ann's mother had initially been horrified when she heard that her daughter and son-in-law were going to be spending most of their day at a shelter for the homeless.

"You'll get your purse nicked," she screeched, then it was followed by, "watch out for the druggies and the crazies," and then finally came her favourite line, "are you sure you've thought this through our Ann."

It was Jon who calmed her parents down, in his usual stoic fashion he patiently told them not to worry; it would all be perfectly fine and a worthy way to spend a different Christmas day.

"It'll be different alright," Charlie her dad quipped, "but at least it will make a change from all the hype and commercialism that's for sure. Christmas just ain't what it used to be. I was lucky to get a colouring book and…"

"An orange and be thankful for it," Ann finished for him with a grin. She had heard that old chestnut so many times too.

The conversation had then predictably turned to religion and her mother had proclaimed how the true spirit of Christmas was well and truly dead.

"But our Ann," her mother said with a wipe of her brow, "you sure get some wild fancy ideas in that head of yours, who's she tek after Charlie?"

Her dad looked as nonplussed as ever and retreated behind his evening newspaper with a snort of acceptance.

"none of this was my idea," Ann said with a supercilious smile.

Her mother stared at Jon with her mouth gaping open, "and I always thought you were the sensible one."

Jon laughed heartily, "it was Anton and Lulu's idea."

"Who they heck are they?"

"University types no doubt," Charlie remarked distastefully, peering over today's headlines.

"Wrong again." Ann snapped, "they're Samuel's foster parents, remember? I told you all about them, how kind and lovely they are."

"Oh yes," Betsy, Ann's mom clicked her fingers, "the hippies. So, they talked you into it then?"

"Of course not," Ann scoffed, "since when have you known me to be talked into anything by anyone? I wanted to help, I mean *we* wanted to." She looked at Jon who was swinging his car keys and nodding his head towards the door. "Now I've gotta get back home and wrap the presents." Ann had left her parents wondering what they had done to deserve such a charitable daughter.

On Christmas morning they had driven through the quiet streets of Chattlesbury with Samuel strapped in the back. He had insisted on coming with them instead of his foster parents and chattered non-stop while Jon drove aimlessly around the city centre. Finally, they found the hostel, tucked away down a side street, opposite the council offices.

Samuel was wearing his new football shirt and had gelled his hair into spikes with the pampering set that Lulu had bought for him. His foster parents were already waiting outside for them with bright smiles on their faces, both were gushing with ebullience.

"You are going to love it," Lulu said to Ann as she settled back in her wheelchair, "but I hope you've brought a hankie." She then went onto give them a pep talk, a speech that was designed to tug at your heartstrings by highlighting the satisfaction gained from helping the less fortunate at Christmas.

Now they were sitting in a cold white canteen waiting for Penny the manager to brief them on the days itinerary. A large man sat next to Ann, covered in a checked apron and sporting a hair net. Harold had been a cook in the army for thirty years. Now retired, he liked to escape the nagging wife by helping out once a week at the Good Hope Hostel.

"Are there many erm, homeless staying here?" Ann asked.

"It can vary, there's the regulars who come and go, then there's some who stay for one night, have breakfast then up and leave never to be seen again."

"I see." Ann nodded, "do they get permanent accommodation?"

"Unlikely," Harold pursued his lips, "probably holed up in a doorway with a blanket and a tin can for company."

"That's so sad," Ann sniffed. Lulu had been right to warn her, she could feel herself welling up at the thought of anyone sleeping rough, especially during the long chilly winter months.

Harold popped a stick of gum in his mouth then offered Ann one, "after you've been here a few years you become hardened to it. You have to switch the feelings off, otherwise it would drive you mad with sorrow."

Just then a tall lady with long silver hair breezed into the kitchen carrying a large box of assorted vegetables, "hi folks," she went to kiss Anton and Lulu, "nice to see you again."

"I've brought friends," Lulu said bouncing on her seat with excitement, then she introduced everyone.

"You are very welcome," Penny said warmly, "the more the merrier. So, we have eight volunteers in total, which should be plenty. Janet's not here yet; her car's broken down so she's waiting for a lift."

"Janet's a cook too," Harold whispered, "not as good as me mind."

"I'd just like to thank you," Penny continued, leaning against a table, "for giving up your Christmas day to help our residents. Without the kindness of our volunteers, this hostel wouldn't be running. It's very much appreciated, so thank you once again," there was a light round of applause, "so shall we put some Christmas music on and get cracking?"

Penny organised jobs for them all and they set to work. Ann was busy in the kitchen, helping prepare the food. She peeled the vegetables which were gloriously fresh, donated from a kind farmer. Jon and Samuel went off to help Lulu decorate the canteen and dress the tables. They all worked hard, stopping for a tea break at eleven and then ploughing on until lunchtime, when the delectable bronzed turkeys were taken out of the oven and sliced on foil platters. Ann emptied the hot vegetables, stuffing balls and pigs in blankets into trays for people to help themselves and then ladled the vat of thick gravy into serving jugs. Pots of bread and apple sauce were laid out on each table along with sparkling water, squash and reindeer covered napkins. The stark emptiness of earlier had been transformed into a room of radiance and colour. Tinsel was draped haphazardly across the walls, red, gold and green stars hung from the ceiling and a small twinkling, fibre optic tree had been erected beside the doorway.

"It looks lovely," exclaimed Ann, "very festive."

Penny smiled, "this year we've been extra fortunate. We've had a batch of presents donated to us, as well as these Christmas decorations."

Sam was shuffling his feet, "don't they get presents off their families?"

"No not usually," Penny was shaking her head, a sad look on her face.

"That's crap," Sam decided. He looked upset, Ann placed a comforting hand on his arm. Then the first of the residents were filtering in and they all pitched in to help with the serving of the meals.

After everyone had been served a tray of Christmas dinner, Penny asked Ann if she would like to distribute the presents. Ann split the gifts into male and female piles and enlisted Samuel to help her. The canteen was noisy, people were laughing and talking loudly and some were singing along to Slade's 'Merry Christmas Everybody.' Harold came from behind his counter complaining about his aching feet. Janice followed him, whacking him on the shoulder and telling him to stop bellyaching. They were laughing boisterously, and Jon joined in.

Ann wheeled across the room to a lady who looked to be in her sixties. On closer inspection Ann realised that she was younger and that it was her lank straggly hair and dirt smeared face that had added years to her.

"Merry Christmas," Ann said cheerfully, passing over a square lumpy gift.

The woman looked up from her food and grimaced, "don't expect any thanks off me!"

"Oh. Okay, well I hope you like it anyway."

The woman prodded it suspiciously, "let me finish my dinner then I'll open it I suppose."

Ann nodded, "have you always lived in Chattlesbury?" There was silence, "I mean were you born here?"

"I were born in Yorkshire, but I got dragged down here by a wicked step-mother and a fool of a father," she snorted, "I suppose you think I'm rude."

"Not at all," Ann said with sincerity, "actually I prefer straight talking people."

"Good job," the woman snapped, but her face softened slightly, "it's my way that's all."

"Are none of your family around?" Ann probed, feeling desperate to keep up the conversation.

The woman placed down her cutlery with a clatter, "I hope you're not one of them do-gooders, always trying to fix up a happy ending. 'Cause believe me they're ain't one."

"I can assure you I'm not," Ann looked down at her wheelchair with disdain, "I'm as bitter as they come."

The woman seemed to like this answer and smiled, showing chipped yellow teeth, "what's your name lass?"

"Ann. Short for Annette."

"A nice solid name. I'm Frances, but you can call me Goldie."

Ann looked blankly at her.

"On accounts of my back gold teeth," Frances said with an exasperated sigh, "I was friendly with a dentist a long time ago. It's the only thing of value I have left."

"Frances is a lovely name," Ann said, "would you like a drink?" She reached across to pour them both a tumbler of squash.

"Aye it is," Frances agreed, "it were my late mothers. She died in childbirth. I've been on me own ever since. No one has ever really given a shit about me. Apart from the staff here and those two," she pointed her knife at Anton and Lulu who were singing spiritedly.

"They're treasures aren't they?" Ann glanced over at them.

"Yep. Reminds me that there are some good folk left in this world. Lulu's forever bringing clothes here, food too. She bakes these amazing muffins with chocolate chips and icing sugar. We have them with afternoon tea, pretend we're all posh," Frances laughed and Ann thought at that moment how young and carefree she looked.

"Were you born like that?" Frances enquired, head cocked to one side.

"You mean disabled?"

"Aye."

"No. I was in a motor vehicle accident in my early twenties. I haven't been able to move my legs since."

"Well don't expect any sympathy off me. I've got enough problems of me own." Frances smacked her lips together, "that were lovely. Did you cook it?"

"I peeled the veg," Ann replied with a wide smile.

Frances sat back and pulled an e-cigarette from her trouser pocket, "so what you doing here on Christmas day? Come to have a gawp at the homeless have ya?"

"We were talked into it."

"Blimey," Frances coughed, "and I thought *I* was blunt. Well, it ain't too bad here, everyone's nice enough, apart from that one there," she pointed at a poker-faced man who was shovelling Christmas pudding into his mouth, "used to be a pickpocket. Says he's reformed but a leopard never changes its spots. Watch your handbag around him." She leant closer, "now don't mek it obvious by looking, but the man with the turban on the next table smokes wacky backy, drinks cans of cider for his breakfast, he's had a hard life though, even bought a tear to my dried up old eyed, knowing what he's been through."

Ann was just about to enquire in whispered tones what that was, when Penny stopped in front of them.

"Hello Frances, are you going to open your present?"

"I suppose I should, before someone nicks it. Does the mayor know you've been splashing out like this?"

"The mayor gives me what I want," Penny said with a playful wink, "I know *a lot* about what he gets up to in those posh chambers of his."

Frances guffawed at that, "the man's a high and mighty hypocrite. Bent as a ten bob note."

"Aren't all men in power?" Ann said drily.

"You may be right there lass," Frances tore off the wrapping and stared down at the pack of lip glosses and Belgian chocolates.

"What the hell! Whose idea was it to give the homeless a set of fancy lipsticks? A pair of socks I could understand, a warm blanket yes, but these," she stared down at them, "peony pink and sizzling scarlet? Who've I got to impress around here?"

"Well I think they're pretty," Penny replied calmly, "it's the thought that counts Frances."

"Aye it is and you know what thinking too much leads to...a right blinding headache."

Ann sniggered behind her closed fist.

"These here chocolates look tasty though," she looked around furtively, "better hide 'em," up her jumper they went, along with the offensive lip gloss and a piece of Christmas pudding which had been left on a discarded plate, "now I best be off for a walk. I ain't got the time or inclination to socialise," she got to her feet and looked at Ann, "it were nice meeting ya. I wouldn't say I'd like to see you again though."

Ann burst out laughing, "merry Christmas Frances."

After Frances had ambled off, Ann turned to Penny and confessed, "at last, I've found someone ruder than me."

After all the presents had been dispersed, and the food had been devoured the whole canteen participated in a Christmas carol sing-a-long. Then a press photographer appeared and took pictures of them all wearing reindeer antlers and Santa hats, while grinning manically. Finally, at four o'clock the residents had all wandered off and the volunteers were able to sit down with their own Christmas dinners and a glass of cheap plonk. And it was the best meal Ann had tasted in a long time.

Chapter Twenty-Two

As usual Will was up early, searching in the kitchen for nappy sacks.

"They're in the utility, along with Esme's other stuff," Flora patiently told him, after he had grumbled about not being able to find anything.

Max strode into the room, his new velour dressing gown flapping open.

"Oh love, go back to bed," Flora admonished, "you're on holiday."

"I'm up now," Max was rubbing his temple, "I've drank far too much this Christmas, have we any Alka-Seltzer?"

Flora pulled open a cupboard and passed him the box.

"Now I really need to get on with cooking the food," Flora's tone was uncharacteristically bossy, "I've got a freezer full to prepare."

"Are you sure this New Year's Eve soiree is a good idea?" Max poured himself a glass of water and they all stared at the fizzing tablet. "Why couldn't we have gone to the local quiz like we usually do?"

"Stop complaining Max. Isn't change a good thing? At least that's what you keep telling me."

"I was referring to the world of education Flora," Max replied primly.

Will stuck his head round the door, "take no notice Mum, I think this party is an ace idea."

"Only because your kind-hearted Mother has invited some of your friends," Max berated.

"At least I have friends," Will said out the corner of his mouth.

"What was that?" Max slugged back his drink and then sat down at the kitchen table.

"Will's just joking," Flora threw her son a stern look, "they'll be plenty of people here you know love. Brenda and Tony, Uncle Evan, Father McGregor and both sets of neighbours have said they'll pop in too."

"Father McGregor?" Max looked astounded, "shouldn't he be attending to his role and duties as a priest? Really Flora, what if Will's friends get drunk and rowdy. I won't be able to look him in the eye again at mass."

Flora laughed, "Father McGregor has a brilliant sense of humour love, please stop worrying about things that haven't even happened!"

"Don't worry Dad," Will said with a wink, "I won't tell him what *really* goes on at that school of yours."

"Speaking of St Mary's," Max scratched his stubble covered chin, "I was very disappointed that your friend Sophie has stopped her voluntary work there."

Will yawned, "she needs to earn money Dad, she's looking for a job now that she's separated."

"Will she continue with her studies love?" Flora's head was in the freezer, trying to find the onion bhajis and pakoras.

"I guess so," Will shrugged, "I mean it would be such a waste, we're almost at the end of the second year and her grades have really picked up."

"So how are *your* grades doing?" Max asked.

"Not bad," Will replied, "mainly b's and a few c's so far."

"Good," Max nodded, "so you're on course for a 2.1."

"Yup. Looks that way."

"Are any of your university friends coming tonight?" Max pulled his robe tighter.

"I've invited them but I doubt it. Sophie and Evelyn are going for a meal, Ann's busy with her own family and I think Jules mentioned something about having to work."

Will thought briefly about his own job as a barman at the Student Union. His doctor had given him a sick note that lasted until the new semester started, so luckily, he was off New Years Eve. He tried not to dwell on the fact that that was the place he had been stabbed. Will had been suffering flashbacks since his release from hospital, mainly at night-time when he was in bed trying to sleep. He would lie still and try to think of something else, but that would make him more anxious and he very often broke out in a body drenching cold sweat as he visualised Hema's cousins face; contorted with hate and rage and the silver flash of the knife as he plunged it towards him. Will shuddered, he didn't realise that his Mother was asking him a question until both her and Max had turned to stare at him expectantly.

"Sorry Mum what was that?"

"I just wondered if Hema is free today maybe she could help me prepare for the party?"

"Yeah sure," he bent to retrieve a fallen nappy sack then went back upstairs to his girlfriend and baby.

* * *

Will was busy for the rest of the day; mainly looking after Esme, while Hema and Flora cooked everything edible in sight. But in-between the quiet periods, when she was napping, Will lay on the bed, plugged in his i-pod and read. Jimmy had messaged a few times during the day. Firstly to tell him that they were coming to the party, then he text him an hour later to inform him they weren't. Finally, late afternoon, Will received a simple text stating that him and Sadie were definitely attending and would bring beer. Will emitted an irritated sigh, Sadie, Jimmy's fiancée had been pestering Hema over the Christmas period with her personal problems. From what Hema had told him he understood that their recently engaged friends had had an almighty row on Christmas day involving in-laws and wedding plans. An argument to end all arguments, Jimmy had insisted the engagement was off. This had resulted in a bout of late night hysterical calls from Sadie who proclaimed she couldn't live without 'her Jimmy.' A week later their rocky relationship was back on track again and they were 'stronger than ever.' Will had his reservations, he had given up trying to decipher the pair of them and he advised Hema not to get involved.

Esme stirred in her crib and he unplugged his ear phones, rolling onto his side to look at her. Today she was wearing a white cotton romper suit with the words 'I Love My Daddy' emblazoned across the chest. Will thought she looked seriously cute, her hair had grown since her birth, it curled around her face in soft dark curls and she had grown in length and weight too. Will wondered if she was going to be petite like her mum or lanky like him.

"I thought you were studying," Hema stood in the doorway, a bright smile on her face.

"I was," Will countered, "isn't she beautiful?"

"Gorgeous," Hema moved to stare down at her daughter, "I still can't believe she's all ours."

"It's mad," Will agreed, "she's changed since she was born, we should video her more."

"What – so we can embarrass her on her eighteenth?" Hema laughed, "but yes we should definitely record her milestones, she's almost rolling over Will, next she'll be sitting up and can you imagine what she'll be like when she's walking?"

"She'll be everywhere," Will picked Esme up, she stared at him with Hema's golden eyes, "let's just enjoy her now, as she is."

"Let's cherish this time Will, it's scary how the time flies."

He lay her on the bed and she kicked her chubby legs and emitted a disgruntled cry.

"I think that means food time," Hema lay beside her, blowing gently on her face.

Will stretched, making his t-shirt ride upwards exposing his stomach. He noticed Hema staring at his purple scar then quickly looking away when she noticed his eyes on her.

"Is it still sore?" She asked, her tone soft.

"A bit," Will winced as he ran his hands over the puckered skin, "I was lucky huh?"

"You were brave," she replied with more firmness, "Will, I…I think he meant to stab me not you. I really think he wanted to kill me."

Will placed a finger over her lips, "don't think about it. It's over now, he's in jail and he can't hurt us anymore."

"But what about when he's released? He might get off lightly, he might come and try to…"

"For attempted murder?" Will shook his head, "that's serious shit Hema, I think he'll be put away for a long time."

"I hope so."

Will grabbed hold of her hand, "c'mon, it's New Years Eve. Let's look forward, let's be happy. I'm going to feed Esme, and you're going to get yourself ready and we're going to dance and mingle and enjoy ourselves, okay?" He kissed her lips and playfully slapped her derriere. "So, how's Mum got on with the food, has she burnt everything?"

"Let's just say it's all well done." Then they were both grinned and the strained atmosphere was lightened as their laughter rang around the house.

"Actually Mum, you've done well," Will pulled back the clingfilm and took a hearty bite of a samosa.

"Do you think there's enough?"

Will's gaze swept over the long table creaking under the weight of trays of food. There were all sorts: sandwiches, quiches, pizza, chicken drumsticks, spring rolls and of course the obligatory cheese and pineapples.

"Yep. I think we might be eating this for the next week or so."

"That's not everything," Flora said proudly, "there are four different desserts in the fridge."

"Banoffee pie?" Will's eyes were alight with anticipation.

Flora nodded, "with squirty cream."

Will sank down in the chair and pulled a breadstick from a pot, "I think I might just stay here for the evening."

"Will Bentley are you eating again?" Hema came into the kitchen, bouncing a freshly bathed Esme on her hip, "now I know where this little one gets her appetite."

Flora wiped her hands on her apron and went to fuss over her grand-daughter, "and don't you look posh."

The letterbox on the front door flapped open and a male voice shouted through, "open up." It was uncle Evan, punctual as ever. No one in the kitchen moved, making an annoyed Max, who was sitting in the lounge, fold up his paper and go to answer the door.

"Took your time old boy," Evan strode down the hall, heading for the kitchen, his lady friend trailing behind him. He saw the food first and made a beeline for the egg and cress sandwiches, but Flora intercepted him, steering him towards the seating area.

Evan patted Will on the shoulder without his usual brute force and leant over to gently kiss Hema and Esme.

"How are you bearing up?" He asked Will, no nonsense as usual.

"Okay I guess."

"Want me to send some squaddie mates of mine round his house, do the bastard over?"

"Evan!" Flora gasped at his casual use of profanity, "don't you dare! He's in custody now, so let the police and the courts do their job. We don't want you and your army buddies jeopardising the case."

"Pah," Evan snorted in disgust, "let's hope he doesn't get some do-gooder liberal leftie then. They'll have the jury feeling sorry for the swine instead of the victim."

"There isn't going to be a trial," Flora explained evenly, "the man has pleaded guilty, so we need to support Will by keeping quiet about it. We've already had press hanging around outside the house. Don't stir things up Evan and whatever you do, don't get mouthing off to them like you just did to us."

"Okay, okay," Evan glanced at Flora, "since when did my sister become such a firecracker?"

"I blame Facebook," Max said with a disapproving shake of his head, "social media and working again is turning Flora's brain."

"Maybe it's that thing that women go through," Evan replied with helpful intentions, "the strange time of life, begins with an m…"

"I am here," Flora said crisply, "and if it's the menopause you're referring to that is nothing to do with it. I've just gained in confidence these past six months that's all and Max you know very well I love my job."

Hema and Evan's lady friend gave her a grinning thumbs up.

"Go Nana," Hema said, "this little one needs strong female role models in her life." Esme let out a gurgle of agreement invoking a chorus of ah's around the kitchen and the conversation was forgotten.

An hour later the house was full. Will had set up station in the lounge, he flicked through the music channels until he found a caters for all programme, playing back to back hits with no ad breaks. Sadie and Hema had pushed back his dad's favourite chair and were dancing in the middle of the room. Esme was watching from her bouncy chair, kicking her legs in time with the music.

"Your daughter is cool Will," Jimmy smiled down at her, "she's got natural rhythm."

"Of course she has," Will said proudly, "she takes after her old pa."

"Her mother more like," Hema laughed, shimmying provocatively.

Max watched from the doorway, arms folded across his chest. Hema stopped dancing and Will quickly turned down the volume.

"Is it too loud?" Will asked, anticipating a lecture.

"Not at all," Max replied with a smile, "I was just thinking how nice it is to see my son fit, healthy and enjoying himself. Ah, there's the doorbell again." He went to answer it with a bemused Jimmy gaping Will's way.

"Was that your dad just?"

"I know," Will laughed, "since we've had Esme he's really started to mellow out," he lifted his daughter up into the air, blowing raspberries on her toes.

Sadie had stopped dancing and held out her arms for Esme, "she's the most beautiful baby ever. Oh Jimmy imagine what our baby would look like?"

Jimmy swallowed in response, "you said you didn't want kids!"

"Well not yet but after we're married, who knows…" Sadie kissed Esme's chubby cheeks and looked across at her startled boyfriend.

The nervous look on Jimmy's face made Will throw back his head and laugh.

Jimmy eager to change the subject was listening to what was going on in the hallway, "shush," he said, "I think your dad's shouting Will."

Will muted the music and listened. He was right, there was a hullabaloo going on, he could hear his dad talking in a firm tone, telling someone to leave. Will peeped his head around the architrave, wondering who it was. He was shocked to see Hema's parents; Mr and Mrs Kumar standing on the doorstep pleading with his dad to be let in. Swiftly he ducked back in the room, "Hema," he whispered, beckoning her over, "your parents are here!"

"Okay," she didn't look surprised.

"Did you invite them," Will's hand raked through his hair.

"They asked me if they could come Will, what was I supposed to say? They want to talk to you."

"You should have told me. I've nothing to say to them."

"Then let me do the talking. Let *them* explain. Please let them in Will, we can't carry on like this," Hema swallowed, "I was just getting back on track with them, they had accepted us and they were starting to love Esme. She needs them in her life Will…please."

He looked down at her imploring eyes and softened. *The stabbing wasn't their fault* a voice inside argued *be the bigger man for your family.*

Will nodded and Hema rushed out of the room.

"If they dare cause any trouble," Will's hands had balled into fists.

"Chill," Jimmy soothed, "they ain't gonna start anything here and if they do I'll chuck em through that window."

"You two need to stay calm," Sadie's shrill tone had Esme's mouth turning down, "look, she's picking up on the bad vibes!"

As Mr and Mrs Kumar came into the room Will blinked in surprise. Mr Kumar was wearing jeans and a trendy spotty shirt that wouldn't have looked out of place on a shop window mannequin. While Mrs Kumar was wearing a posh black lace dress that hung to her knee. Will reminded himself to refer to them as Shivani and Daljeet, they were all adults here and he had the battle scars to prove it.

"Mum where's your sari?" Hema seemed just as surprised by their appearance as Will was.

"I wanted to wear something modern, something a western woman would wear."

"You look…" Hema glanced over her, noting the brightly painted red nails, the blingy costume jewellery, the nylon tights and shiny stilettoes, "you look stunning."

"Thank you. Your dad thought so too. He almost keeled over when I came out of the changing room."

Max was hovering behind them, with a concerned looking Flora.

"We don't want any trouble," Max warned, "Will's been through enough."

Shivani turned to Flora, "I brought gifts for New Year. I hope you had a good Christmas."

"Well all things considering, no we didn't actually," Max blustered.

"Max!" Flora remonstrated, she stepped forward to embrace Shivani, "we had a quiet Christmas. Thank you for the gifts, you really shouldn't have."

Will stared down at the gift bag which had been thrust in his hands. Hema was nodding at him, encouraging him to graciously accept the token, or peace offering, whatever it was meant to be. Slowly he opened a box. His sharp intake of breath had them all craning their necks to stare at the gold and chrome designer watch. It must have cost hundreds, maybe even thousands. Six months' salary at least he thought, he should be feeling gratitude but instead he felt a growing sense of rage.

"Oh my," gasped Flora, "that's very…generous of you." There was an uncomfortable silence. "Will?…"

"Thanks," he mumbled, trying to stop his mouth from twisting into a sneer.

"So, I guess I'll open mine," Flora said brightly, tearing off the gold shiny paper. There was carefully folded tissue which revealed a pretty satin clutch purse, "oh how pretty. What have you had love?" She turned to look at Max whose face was taut with the exertion of suppressing anger.

"This is what I think of your pathetic attempts to assuage your guilt," he threw the box down on the floor. Esme thinking it was some sort of game let out a gurgle of laughter.

Flora was on her knees, "oh no it's ruined," she picked up the present, frantically trying to smooth out the dents.

Max erupted. "You think you can come into my house after what's happened to my son?"

"Love it wasn't their fault," Flora protested.

"Yes, it was," Will cut in, as a coldness settled over him, a determination to have his say, "for once I agree with Dad. If you had accepted that we loved each other, none of this would have happened."

Mr Kumar held up his hand, "I don't think…"

"You just couldn't let us be," Will continued evenly, "you stirred up hatred and division. Turned others against us. You…" he jabbed his finger at Daljeet, "had the power to calm the situation, but instead you created more trouble and turned a blind eye to the repugnant thoughts of your bigoted family. And why? Because you couldn't stand the idea of your daughter being with a white catholic. You hated that she had her own mind and chose me above you."

Mrs Kumar's mouth was flapping open, "my husband is very proud and traditional. Family is everything to him. He adores Hema and he wanted to see her settled in a good Hindu family – is that so bad? To want the best for your daughter? It was never about the colour of your skin Will."

Will lifted his shirt to reveal the purple scar, "this is what you've done to my skin. This is what your tradition and pride did to me."

"He could have died," Max shouted, thumping the table, "and you think a watch is going to make it alright?"

Mr and Mrs Kumar began speaking at once; jabbering apologies.

"Mum stop," Hema snapped, "for once will you let Dad speak for himself?"

Shivani closed her mouth abruptly.

"Dad please tell Will what you told me."

Mr Kumar took a handkerchief from his pocket and blew his nose. Tears were forming in his eyes and he looked completely broken.

"I'm ashamed Will. I'm ashamed of how myself and Shivani have treated you. And yes you're right, I didn't defend either you or Hema to my family and for that I will be eternally sorry. I can see that you love my daughter. I've heard about the valiant way you defended her. But please believe me I didn't have anything to do with the stabbing, it was my brother and his sons and for what they have done I will never forgive. But I'm here to ask your forgiveness Will. I'm so sorry I doubted you. I'm sorry I've treated you so badly. You too my darling," he turned to Hema, who had tears in her own eyes. "Please forgive me." He hung his head and wept.

It was Flora who moved first. Driven by her benevolence and geniality, she would her arms around Mr Kumar, hugging him tight. Hema joined her and then Shivani to become a tight comforting circle around Daljeet. While he hung his head and repeated his heartfelt apologies, Will's anger drifted away to be replaced by sympathy. He glanced at his dad who smiled and nodded his way.

"Mr Kumar," Will held out his hand, "apology accepted." Slowly they shook hands, while all the women in the room cried tears of relief, "truce?"

"Truce." They all shouted at once.

Max held a wine bottle aloft, "so here's to a peaceful New Year. Would anyone care for a drink?"

Chapter Twenty-Three

Sophie's number one New Year's resolution was to bag herself a job. So, on a bitterly cold January day she laid the local newspaper out on the floor, grabbed herself a red marker and began circling any vacancies that took her interest.

"Shop worker – yes!" Carefully she marked it, gasping at the remuneration package that came with the requirements of being trustworthy, reliable and punctual. "Is that the going rate for the minimum wage now? - Appalling!"

Sophie stretched a foot out in front of the topaz glowing fire. Her feet were cold, even though she was wearing a pair of bed socks that Evelyn had made for her.

"Shall I turn the heating up?" Evelyn put down her knitting needles and frowned at Sophie.

"No no, it's just the dogs are taking all the heat," she shoved at the Labrador who lifted his head and winked sleepily at her.

"Where was I?" Sophie rustled the paper, "ah care worker, this sounds promising: caring, diligent, professional manner. No experience necessary. Competitive rates of pay. This is a definite maybe." She squiggled a star next to the bold advertisement. "Oh. It says applicants must be available to work nights and flexible with hours, ranging from twenty to forty per week."

"Could be tricky," Evelyn said, "how will that work around university?"

"Exactly. What I really need is set hours, no more than twenty per week. Oh here we go; part time call centre assistant, full training given, city centre. Previous sales knowledge would be desirable but not essential. Sounds promising, yes to that one. There's an open day next week Evelyn."

"You know you don't have to worry about paying me rent dear," clack, clack went Evelyn's knitting needles, "this house is all paid for and I'm not short of money. Mam saw to it that I would be okay financially."

"I *do* have to pay my way Evelyn. I'm not going to live here rent free. You've been so kind, but I really want to contribute." Sophie sat up, "it will do me good to get a job, I need to be self-sufficient and independent like Jules."

"Well okay, but there's no hurry. Please don't just take the first thing that comes along. You have to enjoy your work, even if it pays peanuts."

"Well that would be a bonus I suppose. Oh here's another; a perfume counter sales person at that new department store in the city. That's perfect for me huh? No." Sophie folded the newspaper with a determined look on her face, "that was the old Sophie. I want to do something different, something challenging. I'm going for the call centre job; the pay is good and there's all sorts of perks and bonuses."

The conversation turned to what they could have for tea, "shall I do us a roast Evelyn followed by an apple crumble?"

"Actually Sophie," Evelyn's face and neck had turned pink, "I'm going out to the pictures."

"With Jacob?"

"Yes."

"You guys are so sweet together. He's more than a friend now isn't he Evelyn?"

Evelyn nodded, "I'm very fond of him. He's a fine man."

"You're perfect for each other," Sophie grinned, "do you want me to do your hair for your hot date?"

Evelyn chuckled, "okay Sophie, but please no diamante clips this time and definitely *no* red lipstick."

* * *

"You want me to be your birthing partner?" Juliette was standing in her kitchen, hands splayed on her hips.

"Yes," Marie replied, "that's if you don't mind?"

Juliette squealed, "of course I don't mind!" She rushed over to hug her sister, "but what about Dave?"

"Dave?"

"Your husband, remember him?" Juliette tutted.

Marie waved away the mention of him, "oh he'll be there of course, but I doubt he'll last, you know how squeamish he is Jules, he can't even watch Harry Potter. How will he cope with all the blood and mess that comes with giving birth?"

Juliette touched her shoulder, "I think he might surprise you."

Marie bit her lip, "I'm not convinced. I've booked a water birth anyway. They're all the rage now you know. Although if I decide I need pain relief I'm damn well going to have everything they've got."

"It's the kind of pain you soon forget," Juliette said, wanting to put her mind at rest, "you've got this little bundle of joy at the end of it so it's totally worth it."

She then diverted the conversation onto a different topic; their parents surprise ruby anniversary party. They had married on valentine's day and luckily this year February 14th had fallen on a Saturday, a perfect day for a party. Juliette had booked the social club where she worked. They had hired a DJ but were doing the food themselves. Invites had been sent out to over a hundred guests, the majority had already confirmed they were attending, they were expecting a good turnout.

"So, are you bringing Ben?" There it was, direct and simple.

Juliette nodded, "I've asked him."

"That's great," Marie enthused, "Mum and Dad have been driving me potty asking about him, they're desperate to meet him and what about the kids Jules, haven't they met him yet?"

"No. I wanted to wait. I wanted to make sure."

Marie let out a sigh, "make sure of what? To me it's simple, you love this guy, it is serious isn't it? On his side as well as yours I mean?"

"I think so yes," Juliette replied, "I just don't want to be one of those women who has a string of different boyfriends coming and going. The kids need stability."

"They already have it," Marie said softly, "you're the most self-sacrificing mum I know, but you need to be happy Jules, and if this guy messes you about he'll have me and Dave to answer too."

"He makes me very happy," Juliette said with a laugh.

"I can see that. So, let all the family meet him properly, we're not going to bite him or scare him off. He'll love us."

"Humph," Juliette teased, "not sure about that one."

Marie socked her playfully on the arm and they walked through the kitchen to flop down on the couch with cups of tea and biscuits, having a good gossip about what was good on TV at the moment and life in general.

* * *

On the day of her interview Sophie was extremely nervous. Her slot wasn't until eleven in the morning, but she had been awake since six worrying over what clothes she should wear. After taking the boys to school she rummaged through her minimalised wardrobe until she finally settled on a black pinstripe suit, smart ruffled blouse and shiny shoes. Then she applied a light sheen of makeup and tied her hair back into a sophisticated bun.

"How do I look?" She asked Evelyn.

"Very professional," Evelyn replied, biting into her toast and marmalade, "have you prepared for the interview?"

Sophie looked blank, "in what way?"

"Researching about the company, practising interview questions?"

Sophie clamped a hand over her mouth.

"Have you done *any* preparation Sophie?" Evelyn asked, "surely you've been for an interview before?"

"No, I haven't," Sophie squeaked, "I've never had a job before."

"Not even a Saturday job when you were a teenager or a paper round even?" Evelyn looked at her with incredulous eyes.

"I helped my friend sell cosmetics once – does that count?"

"Not really," Evelyn glanced at her watch, "well it's too late now. You should be setting off soon."

"Actually, I need to go now. I've no idea where it is so I thought I could park by the uni and ask a passer-by the way," Sophie grinned at a doubtful looking Evelyn, "I've got a really good feeling about this job. How difficult can answering telephones all day be?"

"Well you certainly love chatting. Good luck anyway dear."

"Thanks," Sophie checked her handbag, "and what have you got planned for today?"

"Housework this morning then uni work later."

Sophie smiled, "I'll try and fit in some study time before the kids come out of school, but anyway, have a lovely day Evelyn, I'll see you this afternoon," she waved and hurried down the hall and out into the blustery morning.

The call centre was located on top of a very steep hill. Sophie staggered up rueing her decision to wear high heels. Yes they looked nice but were totally impractical for every day wear. The blasted things kept getting embedded in the soft gravel and more than once she twisted her ankle painfully. To make matters worse when she was halfway up the hill, the heavens decided to open and a tumultuous explosion of water showered down on top of her. Guess what – no umbrella! This day was turning into a disaster she thought, as she trudged up the crest of the hill. The rain in its infinite wisdom became more intense and Sophie actually ran along the drive and through a packed car park. The call centre itself was quite small. She had envisioned a towering block, but in reality it looked more like a country hotel. She wiped at her damp face with a tissue and smoothed beads of rain off her hair before pushing through the revolving doors that took her into an impressive marble lobby. Sophie glanced at her reflection in a wall of mirrors. She looked windswept and that was putting it mildly. As she was looking around for a toilet to spruce herself up in, a snooty receptionist enquired if she could help her.

"I'm here for an interview," Sophie gasped, her breath was shallow after her sprint up the embankment.

"Fill this in please," the perfectly coiffed employee thrust an application form towards her. "You do have a pen?" She snapped, when Sophie paused.

"Oh yes, yes, I'm fully prepared." Sophie bit the wall of her right cheek; a punishment she told herself, for fibbing.

Then the telephone rang and the receptionist turned her haughty attention to what sounded like an irate customer. She turned away from the desk and made her way over to a tan leather sofa which enveloped her as she sank down into it.

Sophie pulled herself upright, crossed her legs and delved in her handbag for a half chewed biro. As she was filling in the form, a few other people filtered in; a man and two younger looking women were given forms to complete and came to sit beside her on the sofa that was more like a bed.

When they had all completed their applications and handed them back in to Mrs Snooty, they were made to wait in silence for another half hour. At one point Sophie did attempt to initiate a conversation but was given such a withering look from the robotic receptionist that she fell silent again. Finally they were led through into a posh looking meeting room that smelt of polish. A man was sitting at a computer tapping away. He was wearing an expensive looking suit and reeked of cologne. His name tag revealed him to be Andy, Head of HR.

"Howdy folks," he had an unmistakeable American accent and the whitest teeth Sophie had ever seen.

They all said a polite good morning.

"Please sit down," Andy motioned to the chairs which had been placed in a strategic circle.

Sophie's stomach squelched with nerves. The fear of the unknown gripped her as she wondered what they would be expected to discuss. She had presumed she would have a short informal interview with one person maybe two. Now the realisation that this was a group interview heightened her nerves. *Please don't let me make a complete prat of myself* she prayed inwardly. Andy pulled a board into the centre of the room. It had a blank flip chart and a permanent marker pen that reminded Sophie of school.

"Well I'm Andy, it's great to meet y'all. Can you introduce yourselves to me, with a brief bio?" He then proceeded to make each candidate stand up and state their names and a brief background history. When it was her turn, Sophie omitted the part about being separated to one of the most well know Midlands strikers, but did tell everyone about her status as an English student.

"Of course the American universities are huge compared to your little English ones. But then everything in the UK is tiny, I suppose you guys could call it quaint." He laughed, while everyone remained silent. Andy then proceeded to explain about his reasons for coming to the UK. It seems he had been headhunted by a top London agency who had put him forward for the job as Human Resources Manager.

"I was chosen from ten strong candidates. They practically begged me to take the position. I have a basic salary of 70k plus bonuses and a bigger company car then the Managing Director," he pointed at a portrait of a stern looking man smoking a cigar, "that's him," his voice dropped to a whisper, "rumour is that the board want him replaced by yours truly," he pointed two thumbs at himself and gave everyone a cheeky wink. Sophie felt herself relaxing, with the superior realisation that Dandy Andy was a bit of a plonker.

"So can any of y'all tell me what we make and sell here at Hanley and Hanley?"

There was silence and Sophie felt relieved that she wasn't the only one who hadn't done any research on the company.

"You!" He pointed at Sophie.

Sophie opened her mouth and then closed it again. Her stomach grumbled, reminding her that breakfast had been hours ago.

"Toasters?" The word popped out without thinking.

"Toasters?" Andy looked amused, "think again sweet cheeks."

"A-Another electrical appliance?"

"You're getting warmer baby."

"Coffee makers," the man sitting next to Sophie said with a triumphant grin.

"Nope." Andy scratched his chin, "let me give you a clue. It begins with a V."

They all looked at each other perplexed.

Andy did a pushing and pulling motion with his hands, "it likes to suck. Do you gettit now?" Then Sophie had 'got it'.

"Do you mean a hoover?" She asked, trying to quell her snigger, "or is that a vacuum cleaner in America."

"Vacuum cleaner is the correct terminology," he confirmed, "man the UK need to catch up with the lingo."

"Of course!" Sophie erupted, "I've seen the adverts – Hanley's Hoovers, I mean vacuum cleaners."

"I helped create those ads," Andy boasted, "the MD was all for radio marketing, but I said nope, TV is the way to move forward and look you're proof that it's worked, you've remembered the ad! Do you have a Hanleys hoover, I mean vacuum cleaner?"

"No," Sophie shook her head with regret, "but it's on my to get list."

"Cool," Andy nodded with approval, "there's a great sale on, twenty percent off until the end of Feb, so you guys better hurry!" His exuberance for the product was contagious and Sophie felt excited by the prospect of buying herself a top of the range Hanley's Hoover, when she had her own place.

Gregarious Andy clapped his hands to signify that the interview would now be officially commencing. He fired off a barrage of questions: do you have any experience in a call centre? How would you deal with an irate customer? Are you able to cope well under pressure? Can you multi-task? Please give examples. He jotted down their answers, humming to himself as he did. Then they had a brainstorming session which involved Andy pacing around the room, encouraging them to shout out words to describe qualities that would make a fantastic call centre operative. Sophie politely held back while the others flung words at Andy: warm, friendly, good listener, persuasive. When there was a break in the adjective flinging, Sophie raised her hand and said tentatively, "you should be passionate about the services and products that you sell." This carefully thought out answer made Andy almost orgasmic with delight. At one point, Sophie was worried that he was going to jump across the table and kiss her.

"Fantastic Miss Sophie," he beamed her way and Sophie basked in his unexpected praise. *I could do this* she thought, *I could really sell hoovers.*

"Why do you want this job?" He stopped pacing and stared directly at Sophie.

This question floored her and she paused to think, she could give him the usual bull about what a wonderful company she thought Hanley's was, but Sophie felt overwhelmed by the urge to be honest with him.

"I desperately need the money," she replied, "and I think…I think I could be good at it. I mean I'm super friendly, polite, I love chatting and I'm enthusiastic and positive. I'm a quick learner…" she trailed off, blushing.

"Keep going," Andy gave her a cheesy thumbs up, "jeez you English are all so humble."

"I er," but Andy had already moved onto the next candidate.

The last question he asked, Sophie *was* prepared for. She had anticipated it on the drive over here – "where do you see yourselves in five years' time?"

She listened to the others gushing about being wealthy, moving to Australia, reaching management level within Hanley's, the male interviewee even proposed that he would be leading his own company.

"So. Y'all extremely ambitious by the sounds of it," Andy smirked, "I better watch my back." There was a silence, where everyone wondered if they had been over zealous.

"What about you Sophie? You've gone awful quiet," Andy was gazing at her with interest.

Sophie swallowed, "I know it sounds corny but I just want to be happy and healthy."

"Not corny at all," Andy said, "carry on Princess."

"I'd like to have completed and passed my English degree. I'd love to be settled in my own home and have a secure job that I enjoy, and which pays me enough to live comfortably on."

"Wouldn't you like to be rich?" One of the women asked, looking surprised.

Sophie shook her head, "I've done wealth and believe me the old saying is true – money definitely can't buy you happiness."

"Very admirable," Andy smiled, "so, now I'm going to reveal what Hanley's can offer *you*."

He wrote a list on his flip chart: a good basic rate of pay, excellent commission opportunities, a fast paced dynamic environment to work in, fantastic career prospects and a great team of colleagues.

"It's all about teamwork," he said proudly, "let me show you."

He took them outside onto the main open plan office floor. There must have been at least thirty employees sitting at desks typing, answering phones, chatting over the water machine. Sophie noticed that everyone looked happy and there was a nice ambience in the room. Andy showed them the staff room, the meeting room, the posh ladies powder room, all the while he chatted about what a fantastic company it was, how good staff morale was and how approachable the management team were.

Finally the interview was over, he took them back down to reception, thanking them profusely for attending. "There should have been seven candidates here today, obviously a couple couldn't be bothered to turn up so thank you for making the effort."

Sophie was breathless with excitement and found herself hoping that she would get this job. Andy's enthusiasm had rubbed off on her and she had a good feeling about this place. Her hopes were a little deflated however after he regrettably explained that they would only be able to take on two new employees.

"If it was up to me I'd employ you all," he flashed his pearly whites, "you've all been real impressive today, but I'll be in touch within the next forty eight hours, so in the meantime, have a nice day y'all." He shook their hands and then walked outside with them, where the storm had passed and a beautiful rainbow was lighting up the sky. Sophie literally skipped down the hill, her adrenalin flying. She had survived her first formal interview and she'd done pretty damn good too.

Chapter Twenty-Four

The Christmas break was well and truly over, and the English students began exam preparations, dissertation meetings, as well as the new modules for semester two.

"I can't believe the second year is almost over," Juliette said to the others as they ate lunch in the canteen. The conversation was centred around their little table, but her eyes were elsewhere. Across the room seated with the other lecturers she could see him, looking as handsome as ever.

"I'm feeling the pressure," admitted Evelyn, "so much reading, so little time."

"How are you feeling?" Ann's question was directed at Will, who was toying with a tub of Flora's homemade pasta salad.

"Not too bad," he replied, "I still can't believe what happened here at Christmas."

"You were so brave Will," Juliette said, "are you sure you're okay to come back to uni so soon though?"

"Yeah I'm fine physically," he replied, "the docs given me the all clear. I've just been having a few nightmares and flashbacks, but that's expected when you've been through trauma apparently." He relaxed back in his seat, "anyway, I'd rather keep busy. It's no good to dwell on things. Where's Soph by the way?"

"Here she is," Ann commented drily, pointing to the entrance.

An excited looking Sophie was hurrying their way, "morning guys, I've got some great news to share – have a guess what?"

"Erm, you've won the lottery and you're sharing it with us?" Juliette was laughing.

"I wouldn't want to," Sophie stuck out her chin, "actually, I've got a job. You are looking at the new Hanley and Hanley's employee."

"Oh Sophie, well done," exclaimed Evelyn.

"Wow!" added Juliette, "well sit down and tell us all about it."

Lunchtime passed quickly and then it was timetabled for the second year English students to meet in the main lecture theatre for a dissertation meeting.

Juliette, Sophie, Will and Evelyn sat with Ann on the front row, pens ready and poised as the course leader Tarquin Haverstock hopped up behind the podium and began a talk on the dissertation process.

"So the topic and the books chosen are entirely up to you folks. This is your baby so pick something you're going to enjoy, choose something you feel passionate about. Hopefully your personal tutor will be able to mentor you, but if it's a theme they're not familiar with, we can swop you around with another lecturer. Now then, Dr Rivers is going to give a brief talk, showing you examples of some of the dissertations he's overseen. Then at the end we'll have a question and answer session." He nodded at Ben who flipped on his computer screen and began discussing a dissertation on the poetry of Byron.

After it had finished, the students filtered out of the lecture theatre, some heading for home, others for more study in the Learning Centre.

Juliette was trailing towards the exit, after the others, when she heard Ben calling her.

"Miss Harris, can I speak to you?" He was gathering his papers together and gazing her way with a grin on his face.

"Of course Dr Rivers," Juliette let the door swing shut.

The lecture theatre was now empty and she felt strangely nervous.

"Don't look so worried," he moved towards her, "are we still okay for the weekend?"

"Yes," she replied with a blink, "of course. I...I've told Harry and Molly you're coming and they're excited to meet you, especially Molly."

"Who did you say I was?" Ben was suspicious.

"I told them you were my...my boyfriend," her cheeks became hot under his scrutiny.

"Well well Juliette," Ben teased, "I expected you to introduce me as a friend."

"I think we both know you're more than that."

"Yes." He lifted her chin with his strong fingers, "a lot, lot more." His lips swooped down onto hers and then she was in his arms kissing him fervently.

Suddenly there was a loud bang and they broke apart, both staring towards the sound of the noise. Gladys the cleaner stood in the doorway, duster in one hand, polish in the other and a look of utter shock on her face.

"Dr Rivers," she mouthed, "I'm so sorry to interrupt."

"No worries Gladys. We were just erm, finishing up here."

"I can see that," she said with both eyebrows raised, "I can always come back later if you want to carry on with your studies." She began wiping at the walls with vigour.

Juliette's hand flew to her mouth as she stifled back a titter, "I should go," she whispered, "see you Saturday?"

"I'll be there," Ben grinned, his boyish, gorgeous grin that made Juliette's stomach flip with happiness. Reluctantly Juliette released his hand and walked towards the exit, inwardly thinking how little she cared what anyone at this damn university thought of their relationship anymore. All she was bothered about was him. Determined to prove this, at the door she turned and shouted, "I love you Dr Rivers!"

He stared her way with surprise, then his whole face lit up with happiness and the breath caught in her throat. "We're in love Gladys," she yelled towards the open mouthed cleaner, "he's not gay, he's not bi, he's all mine – isn't that just perfect!"

* * *

Evelyn decided to have a lie in on the weekend. The past couple of weeks had been tiring, with exams to prepare for and essays to complete, she was tired and the biting cold hadn't helped her flagging energy levels either. So here she was on a drab Saturday morning lazing in her warm bed, while downstairs she could hear Sophie chastising her children to be quiet. Oh but they were good, thoughtful boys. They had settled in well in their new home and didn't seem at all bothered that they were living with a lady who was old enough to be their Grandma. Last night they had showed her how to play her very first computer game. Evelyn had been transfixed with the bright colours, the loud noises and fast moving characters. It had taken a while for her to get used to it, but after an hour or so of patient tuition and whoops of encouragement, she had become quite nimble on their handset and tonight they had challenged her to another game. Evelyn could understand now why they had a reputation for being so addictive. She had even been dreaming of the computer game characters.

There was a soft knock on the door. Sophie's voice drifted through, "Evelyn, are you awake?"

"Yes dear," Evelyn struggled to sit upright against the headboard, "come on in."

"I brought you tea and crumpets," Sophie pushed the door open and came in balancing a tray.

"Breakfast in bed? My you are spoiling me Sophie, I could become used to this."

"You deserve spoiling," Sophie set the tray down on the bed, "you've had a fair bit of mail this morning."

"Oh it's probably just bills," Evelyn scanned the pile of envelopes, "can you pass me my spectacles please," she motioned towards the dresser, where they rested in a floral case, "is all this mine?"

"Yes," Sophie replied, smiling with excitement, "but I did have one letter; a confirmation of my employment at Hanley's and Hanley's. I start next week Evelyn," Sophie gripped the duvet with excitement.

"Well done Sophie, I'm proud of you," Evelyn paused to polish her smudged glasses, "have you told your mum?"

"No!" Sophie shook her head, "and I don't intend to either," she rolled her eyes at Evelyn's look of reproach, "not while she insists on siding with Ryan O'Neill."

Evelyn sighed, "fair enough. What's your maiden name Sophie?"

"Fletcher. Originating from the Fletchers of Bristol, who moved up to the Midlands in search of work in the industrial towns," Sophie helped herself to one of the crumpets, "when Mum was well, before Dad did a runner, she investigated our family tree. Apparently my great, great grandparents were innkeepers, in a public house of ill repute."

"Really?" Evelyn's eyes widened with surprise, "you have a dark past Sophie." Evelyn chuckled and bit into her breakfast. "My Grandparents were potato farmers up North, their Lancashire hotpots were famous. Granny Cooke sold them by the tubful in her farm shop. She was a nice lady, kind and caring. Seems like folks have lost interest in kindness now-a-days. This world needs more of it, don't you think?"

"You could be right there Evelyn. Well I'll leave you to open your mail," Sophie backed towards the door, "I'm taking the boys and the dogs out to the park now but I thought later we could go out for lunch, my treat, an excuse to celebrate my employment."

"Sounds heavenly," Evelyn smiled her way warmly as she left the room.

She put her glasses on and began opening the morning's mail. The first letter was a plea for donations from a wildlife charity. Evelyn wondered how they had gotten her name and address details, with a shake of her head she put it on a pile to be binned. The next was a bank statement, showing Evelyn that she had a fair pot of money accumulated and gathering interest in her personal account. Then she picked up a thick cream envelope with swirly calligraphy style writing and a London postmark on. Her interest was piqued and she slit open the envelope. The paper felt posh beneath her fingers and there was only one sheet. Quickly she scanned it, gasping as she read the words.

Dear Ms Cooke,

We are pleased to inform you that after careful consideration, we are interested in reading the full manuscript of your novel, 'A Journey Into The Unknown.' We therefore look forward to receiving your completed manuscript as soon as possible.

An email address had been provided and it was signed kind regards from the director of the company. The letter fell from her fingers as Evelyn began hollering for Sophie to come quick.

"Evelyn what is it?" Sophie burst through the door, "are you okay?"

"I'm absolutely fine Sophie," the excitement shone on Evelyn's face as she sprang from the bed and danced a jig around the room, "in fact I'm absolutely wonderful."

* * *

"Right then, that's the last of the food taken to the social club," Marie stood in Juliette's kitchen, eyeing the mountain of washing up with unease, "Jules, why don't you let me buy you a dishwasher?"

"That's for lazy arses," Juliette replied, pulling on her rubber gloves with a twang, "come on, it won't take us long to get cleared up."

"Well okay," Marie grumbled, "but then I must go, I need a shower and I still haven't decided what to wear yet. Nothing fits me anymore!"

Juliette looked at her sister with sympathy, "you *are* eight months pregnant."

"Nine almost," Marie corrected, as she patted her baby bump, "and I refuse to wear those horrid dungarees that Dave's mother bought me. I look like a farmer whose beer belly has got seriously out of hand."

"I gave you some maternity dresses," Juliette replied patiently.

"I'm not a dress kind of girl – you know that! You've got the gorgeous pins and the cleavage to pull a dress off, whereas I'm short and dumpy and even more so now I'm pregnant," Marie sniffed, "sorry to moan, I don't know what's wrong with me just lately."

"It's your hormones," Juliette pulled her into a warm hug, "and you'll look lovely whatever you wear, so stop stressing."

Marie was still looking down at the floor.

"Go on home now and have a rest. You've been on your feet a long time, you'll be too tired to dance with my boyfriend if you're not careful."

"You mean that?" Marie's mouth hung open, "I can have a dance with him?"

Juliette laughed, "as long as you don't try to snog his face off."

"As if that's going to happen," Marie rolled her eyes, but her spirits were lifted, "maybe I'll get off then, soak my feet and ask Dave to polish my nails. So I'll see you later. You won't forget the…"

"Flowers and the presents?" Juliette cut in, "it's all in hand, now get off with you." She gently pushed Marie towards the door.

"Tell the kids I'll see them later," Marie called over her shoulder, "where are they by the way?"

"In their rooms I think," Juliette waved as Marie slowly made her way down the concrete stairs, "bye sis." She closed the door, leant against it and smiled, "time for operation beautiful."

Operation Beautiful consisted of making not only herself presentable but also her livewire children. She interrupted their game of hide and seek to frogmarch them into a strawberry scented bubble bath. While they were soaking, she laid out their clothes; a sparkly dress with matching ballet pumps for Molly, and a smart shirt and trouser set for Harry. She wanted them to look lovely for their first meeting with Ben. She hoped he would take one look at them and fall in love, well maybe that was being a little bit unrealistic, but she was so eager for them to get on. Otherwise a serious relationship between her and Dr Rivers was going to be a definite no-no. It was simple; her children came first and always would.

"Mum," Molly hollered from the bathroom, "Harry said your new boyfriend is going to hate me."

"Did he now?" Juliette walked through splashing Harry with bubbly water, "he's teasing honey, Ben is going to love you, especially when he sees you in your posh new frock."

"Maybe *I* won't like *him*," Harry grumbled, his mouth turned down, "is Dad coming?"

Juliette sighed at the mention of her ex Marty, "no, your Father hasn't been invited love. Granny and Granpops aren't his family. Remember I explained that to you."

"I thought you were friends now?" Molly cocked her head to one side and gazed up at her with wide eyed innocence.

"We are," Juliette began, "I mean, your dad and I are. But Granny, Granpops and Auntie Maz are still angry at him because of the way he's behaved."

"Oh," Molly shrugged, blowing a bubble in Harry's face, "okay then."

"Where *is* the toothpaste?" Juliette scrabbled in the cabinet, found it behind the out of date sun cream.

"Mum, is your new boyfriend handsome?" Molly asked.

"Oh sick!" Harry made retching noises.

"He's very handsome," Juliette replied with a cough, "and he's clever and funny and kind."

"What you asking that for?" Harry demanded to know of his sister.

"Because," Molly drew out the word, giving Harry a withering look, "my friend Lucy told me her mum has been having an affair with Mr Probert the butcher."

The toothbrush clattered out of Juliette's hand, "she has? Are you sure Lucy's not making it up sweetie?"

Molly shook her head, "Lucy's Dad keeps shouting, he's real angry and he's moved into Lucy's bedroom with her."

Juliette was astounded by this revelation. Lucy's mother went to church every Sunday and Mr Probert had always seemed such a reserved guy. The stiff upper lip type.

"Lucy said it's because Mr Probert's really handsome and he gives her nice meat."

Juliette stifled a laugh.

"So do you think Mr Probert's handsome Mum?"

Juliette swilled her mouth out, "no I don't think he's handsome Molly. Not every woman finds the same man attractive."

"Are you having an affair Mum?" Harry's nose wrinkled with distaste.

"No! At least not in that sense. Ben isn't married, and if he was then I wouldn't have anything to do with him."

"Even though you think he's real handsome?" Molly looked at her with suspicious eyes, "is Lucy's Mum a bad person then?"

"No of course not," Juliette sighed, "sometimes people make mistakes honey, sometimes people are so sad they make bad decisions. We should try not to judge, we should try to be compassionate. It's no one else's business anyway Molly, I'm sure Lucy's Mum and Dad will work things out. And you definitely don't need to worry about it. Now come on love, hop out, let Harry finish off in here." She held a bath sheet out for her daughter, enveloping her in a soft cotton cocoon.

"And you two, please stop worrying about Ben. He's a real nice guy and he just wants to be your friend – not your dad. Okay?"

"Okay!" Both children shouted in unison and the conversation was forgotten.

* * *

"Are you sure there's enough?" Juliette ran a critical eye over the tables full of buffet food, "I still think we should have bought more desserts."

Her brother-in-law cast her a look of surprise, "are you joking Jules? There's enough here to feed a bloomin' army."

Juliette wasn't convinced, but it was too late to harp on about it now. She glanced at her watch; the guests would be arriving anytime now.

"What's she moaning about?" Marie plodded towards them, puffing and panting.

"Nothing," Juliette crossed her arms, "how are you feeling?"

"Okay I suppose. I've been having a few twinges; those damned Braxton Hicks are a nuisance."

"You need to take it easy," Juliette looked at her with worry, "please don't request Grease or Saturday Night Fever tonight. I don't want to be picking you up off the dancefloor."

"I can still dance!" Marie protested, "I'm not ill you know. Baby will love a bit of John Travolta," she rubbed at her protruding stomach with a tender hand, "what time's Ben coming?"

"He's just left," Juliette's stomach fluttered with nerves and excitement. This was it, he was finally meeting her family, "please don't embarrass me."

Marie's mouth hung open, "as if I would."

"She's going to be on her best behaviour tonight," Dave pulled Marie close, "aren't you love?"

"I suppose so," Marie mumbled.

They all turned as the door swung open and the first guests filtered in. Half an hour later the room was almost full with family and friends. Her brother Ray went up on the stage and explained what was going to be happening.

Juliette's parents, Violet and Frank, were under the false impression that they were coming to a soul night with friends. They were a few minutes away, so the lights were dimmed and people took their seats in anticipation.

Juliette sat with an excited Molly bouncing on her knee, watching the door as it slowly creaked open and the most handsome man stepped into the room. Ben Rivers scanned the room for her.

Juliette jumped up, dragging Molly with her by the hand across the dance floor.

"Ben," she whispered, "come sit down, Mum and Dad will be arriving anytime now." She noticed, that quite a few women were craning their necks to gawp at the delectable Dr Rivers. She led him back to their table and they sat silently as the DJ pointed at the door. Moments later her parents stood there in the entrance, blinking at the darkened room in front of them. Lights were snapped on and a swell of "surprise!" rang around the room. Streamers popped into the air and balloons cascaded from a ceiling net. Violet's hand flew to her mouth, while Frank looked completely astounded by what was transpiring in front of him. Juliette went with her brothers and Maz to greet her parents.

"What the hell you done our Maz?" Violet Harris demanded to know.

"It's a surprise anniversary party of course," Marie replied, hugging her mum, "now you better get out there and mingle."

Juliette stood on the dance floor watching her parents as they were inundated by guests eager to pass on their well wishes. She looked round for Ben, he was still seated at the same table, his head was bent as he spoke to Molly. She watched as he took Molly's tiny hand in his and gently shook it. Molly was giggling and chattering away animatedly. Juliette walked back towards them, the nerves had completely dissipated now to be replaced by an intense feeling of happiness and the certainty that she had made the right decision allowing Ben Rivers into her tight family unit.

* * *

Harry wasn't quite so friendly as Molly, but Juliette had anticipated that and had warned Ben beforehand. But Ben was so good with him; he was warm and friendly asking lots of questions about Harry's hobbies, his likes and dislikes. Slowly Juliette could see Harry thawing and she left them embroiled in a conversation on Chattlesbury FC's chance in the Premiership. She took her purse up to the bar and ordered a round of drinks for them all.

"He seems alright your bloke," Gary her eldest brother shouted into her ear.

"Go and say hi," Juliette replied with a smile, "I think you'll be impressed."

"Lucy already is," he pointed at his wife, who was staring at Ben.

"Jules he is gorgeous," Lucy squealed, grabbing hold of her arm, "where have you been hiding him?"

"We haven't been together that long," Juliette replied with a smile, "I wanted to make sure before I unleashed him on you lot."

"As sensible as ever," Lucy laughed, "I don't blame you keeping *him* under wraps, he's like a movie star heartthrob."

Juliette nodded in happy agreement.

"Mum told me he's your teacher," Gary huffed, "that don't sound very professional to me."

Juliette sighed, "oh please stop with the over protective brother. Ben is a lecturer, a university lecturer. We're both fully grown, consenting adults. He's utterly lovely, he really is."

"Leave her alone," Lucy nudged Gary, "Jules is happy so we should be too. Now go and say hello to him ya great big lump and be nice," Lucy gave him a warning look.

Gary ambled off, pint in hand.

"What do your mum and dad think of him?" Lucy asked.

"They were friendly enough, a little wary maybe."

"It's cause you're the baby of the brood. They're just being protective, that's all."

"I know," Juliette looked over to Ben who was arm wrestling with Harry, "they'll stop worrying when they get to know him."

"Well, I'm over the moon for you honey. You deserve to be with someone nice, someone romantic and dashing. I just wish he had a twin brother," they both laughed.

"Shall we dance?" Juliette asked, eyes shining. As they took to the dance-floor, Ben's eyes travelled over her, watching her as she shimmied to Beyonce's 'All the single ladies,' her gaze caught his and she was transfixed by the happiness and love that emanated from him. Dr Rivers the university heartthrob, the sought after bachelor was officially her partner. He was all hers and she couldn't be happier.

Chapter Twenty-Five

Jon and Ann picked Samuel up early on a mild Saturday morning.

"He's so excited," Lulu whispered, as they waited underneath the shade of a towering Sycamore tree, "he was up till late last night finishing all his outstanding homework so he could stay later with you guys on Sunday."

"Thank you for agreeing to let him stay overnight," Ann said, a happy lilt in her voice.

Lulu cocked her head on one side, "what are you planning on doing with him?"

"We thought bowling, followed by lunch of his choice. We'll have him back Sunday morning if that's okay?"

"Absolutely fine," Anton passed his overnight bag through the car window. "Here he is now."

Samuel ran down the drive grinning widely, he tugged the back door of the vehicle open and was just about to hurtle himself in when Lulu stopped him.

"How about a kiss," she said softly, "I'll miss you Sammy." Slowly he backed out and gave her a perfunctory peck on the cheek.

"Have fun guys," Anton pulled Lulu into a waist hug.

Ann and Sam turned to wave while Jon reversed off the drive.

"So, where does your girlfriend live then?" Jon smiled in the mirror, pushing the gear stick into first.

"She's not." Sam replied, "my girlfriend I mean."

"You'd like her to be though right?" Jon countered.

"I suppose so," Sam shrugged, looking down at his hands.

"Jon!" Ann chastised, "don't embarrass him. She lives close to the bowling centre, so head in that direction." She turned to look at Sam, "she knows we're coming right?"

"Right," there was an infinitesimal pause, "thanks for inviting her. She was well happy the other day at school when I asked her."

"It's a pleasure," Ann smiled broadly, "how is school going?"

"Not too bad," Sam replied, "I-I've been entered into a regional spelling competition."

"Sam that's brilliant," Ann gushed, "well done!"

"I guess," another shrug, "spellings not as cool as playing footie though."

"It's cooler," Ann answered, "no one's teasing you are they?" She stared hard at him with concern.

"Not really," he replied, "no one important anyway."

"They're just jealous," Jon said, his tone light, "don't let them put you off."

"Don't you dare Sam," Ann leaned across to rub his arm, "spellings such an important skill to be good at. You go for it."

"Thanks," Sam glanced up from underneath his fringe of curls, "you can come watch me if you want. With Anton and Lulu I mean."

"Oh, we would love to," Ann nodded eagerly, "just let us know when it is and we'll be there."

"So tell us how your weeks been?" Jon said as he flicked on the cool air. They settled back into an easy conversation and in no time they were at Beth's house and he was out, running up the steep drive, banging on the door knocker, laughing with her and helping her into her jacket, before they made their way down towards the car, and they sped off up the road, following the signs for Chattlesbury city centre.

* * *

"So it appears I've been left in temporary charge of a flower shop," Flora was spooning scrambled eggs onto charcoaled pieces of toast, "I'm so nervous."

Will gazed at his mum with a mixture of pride and trepidation.

"Flora explain to me again why this has been left down to you?" Max was pulling one of his belligerent faces that had his wife tutting with annoyance.

"Marie obviously trusts me Max, that must be why."

"It's a lot of responsibility Flora," Max pursued his lips, "and you haven't been there that long, how will you cope?"

"Mum will cope just great, won't you?" Will took his plate of eggs and sat down at the table with them.

"I suppose I'll have too," Flora chewed her bottom lip, "they'll be another staff member to help me and Marie said she'll pop in as much as she can."

"Well how long will she be off?" Max demanded to know. "hopefully not for too long!"

Max! For goodness sake, she's just had a baby, she needs time to recuperate."

"Sounds like she had a bad time of it too," Will said, between mouthfuls of food, "Jules was telling us the other day at uni that she was induced. She ended up having an emergency caesarean, after spending hours in labour. Pretty horrific by the sounds of it."

"Hema was the opposite," Flora reminisced, "no pain relief from what I remember."

"Only because she was too far dilated," Will said with a rueful smile, "they wouldn't let her, but I think she would have had anything going."

"What have they called the baby Will? I should send them a card."

Will scratched his head, "not sure, I know it's a boy."

"James," Flora clicked her fingers, "that's the one, such a nice traditional name." She scribbled a note down on her weekly shopping list. "So anyway Max, please don't worry, I'm pretty savvy in that flower shop now, I'm sure I'll be fine."

"I hope so Flora," he cleared his throat, "you can always call me at work if you're struggling though."

"At St Mary's?" The shock was evident in Flora's tone.

"Yes at school."

"Oh okay," Flora looked happy, "I'll keep that in mind. I suppose you're working today love?"

Max unfolded the morning newspaper, "actually I'm having a weekend off. St Mary's will have to cope without me."

Will raised an eyebrow at Max's tone of indifference, what was going on with his Dad? He wondered.

"And what are your plans?" Flora asked her son.

Revision," Will pulled a face, "exams start soon. I tried to avoid the modules with exam assessment in, but the majority of the second year modules unfortunately have them. Give me an essay or a presentation any day."

"It must be nerve wracking," Flora glanced with sympathy at her son.

"It's not so much the nerves that bother me," Will admitted, "my mind goes blank and I have a tendency to waffle."

"Just try your best love, you might surprise yourself."

"Exams are the bane of my life," Max grumbled, "think of the seven and eleven year olds at my school having to sit SATS."

"Poor wee souls," Flora sipped at her orange juice, "surely there must be some other way of assessing the children."

Max shook his head, "unfortunately not according to this government. Some children cope with it okay, but from my experience, the majority stress themselves out worrying they're going to fail. However, a good teacher does have strategies to help combat this. It's the anxious parents *I* have to deal with. The competitive ones who want their child to get top grades no matter what, and those are the type who blame the school when they don't."

"I'll be proud of Esme, no matter what SAT score she gets," Will deposited his empty plate into a bowl of warm, soapy water.

"Ah yes, your mother told me you don't intend on sending Esme to a faith school?"

"That's right," Will glanced at his dad warily. He had been expecting a showdown on this, but Max merely nodded.

"There's some very good community schools nearby, I could show you their Ofsted reports if you wish.

"Actually Dad, Hema and I want to go and visit the schools ourselves, get a feel of the atmosphere. We're not bothered about league tables and Ofsted reports. We're bothered about how the adults interact with the children, whether it's a happy environment."

Flora looked his way with admiration, "you've got a while yet before you have to decide, Esme's not even walking."

"You'd be surprised how quickly school places fill up Flora," Max rose to his feet, "now I'm going for a swim and when I come back I'm sorting out the garage, it's a mess. And Flora, I thought this evening we could watch a movie with a takeaway?"

"On a Saturday love? We usually have steak."

"Let's do something different tonight, I'll treat us all, you and Hema too," he nodded at Will then disappeared out the kitchen whistling.

"Blimey," Will stared after his dad's retreating figure, "what's got into him."

Flora looked as bemused as Will, "don't knock it Will. Whatever it is I like it and I'm hoping it continues."

"Here, here," Will grinned at his mum before walking steadily out of the kitchen and up the stairs to Hema and Esme.

"I'm going stir crazy," Will banged the book shut and pushed it away with some force. Hema was standing behind him, kneading his shoulders, trying to release some of the tension that was coursing through his body.

"You need a break," she suggested, "why don't we go out this afternoon."

"Where to – the pub?" Will's eyes literally lit up at the thought of an ice cold cider.

"Not exactly," Hema shifted her weight onto the other foot, "we *could* go and see Mum and Dad?"

There was a silent pause, quickly she continued, "no, silly idea...let's go to the park, it's a glorious day, we could take Esme on the boats and the..."

Will silenced her with a pat of his hand, "we'll go see your mum and dad."

"Is – is that okay?"

Will swivelled round on his chair, "they're your parents Hema, I'm not going to stop you seeing them."

Hema bit her lip, "but how do *you* feel about seeing them?"

Will shrugged, "honestly it's fine. I'm not going to hold a grudge against them. Your dad apologised and I believe him when he said he had nothing to do with the stabbing," a cheeky grin warmed his face, "besides, your mum makes the best Indian food I've ever tasted. My stomach's more important than my pride."

Hema bent to kiss his lips, "you are a kind, forgiving person."

Will laughed, "a proper Catholic huh? Now go and see if Hema is awake and I'll finish off up here."

An hour later Will crossed his Dad on the stairs, telling him briefly what they were doing.

"Very magnanimous of you," Max patted his shoulder, "good luck."

"How was your swim?"

Max flicked back his wet hair, "relaxing. I'm determined to make more of an effort on the exercise front. I need to get fit. Being a headteacher is draining the life out of me. There's more to this world than work eh son?"

Will stared after his Dad as he bounded upwards, "yeah… I suppose." He turned to gaze at Hema who was looking as puzzled as he was.

"Is he okay?" Hema mouthed.

"Must be a miracle," Will chuckled.

Hema hooked the changing bag over the handlebars of the new pushchair they had recently purchased. It was a trendy contraption, that allowed them access to sit Esme fully upright. She was crawling now – to the eight month old the world was a wondrous, unexplored place. To Will and Hema it was full of danger for their precious child. As a precaution they had installed safety measures throughout the house; a stairgate, wall socket protectors and a fire guard – even though the fire was rarely used.

"Don't you look pretty!" Will admired his daughter in her cute gingham frock and matching sun hat. Thank God for warm April sunshine. The vestiges of winter were being slowly shaken off, allowing spring to unfurl over the land. Daffodils lined the garden, a yellow injection of rebirth following a season which had been cold and unforgiving.

Will noticed Hema had made an effort with her appearance also. She was wearing a spotty cotton maxi dress and smart shoes. She had styled her hair up into a classic bun and her face was carefully made up.

"You look as though you're heading for church," Will joked.

"Do I?" Hema frowned, "is it too much?"

"I'm kidding," Will squeezed her waist, "you look really hot actually," his hand travelled down towards her pert buttocks.

"Let's go," Hema slapped his hand away with a wry grin.

"Are they expecting us?" Will felt into step beside her.

"Yes. I messaged Mum earlier. It's her day off and Dad's on his way back from the cash and carry."

"And they know I'm coming too?"

"Of course Will, they've accepted we're a partnership."

Will silenced the voice of nagging doubt within him and changed the subject.

Hema chattered about the summer, she was already planning where they could take Esme for trips out. It was a nice stroll, along tree lined streets, through the busy park and past a row of cosmopolitan shops on the high street. They gazed at the window displays, while Esme gurgled at passers-by and pointed towards dogs scooting about in the distance. Eventually they turned into her parents street. Will could see Mr Kumar on his drive washing his car. Soap suds ran in rivulets out onto the road, mingling with fallen blossom that clogged the drains. Daljeet had his back to them, he was bent over the boot, swiping at the rear brake lights. Will noticed his hair was peppered with more strands of gray and felt a pang of sadness that they had wasted so much time at loggerheads. But hopefully their relationship was on the mend.

"Dad," Hema called.

Daljeet dropped his chamois into a bucket and spun around to take her in his arms.

"My daughter," his eyes were moist as he held her at arm's length to look at her, "are you well?"

Hema cast a furtive glance at Will, "I am."

"Will," Daljeet took his hand in a firm grip, "it's good to see you."

"Hello Mr Kumar," Will replied politely.

"Please... call me Daljeet, let us dispense with formalities. Where is my poti?"

Esme screamed with excitement as he lifted her out of her harness. Daljeet kissed her rosy cheeks, smoothed back her unruly hair, "she has grown since New Year," his voice was choked with emotion, "come and see your Grandma little one."

Shivani was standing in the kitchen pressing an iron over a pair of her husband's long trousers. The radio was playing; a cacophony of sounds that Will could only conclude as being Bangra. Hema skipped through the door, her hands twisting in time with the beat.

"You came!" Shivani's face lit up with happiness.

"I told you we would Mum," Hema brushed her cheek with a light kiss, "these are for you." She thrust a bunch of tulips at her mother.

"Thank you," Shivani sniffed the flowers, inhaling their sweet fragrance.

Hema nudged Will surreptitiously, he stepped forward, "hello. It's good to see you."

"You too Will," Shivani clasped his hands, "how are you feeling?"

"Much better," he replied brightly, "I'm back at uni, working hard."

"Will's preparing for his exams. He's almost finished the second year," Hema was gabbling with enthusiasm.

Shivani studied Will's face, "you look tired. It will be good when the holidays are here so you can rest."

"Shivani just look at your Granddaughter," Daljeet was bouncing a very happy looking Esme on his hip.

"Oh such a beauty," she stretched out her hands, taking Esme from her husband and kissing her on both cheeks, "thank you for bringing her."

Hema was rummaging in her bag, "I brought you these," she held a pouch of glossy photographs – Esme when she was a new born and at various stages of her young life.

"This," Hema pointed to a picture of Esme wailing, "was the day she cut her first tooth."

"Show them the one of her rolling over for the first time," Will grinned, "it's a cracker."

Shivani clutched her bosom, "these are for me to keep?"

"Yep," replied Hema, "we've bought a DVD to show you too."

"Come come," Daljeet ushered them down the hall, "let us look at them over tea."

It was a pleasant afternoon. Shivani had made a buffet full of Indian finger foods that had Will's stomach grumbling with appreciation. There were samosas, bhajis, chicken tikka on skewers, lemon flavoured rice and an array of traditional Indian desserts. While they were eating, the neighbours called round - a Jamaican couple who were loud and friendly and who plied Will with generous shots of Caribbean rum. When Will got to his feet to leave he felt woozy and dizzy from the effects of the strong alcohol.

"Woah!" Hema placed a steadying arm around him.

"Daytime drinking – no good," Will could hear the slur in his words.

"Are you going to be okay walking home?" Hema asked, giving him a doubtful once over.

"Fresh air will do me good," he almost fell on top of Shivani when she embraced him goodbye.

The warm afternoon air actually made Will feel worse. He stumbled down the street, tripping clumsily over his own feet.

"Hold onto the pushchair," Hema advised, steering him away from the gutter, "you're not going to be sick are you?"

Will belched then shook his head, "have I ever told you that I love you?"

Hema chuckled, "silly Daddy is drunk," she sing-songed.

"No seriously," Will screwed his face into a deadpan pout, "you two are my world."

A couple on the other side of the street had stopped to stare at them. Will's voice had grown louder.

"Hush," Hema said with embarrassment, "I know we are, you tell me almost every day."

Will flung his arm across her shoulder, pulling her close, "I'm going to make something of myself Hema. I'm going to pass this bloody degree and get the most awesome job ever. You are going to be so proud of me."

Hema looked up at him lovingly, "I already am. But what about me Will, I have dreams too."

"You wanna go back to uni?"

"I think so," Hema huffed, "but I don't want to leave Esme, not yet anyway."

"Well," Will hiccupped, "you're only twenty, you have all the time in the world. Do you still want to be a social worker?"

"Yes." Hema nodded, "but for now I'm happy to look after Esme, she's so tiny, she needs me. And I want to support you Will. I'm here for you one hundred per cent."

Will stopped walking and turned Hema so he could stare down at her, "I'm so lucky to have you," he inched his face closer and she puckered her lips in anticipation. Then suddenly he stopped, drew back.

"I feel a bit...I think I'm going to be..." He stumbled towards an overgrown hedgerow where he unceremoniously lent forward and barfed.

* * *

"These are the best fish and chips I have ever tasted," Jon speared a succulent piece of cod, holding it aloft before dipping it into a pot of mushy peas and devouring it.

"Uh-oh," Ann shook her head, "the best we had were on Blackpool promenade with the fresh smell of the North Sea as an accompaniment."

"Ah yes," Jon agreed, "the cawing of the ferocious sea gulls scavenging at our feet for scraps. The snorting of the donkeys parading on the beach in front of us. The screams of the Pleasure Beach wafting from behind us."

"Blackpool is awesome," Beth gushed, shifting along the bench they were sharing in Chattlesbury city centre, "the Pepsi Big One is the best roller coaster *ever.*"

"I've never been," Samuel lobbed a chip at a flock of squabbling pigeons.

"Where did you go on holiday then?" Beth asked.

"Nowhere," Samuel replied candidly, "I've never been to the seaside."

"Really?" Beth's mouth hung open in shock, "that's so sad."

"We'll have to remedy that then won't we," Jon stood up to put his chip wrapper in the bin.

"When can I come live with you?"

The words were uttered so quietly that at first Ann thought she had misheard.

"You want to live with us?" Ann's voice was a tremulous whisper, so different from her usual authoritative tone.

Sam nodded, averting his eyes to the floor, "Anton and Lulu are cool, but I know I can't stay with them forever."

Ann swallowed, this adoption was really going to happen. They had passed all the checks, the red tape, the rigmarole of endless paperwork and meetings. Now most importantly Samuel himself seemed keen on the idea of living with them permanently.

Ann cast Jon a warning look, *don't get too carried away* she conveyed with her eyes. A lump of emotion had formed in her throat and she coughed, before asking him the all-important question.

"Would you like to come live with us?"

The words hung in the air, a sincere life changing invitation.

Samuel scuffed his feet, "yep. I think you're both awesome."

Ann's spirits soared with happiness, "You're pretty ace yourself mister."

Jon was grinning widely, he looked so happy that Ann's heart hammered with excitement.

"We need to talk to the social worker," she explained, trying to keep her tone neutral, "it will be a slow process but we have to do things properly – okay Sam?"

Sam nodded to show he understood, "if I come live with you I won't have to move again?"

He looked so vulnerable that Ann had to quell the urge to fling her arms around him, "no Sam, you won't ever have to move again."

Then Beth was pulling him to his feet and they were chasing each other around a gushing fountain, dipping their hands in the water to create arcs of spray that soaked them all.

Chapter Twenty-Six

It was the morning of the first exam and the university refectory was full of nervous students scanning books, trying to cram in a few precious more minutes study. Sophie sat with Juliette, waiting for the others she tapped her pencil against the edge of her polystyrene coffee cup.

"Jules I'm so nervous I've been up half the night."

"Me too," Juliette lifted her mass of red curls, clipping them at the nape of her neck. She was sweating and felt a little bit light headed. Pushing back her chair she stood up.

"I need food. Want anything?"

"No thanks," Sophie took a gulp of water and watched Juliette as she joined the queue for the breakfast section.

Evelyn returned from her jaunt to the toilet looking remarkably calm and composed. She slipped into the seat opposite Sophie and they both turned to wave at Will who was weaving around the tables towards them.

"Morning ladies," his demeanour was as friendly as always, "are you ready for this?"

"No," Sophie's voice was shrill and wobbly, "I don't feel confident about this at all. I'm going to fail, I just know it."

Will passed her a stick of chewing gum, "the secret is to remain calm. Don't stress yourself over it."

Sophie was amazed at his aura of laid back relaxation, "do you *ever* stress about anything Will."

Will laughed, "not really."

Sophie took a deep breath, trying to squash her rising feelings of anxiety.

"Don't worry," Evelyn said in a kind tone, "you've attended all the prep sessions and you've been studying hard for weeks."

"Yes I know," Sophie exhaled shakily, "I'm worried my mind is going to go blank though and I'm going to forget everything."

"Just stay calm," Will reiterated. To him exam nerves had never been a problem.

"It's alright for you, Mr Cool," Sophie bobbed her tongue out and some of the tension was relieved by their laughter. "Oh here's Ann," Sophie stood up and waved.

"Good luck," Jon said as he bent over to kiss his wife, "let me know how you get on."

"Thanks and I will…" she smiled as he jogged away, eliciting appreciative glances from a group of loitering female students.

Melanie appeared as if by magic from behind a wilting Kenita Palm plant.

"Are you okay?" She enquired with a bright smile.

"Yes I'm fine," Ann replied, "just a little nervous."

"Did I tell you about the time when I was sitting my psychology exams?"

Ann shook her head, "go on."

"I was a year two student like you," Melanie reminisced, "and I was so nervous I was sick before I even left the house. Then on the way to uni I was so distracted that I left my handbag on the bus. It had my keys, my phone, pens, everything in. When I arrived here I was in such a state, Ben Rivers found me wandering aimlessly on the third floor in floods of tears. He sorted everything out for me of course; made me a herbal tea, rang the bus station, gave me a pep talk on how to cope with exam stress. I went into the exam and you know what, it wasn't too bad. After all that worry I passed with flying colours."

Ann smiled at Melanie's trip down memory lane, thinking how much Juliette would like that anecdote.

"And I know that you can do it Ann. You've done so well with your essays. You're going to smash it."

"Thanks for the vote of confidence," Ann replied gratefully, "I'll try my best."

"That's all you can do. Blimey," Melanie stopped walking, "Sophie looks almost green."

Ann looked across the canteen where Sophie was almost hyperventilating with anxiety.

"You need to work your calming magic," she said to Melanie.

"I'll try," Melanie picked up the pace, "hi everyone," she took a seat next to Sophie, "you don't look too good, had a rough night?"

Evelyn leant forward, "she's hardly slept."

"Sorry everyone," Sophie swiped at her damp forehead, "I am absolutely ter-rified. You must think I'm such a wuss."

"Not at all, it's perfectly normal to feel like this," Melanie patted her hand, "why don't we go somewhere a little quieter and I'll run through some calming techniques."

Sophie sprang to her feet, "great idea," she followed Melanie out of the can-teen, towards the courtyard.

"Poor Sophie," Evelyn stirred her tea, "why are we putting ourselves through this torture?"

Will tipped his chair back so he could rest his feet up on the table, "I suppose it's because we want to make something of our lives."

"To fulfil our dreams?" Juliette suggested.

"For personal satisfaction and progression," Ann chipped in.

Evelyn smiled, "I have something to tell you. Sophie knows but I swore her to secrecy."

All eyes were on Evelyn.

"Spill, spill," Juliette urged.

"My novel," Evelyn began, "I've been sending it to agents and I've been re-ceiving rejections, lots of them. Some of them gave me some really nice feed-back, some didn't say much at all. Anyway, I was feeling pretty despondent and was considering giving up on the creative writing. Then a few weeks ago I received an email of interest from a London publisher."

"What?!" Ann exploded.

Evelyn nodded, "yes. It seems they liked my book. Anyway, I sent them my full manuscript and they... well it looks like... they might be publishing it."

Nobody spoke for an excruciatingly long minute.

"Are you serious?" The shock was evident in Will's voice.

"Jacob and I have been researching the company and they seem reputable," Evelyn sipped her drink, "I was a little apprehensive. There are so many sharks in the publishing world. I suppose I was afraid that I'd be conned."

"But they're good?" Juliette asked with bated breath.

"They're good. In fact I've been invited to London for a meeting with them this weekend."

Juliette gazed at Evelyn with pride, "well done Evelyn, that's so fantastic."

"I knew you could do it," Ann said, "how wonderful."

Will let out a low whistle, "my mate's going to be a famous author."

"Please can we keep this between just us for the time being," Evelyn's hands were trembling slightly, "I can hardly believe this myself. It's a dream come true, but I need to speak to them and sign the contracts first."

"Of course Evelyn," Juliette clapped her hands together, "this is so exciting. You are validation that hard work, perseverance and talent pays off eventually – I'm so happy for you."

"I'll ditto that," Ann held her water bottle aloft, "here's to Evelyn, here's to dreams coming true."

* * *

Jacob picked her up in his shiny red car early on Saturday morning. Sophie stood with her wrapped in a fluffy dressing gown, waiting on the doorstep while he parallel parked between the neighbours vans.

"Will you text me when you get there?"

"Yes," Evelyn turned into Sophie's warm hug, "I've jotted down the hotel contact details if you need me."

Sophie smiled at Evelyn's thoughtfulness, "be confident. Show them how talented you are."

"I'll try," Evelyn's lips curved upwards, "what will you do this weekend?"

"I'm taking the boys to the cinema. I think I deserve a weekend off after those stressful exams, we all do."

Evelyn nodded, "see you Sunday evening." She picked up her overnight bag and walked down the path. Jacob, as chivalrous as ever, had opened the door for her. She slipped into the seat and buckled up her belt, then waved until Sophie was out of view.

"Evelyn I'm still shocked that you have never been to London, our great capital city."

Evelyn pulled open a bag of mint imperials, "I've seen it on the television of course."

"That's a poor substitute for the real thing. You are going to love it. I've got all sorts planned."

He turned right at the end of the road, following the signs for Chattlesbury city centre and the train station. Evelyn pulled her visor down to shield her from the glare of the morning sun and settled back in the seat. Her stomach was churning with a combination of nerves and excitement, but she was happy and her thoughts turned to her beloved Mam. *Hope you and Dad are proud of me up there.*

* * *

They had been on the train for a few hours now. Evelyn watched the English countryside whizzing past; a blur of patchwork fields and pylons.

Jacob was snoozing in the seat next to her and opposite her a young mother sat with two children. Evelyn smiled at the little girl in the yellow dress whose hands and mouth were covered in chocolate. Her mother was tutting with exasperation, rummaging in her bag for the wet wipes that she had forgotten.

"Here," Evelyn passed over a packet of tissues and the lady gave her a wide smile of gratitude.

"Thanks," she wiped at her daughter's mouth, "are you travelling for business or pleasure?"

"Oh both," Evelyn replied, "how about you?"

"Visiting family. These two here are determined to get me on the London Eye?"

"It's my first time to London," Evelyn admitted, "all I know is that the Queen lives here in Buckingham Palace."

"Wow!" The other lady was astonished, "your first time? There's so much to see and do in London and it's huge compared to Chattlesbury. Do you like history; churches, museums that kind of thing?"

Evelyn sat forward, "I do. Can you recommend places to visit?"

"St Paul's Cathedral is amazing. Then there's the Natural History Museum which is really interesting – the kids love it there. Here," she delved in her bag, passing Evelyn a guide book, "have this. I've been so many times I can navigate myself around without it now."

"Thank you dear, that's very kind of you."

"It's a pleasure. We're here now." She pointed out the window where a sign for Euston station flashed by, "have a great time."

Evelyn thanked her again and gently shook Jacob.

"Here already?" He rubbed his eyes and stretched out his long legs.

"You've been asleep for most of the journey," Evelyn teased, pulling her bags from underneath the seat. The train slowed to a gentle rock as they glided into the station. They joined the line of people waiting to disembark. Evelyn was jostled onto a crowded platform where people rushed in all directions.

"Oh my it's so busy," she said.

Jacob chuckled, "wait till you get on the tube," he took hold of her hand and they set off.

After an exhilarating tube ride that left Evelyn shaking with excitement, they found themselves in a pleasant area of North London. Jacob pulled out a street map and leant it against the plastic pane of a bus shelter as he tried to pinpoint exactly where they were. Evelyn was staring wide eyed at the iconic red bus trundling down the road and the quintessentially English red telephone box just yards in front of them. She rummaged in her bag and began clicking her camera, catching Jacob with a puzzled frown on his face.

"What's wrong?" She asked.

"I can't seem to find the street we need," he replied with a shrug, "this map must be outdated."

"Well look," Evelyn pointed at a figure on the opposite side, "there's a policeman I'll go ask." She hurried across the road with Jacob trailing after her.

The policeman knew straight away where they needed to be heading, "take your first left into Raglan Street and left again. It'll take you up a hill and that's where you'll find your destination. Cheerio now," he touched the tip of his helmet and carried on strolling, with his walkie talkie blaring from his pocket. Off they went.

"There it is!" Evelyn pointed to a small glass fronted building which was sandwiched between a bank and a pub.

"Wait up," Jacob had his hands on his knees and was panting with the exertion of climbing the steep incline. The road was busy so they retraced their steps to use a pelican crossing.

"We're half an hour early," Evelyn said as she glanced at her watch.

"Good," Jacob replied, "that will make a favourable impression." A driver in a blue metro honked his horn to let them know he was stopping, hurrying them across.

Evelyn thought of the laid back atmosphere of Chattlesbury and was glad that she lived in a slower paced city.

"If you think this is bad, then you should see the driving around central Paris. Complete nutters," Jacob said after she had voiced her opinion.

They approached the modern looking building which was in sharp contrast to the old style architecture of the adjoining pub. It reminded Evelyn of the Queen Vic in Eastenders, a proper London boozer with its window boxes and booming jukebox. Evelyn stared up at the gold embossed letters of Willow Publishing, waiting for Jacob to pull open the door. She stepped inside a marble foyer dotted with arm chairs and potted plants. Classical music swooned from above, creating an ambience which was calm and sophisticated.

"Can I help you?" An attractive blonde haired lady in a pin stripe suit smiled at them from behind a high counter.

Evelyn pulled a crumpled letter out of her handbag, "I have an appointment with Mr Frost."

"I'll let him know you've arrived," Jenny the receptionist picked up the phone, "you're from the Midlands right?"

"Is it that obvious?" Evelyn winced.

"Yes and it's all good. My Grandparents live in Birmingham. I go visit them when I've had enough of the hectic pace of London. Please sit down."

Evelyn squashed next to Jacob on a two seater sofa. They watched a cleaner struggling with a thrumming buffer machine.

Jacob squeezed her hand, "are you okay?"

"I actually feel remarkably calm. I think it's partly because the exams are over."

"How did you find them?"

"Not too bad. At least they were easier than I thought they would be."

Jacobs eyebrows lifted involuntarily, "and Sophie?"

Evelyn sighed, "she struggled with them. She had worked herself into a state before we even got into the exam hall. Now she is convinced that she's flunked them."

"The true sign of intelligence is not knowledge but imagination," Jacob said, "that's Einstein by the way."

"I think he was right," Evelyn agreed, picking up a tourist phamphlet and leafing through it.

"Ms Cooke?" A statuesque, gray haired man strode towards them, "please come with me."

Evelyn and Jacob followed him up a long flight of steps, into an office with sumptuous scarlet curtains and a fantastic view of the city.

"My name is Frost, Charles Frost. I am the Managing Director here at Willow Publishing," he spoke with a rich plummy accent that reminded Evelyn of royalty.

"Th-this is Jacob," she stammered, remembering her manners, "a very good friend."

"Pleased to meet you. Sit down," he instructed in a calm authoritative manner, "I hope you had a pleasant journey. I believe you reside in Chattlesbuy? I've passed through there many times while en route to our other office."

"Oh," Evelyn wondered where that could be.

"Manchester," he revealed, as if reading her mind, "now then, let me order us refreshments." He pressed a buzzer and smiled across at them, "are you journeying back to Chattlesbury today?"

"No," Jacob replied, "this is Evelyn's first time in London. We decided to make a weekend of it."

"Excellent," Mr Frost nodded with approval, "after our meeting you must explore this great city."

There was a soft tap on the door and a lady entered, pushing a trolley laden with food and drink.

"You are a darling," Mr Frost beamed at his secretary. "Gloria has been with me for over twenty years. I couldn't cope without her of course."

The lady in the tight burgundy pencil skirt and ruffled blouse poured tea into dainty china cups, "would you like a sandwich?" She offered them the tray and Evelyn picked up a tuna and cucumber one.

"We thought you may be hungry after your journey here. Have a cake too."

Evelyn slipped a mini victoria sandwich onto her plate.

"Now let me tell you all about Willow Publishing."

Later that evening Evelyn kicked off her shoes and rubbed her tired feet. The meeting with Mr Frost had been a resounding success. Willow Publishing were a bona fide company who represented an impressive list of well-known authors. Evelyn had almost squealed with excitement when he had produced a contract for her to sign. He told her that the staff loved her book and were touting her as a new emerging talent. Evelyn had left the building dizzy with euphoria and disbelief. She had wandered around London in a haze, not able to take in the grand opulence of St Paul's Cathedral and the beauty of Kensington Gardens. They had finished with a river cruise down the Thames, where Jacob had took what seemed like hundreds of photographs. Now they were in separate rooms, getting ready to see London in the evening.

Jacob was waiting for her in the bar of the hotel. Evelyn stood back a little, surveying him wobbling on a twisting stool with a pint of beer in his hand. She thought how handsome he looked and how disappointed she had been to be given the keys to a single room. Then he turned and smiled at her and with her heart racing she made her way over to him.

"Where are we going?" She asked him.

"It's a surprise," he replied, pulling out a stool for her so she could clamber next to him, "you look lovely tonight."

Self-consciously she smoothed her new lilac dress, a mad spur of the moment buy which had been encouraged by Sophie "thank you."

"Forget about sherry tonight. Would you like a cocktail Evelyn? There's a menu here with dozens of them on."

Evelyn scanned the list, "why not. Is there one which you recommend?"

Jacob called over the bar tender, "a Margarita please. You are going to love this Evelyn."

Jacob was right. The drink consisting of tequila, triple sec and lime was served in a salt rimmed glass and was delicious. Evelyn drank it quickly and then had another. Then they left the hotel and headed for the tube. It was quieter on an evening, not so manic.

"This is our stop," Jacob said, "Westminster."

He tucked her arm into the crook of his and they set off, weaving around the tourists and the street sellers.

"Have you a head for heights Evelyn?"

"Well I enjoyed flying," she replied, feeling bemused by all the subterfuge.

"Good, because we're going on there." He pointed to a massive steel structure revolving slowly against the skyline.

Evelyn gasped, "the London Eye!"

"Did you know this is the world's tallest cantilevered observation wheel?" Jacob led her into one of the capsules, "it was built to celebrate the millennium year."

"It's amazing," Evelyn gripped onto the handrail as they began to lift into the sky.

Jacob pointed out the Houses of Parliament and other famous landmarks. It was a clear evening and the visibility was excellent. Evelyn gazed down at the boats chugging along the Thames, gasping in wonder.

As they moved higher Jacob placed his arm around her, pulling her close.

"How beautiful," Evelyn murmured.

"Evelyn," Jacob cleared his throat, "I need to tell you something."

"What is it?" Evelyn said, distracted by the sight in front of her.

"I-I wanted to tell you how much I love your company. You make me very happy."

Evelyn turned to gaze at him, "you make me happy too Jacob," she was surprised to notice that his cheeks had turned red and he seemed really nervous.

Jacob grasped her hand, "Evelyn... oh bother, this is so hard to articulate. What I'm trying to say is that... I love you... with all my heart."

Evelyn gasped, time seemed suspended as she waited for him to carry on speaking.

"I've loved you for years, from the first time I saw you really. I love how kind you are, your happy personality, the way you look. You're beautiful Evelyn, inside and out."

Heat coursed through Evelyn's body, "J... Jacob," she stuttered, feeling overwhelmed by his declaration.

"I want to spend the rest of my life with you." He paused to draw in a gasp of air, "will you marry me Evelyn? Will you be my wife?" From his pocket he produced a box which he opened with shaking fingers to reveal the most exquisite diamond and topaz ring Evelyn had ever seen.

There followed an excruciating silence, Evelyn's heart was hammering in her chest like thunder and her mind was whirring as she contemplated the possibility of a future life as Mrs Clarke. She glanced out at the night sky, at the hundreds of stars twinkling around them and she was overcome with emotion. Tears glistened in her eyes as she thought of all the trouble Jacob had gone to making this weekend the most perfect ever. What a decent kind man he was. How could she have not realised she loved him also. The feelings had been there all along, buried deep behind the walls of protection she had built around herself. Evelyn took a deep breath, composing herself both physically and mentally. Then she squeezed his hands, looked directly into his warm eyes and said boldly and with certainty, "I will Jacob, I will."

He laughed with relief, gathering her in his arms and kissing her, while around them the other tourists cheered and clapped and Evelyn whispered softly into his ear, "can we swop to a double room now?"

Chapter Twenty-Seven

"The End!" Will typed the last words of his final year two essay with a mixture of relief and pride, "thank Christ for that."

"Yay!" Hema massaged his knotted, tense shoulders, "another year over. Well done my love," she bent to kiss him.

"This calls for a celebration," Max looked up from his crossword puzzle, "we'll go for a meal, my treat. No expense spared, you can even have a pudding. Flora, where shall we go?"

"How about the pub that's just been refurbished? It's not too far," Flora wiped the soap suds off a clean dish and placed it back in its rack.

"What do you think angel?" Will lifted Esme out of her playpen, she gurgled and kicked her legs with delight.

"I think that's a yes," Hema said lightly, "I'll go change her."

They found a perfect spot in the beer garden, underneath the shade of a majestic oak tree. Hema laid a blanket out with some toys for Esme to play with and they sat at a bench watching her.

"I think I'll have the steak," Will scoured the menu for the most expensive cut, "as Dad is paying."

"Go ahead," Max said with a chuckle, "but you're buying the first round of drinks." After they had ordered they relaxed into an easy chatter.

"So year two is finished?" Max enquired, "no more lectures?"

"Nope," Will wiped the beer froth off his upper lip, "and I'm relieved it's over. It's been a funny old year."

"Lots of ups and downs," Hema smiled and lifted her glass, "I propose a toast: to my handsome, clever, courageous boyfriend, may his third year at Chattlesbury university be happy and calm."

"May I also add to my infuriatingly strong willed, rebellious son. Well done on finishing another year of study."

"And," Flora piped up, "my Will, who makes me proud every day."

They chinked glasses, "to Will!"

After they had finished a delicious meal, Max surprised everybody by lying on the blanket next to Esme. He squinted up at the bright sunshine, quite content for his granddaughter to crawl all over him.

"I have a declaration," he began, clearing his throat, "I've decided to leave St Mary's. I finish at the end of this term and I'm never going back there."

Flora gasped, "Max, what are you talking about? You're the headteacher, you can't just up and leave!"

"Yes I can Flora. I've been thinking about it for months now and I'm sure I'm making the right decision."

"But Max," Flora was white with shock, "you love your job and you're so good at it. Whatever has come over you?"

"I don't love it," Max said firmly, "maybe I did when I was younger and thirsty for success but not anymore. I've become blasé about education and worse still; indifferent towards St Mary's and that is not how a headteacher should operate." He sighed, "I've lost my drive Flora. I used to have a passion for that school but now – nothing. I love the children of course but that's no longer enough. I don't want to work in education anymore. I want a complete change."

Flora stared at him, open mouthed, "I – I had no idea you felt so strongly."

Max shrugged, "I didn't want to worry you."

"I knew you hated it there," Will said, staring at his dad with renewed respect, "it took over your life and made you miserable."

"It did and I took it out on my family and for that I'm truly sorry."

"Is it the staff love?" Flora placed a warm hand over his.

"Partly," Max admitted, "they're a motley crew: ruthless, hypocritical, out for number one. I used to be like that too," he frowned as the sun disappeared behind a cloud.

"You've changed," Flora said briskly, "and it's a change for the better. Leave Max, you have my backing and my blessing. You never truly belonged at St Mary's anyway. You worked so hard and they never appreciated you. Maybe you shouldn't have gone there straight from university, maybe you *should* have lived a little, but hindsight is a wonderful thing isn't it. Leave them to bicker over their precious power and their fake friendships. Give up on them love, give up on them."

"That's good advice there," Will flashed a grin at Flora, "but erm...Dad, what are you going to do?"

Max kicked off his shoes and wriggled his bare toes in the damp grass, "who knows? Something that pays peanuts? Something that helps me sleep at night?" He laughed, "something I truly enjoy? All I know is that I need some time out. I need a rest Will, I feel so tired, even my soul is weary."

Will swallowed a lump of emotion, "you can spend more time with Esme, she adores you Dad."

"And I her," Max stretched to pick up Esme and cuddle her, "no job is as important as family. Flora!" He startled his wife, who was secretly wondering if Max was going through some sort of male menopause, "I'm taking you around the globe, we're going to travel. We're going to have fun."

"Oh Max," Flora blushed, trying not to let herself be carried away by his wild abandonment, "where will we get that kind of money?"

"Our house is almost paid for darling. We have thousands in the bank. Neither of us really need to work. Let's enjoy life for a change. Let's live!"

"I think this calls for another toast," Will declared, pulling Hema closer, "here's to love and family. Here's to living life properly. Here's to new beginnings."

* * *

The Family Fun Day was held on a hot sunny Saturday in June. It had been the brainwave of the eternally enthusiastic Enabling Centre, who wanted to hold a celebration for Chattlesbury's hard working students. The grounds of the university and an adjoining field had thus been transformed. There were fairground type stalls, food vans, go-karts and bouncy castles, children's entertainers and a crazily energetic DJ, who ran around the field, coaxing people to dance their cares away. The Learning Centre and the lecture theatres had been locked up for the summer break. The staff were officially on their break; lecturers, catering assistants, cleaners and security guards, happy that another year at Chattlesbury University was done and dusted.

Will, Evelyn, Ann, Juliette and Sophie stood at a makeshift bar, congratulating each other on finishing their second year.

Nearby on fold up seats sat their loved ones; their children, partners, their betrothed.

"Sophie, how could you sneak into my bedroom and pinch one of my rings, you are so sly, I hadn't suspected a thing." Evelyn chuckled, looking fondly from Sophie to Jacob.

"With difficulty. Do you realise how hard it was to keep you sitting still and out of the way." Sophie replied, "Jacob was desperate to find out your ring size. I had to make sure he got it right."

"It's perfect," Evelyn held up her hand and they all admired her engagement ring.

"Hey you guys," Melanie ambled towards them, "the Dean is making a speech, you don't want to miss *this*."

"Where's Ben?" Juliette had received a text telling her he was on his way and she had thoughtfully ordered him a pint of lager.

"With the other lecturers of course – come on!"

She spotted him chatting to the DJ and as usual her stomach flipped over. He looked so casually good looking that most of the females on the field were openly drooling over him.

"Don't worry," Melanie said with a huge eye roll, "this is one female that isn't going to faint at the sight of Ben Rivers. Besides he ain't interested, that guy is well and truly taken."

Juliette laughed at her teasing, "it's very early days Melanie."

"Oh you can't kid a kidder," Melanie shook her head, "you both adore each other. It's so sickeningly romantic, it's almost like a fairy-tale."

"Proper Mills and Boon," Sophie said with a sigh.

"Will you stop it!" Juliette protested, gulping as he strode towards her.

"Where have you been?" He asked, pulling her towards him.

"Looking for you!" She remonstrated, "I got you a drink."

"As considerate as ever," he lifted her chin, "this is why I love you."

"Is that the only reason?" Juliette whispered, running the tip of her tongue along her lower lip.

"Juliette…" he warned, as Harry and Molly hurtled towards them like mini whirlwinds.

* * *

They gathered before the makeshift stage, waiting patiently for the Dean to take the microphone, adjust his tie, smooth down his hair and smile.

"Welcome. Welcome everyone to our university fun day. On behalf of the staff of Chattlesbury university I would just like to thank you each and every one of you for your commitment to studying at this great establishment. The lecturers and myself are amazed each day by your hard work and your determination to improve your lives and to reach your goals. We are a university which prides itself on its student support. We're here to make your journey here as enjoyable as possible. So this fun day is our thank you to you – the ones who strive to do better, the ones who smash the stigmas and stereotypes. Amazing students like you! Never forget how much potential you have. So enjoy yourself today, after a year of hard work. And never forget our universities unique motto…"

Will, Ann, Juliette, Sophie and Evelyn gathered in a tight circle, hugging each other and joined in with the roar of the crowd - "Learning enables us to be free!"

THE END

Note from the Author

Thank you for taking the time to read this book. I hope that you enjoyed it ☺
I would be very grateful if you could leave a review on Amazon or Goodreads.
I am currently working on the fourth and final book in the 'school of dreams' series.

About the Author

Julia lives in Wolverhampton, England with her husband, two children and dog.
When she is not busy writing, she works part time in a primary school.
Julia loves swimming, reading and watching films.
You can follow her on Twitter and Instagram at: Julia Sutton@sparklyauthor

CPSIA information can be obtained
at www.ICGtesting.com
Printed in the USA
LVHW112216170521
687667LV00009B/594/J